Pevanese Mosaic

Mark Nelson

Trade Paperback Edition

ISBN 978-1-7350938-1-9

Other editions Available:
Ebook

Edited by Katherine Marchlewski
v1.0
Published in the United States of America, and worldwide by
Hadley Rille Books
Kansas City, USA
www.hrbpress.com
contact@hadleyrillebooks.com

For my Grandmother Nina Eldridge, Joey Barat, Grace Gabriel, Tom Vandenberg and all the other artists too numerous to list whose lines, shapes and colors have intersected in my life. Art is the connective tissue of Hope.

Acknowledgments

This tale's germination began with an off-hand comment from a character in book three of the Pevanese cycle, The Poet King. Apparently, that character had a tutor from a place called Esda. I spent the next year pushing The Poet King out into the world, teaching through some troubling times in education, helping a daughter navigate the excitement of getting married, and contemplating retirement. New characters attached themselves to that offhand comment. Exploration beckoned. The story came in sections separated by months of inactivity, a completely different experience from earlier novels. It sat, taunting me, while the publishing world began to change rapidly, folks with whom I had worked closely moved on to other projects and genres. I found myself picking apart my story, afraid that I had lost my motivation and discipline, unsure if it was even a Pevana story at all. One day while tinkering with two passages a pair of precocious royal twins showed up along with a cat, and at that point I knew. I had delusions of a sprawling, multi-faceted stew, but I realized in the end such a grand design would not work. This novel had to end where all the others started. I am satisfied with it. If the piece has flaws, at least they are honest. I take full responsibility.

I want to thank a few important folks who helped Pevanese Mosaic along the way. Jessica Carter, Kathy Johnson, and Tom Vandenberg were all early readers and offered steadfast encouragement. Tom's work has graced all my covers. He is truly outstanding. Before her own burgeoning career took her away, Terr-iLynne DeFino offered cogent, insightful criticism bounded by wonderful friendship. Later in the process, Kathleen Marchlewski from Hadley Rille Books offered excellent ideas to further strengthen the text. A special thank you goes out to Eric T. Reynolds, owner and publisher of Hadley Rille Books, for continuing to believe in my words. Publishing models change, and I am thankful he can still find a space for romantic fantasy.

None of what I have accomplished with these four Pevana novels would have occurred were it not for the love and support from my wife, Carol. We will celebrate thirty-four years together this winter. She has read every word, served as early proofreader, question-asker, and first audience. In a real sense, this novel owes its life to her belief. Thank you, my dear.

Prologue

The Goddess Renia glided over to the edge of her terrace set above the ether and gazed down at life's roil spread below. What she saw pleased her well. Healing and husbandry waxed strong, replacing war's riot and the baser emotions to which Man seemed ever subject. She sent her thought outward, searching for and not finding Tolimon's taint anywhere. And so Mischief receded before the progress of enlightened rule and peace. Green and growing things swelled the slopes above the city by the bay. Tendrils of cook-fires leached heavenward, signals of pattern and content. Along the sea paths and inland roadways activity showed as lines of connection further knitting a region into a multi-faceted, hopeful, human tartan.

This was life with a difference.

She blinked, and a single tear welled against her ethereal lid to hang suspended with otherworldly tension in her sepulchral lashes before slipping down her regal cheek to fall to the lands below.

"One tear," she marveled aloud. "One only for Pain? Just the one for Man's mortal coil, for all the aged, the lost and the wanting? For ever are those things attendant to Man, surely?"

Her familiar, Minuet of the Arrows, joined her. At her back, her quiver of shafts hung replenished and ready. She sighed, a sound that spoke of her long effort in support of her Lady's grand design to pin the fates of Man to higher sensibilities.

"The days are bright below, mistress," said she. "And things well-begun gather pace under the light."

"Tears and labor, Minuet, much labor and well-done," the Goddess responded. "Was it enough?"

Minuet swept her hand in a gesture that included all above and below.

"More than enough, my lady, for look! Your house is restored by folk returned to faith and observance! See the life below, hear the voices raised in song. What was false before has faded to piety and understanding. I sense joy below, mistress, such as has never been before."

"But there is change, also, and I doubt, ever."

"Choice, my lady," Minuet averred. "We always left them that, and look how they have chosen! There are many pathways to happiness." She hefted her bow of adamant. "And I have the means of wending them so, regardless."

The Goddess let a ghost of a smile, and ageless expression, grace her alabaster features. "You encourage me, little one. We have wrought well, you and I."

A low chuckle disturbed their peace, and Tolimon, god of Mischance, sidled into view from the shadows of a pillar behind them.

"What now, miscreant?" Renia demanded. "I thought you removed to other lands, your hopes failed, here."

"My lady jests, surely," Tolimon retorted. "Your talk is full of self-satisfaction, but you forget in whom you place such hope. Choice," he scoffed, rising up and facing them directly. "Pinning fates to peace. I warned you that Man is temporary, his loves finite and his hates malleable." He pointed, eastward, to where a new sun rose, a dark sun whose shadow lapped against the shores of light. "Look now at what your 'choice' has wrought."

"What have you done?" Renia asked, flowing over to confront the view. The other two followed to stand, light and dark, on either side.

"Done?" Tolimon asked. "You grant me more power than I possess, mistress. That is nothing of what I have 'done'. I but allow Man, just as you, to choose."

"But you lie and deceive," Minuet asserted. "You whisper falsehoods in dreams."

"Do I?" Tolimon hissed. "You've your pointy reminders; I've my own means. Are they so different? If we grant Man choice, then we must allow him to interpret the messages in his dreams. And here, mistress, is where Man will always fail you, for he chases demons and darkness in his nightmares. Give him all the light you wish, horrors still accompany Man in his repose."

"But dreams count for naught," Renia contested.

Tolimon chuckled, a low, sinister, victorious sound that seemed to well out from his being in response to the growing shadow in the east. He let it fade.

"Perhaps," he sighed, cruelly contented. "For most that is true, but some give birth to monsters in their dreams...and become them in their waking life."

All three fell silent for a breath, two, a third.

"What kind of life," Minuet mused, "could grow under such a dark sun?"

The Goddess Renia shuddered and tiny fractures appeared in the pillars behind and along the railing against which they all stood. New tears oozed from her eyes to flow downward, dripping points of light against the gathering eastward grey-black wave.

"Evil, my Minuet, what else but evil?"

"What are we to do, lady?"

"You can do nothing against Man's lesser haunts," Tolimon chided, slinking back to his shadows behind the pillars.

Renia wept at the growth of fear.

"String you your bow," said she, "and prepare thyself for toil."

Chapter 1: Windblown Memories

Jeril Tandori placed the last carrot from the row in his basket and struggled to his feet. He liked to cook, but his knees had begun telling him that it might be time to consider letting someone else look to the produce. He arched his back to relieve the tightness that always came when he spent too long pottering about on his hands and knees. A sea breeze cooled his sweaty brow and lifted his mangy, black hair streaked with grey into a subtle air-dance.

Tall enough to see over the stone wall that protected his garden, he stood for a moment to take in the view. The sea surrounded his ramshackle home on three sides. North, south and east the swelling blue stretched away to forever. To the West, along a narrow path off the spit where his house perched, lay the gentle arch of the bay and a small fishing town the locals called Piling, so called for the effect of the broken rocks at the bay's northern end. These ran down to the shore in a jumble as though they were blocks fallen from a giant child's failed construction.

Jeril rested a hand on the top of the rock wall.

"Town," he scoffed. "It was a village when I lay the first level of this wall. So much time. The same yet not."

He removed his hand to rub a last tight spot and walked from the garden to the side door of his house. Entering the kitchen area, he put the basket on the counter, checked to make sure he had the spices he needed, and poured some water into a basin and began washing the vegetables he collected. His hands moved rhythmically, unconsciously economic from decades of the mind-resting activity, giving each separate piece a caress of cleansing water before placing it on the cutting board.

He stared out the window, the only clean pane in the house, east, back towards his past. He liked to cook, but cooking gave him time to think, time to look out that window, time to remember and grieve or rage depending on his mood and stamina.

Time. It was in moments like this that he realized he had spent half his life thinking. Once, there had been a time when he acted, often without thinking, but that was an old, old life that now resided in memory only. He gazed out the window and once again vowed to let it grime opaque like the rest of them, but he knew he would not let that happen. The next time he turned pensive and creaky, he would find himself back in the same position, and the window would be clean, and he would remember.

He sighed, reached into the basket but encountered emptiness, so he reached out with his left hand and found the haft of the knife that was always where it needed to be and began cutting his vegetables into size to add to the stew bubbling over the fire. Cutting was better. He always found a kind of symmetry, an artistic violence in the action. Cutting. Down with a short, precise plunge, a slide to the side, a return to set the blade against his knuckles. There were calluses there no amount of dishwater could soften. He ran his fingers over the surface of the cutting board, decades of use left it sliced and pitted.

Sometimes the anger seeped back in.

Today, however, the anger left him alone. It receded like the morning tide, leaving his better sense exposed and dry. That meant today's stew would be a gentle stew. As if in response, the wind gusted and his house began to sing. When the wind came from the northeast, it found its way through the walls and under the windows, creating eldritch, musical sounds in the draft. Better sense said to plug those holes. The music could get cold in the winter, but he kept things as they were, preferring the sounds and keeping extra blankets handy. He chuckled sardonically as he swept up his partitioned bits and dropped them into the pot. He gave the mass a solid stir. Chunks of lamb swam to the surface: a gift from a grateful parent from the town. A number of them sent their children to him for schooling. He taught them their letters, and their parents gave him cuts of beef or lamb, messes of fish, and thanks with an occasional coin.

There had been nearly ten years of such a sequence. He tasted the broth, added some salt, and nodded in satisfaction. He ate well, but he savored the thanks more. He did his best for the youngsters of Piling because ten years ago a storm blew him up against the rocks below where his house now stood, and the people let him stay and never asked him questions about where he came from.

That had been a kingly boon; one worth treasuring over the years. People took to calling him 'the tutor from Esda' because of his olive skin and different cast to his eyes, which were slightly more rounded than the Perspan norm. He let the myth take hold.

Part of the myth was true; he was from Esda, the sprawling empire across the eastern sea. But they were wrong about his eyes. Few in Esda boasted such deep, sea-green eyes with a rounded shape to the lids rather than the more obvious oval.

Jeril Tandori had royal eyes.

Jeril's father, Esandor Tandori, had been Emperor of Esda before his untimely death. How that led Jeril Tandori to wash up on this western shore was the deeper, most secret part of the myth Jeril fostered about his past. Jeril's brother, Jorian, wore the diadem of ultimate power in Esda.

Half-brother. And younger.

Jeril left the stew pot to its own bubbly devices and moved across the room to where his books were stacked on a table. Maths, histories, story collections, and philosophies crowded the space. Many of the books showed the effects of use and time; the result of his efforts on behalf of Piling's children. The people were proud of their tutor, but they did not boast of him to others. For ten years, no one had ever bothered Jeril from up or down the coast. He had been left alone to construct what life he wished.

And he did, collecting students and books by degrees. His hair showed grey early, and he let his beard get unruly. Old hurts turned arthritic early as well, but he chose to accept everything as it came. He had his books, his garden and his house, and that was enough for him. Though not yet fifty, folk considered him old. He found it expedient.

Let his brother have the troubles of empire. He would concern himself with worms and bugs, writing slates and readers.

He picked up the newest volume in his small library; a collection of poems from the poets of Pevana, selected and analyzed by none other than the queen of Perspa herself, Eleni Avedun. He admired the scholarship, but he admired the culture that let such a thing happen even more. His early students had been almost all male, but the odd girl child found her way to his house over time, and the numbers increased once Donari Avedun ascended the unified throne of Perspa three years ago. Later that day when the children showed up, he expected the tally to be nearly even.

Such a thing would never have happened in Esda during his father's reign, and he suspected his brother kept up the taboo. Eleni Avedun broke tradition and prospered.

He thumbed through pages of the volume, idly, scanning words without taking their meaning, his thoughts captured once again by his own history. Tradition sent him bouncing over the sea westwards. Tradition kept him from the throne of Esda. In the empire, it was always a question of inheritance. His father had two wives. Allanya, his first wife bore him two children before dying in childbirth that took the third. The eldest had been a daughter, Jorilla, married off to a sub-king at twelve. Jorian came two years later. Jeril's mother gave Esandor just the one child, him, a year senior to Jorian.

And there lay the question: younger son of a dead first wife or elder son of a living second? His father had not lived to make a choice, so Jorian made it for him.

Jeril settled back in a chair to wait out the pot simmer. He closed his eyes and, reluctantly, remembered. Jorian's supercilious voice and those horrific images paraded before him again like some fatal play.

"If you want to live, you will leave with tonight's tide," Jorian said, holding up the vial of heartbane and gesturing to the queen, Jeril's mother, laying rigid in death on her bed.

"You will let me go?" He expected a forced dram from that detestable liquid, but Jorian only smiled, wanly.

"For the sake of our childhood. I was lonely after mother died," he said stepping back to leave. "These three will wait for you to say your good-byes to your mother. Don't worry. I intend to inter her with all grace next to father."

"You are the picture of propriety," Jeril snarled, grief swelling once again.

Jorian shrugged good-naturedly. "It's a gift, I suppose." He moved to the door, two other guards entered the room. "There is a boat waiting with some food and water at the private jetty.. Make use of the tide, brother, for if you are still in sight by morning I will send a galley after you with instructions to tie a stone to you and sink you to the bottom. Crude but effective, saves me the trouble of killing you here and having to explain."

"So you will concoct a lie."

Jorian's supercilious grin returned. "Well, I have gotten rather good at it, haven't I? Farewell, brother. I hope to never see you again."

Just as Jorian said, a boat lay tied at the end of the small jetty. Two of the guards pushed him into the craft, untied it, and shoved it off. The third swung a bag that landed with a metallic tone at his feet.

"Ballast?" Jeril asked.

"Enough silver and gold to make a start," the man answered. He bore a scar on his right cheek and sported cold, brutal eyes. "Your brother really does not want your life. I, on the other hand, would relish a chance to stick you."

Jeril looked closely at the man but could not draw his name from memory.

"I don't know you," he said. "I assume you are one of my brother's dregs raised. Maybe one day I'll give you your chance."

The man spat. "My name's Tacidus, captain of Jorian's guard. Remember that."

Jeril stared balefully at the group, reduced to looming shadows as the boat drifted away.

"Remember, Lord," Tacidus continued. "Out of sight of land by dawn or face the consequences."

He sailed away as told. Revenge was out of reach. All he could do was live, so he tried. But every time he tried to settle in a place, Jorian sent death as a warning to keep moving. The first time it was a tiny fishing village on one of the islands of the archipelago. Everything had been burned, bodies piled in a clump, all made to look like raid for plunder, but before the mess a spear thrust upright, bearing the carefully engraved image of Jorian's sigil: a sprig of heather in flower.

The next time came months later, another backwater village. He had awakened to the sound of the decapitated head of the village elder, Jeril's one friend in that place, flung against his door with a note stuffed in the mouth: Go.

After the third time he almost despaired and considered risking a voyage home to put an end to the driving madness.

Instead, he sailed west for nearly a month. His food ran out. His fishing lines broke. His water ran dry. He grew weak but sailed on, fused to the bench, fibrously connected to the boat's timbers as though drawing sustenance from them at the pinch. He barely noticed the storm that snapped his mast and threw him on the rocks below a western headland.

He lived, succored by the locals, who called their town Piling. And over time he lost all thought of running.

A larger than usual gust of wind made the house song surge, breaking the spell of his dark reverie, returning him to his scholarly, craggy present spent and sorrowful. No matter how many years passed, every time he revisited that night, the pain waxed fresh and poignant. The other memories faded to a constant darkness. He rubbed his eyes and shook off as much of the mental drek as he could. Rising, he replaced the volume of Pevanese poetry and went to check the condition of his stew.

He tasted, then added a pinch of salt from a jar on the window sill. The afternoon light filtering through that window snagged his attention. He turned from his cooking to contemplate how the light fell on his newest canvas. And this, too, was an element from that old life, perhaps the only part that escaped ultimate bitterness. As part of his herb study, Jeril's mother taught him how to draw, both for his studies and for his aesthetic. She populated the walls of the royal residence during his youth with her drawings and paintings, claiming that tapestries of dieties and scenes of war needed her pastoral studies for civilizing balance. Father had laughed at her insistence but humored her by giving her efforts space on the wall.

Jeril moved now to his most recent effort, a seascape with a looming squall line. Always, when he fell to remembering the past, he would turn to his colors, and with deft strokes slowly reconstruct his calm. Paintings permeated the clear spaces in his house and served as a testament to how many times he faced down his past in the last twenty years. He took up his palette, tested the texture of the colors there and found them still pliable enough for use. He set brush to a small blob of burnt umber and carefully administered a few gentle dabs to allow a spray-washed rock to take shape. He worked quickly, for this was a well-remembered pattern.

He had done those rocks before. Ten years ago the sea flung him and his boat against them in that storm. Despite the darkness and the flying water that night, he never forgot those rocky contours, revealed in a lightning flash seconds before a surging wave sent his forehead smashing against their unyielding surface.

That had been a deep, deep dark. Those rocks showed in almost every seascape or inland rocky outcropping he painted. He gave a final touch of the brush, satisfied, and yet half-aware of the mania behind the creation. He straightened, rubbed his aching hip, and put down the palette and brush. The light faded, changing the effect, but the rock remained.

"I know I am part mad," he whispered aloud, "but it's still a fine, fine rock. And it did not kill me, and that is worth the honor of a portrait or two…or a hundred."

He stepped back, scrutinized the now completed painting. "My sea," he grumbled forcefully. "My rock." He went back to check the pot; his mood improved. "And my stew, my wine, my books, my view," he sang in a lilting sing-song voice to the petite calico cat perched on the counter. He swept her up, settled her in her familiar place in the crook of his left arm, and reached up into the cupboard for a bowl. He set it on the counter and ladled a portion, spilling a bit in the motion. The cat took instant notice and leaned down. He let her go and each settled to their respective tasks.

"And my cat," he said, gently blowing on the bowl before taking a tentative morsel. He chewed thoughtfully. "Or perhaps I'm hers? Which is it 'Gel?"

The cat, Angel, ignored the familiar contraction of her name. He took that for an answer, however, and accepted his subservience. He spooned a little meat out of his bowl and added it to the spill. Then cat and human coexisted in masticating silence while the wind sent faint notes wafting through the house.

The weather gentled before sunset. Jeril walked back along the spine of the headland that separated his home from the arch of Piling's small bay. The path climbed up through a rocky bulge overlooking the town. In a cleft amongst the mass he found his accustomed spot that looked north over the town and west up the valley to the highlands inland. The sun still hung above the horizon, a red-gold orb sinking beneath a darkening sky. Jeril liked the view and the way the light changed the town's character. Piling lost some of its shabbiness at sunset. The patchwork on the house walls faded. The fishing boats morphed into noble shadow shapes. The place took on a kind of homely consistency despite its hardscrabble truth. The sea gave up her treasures but exacted a price. Jeril looked over the line of boats drawn up on the beach. One went missing in the spring; there had been a half dozen others over his time there.

Piling had its share of fatherless children. When one of them found their way to his house for lessons, he made sure they got his best.

He had experience dealing with loneliness and want.

He fished out a pipe and a small bag of tobacco from his shoulder pouch, stuffed the pipe full, struck a spark to some tinder and lit it. He settled back in his rocky seat, puffing contentedly as the sun made its final plunge. Darkness settled around him like a blanket. He chastised himself for falling prey to his memories once again, but at least he returned to himself in time to see to the rest of his day. There had been several episodes in the past that had stretched longer. He had awakened to singed pots and a mewling Angel. Once, his students pounding on his door brought him back and scrambling. That had been another dark day.

He puffed a smoke-ring into the last of the light and sighed. There were times when he felt trapped within the limits of one of his landscapes. No matter how much detail he might add to the scene the result was the same: a trigger, a lapse into the past, followed by a return to his recriminating present. He had forged a life here in Piling, but his past kept him from living it. He stayed until the stars rode high and walked home beneath their winking observation and the light of a quarter-moon. His shadow feet found their footing on the shadow path as if by their own accord.

He slept. Thankfully, he did not dream.

The next morning Angel woke him up in time to watch the fishing fleet warp its way out of the bay. A small line of children come to study snaked along the path as if following the small flotilla. Some of the children shouted and waved at the departing craft. He looked at the approaching group, noted the missing, and accepted the absent as a fact of daily life. None of the kids nearing his gate were older than twelve. In Piling, when a child hit their teens they hit the waves, even girls. The town liked and admired their strange tutor from Esda, but fish always held first position.

Jeril did not mind the town's partial interest in the education of their children. Of all the things his life had taught him, the one that stood foremost was that one did not push unless one felt confident in the result. He could have insisted, but then he would have been ultimately responsible for the results. Twenty years ago he made a choice not to push and let his brother and the world's currents push him away from a conflict he could have never won. He lived. Harsh lesson well learned.

He went to the door, opened it and welcomed his daily charges, who trooped in like a flock of starlings, fluttering to their places with the facility of familiarity. Variations of "Good morning, Master Sandre", the name he went by among them, attended their entrance, and Jeril's mood lightened as it always did when the kids came. He chuckled into his beard as he took his accustomed place at the head of the table. Theirs was an informal tutelage, the mass of them clustered about the table with slates and precious paper, sharing books or listening to his readings.

"What will we do today, Master Jeril?" piped a little blonde waif named Seri. Her mother ran the kitchens at the town's one tavern. Eleven-year old Seri, freckled by the summer sun and altogether curious and spunky, hardly ever missed. Her older brother had been one of Jeril's most promising pupils in his day, but he followed his father out after fish at thirteen. Two years later the sea took both of them. Seri started coming just after, early, only five at the time, and had functioned like a human sponge ever since.

Jeril gave her a fake scowl, also part of their morning ritual. "We will do as we have always done…"

"Sums, reading and stories," the children finished for him, their voices forming an audible counterpoint to the faint wind-music from the drafty spaces.

"Today is Dem's birthday," Seri asserted. "We should do something different."

Jeril considered, gave a mock withering glance at the shy and awkward Dem, a shaggy haired lump of just turned ten, a slow but diligent pupil whose father always led when the fishing boats set out.

"So, you've reached double digits then, Dem?" The boy reddened appreciably. "Such a felicitous number. Something different, hmm." He paused, looked at Seri, who winked at him and tilted her head in the direction of Jeril's paints.

"Come on, Master Jeril," she urged. "Please?" She reached into her pouch and pulled out a large wad of the rough paper used to wrap up fish. "See? My maman gave me ALL this for us to use."

"Fish paper?" Jeril scowled. "What will we do, play connect the dots with the blood and guts stains?"

Seri frowned, waving the mass upside down. "No silly, just the back sides! See? No stains, no scales. Perfect!"

"But the smell," Jeril protested, which brought peels of laughter from all of them.

"What smell?" asked the smallest of them, little Taina, a red-haired bob of sauce.

"Really, Master," added another, brown-eyed Beyn, the cooper's son. "We don't mind the smell."

Seri shook the wad meaningfully. "Well?" she demanded. "Since when do you say no because of a smell?" She sniffed elaborately. "This place smells like last week's cooking mixed with Angel's hair. Really, I should come and help you clean it up one of these days."

Jeril leaned back, laughing, in his chair, quite convinced. *Such promise.*

"Fine," he said, reaching for the mathematics text. "Sums, reading and stories, as usual, but…" He paused for effect, sweeping his glance around the table to stop, pointedly, at Dem. "After, and if you do your best, we will put Seri's paper to good use with some drawing practice."

"And paints?" chirped Seri.

Jeril flipped open the book. "And paints! Now, slates everyone. Attend to these numbers. First one done gets to give Angel her morning treat."

The children ran through their lessons with commensurate zeal. Jeril beguiled them with a story about Minuet from *The Queen's Book of Tales*, a collection of Pevanese folklore compiled by Queen Eleni Avedun during the first year of her marriage to the king. After story-time Seri distributed her hoard of smelly paper and for an hour the house fell into a quiet rhythm of scratching pencils and charcoal sticks, whispered commentaries balanced by the occasional giggle, and all laced with the musical whistle from the house walls.

Jeril mixed up measures of paint on an old cutting board for a communal palette and let them have a go at using colors on their drawings. Once again, Seri showed her potential. Where the other children dove for the primary colors, she took her time, dabbing carefully, mixing pigments together in unique ways before applying them in layers to her canvas. She worked a different subject as well. Most of the others drew rocks or approximations of the headlands or their houses or their father's boats. Seri focused on Angel, who had perched herself on the windowsill to watch the proceedings. Jeril kept half an eye on her progress as he pretended to help the others. Right away, he could tell Seri possessed an instinctive connection between shape and color as she captured Angel's regal bearing.

She deserves a proper school, he thought, pausing to look closely at her results. *I will need to send a letter to Pevana. Perhaps I could find her a place in one of the Queen's new schools. She can do better than wasting her youth on the boats or mucking out the tavern kitchens.*

"Well done, Seri," he murmured over her shoulder. "You've got her eyes just right. And I really like how you've feathered the tan, sienna and black for that patch on her flank."

"I like to draw things," she replied. "Dem's father says once the weather shuts down the season, he will let me paint a design on his boat."

"Really? What do you have in mind?"

Seri glanced up at him, as if startled by the frank tone of his question.

"You sound different," she said.

"Do I? Perhaps I'm just surprised at your skill."

"So you think I have some?"

"Absolutely. And I'm not the only one it seems." Angel, after a leonine stretch, jumped down from the sill to examine Seri's painting, coming close to sniff at a corner.

Seri giggled. "Do you think she likes it?" She reached out a hand to pet the cat, who responded by arching into the stroke and purring.

"I'm sure she does," Jeril answered. "But one never knows with cats."

Angel allowed one more stroke before moving on with a last definitive twitch of her tail. The movement seemed to break the magic. Voices rose as the others compared compositions. Dem and Taina clustered close to admire Seri's.

Jeril backed away to grab the water bucket from the sink. He poured some into a basin and brought it back to the bench.

"Right!" he bellowed. "Paint time seems to be over. Brushes here. Tack your paintings over there with the pins you see sticking out from the cork-board. Then all of you head outside to the rain barrel for a wash. Clean up, and after we'll have a bite while things dry."

It was a different group that left later. That morning they arrived an organic mass of arms, legs and energy. That afternoon they left in a line, almost solemn, each one carrying their piece of art as if it were some votive offering to their house gods.

Later, the fishing boats ghosted home. Jeril counted them with half a thought as he always did, reassured once again as the numbers added up. The light slowly faded on another day of his life in exile. He glanced out the seaward window just before true dark and blinked, once, twice, unsure. It might have been a last reflection of the sunset, but he thought he saw red…and it was moving.

Chapter 2. A Task Set...

The absence of sound woke Jeril in the middle night. No wind teased through the thin spaces, and the light seemed all wrong. He blinked himself alert, rose and paced to the north-facing window. The area below seemed bathed in a red light. Red light and not from dawn's east. He snapped his eyes shoreward, and in that movement lurched into full on panic. Piling was burning, the flames lighting the beach. He looked closer, took in the shapes of three galleys pulled close to the beach and a cluster of moving shapes.

None of it made sense. Clarity came with the sickening flare of another building falling to the torch. Jeril took in the location even as he turned to grab his kitchen knife and rush for the door. He did not have the time to dig his sword out from the storage bench.

Flames that high meant the tavern and its store of spirits.

Seri and her mother.

He ignored the stitch in his back as he sped out through the gate and down the path. The scene below crystalized as the tavern fire grew. The added light gave definition to the strange galleys on the beach.

All three rocked with furled sails, but even in the half-light Jeril could make out their red pigment.

Blood-red, Esdan sails.

Memories flooded to the present, and he began to keen as he ran. Every time he checked his progress, the scene below changed. Sounds now attended the raging fire light. Screams, shouted war cries, cruel laughter and harsh cheering. He made out the metallic glint of helms moving in groups through the small streets. More cries. Sounds of female voices. And, horrifically, the terrified cries of children cut short.

He redoubled his pace, fairly leaping over his rock-pile seat, half-falling, half-flying down the descending path to the beach. With each bound he left behind twenty years of passivity and acceptance. Old military thought patterns from his youth reasserted themselves.

Almost immediately they told him he acted the fool, thinking he could do anything against armed soldiers with just a notched kitchen knife.

But those flames. Those screams.

Seri and Dem and Taina. No!

His feet hit sand. He stumbled, regained his balance, gasping for air, half-sobbing against the rage. He could make out the galleys clearly now, sleek, fast, lethal and made to carry forty to sixty men each.

He did the math.

And slowed down.

Not pirates, obviously, he thought. *But why here? What is Jorian up to? If Jorian is still emperor…*

His ignorance brought him to a dead stop. The screams from the town stopped at the same time. He had no way of knowing, but his innermost hate told him his brother still lived, had ruled for twenty years in his cynical, manipulative fashion, and those ships were killing Piling at his orders. *But why? No treasure but fish.*

He flashed back to their last conversation over his mother's stiffening corpse, the look in his brother's eyes, the way his mouth had worked, shaping a smile that had darkness at its center, the non-choice he gave.

He started moving again in measured strides. He swung inland off the beach to approach the town from behind the low dunes that arched off the shore. His thoughts strengthened with his resolve. *No raid, this. Message rather, but to whom? Me? Why?*

He had accepted his exile twenty years ago, never journeyed beyond Piling once he arrived there. No one knew his whole past. He was the mysterious tutor from Esda. And that brought a chill to his spine. He had never made a secret of his origins.

Fishing boats went out to sea from Piling.

Some of them did not return.

Although improbable, it was still possible that word of the hermit above the headland might have reached inquisitive ears…and Jorian had always been an inquisitive sort.

But that just *felt* wrong. Jorian had dismissed him with impunity. This was larger than a family quarrel. Then he recalled hearing about an embassy last year from the east; he chalked it up to fisherman rumor that filtered up and down the coastal areas. But now those flames and those red sails furled on the beach spoke otherwise. No rumor. Fact. And *that* did make a sick kind of sense, and convinced Jeril that his brother still ruled Esda. This was a message to him *and* Perspa. *No escape. No security.*

"Curse you, brother," he muttered, running a hand through sweaty hair and quickening his pace. "What can one man do against the reach of empire?" He shifted his knife from hand to hand as he walked, mind racing in search of a plan. *Not much,* he thought, *but a brave man would do something. For honor, for pride, for Seri, Dem and the others. Something.*

He reached the first of the town's outbuildings, unburned yet, and hid behind a corner to search out the scene as best he could. The village structures still blazed, and the half-light illuminated the slopes that climbed inland. A line of shadows wound up the beaten way. At least some of Piling's folk escaped the raid. The raiders left them unpursued, which reinforced his earlier supposition. The sight brought a flicker of hope. Perhaps Seri and her mother were among them, but then he recalled the uprush of fire and smoke from the tavern. Hope faded along with courage. He crouched lower, considered leaving and following the survivors, but the need to know drove him to slink away from cover. He made it to the shadow of a hovel with its roof already fully engulfed, peeked around the corner and recoiled when the point of a spear nearly took his eye.

"Stand up," a voice growled.

Jeril rose and instinct took over. He leaned away, swung up with his free hand to deflect the spear, then shifted forward in the same motion to bury the blade of his knife hilt deep in the man's throat. The violence of the blow broke the weapon and sent the soldier reeling backwards in a shower of blood. Jeril picked up the man's spear and turned to face four of his fellows who must have witnessed the affair.

They spread out to encircle him, shouting as they moved.

Behind them, Jeril saw other shapes approaching, led by one with the high helm of an Esdan naval officer, confirming his earlier fears. He ran through his options, found none, and snarled as he flung the spear with remembered skill at the officer. But his body failed him at the attempt, the tightness in his back, grief and weariness all combining to send the spear sailing harmlessly wide.

A glancing blow to the head from a spear shaft sent him to his knees, another against his shoulders sent him all the way prone. Then a booted foot took him in the side. He struggled for air as hands grabbed his arms and hair and hauled him upright. He coughed, tasted copper, felt a sharp pain from bruised or cracked ribs and glared into the eyes of the officer. The burning hovel made the man's eyes dance with yellow and red, lending a surreal quality to Jeril's failure.

"So, one of the rats stayed behind, eh?" the man said, coming closer. "Let's get him over to the square and have a look at him."

Jeril went unresisting as the group moved back through the town. Most of the structures had collapsed in showers of sparks and flames by then. For Jeril the walk was nightmarish, observing treasured familiarity reduced to glowing coals. Bodies littered the ground. He recognized Byrn the cooper, lying spread-eagled with a gaping slash in his throat, his blood-soaked garments smoldering from the flames of his burning barrels. A bit further on he saw Dem's little form impalled to the ground by a broken spear shaft. Jeril quailed but strong arms kept him upright and moving. The heat from the still burning tavern created a slight whirlwind that sucked in ashes and detritus. Stray papers bounced by. Fate sent his foot down on one of them, pinning it. He glanced down, saw Angel's singed features, and vomited blood and bile in a stream that splattered against the back of the guard in front of him. The man spun in surprise and disgust and backhanded Jeril's face. He felt hair and skin rip from the force of the blow, but he did not care. How could he? The signs were clear. Death to all he knew or cared for. He shut his eyes against the pain, afraid that his captors might unknowingly show him Seri's corpse.

They urged him along to the square before the still burning tavern. They bound his arms tightly behind him. He spat blood again and tried to clear his vision. They shoved him over to a post sunk in the ground in the cleared space before the tavern. They lashed him to it with lengths of ship's rope. He sagged there against his bindings, blood still dribbling down his chin. Through his pain he watched half-lit drops plop into the beaten earth to add his contribution to the rest of Piling's effusion.

Someone grabbed his hair and pulled his face upright. The officer came close then to inspect him. Jeril blinked away sweat. His vision cleared. Even in the lurid glow from the fires, he could see the tell-tale olive colored skin, rounded eyes, the creases at forehead and lower chin that spoke of a career wearing authority's helm. This was no junior officer.

"Name," the man insisted.

"I am the tutor for this place." Jeril spoke slowly, carefully forming words around torn lips.

"Then you are a tutor who has had training," the officer replied. "I saw you take one of my men. No lies."

"Luck."

The officer turned and spat. Then slapped Jeril viciously across the face.

"I said no lies!" he snarled. "Who are you, and why didn't you run with the others?"

Jeril shook off the pain of the blow. Thoughts of poor, shy Dem, and Seri, and the picture of Angel, wrinkled and half-burned, swam before his inner eye.

"I have friends here. I needed to see if you had killed all of them."

The officer stepped back, slapped him once again, snapping Jeril's head such that he felt sure his neck might break.

"Wrong answer. Try again. Name? Where did you take your training? Speak or I'll spit you here and now."

Jeril considered telling him the truth then, if only to ensure that the officer might follow through on his threat and end his agony. He hurt, everywhere, but nowhere as deeply as his heart. To see life that he had come to know and share snuffed out with such incendiary alacrity pushed him to the edge. He gathered bloody spittle to make his final comment, made eye contact with the officer…and then spat to the side instead, the instinct for life defeating him. Internally, he cursed his lack of courage even as curiosity took hold. Inspite of being bound and broken, he still wanted to know why.

"My name is Ban," he muttered, dredging up the name of a long lost friend. "I spent a year as a guard in the city of Teirne. I have been teacher here for over ten years."

The officer came close to scrutinize Jeril's eyes, looking for the truth or the lie. He stared for a long, uncomfortable moment in silence while the flames flapped and sparks popped around them.

"You are a bloody mess, Ban," he murmured. "And yet I can tell your skin color. Plus, your eyes give you away, no matter how much you might try and hide them behind all that hair. You've an eastern look about you, friend, and I remember learning the move you used on poor Tanil."

"I'm just a tutor."

The officer smirked. "Not any more, I suspect." He swung his gaze tellingly. "I think we've taken most of your business from you. Sorry."

"Why?" Jeril rasped. "What did Esda want from Piling?"

The officer smiled openly at Jeril's mistake. "Ah! I was right! How did you know that, Ban, or whatever your real name is?"

Jeril glared but held his tongue. The officer came close again. Jeril looked closely and noticed the end line of a scar half-hidden by his helm's cheek guard. And that voice…

"You are correct, of course," the officer continued. "And I suppose you might think this tragic event nothing more than cruel fate, the accidental slaughter of innocents, unconnected to any pattern or purpose."

"Who are you?" Jeril whispered, even though he knew, now, wincing yet again as his ravaged lips protested.

"Jorian of Esda," the officer retorted. "See? I can give a lie just as easy."

"This is madness." Jeril groaned. His knees gave out, and he sagged further against his bindings.

"Correct again." Jeril felt a hand grasp his chin and force his eyes upward. The officer sneered, dropping all false mirth from his tone. "As I said before, your eyes give you away. The only madness about this night, friend, is thinking that you could leave your past behind."

Sickening alarm suffused Jeril's senses, but he could not speak. The officer grabbed Jeril's throat and tightened his grip. Jeril felt the constriction, surged to the edge of panic.

"The emperor sends his regards," the officer said, releasing the pressure and stepping back a pace. "We've always known where you got off to. He made it his hobby to keep track of you. We were going to head to your house once we finished here. You just saved my men a climb, thank you very much."

"That is absurd."

"I quite agree. But the Emperor has his quirks."

"I was never worth such attention."

"Neither was this western land with its petty cities and half-savage kings, but all that changed five years ago."

"I don't understand."

"Living in this backwater, I can see why you wouldn't. All fish and grubby little minds, really, Jeril, for it is Jeril, don't deny it, you've fallen pretty low."

"Scarcely worth such attention." He did not bother to dispute the use of his real name.

"That was always up to the emperor to decide, but you are partly correct yet again. This place has not dulled all of your senses, apparently.

This is a message for the king of this land. Your presence just added spice to sauce Jorian's wit."

"These people were innocent."

"There are no innocents, not anymore."

"So, am I to die, now, at my brother's whim?"

"You have always lived, or died, at the emperor's whim. He wanted you to know that."

"Since when do middling naval officers know the mind of the emperor?"

"When said emperor asks the captain of his personal guard to undertake a special task. I told you I recognized the move you used. I teach it to all new imperial guardsmen."

Raw emotions from past and present swelled like the flames that consumed Piling. The collected recriminations of twenty years lived in ignorance took Jeril and tossed him, spiritually, into the pit. The officer took off his helm. In the flickering light, Jeril saw clearly the scar on the right cheek, and he remembered that voice, those cold, hard eyes. Darkness that was more than just fading firelight tinted the edges of his vision. All dead, everything dead, even illusions.

"So kill me," he rasped, pleading for an end, any end rather than more of the lurid here and now. "Have done and let me go. Tell Jorian I wept and pleaded for my life. Tell him whatever he wants to hear. I don't care anymore."

The officer shook his head with mock sadness and pity. "Sorry, Jeril, but you don't get off so easily. Like I said before, you live or die at Jorian's whim. And for now you will live. Jorian has taken an interest in this land. He wanted to send a message. These flames will do for a start. You will sweeten the deal."

"Strange choice of words for such a bitter business."

The officer gave a barking laugh. "Finally, some of that wit your brother boasted you possessed. This 'bitter business', as you put it, is in deadly earnest. Word of tonight will no doubt spread, but yours will be the better voice to give its proper power."

"Why would the King of Perspa listen to me? I'm nobody to him or his realm."

"That's where it gets personal, doesn't it? You are a nobody, but you know what is coming if Perspa resists. Who better to clarify Esda's power to Perspa's upstart king than Jeril Tandori, the emperor's brother?"

"I left that name behind twenty years ago."

"You were allowed to think so. Time to think again, friend."

Jeril swallowed that bitterness for the truth it held. He should have known. He should have kept moving all those years ago. He let the life he constructed in Piling layer over old wounds, old skills, old responsibilities. His name was a tether he could never completely break as long as his brother lived and ruled. Clarity snapped like a bear trap on the options he once thought he possessed. *No way out save suicide.* Even as that notion oozed up from the slime of his emotions, he knew he could never.

Too much useless honor...

"This land is not worth such bloody instruction," he said, gritting his teeth and steeling his despair to confront life.

The officer turned away, snapped off a series of curt orders that sent soldiers marching off back toward the waiting galleys. Within moments all that remained in the square were the officer, Jeril and the scattered, lumped shapes of Piling's dead.

"Tell this to King Donari Avedun, and do not tell me you will not go. Give him what name you wish. Your personal lies are of no account. Your description of this," and he waved a hand to include the ruins about, "will perhaps coerce a more credent ear from the man. I have left you one serviceable boat for the purpose. Like I said, we watch this coast. If you run, we will just burn the next village up and keep right on going until we reach Pevana itself. You smell like blood and ethics. I do not think you will want that on your conscience. So," he continued, coming close, face to face, to make sure Jeril heard and understood, "say to Donari that unless he agrees to Jorian's demands, we will come with sword and flames and turn his land into a desert."

"What demands?"

"Go to Pevana and find out. And when you find out, be persuasive. Tutor the king to wisdom and save lives."

"Madness."

"You are in no position to define madness. You are a messenger. Deliver it." The officer moved around behind Jeril. He felt a blade slip between his bound hands and cut them free. Then the ropes that bound him to the post fell away, and he collapsed to a sitting position, back against the post, flexing the blood painfully back into his hands. The officer leaned down for one last word.

"Hear this, 'lord'. Do not fail. We can take everything from you whenever we want."

"Why wait so many years?"

"That's the only thing coincidental about all of this," laughed the officer as he turned to go. "You've always been a tool waiting for use. You know your brother. He has not changed in twenty years; still the same focused, magnificient bastard when he sets the bit in his teeth. I rather admire how he has ridden you over the years. By the way, I think you recognized me earlier. No secrets: my name is Tacidus, if you need the assist, and if ever we meet again it will be because you have failed your task. And you will not have to ask for death, then."

The man walked away before Jeril could summon a response. He watched the officer disappear from view, followed the audible progress as the Esdans pushed the galleys out of the shallows and readied for sail. Around him Piling's fires fell to smoking clumps of ruin. Dawn's light silhouetted the Esdan craft as they rowed out to sea. Their red sails blended into a red sunrise. They dipped below the horizon as the light brightened to full morning.

By midmorning, Piling's few survivors slinking back to sift through the rubble found him. They bathed his hurts as best they could, and when he recovered enough he helped them collect and bury the dead. The folk wept and raged at first, asking him over and over why such violence had come to them. And Jeril wept anew alongside them, offering what partial answers he could to explain but keeping the darker, deeper truths hidden. They buried the dead in a common grave above the tide line. Jeril committed to memory each of the faces before pushing dirt into the hole. He paused longest over Seri's pale visage, oddly calm, as if she were only asleep and not dead from the gaping hole in her side.

When all was finished, he returned to his house, staggering in through the gate dazed but determined to lose no time. He rolled several canvases into a tube, stuffed several brushes and favored charcoal pencils into a bag, to which he added a jumble of extra clothing and some of his most precious books. Into a smaller bag he tossed some of yesterday's bread and what was left of a cheese Seri's mother had sent earlier. He moved puppet-like, jerking from task to task with little grace. Even the musical notes produced by the afternoon breeze sounded dirge-like and somber. Almost as an after-thought, he remembered to dig out his sword from its place buried beneath his extra blankets in the storage box. He slung it over his shoulder.

From a hollow underneath a loose brick before the hearth he hauled a leather bag, long untouched and nearly forgotten. It held the remains of the money Jorian sent with him twenty years ago. He hefted its bitter, bitter mass and stuffed it into the bag, finding a fatal kind of irony in how his life had come full circle.

When he finished he blew last night's banked coals to life and lit a stick to which he tied some of his paint-soiled rags. The flames danced colorfully for a second. At another time he would have found that interesting, but he had had enough of fire. He had intent enough for just one more.

He would send his own message to Tacidus, officer of Jorian's guard.

He blew on the flames until they took full hold, then tossed it into the corner where he stored his paints, finished works and extra canvases. Within seconds, the fire found the oiled pigments, and flames leaped from floor to ceiling. As if in response, the wind freshened, and the draft through the weak spaces in the walls and windows fanned the blaze, which spread eagerly along the walls.

He opened the door and watched the flames for a moment. Angel hissed from the kitchen countertop and bolted beneath Jeril's feet, a mottled orange, black and white blur. She waited for him on top of the fence, mewling pathetically. Jeril paused to sweep her up in the crook of his arm. He shouldered his bags and headed back down toward the beach.

Piling's survivors clustered about him as he made his preparations to leave. He answered their questions as best he could.

"Those that did this have charged me with taking word to the king," he said, depositing Angel on the stern seat and tossing his bags amid-ship next to the boat's small mast. "They will not return once I am gone. Rebuild or leave. You choose, but what I told you earlier is true. This was no piracy. Get word south along the coast, if you can. Regardless, our world has changed. Farewell."

He put his shoulder to the hull and pushed. Several others splashed through the shallows and helped steady the boat against the first waves, timing the push to send it into deeper water. Jeril shipped the oars and thrust as quickly as he could away from shore. The ruins of Piling smoldered in the afternoon sun, a mute testimony urging him to action. An odd feeling of symmetry washed over Jeril as he rowed away for the second time in twenty years from everything he had ever known or cared about.

"Goodbye Seri, Dem," he whispered.

The wind freshened when he cleared the bay. He unshipped the oars and raised the sail. Angel took refuge from the boat's new motion beneath the stern seat as Jeril placed the tiller in its brace. He tied off the sail to take the wind on its quarter and leaned into the pull on the tiller to set the boat's bows heading northward.

To Pevana.

He had a message to deliver.

Chapter 3: A new home in someone else's old haunts…

Jeril limped into Pevana's harbor, boat half swamped from a squall that caught him too far from shore to make a run to safety. That storm rinsed the smoke of Piling's burning from the horizon but could not rinse the memories from his mind. A wet and bedraggled Angel hissed at him from underneath the rowing bench. Just as uncomfortable as the cat, he kept to the stern-seat working lines and tiller. If he could have spared the energy, he would have hissed back. Each time he tacked, water sloshed across his boots. While the storm did not carry away any of his belongings, he suspected some of the canvases stashed in their tubes were now waterlogged and ruined. He must have cut a pathetic figure, crawling his way through busy shipping; galleys from up and down the coast crowded the waters just inside the harbor.

Piling burned while Pevana prospered, oblivious of the message held in the pillar of smoke that snaked heavenward as Jeril sailed north.

He avoided accident and tied up next to where a flight of stone steps ascended to the harbor square. He tossed a coin to a boy who had rushed down the steps to help him.

"I have business above," he gruffed, shouldering the bags that held what was left of his life. "Watch her for me. Have a care for the cat. She had a rough time of it. I should return soon. Where would I find the Harbor Master?"

The boy pocketed the coin and pointed up the stairs. "See the building above? That is the office. You should find Master Harbinton there."

Jeril tossed another coin. "For the name. My thanks, and yours?"

The boy smiled, a gap-toothed affair. "Tam, sir, and don' worry. She looks like a nice little thing. I'll scoop her dry for you. An' if you do stay longer, my da' has a mooring with slips for boats her size. What is your cat's name?"

"When she wants to, she answers to Angel. You are a fount of useful skills and information!" Jeril chuckled around the first smile to tease his lips since before Piling. "Are all your folk so industrious?"

The boy's smile deepened. "I wouldna know for sure, but my da' says Pevana has never seen such traffic."

Jeril swept his gaze back over his winding course through the collected shipping.

"I suspect your father is right." He paused, considered, then dropped all but the small bag that held his money, which he stuffed into a pocket inside his coat. "Watch all of it for me, and when my business above is done, perhaps we will go have a talk with your father about that moorage."

He found the office as directed, a small place that shadowed the topmost steps. Entering, he found a hairy round man swathed in a stained, worn green jacket seated behind a table, one meaty finger of one meaty hand holding open a ledger; the other clutched a pen poised above the page. An ink drop swelled against the tip.

"Name and business?"

"Master Harbinton?"

"Who else? Name and business. I've work to do."

"You are about to drip."

"Drip? What?"

Jeril pointed. Harbinton scowled, noticed, and returned the pen to its well.

"Now, name and business," he said, the tone of his voice just slightly less perturbed. "You were watched coming in. Pretty seamanship."

"I have a few year's experience."

"My man said your boat looked a bit beaten up. Run into trouble?"

"Squall, last night, to the south."

"And those bruises on your face? That split lip?"

"I came from Piling."

That brought raised brows and clipped comments.

"Fishing town, small. Watchers reported smoke days ago."

"Burned," Jeril added. "Most of its people killed or fled. I've come with a warning."

"And so have delivered it," said a voice from behind.

Jeril turned. Framed in the door stood a man dressed in all black, close-fitting clothes, that, to Jeril's memories of his former life, looked suspiciously like an informal uniform. The man advanced closer, smiling, and Jeril surmised him still in his twenties but with steady, steely, intelligent eyes that suggested experience beyond his years.

"And you still haven't given Master Harbinton your name."

The tone, at once jocular but with the hint of authority, raised Jeril's suspicions such that he paused before replying. He had his fill of officers back at Piling. Although this man bore no obvious insignia, he carried himself like a man used to responsibility and authority.

"Who are you?" Jeril asked.

"The one who watched you dance around all those tubs like you knew what you were doing. Small boat, in from the south, unfamiliar cut to her. Not one of our local lot. Got me curious, so I watched. That's my job, watching. My name is Devyn Ambrose, eyes and ears to King Donari Avedun. And who might you be, friend? You say you came from Piling, but by those eyes of yours, I'd hazard a guess you weren't born there."

"Before Piling burned, I was ten years there. Before that…other places. My name is Jeril Sandre. I am a painter and tutor." Memory teased at the sound of Ambrose's name: there were several poems in the queen's collection credited to a Devyn Ambrose.

"And a survivor, apparently," Ambrose said. "Your face says you ran afoul of them. Why did they let you live?"

"I lived on the edge of the place," Jeril temporized, unwilling to reveal all the truth, still trying to process the connection he had surmised. He sensed he was in deep waters here. In all his moves over the years, his explanations had sufficed for the simple villagers he settled amongst, but there was nothing simple about his presence on Pevana's wharf and definitely nothing simple about this Devyn Ambrose. He paused, noticeably, drawing a more piercing look from Ambrose, and made a choice. "Truth: three Esdan galleys beached in the night three days ago. They killed many, set light to everything. I fought back. They left me for dead. Folk who fled returned, cleaned me up and sent me here with word."

"So some lived."

Jeril saw the trap: an inquiry, more questions, but he was committed now. "Some lived," he agreed. "I lost many friends, Devyn Ambrose, and I want the king to hear of this and do something. I am tired, and I do not want any more questions. I taught the children of Piling for a decade, man, and they cut them down."

"Esdans? Raiding our coastline? You are sure?

"Yes. As you said, I was not born in Piling. You noticed my eyes. In another life, I came from Esda, but I am no spy. I fought for Piling. You have lurkers off your coasts."

"Who happen to surprise a village in three galleys. Three."

"Organized lurkers, Ambrose. Mark it. Truth. I came to warn you. I have done so. Now, arrest me or let me go. My world burned three days ago, and I need to rest before I try and build another."

Ambrose looked at him, his blue eyes intent, considering. Then he nodded as if making up his mind. "I believe you," he said, finally. "What do you think, Harbinton?"

Jeril turned back to face the Harbor Master, who had re-dipped his pen and recommenced scribbling in his ledger.

"Plausible," he grunted without looking up. "Some of Casan's rags were left still unaccounted for last spring, but there have been rumors about the tone of the latest trade talks with the Esdan ambassador."

"True," Ambrose responded, reappraising Jeril yet again. "I apologize for pushing at you, Jeril Sandre. King Donari has been busy mending things in the north. Perhaps we should turn our attention now to the seaways."

"That would be wise," Jeril asserted, dumbfounded that Ambrose did not press him further. And yet word had come to Piling of their new king and the changed atmosphere of his rule. People trusted here. They believed. He understood suspicion and possessed ties by blood to manipulation and betrayal that went back generations. Ambrose believed him…astonishing. In the moment he felt a weight leave him. Someone else knew. Someone else could seek the revenge he wanted for Seri, Dem, and all those lost souls sacrificed to his half-brother's perverse ill-humor. He sagged back against the table; weary now more from suppressed grief than the exertions of his journey north. A light touch on his forearm brought him back.

"You look as if you need to rest, Jeril Sandre," Ambrose said with genuine concern. "I will get this news to the king. What are your plans? You say you are a painter and tutor. Perhaps you should consider making a new start here in Pevana. Have you a place to stay? The king will likely wish to speak with you."

Jeril stared dumbly, overcome by the need to make a choice. He had run for twenty years. He was tired of running. He had nowhere else to go. Perhaps he could lose himself in this city by the sea, capital to a newly founded kingdom.

"Yes," he whispered, at first almost to himself but growing louder to include Ambrose and Harbinton as the conviction settled. "Yes, I will stay. I want to stay. I've work to do."

"Don't we all," groused Harbinton, tapping his pen again into the ink. "If Ambrose here is satisfied, perhaps he could direct you, so I could get on with mine."

Ambrose laughed as he led Jeril back outside.

"As it happens I know of a place. See to your boat and baggage, and I'll take you there. It is on my way. The proprietess is something of a friend of a friend, you might say."

Ambrose waited at the top of the steps while Jeril returned to Tam and his boat. The boy had bailed her dry and laid out the sail, the spare lines, and Jeril's bags on the dock to air out. Jeril fingered several more coins and proffered them.

"My thanks, Tam."

Tam sat on a pilon, scratching Angel behind her ears like he had been doing it all his life.

"Did your business go well above?" he asked.

"Well enough. I have a mind to trust you, young man, with the payment of another coin for surety. Where is your father's moorage?"

The boy pointed to a covered shed a small distance off.

"Excellent," Jeril said. "This should be enough for your father's price, yes?" Tam nodded. Jeril marveled at how quickly his voice changed when talking to children. "Good," he continued. "Could you row her over for me, get her all stowed? Tell him Jeril Sandre will return in the morning to talk with him. Just now, I need to find me a room and meal. The man at the top of the stairs says he knows a place."

Tam looked. "Oh, that's Devyn Ambrose!" he piped.

"You know him then?"

The boy untied Jeril's boat and clambered down to the rowing bench. "Everyone knows the poet Devyn Ambrose," he said as he pushed off and set the oars in their locks. "He has the king's ear."

"So I gather. I can trust him, then?"

Tam spread his gapped tooth smile. "Like you trust me," he responded. "I like your cat, Master Sandre! She's nice." He set the boat gracefully in motion.

"She is more discerning than most people I know," Jeril chuckled. He scooped up his bags with one hand, Angel with the other, and turned to go. "Come you, inconstant vixen, let us see what we might make of Pevana."

He rejoined Ambrose at the top of the stairs, who graciously took one of the bags, smiled at the cat and led Jeril through the harbor gate to the city proper. Not far from the gate square, he turned in at a house separated from the road by a courtesy fence with a fragile wooden gate. A decorous sign hung on a post next to that gate: Landare's Lodging House, inquire within.

Ambrose handed him his bag. "The mountainous woman who runs this place is called Gania," he pointed at the sign, "Gania Landare. She growls but keeps a clean house for a fair price. I know she has a room to let. The prior tenant shipped out north just before you limped in. I will take your warning to the king. Rest. You need it, but be ready to talk when I come for you next."

"I thought you said you believed me."

Ambrose let Angel sniff his hand. She hissed at first, then reconsidered, scrunching her whiskers and then giving the extended index finger a quick lick.

"I do," Ambrose said, turning to go. "But I think there is more to you, Jeril Sandre, painter and tutor, with your eastern eyes and cautious manner, a story I would like to know. That is the other part of my job, collecting stories."

"I have not much to tell," Jeril said, wondering what to make of this curious young man.

Ambrose smiled to take any sting from his words away.

"One thing my life has taught me," he said walking away, "is to never be surprised at what people will say. Everyone has a story worth telling. I will get word to you here. Expect it. Farewell for now."

Jeril watched him walk away until a passing wagon obscured his view. When the wagon moved out of the way, Ambrose was gone. Jeril steadied his nerves and his baggage, pushed open the gate and walked up to the door, which opened before he could put down his things to knock.

Ambrose's description proved apt as a female form filled the door space. Jeril recoiled slightly. The woman had a basket on her arm as if she were off to market and took an aggressive step forward before she realized someone was in her way.

"Oh!" the woman exclaimed, "didn't see you there. Sorry. Are you selling or asking?"

"Selling?" Jeril stammered. "I, I…"

"Well, it's obviously not selling. That lot is never at a loss for words, so you must be asking. Looking for a room, are you?"

The woman's raspy voice, as though she had spent half her life breathing tavern fumes, forced Jeril to recoil another step.

"Devyn Ambrose sent me. He said you might have a room to let, Mistress Landare, I presume?"

The woman swept the area with her baleful eyes. "What? Run off already, did he? He's always doing that, darting here and there on the king's business. Afraid of me, that one." She settled back on Jeril. "And he's right to be. Instructive, that is."

"I quite understand," Jeril responded. He could not quite keep the tremor out of his voice. He was tired, despondent, out of his element and knew it, but he took a better breath and controlled himself. "He did have business, in fact. He said you kept a clean house with a room. I'd like to see it, please."

Landare inspected him from head to toe with a scrutiny reserved for dirty dishes. "You look a bit seedy, and I do keep a clean house. I like to put clean people in it, if you get my meaning."

Jeril smiled, sensing a change in her tone. "I've had a rough sail here, trouble back home before I left, and I'm sure I look a sight."

At that moment, Angel perked up in the crook of his arm and gave a piteous mewling sound, which had an instantaneous effect on the woman.

"But you have a cat!" she cooed, her tone quieting and softening the way rain dampened heat and sound. "And she's such a prim miss at that! Sounds hungry. You've just arrived, yes? No time for a meal for either of you?"

Her words reminded Jeril of his own hunger.

"As a matter of fact, yes, mistress. We both could use a meal. I have the coin for it, and the room, if you are willing."

"What's your cat's name?" Landare demanded, some of her gruff returning, even as she gently put forward a roughened finger for Angel's approval. Jeril felt her purring response through his arm.

"Her name is Angel," Jeril answered, "and she is my last friend in the world."

Landare stepped back, opened the door to the house wider. "And that's a good name for that one, if I am any judge of cats, which I am.

You'll learn that well enough if you stay long. I have both room and a meal. Three silver a week, another half for water and food. Can you cover that?"

"Yes, easily."

"Oh, is that right," she scoffed, but with more good humor. "Made of money, are you? What trade have you?"

"Painter and tutor."

That brought a scowl. "Bah, I should have known. Makes sense in a way, given the room I have available. Come in then, have a look, and I'll have my Lyssa get something in a bowl for both of you."

Jeril followed her in through the main parlor of the house and up the stairs to the first room at the top. The room had a window that faced out the back of the house and overlooked the alley. A bed, a small chest of drawers and a single table comprised all the furniture.

"It's a bit spare at the moment," Landare offered. "The last fellow took his extra things with him when he shipped out for the north. I might be able to find a decent sitting chair."

Jeril looked longingly at the bed. "Not at all," he said. "It is perfect."

"Well then, consider it yours, and Angel's."

"Thank you, mistress…"

"Call me Gania. I thought you might like the room. It's seen its share of wickedness," Gania growled. "A lady running away from her husband, a calvaryman who died in Roderran's War, and before that, a foolish boy who thought himself a poet."

"What happened to him?"

"The worst thing possible. He became a hero and married a princess. Still," she sighed, "he was a caution. Been gone now for near five years. He's friend to your Devyn Ambrose, actually." Her expression turned skeptical. "I'm wondering if Ambrose isn't having a joke over on me, but never mind. It is a good room, and I am sure a painter will do well enough in it. Have a rest. I'll go see about some water and food."

Jeril dropped his things next to the bed, heard the door close behind him, and put Angel on the corner by the pillow before sinking down with relief on the covers. His mind whirled like a water funnel, but his body claimed him for sleep anyway.

"First day in Pevana," he whispered to Angel as she snuggled near his chin. "Interesting place, eh 'gel?"

Angel's throaty purr accompanied him into slumber.

The next day he rose late, let Gania attempt to make friends with Angel and went to see about his boat at Tam's father's moorage. Once he finished he dawdled on the waterfront to get a sense of Pevana's pace and timbre. He spent an hour sketching the pier where he first tied off. He liked the pattern in the stonework. The amount of traffic in the roads impressed him, ships of all sizes were tied up at the wharf, lines of dockworkers tramped up and down ramps extended from hulls loading and off-loading goods.

For a man who had made it a point for the last twenty years to live in forgotten backwaters, the place seemed to hum like a beehive. It reminded him of Esda's scope, and yet he knew it just a shadow of that immense capital of empire. He looked at the life presented before him, found it pleasing, but he wondered if it could survive the threat he knew must come from the east.

He wanted to disappear into this place and paint himself into some semblance of peace. He wanted to believe Tacidus's threats empty, designed to get him moving again, and nothing more. Yet Pevana's size and obvious prosperity meant growth Jorian would not suffer. Jeril spent a decade serving on the frontier monitoring the threats to Esdan sovereignty. Esda brought the client kingdoms she controlled to heel when they grew wealthy enough to look to their own defense. During his service, Jeril spent as much time reading detailed reports of metallurgy as he did tending to his troops. Increased yields from the mines meant better weapons down the road.

The history of Esda was a timeline of territorial and merchantile conquest. Jeril himself oversaw the investment and pacification of two of them. As he sketched away, he imagined the great map that hung in the palace chartroom in his youth. Esda on its hill above the sea, homelands stretching in a great arc north, east and south, and the allied kingdoms of Berilia, Semilla, Artsenia, and Tillem also in a great arc south, east and north.

But nothing west. No interest in the upstart, half-barbaric kingdom whose capital perched above the confluence of three rivers, whose lords spilled the blood of generations in small arguments over boundary lines and small trade advantages. No interest in the city states of the south, barely more than fishing villages compared to the empire's major population centers, disunited and squabbling like women cursing over wash-tubs.

To Esda, the west was a land of small places not worth treating with or taking.

A sleek, newly launched galley slipped by under oars, bound for the harbor entrance and the open sea beyond, and Jeril thought he might have his answer. Perspa got a new king, who moved the capital to the coast, brought under his scepter all the lands to the south, and suddenly Perspa became much less barbarous and isolated.

The flames that took Piling, all those slaughtered innocents in the dark, meant that Jorian had noticed, and it was now only a matter of time before he brought the weight of empire against this city and its king. Jeril finished his sketch and took a deep breath of salty air tinged with Pevanese essence, almost a spice. He liked the way Tam had warmed to him so quickly, and Gania had fed Angel tid bits with her coarse yet surprisingly gentle hands.

The thought of hands brought memories of his mother back; her's had been the only gentle touch of his youth. She taught him plant simples and how to sketch, gave him the only peace he ever knew at court, and tried to shield him from his father's worse effects.

"Never let the demands of your place get the best of you, Jer-Jer," she said. "No matter how bright the helm or sharp the spear point. Remember the quiet knowledge. Color, shape, taste and touch. Those will always be your haven in this world."

She tried to include Jorian in that space, tried to act the surrogate for the boy's lost mother, tried to show him how to be different, and failed. Jeril blinked back sudden tears at the recollection: her face frozen in death, vial of heartsbane on the bed next to her.

She had saved Jeril but taught Jorian how to kill her. Perhaps, if the three of them had more time together, things might have turned out different. But Jeril's duties took him to the frontier, the father had died too soon, and the younger son had chosen his time. He sighed back to the present.

Time. He wanted time to live here. He wondered if he should tell all the truth. Surely, Ambrose's report would bring a summons, perhaps a genteel interrogation. Did he owe anyone the truth?

"No," he muttered, flipping shut his pad and stowing the pencil back in his coat pocket. "Truth died for me with Seri and all the others back to my mother. Perhaps my fears misinform me."

But Ambrose sensed more to my story than I told, he thought as he walked back toward Gania's house. *And he had a kindred air about him, as if he understood. I wonder why?*

He chewed on the thought until he reached the harbor gate, and then the answer came and startled him such that he stopped in the middle of the street, much to the consternation of the traffic flow that had to shift around him. *He reminds me of myself when I was his age.*

"Preposterous," he scoffed. "I need lunch to settle my wits."

When he reached Gania's, he noticed a carriage stopped by the gate with a dolphin insignia. The driver stood by the matched pair harnessed to the traces, gentling them. Jeril's artist's eye caught the tell tale tip of a carrot poking out of an immaculate pocket as he drew near.

"Note to self," he whispered. "Word travels fast in Pevana." He paused at the gate, caught the driver's eye. "A fine set," he said.

The man smiled affably. "The best in the city for this sort of work, sir, thank you for noticing."

"I assume there's someone inside waiting for me?"

"If you are Sandre the painter, yes, sir. The queen sent a clerk to take your story."

"The Queen?"

The man's smile deepened. "Quite right, sir. You must not be from around here. The Queen Eleni is the King's wife and official historian. This sort of thing is part of her official capacity."

"How novel," Jeril responded, surprised by the easy tone and ready information.

"Sure," the man agreed. "There's some as don't like it, but many more do. Times are changing here."

"I have been here a day, and yet already I can see your point."

The right side horse nickered then and nudged the man's pocket, tensile lips searching for the half-hidden carrot tip. The jostling startled the man back into decorum.

"Perhaps you should go in now, sir. We've been waiting for you."

"Yes, I suppose that would be best."

Jeril squared his shoulders, marshalled his thoughts to spin as much of the truth as he dared, and walked up the porch and through the door.

The clerk kept him for nearly an hour in the sitting room of the house, taking down his story, making copious notes, asking pertinent questions, not so pertinent questions, far, far too many questions, all the while tacitly ignoring the rumbling from Jeril's empty stomach as it reacted to the food smells coming from the kitchen. Finally, Jeril managed to satisfy the clerk, for the man shuffled all his papers together, topped his ink well and shoved everything into a ponderous-looking satchel.

"Well then, Mr. Sandre," he effused, rising and offering an ink-stained hand. "I think I have quite enough for a clear report. So sorry to hear about Piling. I knew a man from there once. Small place, quaint, kind of out of the way."

Jeril found the man's officious platitudes insulting. "And burned," he gruffed, running his fingers once, decisively, through his beard, "and most of her people dead. You have a problem on your coasts, sir. Make sure the king looks to it."

The man took the hint, bowed his head in apology and moved to leave. Just then the carriage driver entered, munching on what Jeril guessed was the last bit of carrot. He had something tucked under his arm. Jeril recognized the shape of an easel immediately.

"What is this?" he demanded.

The driver nearly choked on his mouthful and stopped.

"Well, um," he stammered. Little orange bits spotted his lips. "I think it's called an easel?"

"I know what it is! Why is it here?"

The clerk clapped a hand to his head and exclaimed. "Ah! I forgot! It was already in the carriage when it came for us. There was a note attached. I put it in my pocket so it wouldn't blow away during the ride here. Jeremi here likes to go a bit too quickly."

Jeremi smiled. "Well, you know sir, you said so. A fine pair like that needs a taste of speed now and then to remember what they are."

"In any event," the clerk interrupted. "I think it is meant for you. Sorry, the note wasn't sealed and I took the liberty." He fished a rumpled piece of paper out of his coat and handed it over. "Welcome to Pevana, officially, Mr. Sandre I'm sure we will meet again once the royals read this report. It makes for quite a chilling story. Again, sorry for your loss and troubles."

The two men left, leaving Jeril suspicious and somewhat dumbfounded. He smoothed out the paper and read the words written there in a spidery, male hand:

Sandre,

I found this forgotten treasure in a storage closet. I thought it might come in handy. Sometimes a person needs a tool to help them work out their grief and fears. A wise man once told me Pevana needs all her poets. Something tells me she will need all her painters, too. Until we meet again,

Ambrose

Jeril ran his fingers through his beard again, slowly, tentatively, as if searching for lost wisdom among the mass. Then he shook his head in wonder, let a smile tease the corners of his mouth, and went off to the kitchen in search of something to quell the chorus in his stomach. As he scooped up Angel, set her on his lap, and dipped his spoon into a steaming bowl, his mind turned to contemplating purchases he would need to make.

Chapter 4: A Commission

Within a week, the bustle of Pevanese life quieted Jeril's fears of imminent invasion. No summons came from the palace. He took parts of several days to wander the streets of the city, getting to know his way about, the location of things and the general temper of the people. Few marked him, for Pevana seemed thronged by folk drawn from all over the kingdom. Opportunities swelled like the morning tide. The king's name was on everyone's lips. Taken together, the effect created a heady brew for Jeril; a different kind of emotional investment he found difficult to name at first. Eventually, he settled on 'hope'; something he lost touch with long ago. Seeing it here suffusing the market squares and coloring the tavern talk caused him some disorientation. But that feeling quickly faded as he assembled painting supplies and set about painting his way into familiarity with the place and its attitude. His room quickly took on remembered smells and clutter, a development Gania took up with him when she came to collect her fees.

"Here now," she grumbled. "I rented you a room and board, not a room and studio."

"I'm sorry, Gania," he responded. "I'll try and keep the mess cleaned up. I find this place inspiring, you see. Can't help myself. Sometimes sketches just won't do, and the markets here have all I need to grind and mix colors."

"I should charge you half again as much for all the work you're making for Lyssa."

"Please, tell Lyssa she won't have to touch any of my things beyond the bed linen."

"I keep a clean house, mister, as I said to you before. I'll not have stains on my floors and walls. Watch your dribblings and keep them neat!"

"Of course, mistress, absolutely. And thank you for your patience."

Gania hefted the coins Jeril placed in her palm, smiling as she made them jingle. "Oh, sure, I've patience enough when certain colors are part of the mix!" She coughed a greasy, good natured chuckle. "Keep it tidy, however, or I will boot you! Make no mistake, Mr. Painter!"

Jeril took up his satchel that included his small pallet and small vials of newly mixed colors. He collapsed the easel and shouldered it.

"See?" he asserted. "I'm taking half my mess with me this morning!"

"Where are you off to, then?" Gania asked, preceding him out the door and thumping down the stairs. "And where is that cat of yours?"

"I'm off to the harbor square to have a go at the waves and shipping. I've rarely seen so much activity," Jeril responded, taking care to avoid scraping the walls. "And I let Angel out at dawn to do her own investigating. Lyssa promised to look out for her should she come back before I do."

Gania gave him a vague wave as she turned to go into the kitchen. "Food at sundown, mister. Be late and you'll be on your own. And watch that easel going through my front door!"

Jeril made his way quickly through the morning market traffic, intent on making the most of the light for his purpose. He went back to the spot just up from the boat moorage. High tide lapped against the harbor waterfront stonework. He set out his vials and sat astride the raised barrier of bricks that served as a sort of railing. Below him, Tam sat bobbing in Jeril's boat, fishing. When he made arrangements with Tam's father about the craft, Jeril gave the boy the freedom to use it as he wished as long as he kept it clean and in good repair. Tam had three poles out, and a line dangling over the gunwale into the water moved slightly, attesting to previous success.

"Ho Tam!" Jeril shouted. "Avoiding work?"

The boy looked up at the sound, smiling and waving. "Got off to catch lunch, sir!" He raised the line; three sleek shapes hung from their gills. "Fishing is much better from a boat than from the dock!"

"So I've heard! Glad you can put my boat to good use!"

The boy took up the oars and began to row back away from the shore. "I'm off to another spot!" he exclaimed. If you are still here when I'm done, I'll give you some of the catch!"

Jeril thought of Gania and her admonition. "Perfect!" he responded. "Good luck to you and watch yourself!"

Tam gave a last wave and set off, and within minutes faded to a spot on the waves obscured by passing shipping. Jeril finished setting up his tray of colors and got to work on his canvas. He deftly laid down a background wash and used his small palette knife to scratch out a series of lines he would eventually turn into masts and the crags of the headland in the distance.

As he worked, the world receded to whispered background noise as the act of creation took him. Colors and shapes, the strokes and adjusted motions, the slow build of depth and substance worked its magic. Sound became the scrape of his palette knife on wood as he blended globs into new shades, pushing light away here, adding it there, creating textures to apply…just there, and there. Touch became the faint moisture on a fingertip that smudged out a missed stroke or the draw of a quickly coagulating swatch on the side of his nose, placed there from an absent-minded scratch. His wrist became an unintended, primitive tattoo. Sight defied real world focus. He *saw* the volume suspended in the bristles, *saw* the transformative magic when color evolved into shape, *saw* everything about the canvas and almost nothing of anything else.

He worked quickly to capture the light's effect, to set time on the surface so that it could pass as it wished in the waking world. Shadow and motion slowed, became fixed in a representation of action suspended yet perpetuated. Hulls took shape in mid-roll, a skeen of sea birds in mid-flight, foam perched on wave tops like frosting on an ethereal cake. He became by stages an extension of his hand, minutely connected to the bristles of his various brushes as he dabbed and stroked order from chaos. He felt the brushes' touch on the canvas like a caress on his own skin.

Beyond his immediate ken a little peace leached into his soul, and a little more of the dark from Piling faded to a new kind of light.

He worked steadily until the westering sun warming his back forced him to stop and remove his coat. When he turned back to the canvas, he paused, scanning its construction with his other eye, the eye that saw pattern, rhythm, connection, and content. He looked up, compared the view with what he had captured and saw the life, the industry, the interplay of lights and darks; a complex, busy weave of what he sensed when he first eased his way into the harbor.

"It is finished," he said aloud, the sound of his own voice sounding unusually loud.

"Yes, I quite agree," said a voice from behind his left shoulder. Jeril spun and stepped back in alarm, chagrined, caught unawares for the second time since he arrived. He drew breath to form accusing words, but they died still-born when he saw to whom the voice belonged.

A woman stood there, admiring his painting. Tan blonde hair fell to her shoulders and tickled the top of a sky blue, light mantle. She smiled at the painting, at him, and her eyes danced with mischief and intelligence. Awareness of his smudged and disheveled appearance rushed back to him. Instinctively, he brushed his beard and grimaced when he felt the half-dried paint adhere to the hair.

"I'm sorry to have broken your concentration," she said. "But when we trundled up and you did not stop, I didn't have the heart to interrupt." She gestured with her head. Behind her, the same carriage from his interview with the court clerk, with Jeremi at the reins, stood at rest on the cobblestones, horses lightly clipping shod hooves in an erratic, equine rhythm. Another woman sat in the carriage, an arm around two little, towheaded children who stood unsteadily on one of the seats looking at the scene before them with solemn eyes.

Jeril turned back to the woman, who bore no outward sign or insignia, but she could be none other than the Queen Eleni Avedun herself. Jeril recalled hearing constant reference to her presence and the twins she birthed. He glanced again at the carriage. *Yes, they look as though they could be five years old.* Instinct drove him to a knee.

"Forgive me, Queen Eleni, I should have recognized you."

"How? We have never met. Up with you, sir!"

Jeril rose. "I am unused to such company, my lady. But I should have known, for your name is on the lips of most of your people."

The queen grinned and gave a casual lift to her eyebrows as if in apology for her widespread popularity. "That sort of thing comes with marrying a king. Can't be helped. I just try not to give them too much silly stuff to talk about. So far, it seems to be working. As it happens, I have had much report of you, too."

"I, lady? But I've only been here a week."

"And yet in that week you've taken to prowling about the city. Folk in every quarter, at least so Devyn tells me, talk of having seen you about."

"Ah, Devyn Ambrose, I see. And may I ask what is said of me?"

"Curious or afraid?"

"A bit of both, lady."

"Well, Jeril Sandre, painter and, tutor was it? Most reports say variations of the same thing: tall fellow with a lot of hair and an intense air about him, but well-spoken with a face that relaxes nicely when he smiles."

The declaration stunned Jeril like an accusation of guilt. The queen must have seen the change to his expression, for she put a hand to his arm, gently, coaxing.

"No need for alarm, Mr. Sandre. We Pevanese are boisterous, nosey types, especially with so much change and news these last months. Call my folk observant, perhaps, but nothing I have heard suggests ill. Relax. Devyn gave the best report of you, if you must know."

"But we spent less than an hour together."

The queen's smile deepened. "Yes, but should it take so long to form an idea of a man? Now that I see you, and those intense eyes of yours, I suspect my Dev's impressions about you are true. He is perceptive to a fault that one."

"He was," Jeril agreed cautiously, quite off his balance, "quite attentive."

"And trustworthy. He wards us with his care. He is off south, checking into your story as part of wider concerns. He should be back soon, but we have had other report of what happened in the south. Troubling."

"I'm sorry to have borne such news."

Again, the queen's self-effacing smile, a motion at odds with Jeril's memories of how royalty tended to act, affected him. He felt himself relax, and that, too, went against the practice of his life.

"We will, perhaps have time later to talk about it in detail."

"Later, majesty?"

She looked again at his painting, squinting as if trying to parse its hidden symmetry.

"As it happens, I have just come from Gania's."

"Is everyone close to the royal family in this city?"

She grinned at his tone. "Not all, not as many as I would like. You will learn my history in time. Gania Landare and I are old friends."

"And she is a formidable friend, I think," Jeril mused, inwardly surprised at his easy shift to informality.

"Oh yes!" the queen agreed. "She is a terror at need, but a kind-hearted soul. From the way you speak, I think you already know that."

"She has accepted my cat into her home more quickly than she has accepted me."

"Oh! So that is yours? What was her name again? Gania told me, but I've forgotten."

The little boy in the carriage must have heard his reference, for he began to bounce joyously, piping 'Kittt—tee, kittt-tee' at the top of his voice.

The queen turned at the sound as the maid gathered him into her arms in an effort to quiet him.

"Arryn! Hush now, mamma has to talk!" She turned back, and Jeril understood, from the motherly blush of pride and embarrassment in her cheeks, why the people of Pevana seemed to love her so.

"I am sorry about that," she said. "The children made their acquaintance with, ah! Now I remember, Angel, over tea and very messy cakes."

"If there were messy cakes involved, I can see why Angel was so friendly," Jeril said. "She's always been a great one for sweets!"

The familial discussion seemed to take away any mystique of the moment.

"She was delightful," agreed the queen. "And I run short of time, sadly. As I said, I have come from Gania's to offer you a commission." She pointed at the painting. "I see you have been sketching. Word has it you have skill, and if you can produce something that looks like that in an afternoon, then I would say you have great skill."

Jeril bowed, a little unnerved by such compliments. "I do not know what to say, my lady."

"What would you say to your own studio? Gania snivveled about the clutter in your room. I have a house near her place. It has sat unused for long enough. I have kept hold of it for sentimental reasons."

Jeril thought of the dwindling supply in his purse. "Queen Eleni, I am not sure I could afford the price of a house just yet."

The queen waved away his reluctance. "The house is beyond price, I assure you. It sheltered my first dreams and my old life. It has some unique features that should work for you."

The idea of a house, space, privacy and security bloomed flowerlike to Jeril as the queen spoke. Such generosity, from such a source, seemed too much good fortune to be real.

"But…but," he began.

"No buts, man," the queen asserted, holding up a hand, instantly royal again but only enough for attention. "Things are more fluid here in Pevana than you must be used to, I suspect. My offer is true, and for payment," she glanced again at the painting, "I have some wall space in our wing I would like to cover. Can you handle portraits? I have a mind for some family things." She gestured back over her shoulder at her still squirming children. "And I think the time is now. Those two have found their legs and only something truly novel will keep them still."

The queen's casual reference to her motherhood and request stunned Jeril. He had hoped in time to sink into some sort of obscurity in Pevana, but here he was, just a week into his residency, making small talk about baby pictures with the Queen of Perspa and the inevitable notoriety such a commission would bring. So much for hiding, and yet there was something in the way the queen conducted herself, something familiar and genuine, Jeril found himself not wanting to hide.

He wanted that house.

He wanted a life, no matter the consequences.

"I accept," he said. "Will I have some time to get settled first?"

The queen clapped her hands happily, as if there were any real chance he could or would refuse. "Excellent," she exclaimed. "And no, there isn't too much rush, of course. I have left a key with Gania. She will take you to look at it. Some of the furnishings are still there, so you wouldn't have to extend yourself finding stuff for the place."

"Your generosity is amazing."

The queen looked at him intently. "I am Pevanese," she said quietly. "And we Pevanese know how to value art. I may be Queen, and a mother, but perhaps above all else, I am one of the poets of this city. Generosity may align with necessity. The people were right, of course, you have eyes that relax when you smile. Welcome to Pevana, Jeril Sandre. Make use of my house. Paint my family. Help me adorn this place with beauty."

She turned on her heel and returned to the carriage. Jeremi raised a hand in salute as he urged the matched pair into motion.

"Bye, bye!" chirped the little girl.

"Kitt-tee!" echoed her brother, Prince Arryn Avedun.

The wonder of it all left Jeril speechless, staring at the carriage as it rolled out of view.

He gathered his things and walked back to Gania's. She scolded him for being late, fed him a bowl of something tasty, and when he finished took him up the street and around the corner, stopping outside a two-story place with a forest green door.

Gania fussed good-naturedly as she fumbled for the key.

"For as long as I've known the little slip, and that is most of her life, mind you, she has always been full of surprises." She got the door open. The hinges squeeked a little. "And this is no exception," she continued, leading him in. At the foot of the stairs she turned on him, scowling or smiling he just could not tell. "But I think this is right, somehow. Her with the babies, the demands of crown and husband. It was time to let this go for final, I think. Besides, I'd have kicked you out next week anyway."

"Kitchen there, sitting room there, privy that way," she said, pointing. "Bedrooms, a covered deck and something I think you will like are upstairs. Have a look with you. I'll get back to the house to help Lyssa trammel up your things. We will bring back some food as well. No sense in going hungry on your first night here. Up! I'm off."

He mounted the stairs, looked into the bedroom to either end of the landing. In between them, with windows and side-by-side doors that opened on to a deck, a spacious workspace with a large table and cupboards mesmerized him.

It was an artist's room. Suddenly, hints of a compelling story welled up like spirits conjured.

Jeril sighed and wished deeply that he had told the whole truth to Devyn Ambrose and the clerk.

He did not receive word from the palace for nearly a month, and during that time he busied himself with outfitting his studio. Most of what remained of Jorian's gold and silver went for canvas and frames to stretch them on, colors ready-made and the means to mix others. He splurged, hired a cart and borrowed Tam from his chores and together they spent an afternoon gathering plants Jeril intended to dry, grind and use for extra pigments.

He painted every day at all hours and in every kind of light, and every day he fell more in love with the home the queen gifted him. Angel settled in as well, ghosting about the rooms and closets, sniffing out the history of the place in her own way. She quickly discovered a perch on the deck railing as the perfect place to survey her domain and keep a cat's eye on him. Jeril sketched roof top scenes from the covered deck, captured sunrise over the headland and climbed on the roof to claim the sunset behind the mountain to the west. The citadel hill loomed above him, and the place the locals called The Maze fell below to the south. He worked feverishly, lining out his own sense of belonging one drawing, one painting at a time.

Work found him; a small, steady stream of cautious requests from some of the wealthy merchant families. Luckily, most of them were simple and swiftly completed. Coins flowed back into his purse. Folk took to nodding at him as they passed. He took to combing his beard and pulling his hair back with a tie; a subtle exposure and a step away from his reclusive past.

When a page dropped off Jeril's summons to the palace, he suffered through a night of doubt. Who he used to be, and how he set himself to live, all that time hiding from royal betrayal flooded back with a vengeance. He picked through his brushes and palettes, organized a sheaf of clean pages for initial sketches, tried to eat, tried to sleep and failed at both.

Gania must have got wind of his appointment for she showed up with Lyssa and another, younger girl Gania introduced as Tasia, an alert, darting-eyed twelve-year old from the neighborhood.

"Here," Gania houghed, tossing him a bucket. "Is your fire up? Good. Tasia, dump your water in the tub there. Lyssa, hang yours over the fire to heat. Right. Good. I'll set a few things to right here while you lot trot off to the well, and mind the spills!"

Jeril did as he was told, amused by the sudden take over. He followed Lyssa and the girl but made sure to take the largest bucket from Tasia once they had filled them.

"I can manage, sir" the girl protested. Jeril started at her tone, hearing hints of fire and spice that reminded him of Piling.

"I'm sure you can," he said, taking the bucket anyway. "But I'd feel better if you'd let me earn the bath Gania intends for me."

Tasia smirked and took up two of the smaller buckets. "My friends and I have watched you a bit. Some of them think you get more paint on yourself than the canvas." She set off.

"Do they, watch me, I mean?" Jeril shifted to take up the other larger bucket Lyssa filled and follwed after Tasia.

Tasia giggled a bit and glanced at him sidelong as she walked. "My friends and I watch everything in this part of the city. We have always done it, since before the great fire. I was six then. You remind me of Kembril Edri, but with him it was dust and dirt."

"You are filled with sauce and mystery, young miss. Who was this Kembril?"

She slowed to make the turn at the corner and up the short slope to Jeril's door. "He was the storyteller. Devyn's friend. I miss him. We all do. Tam especially."

"Ah!" Jeril chuckled. "Tam! Yes. I see now. My first acquaintance. He and this Kembril were close?"

Tasia set down her buckets to deal with the door. "He was as close as any of us from the Maze, Mr. Sandre. We liked Edri's stories. Tam has always been one for listening. He says your paintings are like a different kind of story."

Jeril followed her in, and it felt as if the better memories of Piling were reaching out to him, leaching past the defenses he had erected in the aftermath of the Esdan raid, little tendrils of hope and home and interest.

He added his load to the tub. Tasia waited for him at the door, sidestepping to let Lyssa in with her additions. By the time the three of them had collected enough for a decent bath, Jeril had come to small moment of decision.

"Tasia," he said, as Gania finished her bustling and shepherded the other two doorward, "Thank your friends for watching out for me. Tell them, and Tam especially, that once I get a bit more settled, I will carve out time for any who might like to come and learn their shapes and colors. The Queen mentioned Pevana's poets. Perhaps, in my small way, I might help produce some painters."

Tasia's eyes grew briefly round at the suggestion, quickly suppressed by a sardonic expression.

"You see, Gania?" she said, as Mistress Landare urged her out the door. "Tam was right! He said Mr. Sandre had the look of a teacher. Wait till I tell him…"

Gania paused hand on the latch. "Let the water get nice and hot," she said. "You've an impression to make up the hill, but I canna' see how it could be any greater than the impression you just made with young Tasia. The Maze children are a different lot. Good souls, all of them. You have a care for the splotches in that beard of yours. Can't imagine what they will do to the water!"

Jeril latched the door behind her, tossed off his garments and settled himself in the tub as best he could. He let the water sluice away his fears, and his resolve grew as the water slowly chilled. He finished, rose like a hairy leviathan from the tub, and stared for a long while at his reflection in a mirror fixed to the wall above a basin. Then he took up a pair of shears Gania had left for the purpose and hacked away at the mass of dripping hair, trimming it back to just off his neckline. He shaved his beard shorter, taking care to shape it just so.

He stared at a face that reminded him of the man he used to be. Not the same beardless, naïve, open face of his youth before subterfuge took over his life, but rather a blend of the discerning and the dissembler that life had taught him to be. Right or wrong, it was him.

"This is correct," he said to his reflection. "A man has to own his face in the end."

He dressed in his best clothes, swept up his satchel, and headed up the hill to paint his destiny.

Chapter 5: Royal is as Royal Does…

A flicker of movement brought Jeril out of his painter's trance. The young prince, Arryn, squirmed in his mother's arms, clearly intent on descending from her lap to the more interesting region of the floor. Jeril held his brush poised above a spot just below where he had been texturing up the folds of the queen's dress. He exhaled, made the stroke and backed away. During the time he spent working on the family portraits, that motion had come to indicate an end of the session. Jeril relaxed, shaking the tension from his shoulders as the family melted from their poses. The fluid familiarity of the motion captured his attention anew even as his painter's eye receded to real-time focus.

The sense of unity in the royal family continually struck him as it clashed with his own experience. King Donari, a patient, doting father, took the twin's five-year old chaos with easy grace. And he adored his queen. Jeril picked up that truth early on during the sketch phase of his work, finding the looks that passed between the two royals disconcerting at first. His finger tips tingled with tension as he struggled to process and capture the moment. He marveled at such openness. By comparison, his memories of life in Esda seemed like a closeted, duplicitous fraud. The only moments of light he recalled were the memories he retained of his mother and their early days together when she taught him his letters and the nature of plants and things.

He wiped off his brushes and considered how he would spend the rest of his day. The painting was finished save for some small touches. He glanced around the sitting room, transformed by his work into a temporary gallery. He nodded, satisfied by the scope and composition, reassured that what he saw reflected love's interest rather than ego; the image is enough to reinforce the just rule of a good king, stopping well short of conscious pomposity.

That genuiness formed the main difference between his memories of the east and his appreciation of this western life. Pevana, with its clustered streets, squabbling merchant families, Maze-dwellers and poets had more honesty in it than seemed reasonable or possible. He felt the truth of it the first time he passed through the citadel gates on his way to the palace to begin his commission: careful yet casual scrutiny. He had felt guileless and exposed in his newly shaven state, then, expecting challenge the closer he came to authority. Such emotional reactions faded quickly, however, and by the time of this last visit he held trust and friendship with both gate guards and palace staff.

He never stayed the night there despite working late on a number of occasions. Old, careful habits died hard, and he preferred the lock on his own door and Angel's purr to unctuous servants and helmeted soldiery.

He finished cleaning and packing away his palette. A tug on his pant leg brought his attention downward.

"Kitty?" young Arryn asked. He had learned his consonants since that first meeting. "Angel kitty?"

"She is well, young prince," Jeril responded. For some reason the siblings always brought out his gentler side, and yet he knew that had always been the case during all his travels. He never learned to doubt the veracity of children.

"I want to see the kitty!" Arryn announced, beaming and insistent.

"But what would Angel-kitty do here in this big place?" Queen Eleni interjected, sweeping the boy up and giving him an un-queenly yet decidedly motherly kiss on the cheek. "Perhaps we can visit her soon."

"Want to play with Angel!" Arryn asserted, squirming anew in his mother's arms.

"Kitty, kitty, kitty," piped the other twin, Princess Ailen, who had managed to remove her dress already and hugged her mother's robes while jumping up and down excitedly.

The prospect of a royal visit loomed like a perplexing ordeal. The queen must have read his mind, for she laughed as she let her son down.

"Do not fear, Master Sandre, I, too, enjoyed my cluttered life there. I promise never to drop in on you unawares. We have given the children several pets since that day, but for some reason they still ask after your cat."

"Queen Eleni, you are always welcome in your home. I am just embarrassed at my bachelor's ways."

Eleni glanced around the room, taking in the scope of his efforts. "No, no," she asserted. "Your home now. Your gifts to me and mine are worth far more than mere rooms. I am glad it serves you as it does!"

King Donari came over, sipping on a glass of wine. Here, too, Jeril marveled at the change in his own response to royal proximity. Power flowed out of Donari's eyes like lamplight, undeniable, perspicacious and insistent. And yet laughter more often graced the man's features than worry, despite the demands of active youngsters and a kingdom newly won and in need of ordering.

"She is right, you know," he asserted casually. "These are impressive. You will never want for commissions."

"Thank you!" Jeril gushed, stepping back to bow respectfully, but Donari forestalled him with a gesture.

"None of that now, Sandre. Any man who is kind enough to minimize my wrinkles and gray does not need to bow in the sitting room!"

"My knees thank you, my lord."

"And my backside thanks you for working so quickly. I assume that is an unexpected benefit of having to paint our restless children!"

"This whole experience has been special to me, sire, and I am glad you are pleased with the results."

Donari clapped him on the shoulder. "More than pleased, man, more than pleased! If my wife is happy, and she is, then so am I. Call that marriage wisdom if you like."

"I will remember it, sire, should I ever be so lucky."

Donari beamed at him. "Do, though I suspect your life will hold other joys."

The comment jarred Jeril's calm. Even in jest, the king had a way of pushing at barriers. Jeril continually struggled with his own deception in the face of such perception. Guilt constantly nibbled at him as he worked, unaffected by time or knowledge, a pernicious knot that tied him to his past and kept him cautious and reserved.

Eleni ushered the children out of the room. Donari went out to the balcony, motioning for Jeril to follow. He joined the king at the railing, sharing the view. The afternoon sun bathed the southern and western reaches of the city. Jeril looked down at the streets he had spent a month wandering, learning, sketching, owning. From the stylish red tiles of the hill top estates to the slate roofs nearer the walls and the mottled, shadowy divergence that indicated the Maze, the whole area radiated peace and industry. Jeril wondered if the same held true everywhere in the kingdom. He knew the lay of the land. Maps of the newly united kingdom were plentiful in every shop, and his artist's intuition told him it was so.

It shocked him to realize Donari was what his own father should have been, what he should have been, and what Jorian could never be: a leader. His mother used to tell him that like would know like, always. There lay the bitterness, for he knew himself a failure. All that Donari represented to his people stood at risk because of Jeril Tandori's name and what he knew. He painted faces; Donari built ships and alliances.

Jeril sighed and grew aware of the king's scrutiny. Donari looked at him with piercing kindness.

"You sigh at the view or some memory touched by it?" he asked.

Jeril weighed his words. He owed the king much. The queen's generosity deserved truth. *But not yet. Not now. Not all of it. It would change nothing.*

"A little of both, sire," he answered. "In my short time here I have come to feel strongly about this place. Paintings cannot begin to repay the queen's gift."

"I will take that as a kindness. And the home is well-bestowed, I'm sure. We have come through a bad time, both of us. My city prospers. And you. I have studied your comments about Piling. Tragic. I will have to see to the coasts. Esdan mischief of that sort will not be tolerated."

"I lost many friends there."

"You could go back."

"More than my home burned, sire. Too many faces, good, kind faces, blown away by an ill wind."

"An eastern wind, perhaps?"

Jeril had to fight back fear's rush at the king's question. "My lord?" he asked in return.

"Devyn sent a letter back before heading south. He interviewed some of the survivors. They called you their 'tutor from Esda.' I found that passing strange."

"I am eastern, sire. As others have remarked, my eyes give me away. I have never denied it."

"I did not mean to rankle," the king soothed. "I but ask is all. I have watched you these last weeks, Jeril Sandre, as you worked on this project. I am sure you have come to know something of us as well."

"My lord," Jeril replied, hesitant, uneasy. "I would not presume to such familiarity."

"But we grant it, freely."

"But I am not worthy of…I am just a…" Jeril stuttered, disconcerted by how close the king came to touching on the things he desired most: a home, family, certainty, love.

A disturbance inside broke the mood, thankfully. Arryn, followed by a harassed maid, scampered through the balcony door, screeching "Dad-dee!" and threw himself at his father, who scooped him up laughing. The child twisted around to fix his eyes on Jeril.

"No more sit, sit? Master Jer?" he asked, grinning impishly.

"No more for today, little prince. In fact, I think I may be finished."

The boy settled back in his father's arms apparently satisfied. The maid hung back, waiting for permission to come take him.

"I am sorry, sire. He slipped by me while the queen dealt with Ailen."

"No worries," Donari responded, handing the boy over. "Arryn!" he admonished, ruffling the boy's blond hair. "Mum and I need you and Ailen rested for later when the Lord Hallan comes to dinner. No more screeching! Time for a nap. Off with you."

Arryn accepted his father's words with surprising grace for a five-year old, and again the moment reminded Jeril of the power the king held.

"My lord, I will take my leave. I have taken too much of your time."

"Nonsense," Donari scoffed. "But I do have a meeting I need to make." He led Jeril back into the sitting room. Jeril's gear had been neatly packed into his bag and placed on a chair next to a small table. Donari took up a thick volume from the table and handed it to Jeril.

"My lord?"

Donari gestured at the book. "Jeril Sandre, painter, eastern tutor, you have rare skills, and I am glad you are with us. I stole a glance at some of your sketches awhile back," he smiled in apology, "couldn't help it. Just curious. And, as you mentioned, you seem to have finished our portraits, and I was wondering if I might convince you to do a few more pieces."

Pride, joy and fear in equal parts filled Jeril as he took in the king's words.

"Sire, I am yours to command."

"Command has such a regal pomposity to it. I have in mind some scenes from the history my wife composed about the events that brought me to the throne. I would like a few larger canvases for the main hall decorations."

Conflicting emotions still niggled the edges of his calm, but curiosity took precedence. He caressed the embossed leather cover, read the title: *Path of the Poet-King: An Account of the Perspan Unification by Queen Eleni Avedun.*

"My lord king, this is a precious work to trust…" and at the word Jeril faltered. *Trust.*

"It is precious in its honesty, Master Jeril. Eleni slaved over those pages, and that makes them doubly precious. I want you to read it. There are a few scenes that might serve for a composition, but I would like you to choose which ones your expertise tells you would be most suitable. Make some sketches, send them up with your ideas. No rush."

Jeril bowed himself out of the conversation, took up his bag and left. He walked alone down the hall, bemused and perplexed. He needed a quiet hour with a bottle of wine and Angel's company. As he walked, he grew more convinced Donari's casual manner hid important questions.

Questions that he could not answer, perhaps could never answer.

He paced down the hill acutely aware of how much truth he held tucked under his arm and how many lies he kept hidden away in his heart.

When he got home he made sure to feed Angel. Then he set a drink on the side table next to his chair and settled himself. Angel joined him, taking her accustomed place hemmed between his thigh and the chair's padded arm. Her purring pleasure quickly set the tone.

Then he took up the volume and began to read.

Chapter . 6: Gal from Gallina

Normally, on the anniversary of her mother's death, Grayce Stonesmith awoke from dreams of that tragic day, but today was different. Today a series of images surrounding a face she saw five years and one month ago almost to the day sent her gasping into full consciousness, clutching empty air as though reaching for someone. Who that someone might have been, she had no idea. She had been a stripling of fourteen when she glanced at that stranger's face at the beginning of a market day: a man still young, slightly bearded with intense eyes, sipping tea.

As she focused on this change in her five-year routine, other images from that day returned to her: she and her mother, setting up their small collection of Old Way's statuary, a troop of red-robed priests with armed guards, harsh words, commands. And then that face in passing as the young man moved by their table, quietly apologizing for filching a sturdy representation of the goddess Renia. She recalled watching him disappear in the crowd and then following the arc of that statue as it flew through the air to take the lead priest in the side of the head, toppling him from his mount.

Grayce took a shuddering breath at the memory. As she exhaled, she realized the line of that arcing statue had defined her life since. That face. A scurry of rushing people, cursing priests and guards, pikes leveled and thrusting. That face and the words shouted over the din, "Keep to the Old Ways, brothers!"

A month later her mother lay dead among the ruins of Gallina, lost and burned along with the town, a victim of King Roderran II's invasion of the south. Since then, she had been alone, unsure of who she should hate, love, or even if she were capable of either emotion. She survived the desperate times afterward, when the fugitives from the southern battle rolled through, taking anything left from Roderran's burning in their flight north. Help had come behind. A new start, though tenuous. Then work on the road brought rebuilding and hope.

She swung her feet out from the covers, feeling for her sandals and reaching for her shirt and skirt. It was early spring and a hint of winter's effect remained, so she tied her hair back with a strap and shrugged on a light, thigh length coat with pockets stuffed with charcoal sticks, chalks, a long-handled brush, a small pad and several sheets of larger paper rolled up as a tube. She had to work that evening. Her employer, Staig Motta, though a gruff sort, was still mostly kind. He took her in after the troubles ended. In return for her labor in the kitchens and cleaning tables he gave her wages and a place. At nineteen, worldly beyond her years given her experiences, Grayce felt lucky in many respects. Staig never asked her for more and with his size and reputation provided her some protection from those that did.

Love had died with her mother. She did not have time for it. She devoted all her spare time to chasing shapes around, and tonight she had an assignation with a full moon and the space between two rocky hills west of town. She wanted to draw that moon underneath its light and see if she could capture it in lines and shades. The idea of it sent all thoughts of breakfast packing. She took the stairs two at a time, intending a quick exit to a morning on her own, but Staig's glowering face and upheld ham-sized palm stopped her in her tracks.

"Wait a minute, there," he growled, sleep making his voice raspier than normal. "A word or two, please."

Grayce quick-scanned the common room to see if she had forgotten to wipe anything down. Satisfied, she smiled good morning.

"One too many pots last night, Staig? I saw you there at the end of the bar, head to head with old Liam."

A ghost of a smile slunk beneath Staig's beard to tease his eyes, but it faded quickly to concern. "Ah, now, you leave Liam out of this, missy. It is not the drink that gives me this rasp and you know it. Did you see him last night?"

Grayce took a breath before replying, for the *him* Staig referred to was Earvyn Pickson, a northern emigrant, originally one of the work crew on the road, now a sometime miner. He began to develop an interest in Grayce soon after he arrived. At first, she ignored his garrulous familiarities, but eventually Earvyn took to following her around, slipping in comments meant to be witticisms in a vain attempt to spark her interest. When those failed, he began spending more time at Staig's, drinking and winking, waiting and wanting, becoming increasingly hard to ignore. Staig took notice and began making sure he was always close by when Earvyn came around.

"Earvyn. Of course I saw him," she responded. "And I know you saw him, too, and thank you. I think I can handle him if it came to something, but I know you are there. I'm not worried."

"I'm only *there* when you are *here*. Missy, I don't trust that one. He's too lonely for his own good."

"This town is full of lonely folk, Staig. Many have suffered, and you know it." There were more than a few widows and widowers in Gallina. The five years of the new King's rule, Donari Avedun of Pevana, had brought roads cut through the hills and an influx of northern and southern workers as the mining operation expanded to take advantage of the new prosperity.

Grayce wondered about that prosperity. The old and new blood had not mixed well. Folk who had their roots excised by Roderran's invasion now lived and worked with newcomers who had yet to set down any roots of their own. Everyone delved into the vitals of the hills extracting wealth but little else.

Grayce understood that rootlessness better than most. Old Gallina had been made largely of wood; new Gallina had stone buildings. Foundations were still settling. The place still lacked the cracks and sags that spoke of age, living, use, *home*.

The influx of freshly laid walls and stone fences, all that barren *space* that called to her, were really the only benefit she saw in the new arrangement. For Grayce, Gallina stopped being home when that flaming house-beam collapsed and crushed her mother five years ago. Since then it had morphed into an evolving canvas for her charcoal curiosity. If exploiting those surfaces meant she had to deal with types like Earvyn, so be it for now.

"Earvyn Pickson will tire of me, I'm sure," she said as she made to leave. "I'm not fit company. He has to see that."

"All he sees, girl, are those tits and that shapely behind of yours, no matter how much you try to cover them up."

Grayce smiled at Staig's crude compliment. "I'll have no man, Staig, though it is nice to know you care about my bits."

Staig smiled genuinely in return. "Missy, if I were twenty years younger, I'd be following you around myself. I have watched you these last few years, well, you remind me more and more of your mother. Always liked her, and your da. You need to take care. This place has gotten rough, and you know it. Watch your back when you go out."

"I will and I do."

Staig barked a laugh at that. "Not likely, missy, hard to watch your back when you go about staring at alley walls. Gallina might be new-made an' such, but it still has shadows. Watch yourself, I say."

"I spend my days in the light, Staig, and my nights here wiping down the wine stains on your tables. What could possibly happen?"

Grayce watched Staig take a breath as if to retort, but then he seemed to relent and let it go with a sigh.

"A lot could happen, Grayce, keep half an eye behind you, yes? And since you speak about wiping things down, when are you going to take care of that stain on the corner table?"

The mark Staig referred to was a particularly unique smear of good Desopolisan red, left behind nearly a week ago from a drunken spill by a visiting musician. She could not bring herself to wipe it away yet. She loved the way the deep purple smudge interacted with the oak of the table. The combination was earthen, mineral, and altogether fetching. The wine was the best stuff Staig sold in the place. Grayce did not want to drink it; however, she wanted to paint with it.

"Tonight, Staig, I promise," she said, glancing at the table in question and moving off toward the tavern door. "I'll get it tonight. I have a spot in mind for it behind the hostler's."

"Promise to keep an eye out for Pickson, too, eh?"

"And Pickson, too. I'll be back this afternoon to stir the pots. Fair?"

"Fair enough. Off with you, then."

She bounced out the door and set off for a quick spin around Gallina. To the unenlightened, her route might resemble that of a frivolous child gallivanting about, but Grayce actually moved with purpose. She checked to see which of her drawings still survived. She had been practicing on all the vacant walls and neglected fence facings in town. Most of them got painted over as soon as the owners found out about them, but a few of her favorites still remained. She liked to think they survived due to her developing skills but realized the truth lay closer to ambivalence than admiration. She did not care. She made up her life as she went along, drawing her truths and fantasies as the muse directed. She allowed herself dreams.

But her route today was doubly intent due to the dream that had awakened her. That face. Her mother used to say that insight came to the gifted in their sleep, which turned to truth through artistic expression. If her mother had been correct, then that dream was more than a troubling memory; it was a message.

Grace passed the morning seeing to her remaining drawings. In each one, she found her suspicions realized as she kept finding those subtle bits reminiscent of the images in that dream. Whenever she noticed one of those elements, she found herself re-examining the drawing as a whole, which brought out a charcoal stick for additions and alterations. When she finished, she decided she liked each one even better than before. She found the effect disturbing and yet at the same time invigorating. Such a tiny shift in perspective resulted in something that felt wholly new.

She recalled something her father had told her once when she was very young. He had brought a rock home from the slag heaps. She remembered thinking it was just a plain rock: dull brown and featureless. Her dad had laughed at her when she dismissed it as such. *'Now, G,'* he had said. *'Don't be so hasty to dismiss this stone! All you've seen is its outside. If all miners thought like you, they'd never find anything of value! A miner's life, a miner's eye, always focuses on the inside of a thing. They have to look beyond the start of a seam to feel its potential.'* Then he took that rock and poised the point of his hand pick over a tiny crack. *'You have to pick your spot, you see, and give the thing a little push.'* And then he tapped the crack once, smartly, and the rock split, the newly revealed twin faces a swirling, translucent mineral-laden blue. Grayce remembered thinking she looked at the eyes of the earth itself. Her father's action changed the effect of that small rock forever. Somehow, he had *known* just as she now *knew* what each drawing needed once she found the dream reminder. She missed her father, thought of him buried with his fellows in that mine shaft, and allowed the memory to settle into its safe place for later recall.

She practically ran the back streets after the first one, emotions suspended, attention arrested, oblivious to the world beyond her focus. Between checking on drawings three and four, she munched on a cheesy bun and shared a cup of tea with a young mother and her toddler daughter. In payment, Grayce sketched the little girl's portrait on one of her scraps of paper. She took pleasure limning the child's animated face. While the mother exclaimed over the likeness, Grayce muted her own response. She knew the youngster's right eyebrow was a little thicker than it should have been, and she knew the reason why, too. That face. Subtle reminders.

Then she moved on to check the last drawing, and the whole tone of her day changed.

She turned down Gallina's main street, heading for the back of the stable attached to the Gate Inn, but hesitated in the shadow of a storefront when she noticed a cluster of horsemen exiting the stables and moving out through the gate. Most of the group comprised part of the crews working on the King's Road, but two of the rearmost riders wore the red robes and caps of King's Theology priests. Memories surged. She had heard of the order's reform after King Donari took the throne, but she still had to force down the anger and fear from five years ago. Shouted commands, flying statuary. After the chaos there had been retribution, priestly harangues about guilt and obligation, she never forgot the tones. She made to move back out into the street but stopped when she saw the two priests had backed their mounts just inside the gate. Part of their conversation came clear to her.

"So we are agreed, then," said the one on the right. "You to the south to meet Orlas and get his news from Desopolis. I will take the tenor of the crews on the road."

"Agreed. I just hope he isn't late," answered the one on the left. "The Lord grows impatient."

"Things are moving. Meet me back here in a day. He will be ready to leave. Then we head north."

"A day. If I am lucky."

Both men kicked their mounts forward and passed through the gate before separating.

Grayce waited until the priests were out of sight before continuing, her thoughts roiled by the cryptic back and forth she had overheard. She wondered who this lord was they referred to.

As she stood before her last and largest drawing, a landscape of the hills she intended to draw that night, she found the dream image again; the jaw-line worked into the contour of the left hill, which sent her reaching for the charcoal stick. She lost herself for awhile in a creative, smudgy euphoria. It was only when she stepped back to massage a tight spot over her left hip that she found the other 'new' thing. In the lower left corner, just beneath the edge of where her own drawing began, someone had sketched out a crude representation of a plant she did not recognize.

"Oh, now, that's a fine piece of work that is, right enough. Ha-cough!"

The sound of Earvyn Pickson's voice tumbled Grayce out of her reverie. Caught unaware, she spun around chagrined.

"And I'm sure it's the drawing you mean, Earvyn Pickson?" she snapped, hoping to cover her surprise and put him off.

"Oh, yes, the drawing, too!" he responded, smiling, a gap-toothed yellow stained expression. He loomed above her, breathing like a wheezy bellows, lungs racked by years of breathing underground dust, his face a mask of remembered loss and present desire.

Grayce sidled back a step to give herself some space to run at need, but Earvyn made no overt gesture.

"I knew you drew things, Grayce, but this one is special, in' it?"

"It's one of my favorites, thank you, Earvyn. How did you find it? Have you been following me?"

Earvyn's smile paled momentarily, and he brought his chin up, pride stung and exposed.

"Na, na, lass. Not following! Though you've a shape to follow, ha-cough, and tha's no mistake! I was jus' checking on a mate who works the gate stable, saw you duck in. I thought that a bit funny, so I came to have a look. Didn' want you to come to no harm, you know, ha-cough, jus' friendly concern, yeah?"

"I'm fine, Earvyn."

"Oh ya, ya, you're fine alright, very, very, ha-cough, cough, *fine*. I like fine, I do. I like your picture fine enough, lass, but you're a much finer image, you are."

Grayce moved another half-step back and to the side, Earvyn's eyes followed her hungrily before snapping back to the drawing as her movement uncovered that lower left corner with its strange, added plant.

"Yes, a nice drawing this, girl, but why would you put heather there?"

"*Heather*? You know that plant?"

"Ha-cough! Oh yea, heather, grows all over back home. Used to pick it for my ma on her birthdays. Doesn't grow here. I kinda miss it, I do."

Heather. Northern plant, but why? Why here? Why this drawing? For a moment the questions threatened to perplex her, but her unease over being so close to Pickson, and out of sight from other eyes, brought her back to focus. She sidled away toward the alley opening, which led back to Gallina's main road.

"Thank you for checking on me, Earvyn," she stuttered, struggling to keep her voice calm. *Idiot! Cut and run! Now!* "I've got to get back to Staig's and see to the evening stew pots. Glad you like the drawing. Good day to you."

"I could walk you back to Motta's, ha-cough, yeah?"

"No, no," Grayce eased, walking backward, hand trailing the wall and questing for the corner. "No need, really, I'll be fine."

Earvyn smiled again. "Yeah, fine. Indeed, fine. Then perhaps, ha-cough, I'll see you after my shift, eh? I'll stop by for a mug and a talk, yeah?"

Damn! No way out. "Yes, yes! Of course, see you then." The fingers of her left hand found the corner of the building, and she practically squeezed dents in the mortar as she propelled herself into a mad dash back toward the safety of the main street.

She walked home quickly, her mind a muddle of fear, curiosity and heightened sense impressions that revolved in a circle of weird: Pickson's pathetic desire, the fractured elements of that dream face, a northern plant drawn by someone else, the Priests. It took an act of will to clamp down bubbling questions. She had over-stayed her time away. Staig needed her to prep for that evening. *Earvyn had surprised her!* She spared a quick look behind her. *Staig had been right.*

Grayce wiped the sweat from her brow and paused to stretch the kink out of the small of her back. She had been wiping down tables and setting things to right for the last two hours, trying to finish as fast as she could without drawing complaints from Staig about shirking. She kept her eye on the door as she moved about the room serving and swabbing. Pickson made his appearance later than normal and looked as though he had started on his journey to numbed stupor somewhere else. She noted his look because it was different from his usual, hangdog desperate. She nodded her thanks when Staig moved to intercept him. He settled the miner close to the end of the bar where he could keep an eye on him. Staig kept Earvyn busy with mugs and chatter well enough that Grayce eventually forgot about him. She did not see him leave, but she felt the room's atmosphere ease a little towards last call.

She dipped her rag anew into her bucket and turned to finish her last table but paused when she realized it was the one with the unique wine stain. To remove it now felt like closing a door on the familiar, leaving her stuck on the side that held only the new and troubling. Her hand hovered, and yet the moon would not pause for her. She slapped the rag down and scrubbed hard and quickly, and when she finished not even an outline remained. She took the bucket back behind the bar where Staig waited with a question.

"You don't look like you're heading for bed. Too fast with the tables."

Grayce smiled to hide her consternation at being so obvious. "I'm just efficient," she said, reaching for his bar towel to wipe her hands. "There's a full moon. I figure it will set between the hills in a certain spot. I want to draw it."

"You forgetting something?"

"He's gone home to sleep it off. I watched you slip him several full ones late."

"I tried to get him to pass out," Staig groused. "But the fool holds his drink better than I expected. I staggered him, maybe, but he left upright. I don't like you out alone. Forget the moon. It's full again in a month."

"But not this clear. Not on this line. This one is special, Staig. I want to capture it."

"I've no one to go with you."

"I wouldn't take them even if you did. Sarah and Jan have cooked and served all evening. They are ripped. I'm off to the hills. I'll be fine. It's quite a climb, Staig. Pickson doesn't know where I'll be."

"Don't like it. I—"

"Don't really have a say in the matter," Grayce finished, patting Staig's arm companionably as she moved by toward the kitchen. "I appreciate your concern, but I'll not miss this, Pickson or no Pickson." She ducked through the door before he could stop her.

On her way out the back Grayce grabbed a hunk of that day's bread and several apples. She took her coat with its deep pockets heavy with pens and a pad and within moments was out under the moonlight, breathing deeply to clear her thoughts. Staig's concern perplexed her; it hinted at a change in their relationship. The past event had taken her family, and Staig had not replaced any of them regardless of what he might say. But she sensed he cared, and that changed things.

The early spring air bore a mixed palette of fragrances: unwashed human, the memory of Staig's bubbling pots, the sharp metallic taint from the ore mounds on the edge of town, and, faint yet compelling, the blended aromas of pine and alder. To her mind's eye all such impressions came as images, shapes, shadows and whole scenes, as though her world were a series of stretched canvasses that experience would help her fill.

Whenever Grayce thought about her life, she always came back to the same image: empty spaces, missing faces, gaps that needed substance, meaning, and order. She knew why. Late night scrubbing provided ample opportunity for self-reflection. She was alone, parentless from war, had friends in town, and yet she still felt adrift on currentless waters. With so much of her life made impermanent by permanent loss, she found her drawings the only way she could gain some semblance of control. Acknowledging Staig's latent feelings and Pickson's overt dangers just did not fit into her plans. The urge to draw the moon pulled her like a tide.

She settled her food bag more comfortably on her shoulder, tested the air one last time then hurried off to keep her assignation with a drawing.

The climb left her a little winded. Above her, the moon sailed serenely through a cloudless night. She hurried up the final slope to settle on a flat-topped rock placed by nature as though for the purpose. The moon began its descent while she framed in the scene with feather-light lines that spoke of contours and distance. There was enough light to make out even individual tree branches, arboreal fingers, stretching to grasp the plunging orb. She finished the hills, added a few final touches to the branches and then waited for the moon to place itself for her design. The beauty of it nearly overwhelmed her: a perfect circle in an ink black sky; its glow forcing all other starlight into the background, a respectful, celestial receding. Grayce felt her pulse slow. She blinked once, twice, but not a third time for the moon's glamour turned her into a statue of expectation.

Grayce felt rather than saw her hand moving across the pad. Light washed over her, pale, luminescent, drawing her into the moment she captured on the paper. A smudge here, denser pressure there and light's effect began to take shape. The moon hung before her like a regal dame of the stage, bracketed by a pair of adoring attendants poised to embrace her at show's end. For a precious time the hills and moon made the night a tripart perfection. Then the moon passed beyond the line of hills, breaking the symmetry, stilling Grayce's pencil. The spell faded. Time returned. She sighed and looked at her work as the night deepened around her. *Gone*, she thought, *but I have it, and one day I'll paint it.*

She walked back to town warmed by reverie, floating down the twisting way, barely touching the earth as though she were a sprite uplifted and grown beyond the corporeal. A stone rattling in front of her snapped her back, and a wheezy breath told her she was not alone on the path. She felt her feet root themselves back to ground, and sudden fear rushed upward through her boot soles as she recognized her danger.

A shadow detached itself from a tree trunk, moved through the half-light to confront her, and from it came Earvyn Pickson's voice to complete her chilling return.

"A bit late for a night walk, Grayce, ha-cough, don' you think?"

Grayce's heart hammered in her throat as Pickson's shadow drew closer.

"I was drawing the moon," she whispered. "Please, Earvyn, let me by. I saw how much you had to drink."

"Hours ago, girl, and well tossed off, if you know what I mean." He laughed huskily. Grayce smelled the acid taints of vomit on his breath.

"It's late, Earvyn, Staig will expect me home."

"Staig's snoring like the old pig he is, girl, and you're right—it is late. A bit too late, for you. Now."

"I don't know what you mean."

Pickson moved even closer.

"Don't be stupid," he rasped, his anger and desire at war with his tone. "You know I've wanted you for a long time now, but you don't rise to the bait. We're both alone, girl, why not make a match, eh? It's time you took a man. There's others beside myself who've noticed, ha-cough, so why not me, yeah? Right, why not then?"

Grayce tried to back away but came up against a tree trunk. "Please, please, Earvyn," she stammered as fear overtook her voice. His sweat and vomitous, rheumy breath assaulted her. "Don't do this. I don't want you— or any man right now. Please."

"Please, please," Pickson mocked. "Yeah, girly, that's right, beg for it. I like it when they ask for it. And you been askin' for it for some time now, you have, and ol' Earvyn, ha-cough, is going to give it to you."

Terror took hold. Grayce made a sudden, vain move to escape, but he grabbed her arm and swung her around, pencils, pad, charcoal sticks arcing out from her abused pockets in the motion. She tumbled to the ground on her back, and instantly he was on her, sitting astride her. She slapped him about the chest and face, and he took the blows laughing, secure in his size and power. Grayce felt a scream begin in her core, but before she could take breath Earvyn drew back a hand and slapped stars into her vision. She tried to reach his face to gouge his eyes, but he snarled and struck her with his fists once, twice, a third time until she lay back dazed, arms flung wide and helpless. The copper taste of blood oozed into her mouth from split lips. Her jaw numbed.

She felt his nightmare hands upon her. He ripped her shirt apart with a violent wrench, exposing her breasts.

"Oooh, these are fine, fine, fine," he giggled, grasping one in each hand and squeezing cruelly. "They'd make a nice picture, these would, oh, ha-cough, oh yes. I always thought you had nice tits, Grayce." A calloused finger circled one nipple in a caricature of a caress. "Now doesn't that feel nice, eh? No more waiting, yeah, girly?"

Grayce moaned in pain that Pickson mistook for pleasure. "Oh that's it, enjoy it, G, let Earvyn take care of you like he can, eh? Ha-cough, yeah, like only your Earvyn can do it."

Grayce felt his mouth at her neck, his three day scruff abrading her cheek, his husky breath making her stomach clench. He moved to suck on a nipple. She mewed like a frightened kitten and then gasped in agony when he bit down hard.

"Oh yes, that's it, Grayce-lass," he laughed. "Take it, take it, take it. It could have been nicer, earlier, but now you got it coming to you, yes you do, you little bitch. Paper and pencils!" He spat his cruel consonants into her face. "I've got a nice long, thick charcoal stick for you girly! An' I'm gonna give you a taste of it right now."

Grayce felt his hand leave off holding down her right arm, felt him fumbling with the draw strings to his pants, felt him begin pushing up her skirt. Panic took her fully, and she thrashed from side to side in desperation. He hit her again in response, pinned her legs apart with his own, pressed a meaty hand around her throat to hold her down. She felt his member, stiff, huge, begin sliding up her inner thigh. She tried to scream again but pressure from his hand on her throat reduced it to a choking gurgle. She flung her arm out in a last, futile reach and her hand found something. Her fingers touched bristles: her oversized oak handled paintbrush that she used to temper charcoal lines. She took hold and in the same motion swung it blindly towards Pickson's head. Luck was with her at the last for the blow took Earvyn in the throat. The point, too dull to pierce the skin, still managed to crush her assailant's larynx. Pickson reared back, choking, trying to force air down his collapsed windpipe. Grayce felt his hand leave her throat. With what remained of her strength Grayce swung the brush handle at the side of Pickson's head, and luck was with her again for she struck the ear hole. The handle shattered Pickson's skull, and he fell half-forward on her, gave two quivering, gasping shakes and then grew deathly still.

Grayce lay there for several moments, frozen by her terror and the raw violence. Then she rolled him off her and stared at his ruined features and the ironically tumescent phallus standing more upright in death than perhaps it ever did in life.

Run, run now! Go! Instinct urged her and she scrambled to her feet to comply. She forced herself into a shambling trot, one arm making a vain attempt to control the bouncing of her bruised and ravaged breasts, the other out thrust to fend off tree trunks and branches. All thoughts of her pad and gear left behind forgotten in the need to get away. After awhile her pulse calmed and her balance returned. She started thinking more clearly.

Pickson is dead. His friends will look for him, find his body, all my things. They will see my face. There will be questions, a need for answers. No, no, I can't do it. There will be talk. Staig…

By the time she made it back to the tavern's back door, she had made up her mind to leave. She slipped up to the back door, and discovered that gruff, kind Staig had left it unlocked for her. She stumbled up to her room, flung off her ruined clothes, spared one glance at her ruined face in the mirror before turning away to finish her preparations. She took some clothes, tossed them in a bag she used for market, then changed her mind and rummaged through the pile of stuff Staig stored there and found a light pack he used for hunting. Grayce shoved her clothes in, a pair of shoes, an extra sketchpad she kept by her bedside and several other items she thought she might need. From the bottom dresser drawer she pulled on a pair of pants, salvaged from the luggage of a traveler who could not pay his bill. They would come in handy, now.

She crept back down the stairs. Staig's snores rumbled contentedly from his room down the hall. Grayce went back behind the bar and felt around the shelf below for the spare flint and tinderbox Staig kept for lighting late night pipes and cigars. Back in the kitchen, she took a loaf of day old bread, the remains of a ham and a small bag of apples. These she shoved into her market bag, along with a small crock of lard and a mostly empty bag of flour. She took her things and set them down by the back door. She blew a taper to flame from the coals still glowing on the cooking hearth, lit a candle stub and went back into the bar. She hesitated, weighing the worth of leaving some sort of note for Staig. She found tavernkeeper's accounts pen and ink on the shelf where she purloined the tinderbox. She dipped the pen, held it over the page, but she had no idea what to say, or how it might be interpreted if it came to light. Finally, she decided her best safety lay in brevity.

Staig, You were right. Pickson. I'm sorry. I took your spare strike-a-light. Forgive me.

G

She read the missive over once in the candle light and judged it pathetically incomplete, but she could not spare time for more. She left the note on the strong box, blew the candle out when she got back to her things and added it to her pack. Then she shouldered her burdens and set off.

Chapter 7: Into the Wild

After the first flush of her flight wore off, Grayce doubled back to a dense copse of trees on the slope above town to see what response her trial produced. She settled herself against a tree trunk to wait for morning. Earvyn's shift started at dawn, and she wondered how soon folk would note his absence. The sun oozing over rooftops brought her answer in the form of raised voices and a group gathering at the gates. She watched them fan out, heading for the slopes to the east. She judged she had an hour, maybe two, before they found his body. She stood, stretched, and weighed her options, strangely calm despite the obvious threat of the search party.

When she left Staig's, she meant to abide by the words of her note. She could not stay, even if Earvyn's friends left her alone once the truth came out. And that gave her a chill that had nothing to do with temperature. *The truth. Earvyn dead. Did he talk about me to his friends? Would they believe me if I told them what he tried to do? I killed him? Would they believe that?* The prospect seemed daunting; to have to prove herself capable of dealing with a man as large as Earvyn and expose his rape attempt when, of course, his attention should have flattered her. Running away did not set quite right. She had uncovered a mystery yesterday; that drawing of heather kept coming back to her and counterbalanced her need to get away from Gallina. The shape, and what Earvyn had to say about it, even his tone, picqued her curiosity. *What did it mean? Who put it there? Why Gallina?And those Priests.* The urge to want to find out swept over her like the blue wash she used to set her canvasses.

"Go or stay," she whispered to the morning. A sunbeam, reaching through the maze of branches, flickered wisdom in her eye and she blinked once, twice, a third time, and at the third she straightened her back to miss the gleam and got the point.

"Right," she grinned. "Stay it is. But where?" The notion of lurking in the hills did not seem pleasant. She would have to avoid detection and still find a way to survive. Her father taught her how to make snares and find edible greens and tubers in the lands about, but she would need shelter removed enough where no one would think to look for her. She bent to gather her bag of things purloined from Staig's larder, and by the time the strap hit her shoulder she knew where she would go. The miners of Gallina mixed practicality with superstition. When the shaft buckled that took Grayce's father along with his crew, they closed it and avoided it, but they cut a new one close by. The closed shaft held bitter memories, but it also held a dry floor, a roof, and privacy. *If I keep my wits about me, I might be able to find something out about that drawing. Too many northerners here for it to be coincidence.*

She settled her bag and set off to go make a nest among her ghosts.

She climbed deeper into the trees to make her way as quickly as possible to the mines. The miners had placed a rough barrier in the mouth of the shaft that held her father and his squad entombed, but Grayce had little trouble squeezing past it. Diffused daylight lit her way down the main track, half-choked with stones and broken beams. Dust coated everything. Obviously, the place had lain undisturbed since they called off the effort to rescue her father and his squad without recovering any bodies. Her mother told her the main fall occurred some distance in.

Grayce forced her way in as far as she dared. She came to a sizable alcove carved out of the stone; a space the miners used to take their ease and breathe fresher air. Next to the opening, the remains of a candle, forgotten in the bustle of the failed rescue, still perched upright in its holder. Grayce checked back up the shaft, weighed the risks and fumbled in her bag for her tinder. She managed to get the candle stub to accept a flame and explored the break room by its feeble, flickering light. The place held a table and several chairs, all but one broken. Some cots lined the inner wall, one or two still held straw used as rough bedding. Buckets and a broken water urn held place in a corner. Grayce imagined her father and his men here, eating, laughing, resting, alive. She lost herself for a moment in a scene she had never experienced. The rock walls knew more than she did. The memory clenched her throat, and she blinked back sudden tears. *So much of my life is gone, and Pickson tried to take the rest last night.* Memories of her dead father and the image of what she had done to Pickson last night passed before her mind's eye. *Mother, mother, what have I done? What have I become?*

Her better sense answered her before she lost all control. *You are who you are, not what Pickson and his sort would have made of you. He deserved what he got and more besides, and you know it.*

"I know, so why am I still here?"

You already know that: the drawing. There is more to this than Pickson's attempted rape.

"So what should I do? Where should I go?"

Stay until you know.

She shook herself back into focused silence, grown suddenly aware of exhaustion's grip. She collected what she could of the dried straw and spread it on the sturdiest remaining cot. She tossed her blanket down and used her cloak for a cover. She considered leaving the candle alight, but once again her better sense prevailed and she blew it out, giving herself up to the darkness and unsettling dreams.

She woke up to the faint sounds of picks striking against stone. She blinked in the darkness, gathering what she could from the faint sounds brought to her alcove hideaway through fissures and hollow chambers deep underground. They told her it was near dawn at the least, and work went on for Gallina despite Pickson's death. A draft brushed by her face, carried hints of pine, dust, and early peonies. The combinated reminded her Gallina was the only home she had ever known. She thought it odd that if she were to leave now, she would have spent her last night in what amounted to her father's grave.

She sat listening and breathing for a few minutes, taking stock of her options. Staying in Gallina, no matter what the response from Pickson's death, just did not figure into her thinking. She swung her legs over the edge of the cot, felt for her sandals and the candle stub and tinder. Striking a light, she laced her shoes, ate the rest of the food she took from Staig's and the last swallow from her water jug. Even if she set out that day, she would need supplies, and if she stayed, even more so. The sounds of work going on made her curious. Her mother had never let her come to the mine; she never had the chance to say a proper goodbye. *Father's grave. If I am to go, what better place than this?*

She took her candle, shielding it carefully from the increasing draft. *A vent to the surface from the alcove.* She wondered if it were natural or manmade, for there was evidence that the miners had cooked there. If she were to stay, she could as well. The room was deep enough to mask whatever light she might produce, helped by the slope of the shaft and the jumbled mouth.

She crept down the tunnel and soon found herself picking her way through tumbled stones and dirt. After about a hundred paces, she came up against the fall itself. She held the candle up to take in the scope of the moment that changed her life. An irregular wall of the mountain's bones choked the shaft from floor to ceiling. She stared in a mix of grief, fear and awe, for the barrier before her practically glittered with pyrite and multicolored strains that showed as vague lines cutting through the multitude. She let a deep breath out slowly. Behind those stones, her father's bones moldered, but she could not have imagined a more beautiful headstone. She looked around and found the remains of several torches left behind by the failed rescuers all those years ago. These she gathered and relit, jamming them into stones around the base of the fall. Then she stepped back to give the place a thorough examination. Her candle's effect had only brushed the surface of the canvas before her.

Color reached out, took her grief and fear, and swept it away. Shapes defined by fissures and cracks, swirls and whorls connected to show her a pattern of nature and tragedy. A misplaced strike, a weak seam, a tiny geologic tremble, and the result death and change unalterable.

"And this," she breathed. "And this. Oh, father, you were right, so, so right." For in those broken stones entombing her broken dreams, Grayce saw pictures, tinctures that hinted at wisdom, combinations of shape and shade that suggested whole tales. She put a hand on the nearest boulder, closed her eyes, and saw through her fingertips all the truths her father ever spoke to her. Here was beauty, mystery, rhythm, cadence and song all compressed in a basaltic, adamantine surety. There were seams, fissures, subtle connections all throughout Gallina's hills. She imagined them now as a tracery of lines, realized to her shock how much her drawings reflected that pattern.

Despite her situation and the distance of time, she never felt closer to her father. If she ever had any questions about their connection, the language of the stones answered them forever.

But sounds other than the faint blows of Gallina's miners intruded on her reverie. Voices seaped through to her space from the opposite direction. She had no way of ascertaining how close, but she held her breath and listened nonetheless.

"So you found him in the trees?" The tone clipped, peremptory, cold and commanding even through the filter of rock and space. She did not recognize the voice. The reference to 'him' took her to her knees, crouching instinctively as if to hide.

"Yes, a mess, that." But that voice she did recall; the leftside priest from yesterday.

"He got himself killed. Fool." Again, dismissive, a man out of time and patience.

"We searched the town as best we could. Nothing."

"No matter. We change nothing. Watch them."

"Yes, lord. Absolutely."

"Enough with this skulking about. I am off to meet Edris. We go north, now. Send word of anything new. The road helps us in that."

"Depend on it, sir."

"I always do. Farewell."

The voices faded quickly, but Grayce remained crouched and still for long moments after, deeply alarmed by the obvious reference to Pickson and intrigued by the thought of who 'they' might be. So much change overnight: her world, such as it was, damaged, fragmented, only loosely knit together by her art and work, completely overturned in one night's trauma. She held herself still as dust settled in a tomb, eyes shut tight in concentration, for long moments until sure those voices gone.

She let go a heavy sigh, finally. Eyes still closed, she reached out and found one of the boulders entombing her father, used it to rise, and stood there, blind and communing.

"Goodbye, father," she whispered. "Rest here among your friends. One day," she paused, opened her eyes and removed her hand from the stone. "One day I'll paint this and tell your story to the world."

She gathered the torches, extinguished all but one of them, and returned to her alcove. By its light, she set about unraveling threads from a scrap of rope for snares. Then she snuck up to the mine opening, checked for watchers or signs of those others and scrambled through the barriers heading up the slope to set them in a meadow she knew possessed rabbit warrens. When she finished, she set about gathering a store of edible plants and nuts. By the afternoon, she had eaten most of what she had found and faced a hungry night unless she got lucky with her snares.

While she wandered, the image of the heather on her wall drawing kept coming back to her. She still had no idea what it meant, but it felt northern. It felt wrong, somehow, the way Pickson's attentions had felt wrong; hard to define beyond a feeling. She needed more information, possibly from Gallina, more likely from somewhere else. When her wanderings took her to a rocky outcropping that looked down upon the town, she climbed up and sat down, letting her thoughts follow her eyes as she observed the life she left behind.

Outside of the sketches in her pad back in the mine, the sum total of her days in Gallina were the memories Staig and the others would keep of her and the handful of her wall murals. Folk whitewashed walls, and memories faded faster if they had an unpleasant tinge.

She almost felt sorry for herself, but her natural independence, spiced by the power of her moment with her father in the mine, sent her on a different path.

"I'm alone, finally, no one now but me," she said aloud to the world. "Those people down there might care, might accept me, but what else will there be besides pity and bare walls to draw on?" She let her voice fade to silence, drew her legs up, and rested her chin on her knees. She passed the next hours marking the sun's passing by the shadow her body cast. The wind teased her hair around her eyes, the spring chill faded to a warm afternoon, and still she sat unmoving. Her thoughts etched patterns against her dullness, slowly, as though she watched another's hand articulate the charcoal stick. Then the pattern completed itself with a final stroke that encompassed all her art and the colors her torches had revealed in the mine.

I'm free. I can do what I want. And what I want is to find out who put that bit of heather on my drawing and what it means. But where? North, south, east or west? West just leads to the mountains. East? Ridges and port cities and strange ways. South? No, Pickson said it was a northern plant. Northerners all went looking for him. Desopolis will hold no answers. North it is, then.

She stood up abruptly and took one last look at Gallina before turning to head back to the mines. She checked her snares before sunset, gutting and cleaning the one coney she found, waiting for full dark to head back to town one last time. She slunk in through the kitchen window this time, and hoped Staig would not begrudge her one last run through her room and his larder. She gathered more of her clothes, the pair of boots underneath her bed. Then she hugged the deeper shadows to the gate and slipped through. Within minutes she was up in the woods above town heading north.

"Goodbye, Gallina," she whispered as she jogged along the trail.

Grayce kept away from the road that snaked through the hills, preferring to make her way along the animal runs she encountered. She trended northwards, almost aimlessly, keeping the road on her left and below her. Having no real destination other than away from Gallina and its questions, she spent her time poking about underneath tree roots and tracing the texture of the basaltic outcroppings that pierced the mold. She began to see the region in a new way as she wandered; root and branch at war with stone, a slow grinding, reaching, life pushing against the hard ridges. All formed a lattice of threads that both consumed and wove the earth into a rolling wave of daunting and alluring matter; a canopy of boughs upheld by the rocky shoulders of the world, isolated, dense, full of sound and motion.

All of it went unnoticeable from the beaten way that pushed like a muddied stain through the lowlands below. To people like Staig back in Gallina, that road represented connection, an artery knitting the idea of 'kingdom' together, a way for the new king with his dreams of unity to exploit the highland resources and speed his messengers overland when the sea roads proved untenable.

Grayce sat astride a deadfall in the afternoon sun as a line of wains moved south along that road. She used the root ball for a backrest, trying to catch the light's effect on the ground below her vantage point. Grayce was not sure how she felt about that winding track. Through her younger days 'the road' began in Gallina and ran south to Desopolis. The hills were a barrier, a protection of trees and steep slopes and narrow places, the haunt of deer and elk, a land of more shadows than light. Events five years gone proved such things illusion when those same hills spewed Roderran of Perspa's armed columns with war and rapine against the south.

In burning Gallina, they burned away Grayce's childhood.

And the road that came as a 'gift' of Donari Avedun's peace brought types like Earvyn Pickson south to 'build' that road.

That paradox tantalized Grayce's thoughts as she sat there. *How can they call it 'building' when they destroy so much in the process? Trees felled, banks cut, ground unnaturally levelled, streams muddied and despoiled. For what? A progress of wagons driven by thieves who called themselves merchants? What peace was that?* She looked at her effort on the pad, drew a line through it, decisively.

"Nope," she whispered. "I don't like roads."

A random cloud passed before the sun and dimmed the light, breaking the mood and reminding Grayce it was time to check her morning snares. Her stomach rumbled urgency as she packed away her materials in her pack and scrambled off the fallen tree trunk.

By the time she finished checking all of them her stomach's grumbling turned serious, and the big, fat rabbit snagged in the last one set saliva flowing. She found some mint and a small cluster of mushrooms on the way back to her camp. She spent the rest of the afternoon slowly stewing her dinner, and every time she tasted the broth from the pan she washed away some of her bitter, mid-day thoughts. She ate with relish in a much better frame of mind.

That night she dreamed of colors, and if her hand itched from ill memories, she did not notice.

A desire for a different diet pushed her wanderings westward. She crossed the road under a full moon and felt through the soles of her feet its difference and change. She followed a stream up into the hill folds until she found a series of pools and spent days acquainting herself with fish. The ground there lay quiescent under the early summer sun, the lands about vacant, the canopy undisturbed. She followed deer as they grazed their way benignly through upland meadows. She fashioned a spear, whittled and hardened the point, but never seriously considered using it. She had no way to preserve the venison if she brought one down. Besides, the tone of the area spoke to her differently. She saw no sign of human presence. Tubers populated the area. She found caches of acorns in the hollow spaces in and around trees. She found a large flat rock and used it to cook flat cakes. Fish and nut bread. A stream to bathe in. Mountains in view to the west; to the east rolling tree-woven hills and no sight of the road. Gallina was a thought lingering under a pall of smoke from kitchen fires and the mine works. Everything was distant--especially fear. She drew away all that she was as she filled in the corners of her sketch pad pages, becoming a creature of silence and vision, an extension of the glamor in beauty that exists in and of itself whether man noticed it or not.

She understood the secrets of the cracks in rocks and the inner contours they suggested. She saw the rhythm in the water dance of trout. She followed the manic course of bees and found honey to sweeten her flat cakes. In the amber sheen of the dripping liquid, she discovered altered hues in the sun.

She metamorphosed into an element, a moving insinuation along the palette of the whole, a ghost of intention flowing like water over stones, a new color. She forgot clothes and moved through the area knitting together shape and tone with lines of colored clay and plant resin. She traced whirls and lines all over her legs, arms and breasts; a clay streaked figure of unrestricted expression. She left off checking her traps and snares, munched ambivalently on her cache of nuts and raw tubers and gradually forgot almost all of what she once was. Then one day the wind blew the scent of the sea in her face and she woke up to her own humanity.

She climbed up to the top of a large outcropping that swam like a breakwater against the tide of the forest and looked west. The sea, a line of blue-green just on the horizon's edge, teased at her the way the breeze would lift and sway the tresses of her hair. She swung away from the view and saw with other eyes how she had transformed the area: shapes scratched in the dirt, clay daubed onto exposed rock faces into spatial coherences, new gods and goddesses to grace the milieu. Lines of power revealed themselves to her as fluid web connecting rock, tree, water and sky. She vaguely recalled her mother's bedtime stories about wizards and dismissed them as idle fantasies.

No, mother, here is matter more magical.

"Time to go," she breathed, and started at the changed timber in her voice; deeper, tonally more mature than she remembered. A new truth came to her then about the effect of silence on sound, and that, too, was a kind of color. She scratched idly at a dry patch on her arm and stared in wonder at her decorated nakedness. She bathed in one of the pools in the stream, letting the current leach away the aftereffects of her creative diaspora, taking pleasure in the way her hair floated away from her, frond-like in the water. When the stream ran clear, she rose, dried herself in the late afternoon sun, dressed, and trussed her pack with all she thought she might still need. She left, following the shadows reaching eastwards. She trended to her left, intending to intercept the road further north.

When she neared the line of the road two days later, she paused for a long moment in the undergrowth, staring both ways down its length of worked stone and earth. Again, she sensed its alien quality; a made thing in a place permeated with natural shapes and lines. It even smelled like the sweat of man's labor, and she swallowed down a sudden queasiness brought on by that smell: Earvyn Pickson. Men of his ilk made that thing; a line that meant nature sliced by power, pierced and controlled in a way reminiscent of the way Earvyn had wanted to pierce and control her.

Grayce forced herself forward and crossed, hurrying up the slopes on the other side to denser cover. A sound from south, back down the road, sent her ducking down behind some stones piled together on a shelf. She barely let herself breathe as she watched a lone horsemen, riding at an even steady pace, pass below her vantage. The man, she assumed it was a man, wore black clothing and sported a large hat pulled low down that obscured his face. Saddlebags bulged, lashed to either side, and she surmised he was some sort of messenger. She wondered if he took word of her misadventure to someone in authority, and then thought better of it. She was weeks gone from Gallina; plenty of time for folk to search and question and spread the news north and south. She doubted Pickson would be worth the effort.

Grayce waited until the rider passed out of sight and the sound of his mount faded to silence before continuing. She wandered the eastern slopes, tracing her days in sketches and swirl patterns scratched on moss covered rocks and trees, a wandering line of her expression that knit the hills together with an intimacy reminiscent of home. She made fires, gathered her herbs and nuts as she needed, knew herself but increasingly aware of her connection to all that was 'other'. Nineteen and yet ageless, a living sense impression on the skin of the world, Grayce gathered her past into a precious ball, wrapped her present around it with parchment metaphysical and contemplated her future.

Until a cloudburst drove her into a cave for shelter.

The cave faced northwest and, excluding the road, showed the first signs of human activity Grayce had seen since leaving Gallina. Wood lay stacked along one wall, bracken lay piled in a corner as if for bedding, and a chipped basin nestled atop three round rocks, obviously placed there for balance. The fire pit lay cold and long unused. The place had the look of a hunter's camp.

Grayce took the basin and placed it outside to catch the rain, took some of the dried matter and got a fire going, and set about making herself comfortable. Outside the rain slowed to a gentle, consistent drizzle. She munched on yesterday's nuts, unwrapped some squirrel meat left over from her last set of snares and propped it over the flames to roast warm. She leaned back against a rock the previous tenant placed near the fire pit for a seat and let her gaze wander over the cave's contours. Gradually, the fire's glow compensated for the storm-lost natural light to reveal colors in the stones: reds and greys, freckles of feldspar, smoke stains and cobwebs; and in a crack in a stone set shoulder high on the far cave-wall the tell-tale shape of a tightly folded piece of paper.

Intrigued, Grayce scrambled to her feet and teased the treasure gently out from its hiding place. Time had left the paper brittle, and it cracked a little as she carefully unfolded it. The paper held words written in ink with a spidery hand:

Time Well Spent

Rain makes sluggards of us all and slows us down by necessity
I do not mark the rain or curse it ill, though it forces me to a stillness
Alien and taxing.

It grants me time to contemplate
The many things over-which I hesitate
About choices unpleasant I must make
Whether I would or no;
For now the rain decides if I stay or go.

Forget your innocence. You've no more time for that, my friend
Because the times and their tone won't leave you alone.
The need to act will now drive you into the fray
Hatless and heedful
No matter how fearful or needful,
Or how intensely you might try and pray.

And once you've set your foot upon the path
Irresolution cannot be part of the plan.
Misdirection and misconception
Will seek to trip you up,
But, like a hero, you must drain the cup
Of action and event to which you rise heir—
For just by being,
You show your care...

For some reason, as she read, she heard the voice of that nameless man from her youth. The image of that face came to her as she re-read the poem. Eyes intent yet distant stared out from the mirror of her curiosity. Squirrel meat fat hissing as it dropped into the flames drew her back to the fire. Keeping the page well away from the flames, she used her off hand to remove the meat to cool on a rock.

She reached for her pencil and pad, then paused, thought better of it and turned the delicate page over and began sketching with feathery, whispering strokes on the blank side. Gradually, tenderly, the outline of that face and those eyes took shape. Grayce paused to reshape her pencil with her small knife. Her eyes, focused, transfixed, never left the page. With her sharpened point, working from both memory and interpretation, she drew out the contours of the author, unconsciously adding tell-tell worry lines creasing the area about the eyes, the left partially blurred by a shock of unruly hair.

When she finished she drew a breath like a diver breaking the surface after going too deep. She dropped her pencil and cupped the drawing, her fingers tingling from the contact of the ink on the underside.

"Who are you?" she breathed in wonder. "And who am I, besides an orphan in need of a bath?" Her inner voice came to her, assertive, definite, with part of an answer.

You are a poet who uses color, and you need to find a more meaningful canvas.

Grayce took the page and her added offering back to its hiding place. She spent the rest of that day nibbling squirrel meat and watching the rain. She thought back over her wandering course and its connecting lines and saw her passage as a counterpoint to the road.

The next day Grayce took care to truss her belongings for easy carrying. Her dreams during the night convinced her she was done with wandering the highlands. It was time for a more direct purpose. She looked back once at the niche and its folded, two-sided treasure.

A week later, she crested a final slope and stood staring down at a large, oval valley bisected by a small river that meandered towards a green-blue bay. A gentle salt breeze from off that water cooled her sweaty brow. A walled city perched on a hill to the north of the river's mouth. She recalled overheard conversations at Staig's about Pevana and her white stone houses and red tile roofs and smiled.

Pevanese Mosaic

A city. People. A challenge. But there would be alleys and walls to spare.

A new kind of canvas.

Chapter 8: Threads of Mystery

Devyn readjusted his grip on his mount's reins, willing the beast to stay calm and close to better shield him from the rain that dripped through the canopy of the ancient elm. Thankfully, the winds abated as he took shelter or he would be even more uncomfortable. The rain showed signs of lessening as the light began to fail on the second day of his ride north from Desopolis. He might still have time to find a more sheltered spot to camp, something out of the wind and off the road.

He did not need any more wind. He had more than enough on his sailing journey down the coast to check the status of the city-states turned Perspan provinces. As King Donari Avedun's main eyes and ears, the task fell to him. In truth, he had asked for this trip after meeting the painter Jeril Sandre and hearing his tale of Piling. He needed to check things. It also gave him a chance to reconnect in Desopolis with his old friend, Talyior Enmbron, his wife Lyvia and their child, Devvie, and Lyvia's father, the former tyrant turned king-maker and grandfather, Sylvanus Tamorgen. He looked forward to a good visit, but a squall that took a ship's spar in the sealanes east of the city drenched his hopes, and the rough seas of the gale that blew up after sent him reeling with seasickness and seriously questioning his need to be there.

Thankfully, they managed to rig enough sail to make the tack into the harbor safely. Between the ship's damage and the gale's ferocity, he had his visit. News of unusual developments within Desopolis and ominous enounters in the seas east and south of the coast tempered the pleasures of good wine, good humor, and meeting young Devvie. The six-year old terror was a perfect blend of his father's features and his mother's disposition. Even now, despite the rain and chill, the memory of Devvie and his grandfather rough-housing on the study carpet brought a smile.

But the sum total of what he learned in that week's worth of inactivity disturbed him such that he decided he could not wait for repairs to the galley. He figured he could make good time riding north on his own. As he sat there, hat pulled down as far as possible to spare his neck, he mulled over several items that loomed as the core of a beginning question.

Talyior's private shipping business had thrived in the years since Donari's crowning. Prosperity was tangible up and down the coast, and yet Talyior had mentioned odd encounters on the open sea; ships with red sails showing up on the horizon, several other incidents that, within reasonable limits, Talyior's captains claimed as borderline aggressive.

"Those ships were too well handled," Talyior had summarized, "to be trading galleys. And my folk think they had too many crew for reasonable profit. Didn't add up."

Red sails. Devyn stuck on that fact. From past experience, he had a negative opinion of most things red. There were red sails on the ship that brought the Esdan Empire's pompous, bullying embassy in the spring. And that ship, too, had been smartly handled. And Esdans had burned Piling.

The color also reminded him of the King's Theology, which had never left Pevana. The fraudulent faith emerged after Donari's ascension a reduced and reformed version of the original. It had re-appeared in Desopolis with a small affair near the land gate of the city. Devyn would have missed it completely, but Talyior pointed out the structure in passing as they rode out of the city.

"The King's Theology mission Lyvia mentioned," he had said. "Nothing special."

Devyn eased his horse over toward the nondescript two story building. It sported small windows, simply dressed stone walls bereft of any ornamentation save for some carving above the single door.

"Quite a bit less impressive than Casan's bell tower," he said as they passed. Then he had looked closer at the carving above the lintel and a slight chill tingled the base of his neck.

"Now that is strange." He pointed. "Why heather?"

"Heather?" asked Talyior.

"The only decoration is a northern weed. Remember? We saw whole hillsides of the stuff on our way to Lomillar."

A moment later they passed through the gate, and after a furlong Talyior had turned back, leaving Devyn alone with his thoughts on the road north.

Those thoughts rumbled about at the core of his discomfort as he huddled between his horse and the elm. He sensed threads that started from disparate sources, but how they joined, and what they might make eluded him.

* * *

Gallina came as a surprise when Devyn reached it. A bustling town had replaced the burned out shell he remembered from his last visit on the way back north with Donari, more than five years ago. The place seemed twice its former size, fresher, more prosperous. He made good time getting there, one of the benefits of Donari's Road as the locals called it. He passed traffic on the way: lines of wagons bearing ore south, others carrying loads north. Obviously, Donari's idea of the road as a connective artery for the realm's interior would prove a good one.

The original inn where he and Talyior stayed during their journey south had been rebuilt and expanded along with the town, as had the square where Devyn committed himself to a different life. Even though he arrived just after mid-day, he determined to spend the night and get a sense of the place before moving on. He wandered about the streets during the afternoon. The markets still bustled with folk. The air rang with the sound of smith's and tinker's hammers, the semi-desultory calls of venders still trying to clear their tables. In its previous incarnation, Gallina had been a hardscrabble place Devyn could not help but pity. Now he noticed a different attitude in the faces he encountered, more smiles, curiosity rather than suspicion, a willingness to chat if questioned; in short, folk engaged in a growing enterprise rather than barely hanging on.

What dark looks he got he quickly surmised came from members of the crews working on the road. Many of them were southerners, but Devyn thought he heard some northern accents in the mix, and most of what might pass as suspicious or cautious looks came from them. He outrode the rains and concerns getting there, so he smiled through his unease, refusing to let anything dampen his spirits.

He ducked down several side streets and alleys during his walk, and here, too, he saw signs that suggested this was a different Gallina than before. Several fences and building back walls sported intricate drawings and circular designs shapely and intriguing. By the end of the day, he found himself looking for these artistic expressions so at odds with his former impressions of the place.

The last one he found, an involved piece on the back wall of a building down near the gate, brought those dark looks and those left behind fears back two-fold. For at the bottom of that last mural someone had drawn a crude representation of a sprig of heather. He looked at it closely and decided it could not have been by the original artist.

A carving above a small church door. Northerners among the road crews. This questionable addition, here, close to the gate but nowhere else. A sign. A message.

"A mystery," he whispered. Thoughts, questions and possible connections followed him as he headed back to the inn, lengthening and deepening along with the shadows as the sun set in the west behind the rocky hills that ringed Gallina's valley.

Later, he nursed a last pint of passably good beer and delicately attempted to put those questions to the inn's proprietor, Staig Motta, after the common room cleared at the end of the night.

"You seem to be doing well," Devyn began, sipping from the mug Motta refilled before pouring one for himself.

"And you are a stranger who spent the whole afternoon snooping about the place. What is my business to you? Or Gallina, either?"

"I was here once before. Things were quite a bit different, then."

Devyn met Motta's stare openly, one of the finer by-products of Donari's peace: less need for subterfuge. Before, he would have found Motta's look disconcerting. He smiled slightly, enjoying the novelty of not having anything to hide.

"Sadly, that previous stay was too short, and eventful, to enjoy such fine beer."

Motta blinked once, twice, took a swallow, leaned forward on his elbows across the bar, eyes narrowing in concentration.

"Five years ago," he said finally, decisively. "You and another fellow, horses. The morning we had trouble with King's Theology priests."

Devyn raised his mug in salute. "You have a good memory."

Motta frowned. "And you have a bloody past. Things got bad, after."

Devyn took a long pull, weighing his words. "They did," he agreed, nodding. "But they were going to get bad regardless of what happened in the square that day."

"Folk died, then and after. They burned Gallina."

Devyn gestured toward the door. "And yet you've risen from the ashes nicely. I wasn't part of that burning. I serve the king who rebuilt this place, who began the road that now connects you with the greater realm. Donari wept for Gallina. I'm sure these last five years have proven he's no Roderran."

Motta stared in silence for a long moment. Devyn read the emotions running across the innkeeper's face: suspicion, anger, acceptance. Finally, the man pursed his lips and nodded, his eyes suggesting the ghost of a grin.

"Fair enough," he said. "We have done well enough since." He leaned back, wiped the already clean bar surface with his damp towel. "Better than well enough, actually. We have grown, as I'm sure you've observed."

Devyn reached a hand up. "Devyn Ambrose, eyes and ears to the king. I regret not meeting you before, Staig Motta."

Motta took his hand, gripped it firmly and held on. "You aren't planning on any more market square surprises?"

Devyn returned the pressure. "Absolutely not. Just passing through. I have been on a journey down the coast, and I am on my way back to report."

"And what have you seen?"

"Folk living. More smiles than otherwise. Growth, here, and elsewhere. Encouraging."

"If the king's road helps my trade, that will be enough."

"Gallina has her role to play. She appears to have a resident artist. I noticed the drawings. I also noticed quite a few northern accents during my walk."

Motta frowned. "Road crews, most of them. Miners, others. We have expanded the works in the hills westward. We've drawn men from the north and south looking for work. It has been an interesting mix."

"Harmonius?" Again, a frowning pause, and Devyn leaned in closer. "I noticed a few rough looking characters."

"Nothing we can't handle," Motta responded, scowling. "The road is nearly finished. The two ends will meet close to Gallina. We have had elements from both crews here for several months now. The last few weeks have been difficult."

"In what way?"

"Awhile back, we found one of the northerners dead on a path in the hills above town." Motta paused, took another pull as if swallowing down a bitter memory. "He had a paint brush handle stuck five inches into his ear and a crushed wind pipe. His gang cried murder, but…" He fell silent and stared at the liquid in his mug.

Instantly, Devyn felt a return of that chill he had experienced earlier.

"But you don't think so," he said.

"No," Motta sighed, shaking his head and finishing his drink. "You mentioned those 'decorations' around town. The artist worked for me. Young thing. Spirited. She lost her family in the troubles. The dead fellow took a liking to her. I think he took things too far, and she defended herself. Of course, none of the northerners bought that story. There was a search. The girl has not been seen since."

"I'm sorry."

Motta half-smiled, half-grimaced. "Growing pains."

"You cared for her."

"She was a child of the place. This place."

"And she's gone."

Motta nodded once, resigned. "Gone. Took her things. No sign of her."

Devyn finished his drink, pushed away from the bar. "She's good, you know. I hope she is safe. But, from what you've told me, she sounds like she can take care of herself."

Motta chuckled as he took up the mugs. "Oh yes. No doubt of that. Good night to you."

"I'll be off in the morning. I do have another question."

"Ask."

"Does heather grow around here?"

"Heather? What is that?"

"A plant. Twiggy. Little pinkish flowers."

"Never heard of it. Why do you ask?"

"I'm not altogether sure. Something I noticed in one of the drawings. Good night."

"Will you need breakfast?"

Briefly, Devyn considered the idea, but then shook his head no. For some reason, he felt the need for an early start and speed. By the time he reached his room at the top of the stairs, that feeling had morphed into a full-blown requirement. He had been gone long enough.

He rode out just as dawn began to bloom in the east and made quick time along the road. By day's end he reached the first of the temporary camps where the road crews sheltered. He spent the night with them, trading news for news. Some had seen action in the previous conflict, from opposite sides. Time must have tempered the harsh truths from those days, for the stories were full of exploit and honor to the common soldier, good natured disparage of the southerners, and a romantic sensibility about Roderran.

Devyn decided within a generation folk would see the whole affair as a great victory rather than the chaotic defeat it actually had been. For him, every pace of his horse north brought images and memories of those times back with an aching clarity. There had been offerings on the common gravesites at Lyranden Bridge. For him, the desperate journey in search of Donari's column still felt like it happened yesterday.

He did not begrudge the men their revisions. A man had to find his honor. Peace allowed a man to think, and if a man had to embellish and reconstruct to find some healing, then so be it. Devyn saw no threat there. A man could frame a different opinion and not be labeled a traitor, and that, too, was a by-product of Donari's peace.

A peace whose obvious growth and prosperity now imperiled it.

He met with similar thoughts and reactions with every crew he encountered along the way, but the tone was a bit different at the last camp. This group was engaged in bridging a stream that cut across the road's path. There was a ford, but the grade made it difficult for wagons to pass. Devyn arrived to find the crew putting the final beams in place to span the gap. They said they were behind schedule because they had to search off the road a ways to find suitable timber.

They found the proper trees, but they found other things that sent him off to investigate on his own. What he saw astounded him.

Lines. Everywhere. Lines in the dirt, daubed on rock faces, swirls, shapes, colors, blends and everything dominated by, connected by, lines scratched in the dirt as if some eldritch spirit had taken a fancy to weave its mad pattern visibly on the face of the world. The men sent to cut timber spoke of what they had seen with awe, their superstition and fear palpable, but Devyn, when he found the place, just chuckled. He had sensed something similar during his walk in Gallina, as though that unknown artist had consciously attempted to knit the place together for herself in a familiar pattern.

"Not surprising," he whispered as he knelt down to examine a footprint in the clay at the stream's bank, "for someone who lost everything once."

He cast his thought outward, following the pattern, stretching his senses to see if the artist might still be near.

Nothing.

There had been no rain since he left Gallina, but he could tell the signs about were quite old. The rhythm of the woodlands about felt normal. The girl had been there but had moved on; probably to avoid the crew working on that bridge. He wanted to find this unknown artist who seemed intent to leave her mark but keep her freedom. Motta, though he spoke feelingly of her, never told him her name.

Secrets.

He looked around the area one last time at the lines and patterns. To the untutored road crews, they would appear random, but Devyn saw with eyes that had lived in and survived Pevana's Maze. He turned to go then paused, blinked, and saw it as he had sensed it through the soles of his boots once before: the life threading itself throughout the Maze. Pattern in apparent chaos. Truth beneath the surface.

"No way," he breathed. "She couldn't possibly."

But it was true. He was sure of it as he turned to go, cursing the need for speed that kept him from finding her. Duty called him more intently than curiosity.

He took to horse and spurred north, riding swiftly, wondering if duty and curiosity might connect somehow.

No. Not wondering. Hoping. Who are you, girl? Where are you?

He chewed over such thoughts as his horse pounded out the final leagues to Pevana. When he rode in through the Land Gate, he found the whole city buzzing with talk of another deputation from Esda. He saw fear and concern in the faces he observed along the way. Some in the streets recognized him, but he ignored their shouted questions. He eased through the crowds collected in the city squares and headed for the hill. From the talk he overheard, he assumed Donari would be in council. Devyn's report would arrive unlooked for and timely.

"Trip's over," he sighed. "Time to get back to work."

Chapter 9: Tasia

Tasia Morelli loved words but hated going to school. Her brother, Bastian, who claimed to be wiser, told her school was the best place to find words, but she knew better. He did, too, he just forgot in the flush of his new life as a page in the palace. Regular meals and more frequent baths had changed him from a child of the Maze into something else. He followed 'rules'. Such obedience sent a chill snaking down Tasia's spine as she trotted along one of the narrow lanes of the Maze. The great fire when she was younger took a large chunk of it, and the great events in the early days of King Donari's reign cleaned up other parts. The Maze remained, shifted somewhat from its original location and slightly more prosperous, and that made sense to Tasia. To her, the rabbit run of humanity was as much of the truth of Pevana as the king's banner snapping in the breeze. She first listened to Kembril Edri there and met the poet, Devyn Ambrose.

The Maze meant words, real words, real stories; the kind one could never find within the margins of a book or defined by a teacher. She went to school because her brother and mother asked her to, but she stayed only until she lost interest in the rules and whys of things. Lately that had begun happening earlier and earlier. Today she skipped out after the mid-morning break to wander the back ways of the city. The old woman trying to hold class possessed a wheezy, crackling voice and stumbled over the stories she read to them. She understood many of her friends liked to listen and benefited from the experience. The old woman worked for them but not for her.

Tasia, twelve and timeless, knew more real stories had lingered in the dust that used to collect around Edri's feet beneath the great Tree. More truth now hung in the sounds of Devyn's voice when he brought myths to life. She wanted those words and whenever possible wandered the city looking for them. She found hints everywhere: in the way washing hung from lines, the way vendors called out their wares, in the collection of sounds and sense that typified Pevanese life. Her quest drove her, perplexed her mother, and irritated her brother, but she could not help herself.

Tasia considered herself blessed, or cursed, by expectation of something wonderful. Blessed through Queen Eleni's efforts to educate Pevana's children; cursed in that she already looked higher. Tasia wanted to be a poet of Pevana. The queen's own experiences showed her the way: break tradition if necessary, question, prod and ignore constantly in the search for the heart's desire. That was always her favorite of Devyn's tales; how the queen, in her former life, secretly entered the poetic competition. Through trial and tragedy, she found her words and her love.

To gain her own heart's desire, Tasia knew she had to find her words, by herself. And *that* made even more sense to her because in all the old tales, the hero always had to figure stuff out alone. Why should she be different?

Her flight from school today took her back down the alley that ran behind Gania Landare's boarding house. Tasia earned free meals and a few pennies helping around the establishment. Tasia liked Gania. Where most folk cringed when she let loose her booming anger, Tasia just laughed, seeing the kinder person behind the noise. Gania reserved most of her bluster for the pompous and proud. She lavished patience on Tasia and her friends. Tasia determined early on, with that certainty come from life in the Maze, to keep an eye out for Gania. When she was just a kid, Devyn Ambrose tasked her to keep an eye on things. She got quite good at it. She grew up watching, learning, deciding about things. It was one of the reasons why she possessed so little liking for formal school. Even at twelve, she just knew more.

She pushed through the gate in the low fence that separated Gania's kitchen garden from the alley. She slowed to cull some carrots and a couple of ripe tomatoes on her way to the back door. It was barely mid-day, and Lyssa, Gania's assistant and cook, would be just putting the evening's pot over the fire, and if it was stew she knew Lyssa always scanted on the carrots.

The kitchen smelled tantalizing. Lyssa looked up from stirring as Tasia entered.

"Well, well!" she exclaimed. "Nicely timed, my dear, and with carrots, too! You must have read my mind. Give'em a wash and chop, will you? I'd've already done it, but Gania left me the bedding to see to, and my back, you know…" She left off and rubbed her lower back tellingly.

Tasia laughed at Lyssa's attempt at self-pity, went to the basin next to the sink, and rinsed the carrots and tomatoes off. Deftly, she grabbed a knife, gave the carrots a quick scrape before cutting them into segments.

She quartered the tomatoes, swept up the mass and returned to Lyssa's side to let the vegetables slip through her fingers into the bubbling liquid.

"Shall I finish dealing with the sheets for you?" she asked.

"No need," Lyssa grunted, turning to take a seat at the table. She had a cup of tea there, which she took up and sipped from before continuing. "So, you are even earlier today. What was it drove you from school this time? Sums?"

Tasia stirred the pot, took a taste from the end of the spoon. "No," she answered. "Not sums. Numbers, I can handle. She tried to tell us a story about Minuet and didn't like my suggestions."

"Suggestions?"

Tasia gave Lyssa the look that only twelve year olds possessed when dealing with clueless adults. "For doing it better, of course. She sniffed down her lumpy nose at me, so I left. I've heard better. I can do better."

Lyssa snorted into her cup. "Cheeky, little miss."

Tasia sat down, poured herself a cup, and snorted in return, unrepentant. "I don't care. I don't need her stories. I've enough of my own and to spare."

"Child," began Lyssa.

"Child?" Tasia interrupted. "I may be cleaner these days, Lyssa, thanks to you and Gania, but I know where I come from. Old Mariah means well, I'm sure, but she doesn't know me."

Lyssa put her cup down with a decisive click. "I *know* that! Renia's Grace, girl, listen to yourself! Schooling for the Mazeborn is a new thing. Where's your patience?"

"I buried it in the dirt at Kembril's grave when I was seven."

"Ah," Lyssa mused. "That's right. I forgot. First Edri and then after…"

"Ambrose," Tasia finished. "Yes. I have learned my Minuet, Lyssa, from the best. I want something more."

"But surely you need your numbers and such?"

Again, Tasia fixed her with *that* look. "Numbers? I know what a penny buys. The poor always know. I am sure some in the great houses on the hill could use instruction on money's value. Wasteful nits, most of them."

"I daresay," agreed Lyssa, "but things have been better these last few years. Look at the building going on! Trade from all over in the markets. The schools are part of that."

"Maybe." Tasia pushed away from the table and headed for the back stairs. "I will finish the rooms upstairs for you, Lyssa, and then sweep the front steps."

"I'll have a bowl and a bun for you when you finish."

"Thank you."

"Girl," Lyssa's tone stopped Tasia at the door. "Is school that bad?"

Tasia relented. "No, not really, I suppose. But I am almost thirteen. I want more."

After remaking the beds, Tasia came back downstairs, checked the status of Lyssa's slow simmering stew, and took the broom out to sweep the front steps and walk. The mid-morning traffic clotted the street. Down a ways, some of the local ladies clustered around the well in the square, chatting like a covey of quail as they gathered their second water run of the day. Tasia made a rhythm of her task, sweeping and glancing in turn, observing the pattern in her Pevana world. She imagined Queen Eleni from her palace balcony saw it differently, as did the lords of the merchant houses, and yet to her sense it was all one pattern. She had always felt that way, for as long as she could remember, even when she did not possess the language to express it.

Pevana's dust settled on everyone alike. It was just that some possessed the means to brush it away more consistently.

Her thought reminded her of the old poet, Kembril Edri, and his stories told in the summer dust beneath the Tree. That dust hung over him like a sanctified corona. She traced her desire for words and tales back to him. He was five years in the ground since the great fire, but it still felt like yesterday. He used to say everything flowed downward in Pevana, water from rooftops, money from commerce, dust brushed from the lintels in rich houses; it was all one in the same.

Kembril had worn it all like a cloak of remembrance.

Tasia reached the end of the walk and sighed, not from sorrow over that recalled death, but rather from an odd contentment. Even at twelve, or perhaps especially at twelve, she understood the connections between things. She gave another sweep, satisfied, even if only temporarily, in the insight that life was like dust: though endlessly disturbed by the currents of the world, it always resettled in new and interesting forms and patterns.

Tasia looked up from her work as the gate opened, letting in the hulking form of Gania Landare. She clutched a large basket of late-market purchases under one volumnious arm.

"Have you eaten, girl?" she asked, looming above like a good-natured human cloud.

"Of course," lied Tasia. "You know better than to ask."

"I know better than to believe you when you answer so quickly," Ganai retorted. She reached into the basket and pulled out a sticky bun dripping with cinnamon butter frosting. She took a small scrap of paper from the basket and wrapped it around the bun. "Here, at least put this in your pocket for later."

"Are things so prosperous, then, that you've taken to buying baked goods?"

Gania grinned, a gap-toothed, genuine affair.

"Maybe, but these are better than anything Lyssa or I can make on our own, and well worth it to my way of thinking. I see you've been at the broom. Did Lyssa get you to do the upstairs rooms, too?"

"We did them together."

"Another lie, but thank you all the same." Gania stuck a hand down her ample bosom and fished out a coin and handed it over.

"Silver?" Tasia asked. "For bedding? I'm no palace maid, Gania."

Gania huffed, shifted her basket and moved to enter the house. "We both know you will be back, and you do it better than Lyssa anyway. Don't spend it all in one place."

"Thank you, Gania."

"You have earned it. I'm assuming lessons were cancelled *again?*"

"Shall I lie, *again?*"

Gania laughed outright. "Na, na, and I won't speak to your mother, either. Every time you play truant, I get more housework done. That's worth silver. Eat something before you run off again, and be sure to swing back by at day's end. I'll have Lyssa spoon up a bowl for you to take home."

Gania went inside and Tasia returned to her work, sweeping up the last of the street dust from the steps nearest the gate. The rhythm of her movements recreated her earlier mood: Kembril, dust, Gania, and buns, unmistakable currents in life.

Another current swept up the street from the harbor, disturbing the humanity in the square about the well. A squad of Pevanese cavalry cleared the way. Behind them followed an open-air carriage with the Avedun crest on its doors. In that carriage sat two personages that instantly garnered Tasia's attention. The one on the right, bareheaded and deeply tanned and swathed in flowing yellow robes of an eastern quality, swept the area with darting eyes as the carriage passed. His dark hair, oiled, pulled back and tied severely at the nape into a lengthy pony-tail, swept back and forth like a cat's tail. Tasia remembered him: Piecen, the ambassador from Esda, returned to Pevana.

Tasia remembered the one sitting to the ambassador's left as well. But that memory was a little more distant. When she was little, at the end of the dark days that began Donari's reign, she used to see the man, dressed in priestly red robes, in company with the Lord Prelate. It had been two years since she had seen him last. She followed the carriage, put a name to the face: Reith Simson, head of the Reformed King's Theology. Today, Simson, sporting an understated red cap, sat next to the ambassador looking pointedly straight ahead.

Five years ago, while poking around the trash heap behind the college kitchen, she overheard a conversation between Simson and the head cook. Simson, black-haired, pale, seemed officious and grand next to the old woman, as though he was hiding something. Tasia recalled thinking he reminded her of Tolimon, the mischief god.

And what is he doing, now, in company with that greasy Esdan ambassador?

The procession met the intersection of the Land Gate street and turned north to ascend the hill to the citadel and the palace. There would be rumors and news later, which meant she would have to be nice to her brother if she wanted to know anything. Curiosity banished the unpleasant part of that thought. Tasia took a last look at the carriage as it made the turn and noted the colors: yellow and red, the colors of fire.

The colors of trouble.

She gave the walk a last, decisive sweep.

I need to find Devyn Ambrose.

Chapter . 10: Three meetings

Grayce ignored the rumbling in her stomach and scraped her piece of charcoal against a brick to sharpen its point. Before her, the back wall of the warehouse whose roof she called home lay partially covered in lines and swirls. A week ago, workers applied a coat of white-wash, and Grayce had waited patiently for the stuff to set before she set about changing its plain surface into something sublime. She tried to sketch and plan without success. But the space claimed her attention. She would only have the one night to complete her task.

She had been in Pevana for just over a month. Once she spied out the lay of the place, she gravitated to the warren of slums locals called the Maze. Something about it seemed to speak to her. Plus, no one there painted over or defaced her drawings. She discovered early on that folk in the more prosperous areas of the city tended to look after their fences and back walls more suspiciously than the poorer parts.

She found safety on the roof above her current wall project when her money ran low, forcing her to move out of the cheap boarding house where she had taken a room. Sleeping on the streets proved precarious. More than once, she had to brandish her knife to keep the over-inquisitive at bay. She found her refuge on the warehouse roof after losing the most persistent of them in the Maze. Someone had left a ladder leaning against the wall. She scrambled up, drew the ladder after and watched her pursuer shamble by frustrated and confused.

The building possessed a lofty fronting held up by beams nailed to the roof. In a corner, she found several sheets of roofing felt and some cast off lumber. She piled the scraps of wood against the beams in a roof corner, tied off the felt over three sides of the frame, and in a trice had a serviceable shelter. Through careful thievery, she managed to assemble creature comforts. She built a fire pit with buckets of earth. She collected enough cushions and scraps of cloth to approximate a bed. In many respects, it was far better than most of her campsites on her journey north.

She liked the view the rooftop afforded her. It looked southeast. On the left, a cleared space ran, park-like, back towards the harbor. To the right it flowed like green water up against the Maze manse and its warren of narrow streets and clustered dwellings. Northwards, Pevana's city swelled beneath the dwellings of the well to do, and above all perched the citadel with its palaces and major house estates.

In terms of where the city walls lay, she was in the center of Pevana.

She applied the sharpened charcoal piece and added several flowing lines to her drawing. She took a step back, checked the position of the full moon under whose light she worked, and then began shading and smudging with a will. She worked in a flurry, sometimes inches from the surface, scratching, rubbing, and blowing away excess. Moonlight and her vision combined to transform her into an avatar of creative impulse. She was back in the alleys of Gallina, the wooded hills on the way north, the cave above the Pevanese valley.

She finished just before dawn, coming back to herself with a blink and a shake, fingers sore, back tight and protesting, leaning into the topmost rungs of the ladder. Sometime during her creative trance, she must have hauled the thing over from the alley. She struggled down in a fog. When her vision cleared, she gasped. From ground to feet below the top of the wall stretched a surreal scene: a vast, multi-limbed oak tree spreading its canopy in full spring depth over a grave fenced in wrought iron.

The image astounded her. She knew of the grave located near the center of the cleared space. But the tree. Never. And yet something hinted at her as she took in the arc of the limned branches. More than branches. More than a pattern. Something *other* that suggested memories.

Someone else's memories.

Dumb with hunger and fatigue, she gathered up her various tools, making sure to leave no sign of her work but the work itself. Then she forced herself up the ladder, pulled it up with difficulty, and chewed several mouthfuls of semi-stale bread, swallowing mechanically before throwing herself on her cushions just as the morning sun sent its first beams above the horizon outside Pevana's bay.

The sounds of children's voices raised in surprise and curiosity startled her from sleep. Crawling from her bed to the roof edge, she carefully peeked over to see the first response to her effort.

A group of children, some of them carrying books and slates as though on the way to school clustered in front of her drawing.

"Look!" exclaimed one, a tall, willowy thin girl. "Kembril's Grave. And the Tree. It looks as if we could climb it!"

"Is that really what it looked like?" a little boy asked, reaching out a hand to trace one of the lines.

The girl who had spoken stopped him and gently took his hand in hers. "Yes, Reni," she asserted. "You were just a baby when the bad men burned it, but that is what the Tree looked like. Amazing. I remember being just big enough to reach that lower limb right there."

"And I remember making mud-pies in the space between those ground roots!" piped a red-headed boy. "And then the flames came. Took our house and my sister. Who did this?"

"I dunno, Tren," the taller girl responded. "But I have noticed a number of small things on bare spaces around about. I bet the same person did this one."

"It's so big, Tasia," gushed another little girl, who had come close to the taller one.

Tasia. I have heard that name. I have seen her, and probably these others, too. They are Maze children.

"It is beautiful," Tasia replied, lifting the younger child up. "And worth saving. Let's keep an eye out and see what we can do. Tren, maybe you could ask your brother if he could put together some sort of cover. Those other, smaller pieces were in ink. This one is charcoal and pencil. If it rains…"

"No!" Tren asserted. "This is a gift. I'll see my brother after lessons, but let you also get word to Bastian. Your brother serves as a page. If the King hears of this…"

"Or tell Devyn!" chimed in several smaller children. Others added a chorus.

"Yes, Dev would know!"

"He always knows!"

"Maybe he'll make a story out of it!"

"Yes, yes, tell Devyn Ambrose!'

"Enough!" Tasia said, quieting the children. "We'll be late, and you know how old Moriah feels about that. I don't want to do sums *all* morning."

The group moved off. Grayce eased back from the edge and lay resting her head on her arms, calming her racing heart, for the children's reaction both pleased and alarmed her. Pleased that they thought it beautiful; alarmed that they intended to tell someone in authority about it. Not just authority, but *the* authority.

The King. Road builder.

But other thoughts took precedence. In the back of her head as she waited for the chance to adorn the wall, she knew she risked undue attention, but the moonlight and the space had worked her like a story. There was no other way she could explain it.

Tasia.

She matched the name with a face she had seen several times since she arrived in Pevana. Sharp eyes. Sharp features. Like herself, a survivor. Intelligent.

But who is this Devyn Ambrose?

She crept back to her pillows and rags. Despite what she just observed and heard, she was still weary, and as the adrenaline drained away sleep reclaimed her.

The image of a folded piece of paper stuffed in a niche in a distant cave followed her into repose.

She wandered the city over the next few days emboldened by the steady stream of the curious that came to view her drawing. She always kept to the back of such gatherings, taking a certain amount of pride in the positive reaction. Folk reflected the initial reverence of the children, a number of whom took it upon themselves to act as caretakers. The one called Tren and another, taller boy Grayce took for his brother fixed an old sail cloth above the image. This they rolled up during the day, and always at night one would stop by to loosen the covering. Grayce said nothing but observed intently the range of responses. To her the tree was a dream-truth only, but it was something much more to the folk who came to marvel at it. She quickly noted the emphasis on how they said the term. It tied them to another time and place. She gained a small sense of Pevana's past that way. All her impressions previous had been predicated on the turmoils of the 'northern war' and all its tragedies, personal and public.

The way the people talked about her work brought them to life for her in a new way. She had been in the city for more than a month, had come to know its streets and buildings well enough, but until the Tree she had never bothered to try to know the people.

She started paying more attention and decided she liked them.

She kept on leaving her drawings around the area. The jumbled ways from hill to wall provided her with ample places where she could sketch with near impunity. She turned her passion into a pathway of sorts, moving from spot to spot in a wanderng sequence, touching, dabbing, scratching and rubbing in a near blissful state. Each drawing was different; sometimes a face, sometimes abstract shapes, sometimes a landscape. She let the space dictate to her fingers what it most wanted. She moved in an organic expression of line. That sense of the surreal deepened as her money ran out altogether, and she began skipping meals. Within a very short time, she grew unsure whether her creations came from inspiration or empty belly light-headedness.

At the end of one of her light-headed sessions, she got found out.

A section of wall behind one of the many temples in the city kept drawing her attention until she could not stand to leave it untried. This particular edifice lacked the stained weathering of the other, older buildings, and its rear portion backed up against the first of the Maze alleys. She set to with ink and brushes on a corner near a small door confident she could finish quickly and avoid detection. She worked fast, completely absorbed in tracing out a sinuous, flowering vine that climbed along the doorframe. When she reached the end of her reach, she looked up at the lintel and stepped back, stunned by the sight of a sprig of heather carved into the centermost brick.

Heather. Gallina. Earvyn.

She backed away. The sight of the sigil destroyed the ambience of the place for her.

"Are you finished, then?"

The sound of the voice behind her sent her spinning in alarm to discover the girl, Tasia, staring at her, small smile on her lips and a curious look in her eyes.

"What, who, how…" Grayce stammered, looking frantically about for other eyes.

"I didn't mean to startle you," Tasia soothed. "I just wanted to know if you were finished. Are you well? You look a little pale."

Grayce struggled to regain her composure. "I don't take well to folk sneaking up on me."

"Sneaking? Who's sneaking? I was standing here watching is all. You know, you really do get around."

"Get around? What do you mean?"

Tasia frowned. "I can tell by your style that you are the one who did the Tree. Took me some time to see it. Awhile back I began noticing your other things showing up in out of the way places."

"But you still found them."

"I happen to like out of the way places."

Grayce calmed her jangled nerves. "Just drawings," she said. "I've not the means for paper or canvas these days."

"Just drawings? Hardly, miss…my name is Tasia, by the way. What's yours?"

"I know who you are."

The girl started slightly. "How? I think I've seen you about, but I know we haven't talked."

"I have seen you before the Tree, 'around' as you put it. I heard some of the children say your name."

Comprehension brought a wry grin. "So that is where you hole up! I should have known. You were watching us that day, when we first saw the drawing?"

"You've been looking for me?"

The girl waved away the tension. "Yes. I wanted to find the artist who did all those drawings."

"I did not realize I was that obvious."

"You aren't. Outside of the Tree, I doubt there are more than a handful who know where all your bits are, and you still haven't told me your name."

Grayce paused, unsure, and yet despite the surprise of the moment, she did not sense any threat in the girl. "My name is Grayce Stonesmith. And, yes, I have a spot on the roof of that building."

"Nice choice," Tasia bobbed. "As spots go, that is. I have a few of my own for when I want to avoid stuff like lessons, bullies and the like. I should have guessed. You are good, you know? Your drawings, at least the ones I've found, seem like they tell a story. They make me think about words. That's what I want to be: a poet of Pevana, like Devyn Ambrose and the queen."

Again, that name.

"Who is this Devyn Ambrose? I heard some of the children refer to him that day you found my tree."

"He is the king's servant and my friend. He set me and my friends to watch over things, so we do."

"Have you told him about me?"

"Not yet. Didn't know your name, and I've only seen you a couple of times, remember? Now that we've talked, I think I will tell him about you, but only because I think he would like to know."

"I'm not sure I want that, Tasia."

Tasia shrugged. "Sorry, you don't have a choice, but you've nothing to fear, really. Devyn is a good man, and the king and queen are wise."

"Who am I that a king and queen should bother?"

Tasia looked back at Grayce's unfinished work. "Because of that," she said, pointing. "Like I said, your images make me think. They are like words waiting to happen." She waved her hand in frustration. "I'm not quite getting it, but I think you are an artist, and the royals favor art. At least, that is what Sandre says."

"Sandre?"

"Jeril Sandre. His is one of the places I mentioned before, like your hidey-hole on top of Timmin's storehouse. He's a painter. Showed up in Pevana awhile back. When lessons get too much for me, I go help him with his mixing. He has books and books. He has a cat named Angel who sits in my lap when I read. He is helping me find my words. I think I might tell him about you, too."

"Because I have no choice?"

Tasia laughed. "And you catch on quick! You can't expect to survive here without friends, and you look hungry, if you don't mind my saying."

The girl's perception disturbed her, but just as during that first time, she sensed no threat. It had been months since she had shared so many words. She relaxed.

"Again," she said lightly, "something tells me it wouldn't matter if I did." She checked the light, decided it was too off to continue, and dropped her charcoal sticks into her pocket. "I'm done here for now. Maybe forever."

"Why?"

Grayce pointed out the carving above the door. "That bothers me. I've seen it before."

"It is heather," Tasia offered. "The brothers of the Reformed King's Theology put it above all the entrances to their temples."

"There were no such temples in Gallina, but someone scratched it into one of my works there just the same. I remember those priests. Bad memories."

Tasia came close, tentatively touched Grayce's arm. "They brought flames and death here, too, but after the king came all the bad ones left. They have a handful of small places about the city. My friends and I watch them just the same. Like you said, bad memories."

As Tasia finished, a loud, grating noise came from behind the door, as if someone struggled to wrench back a fouled latch. Grayce backed away, felt Tasia's hand grab hers and yank her back around the corner of the building into the shadows. Out of sight, the door creaked open and footsteps shuffled out. Grayce tensed to run, but Tasia tightened her grip and with a look motioned her to keep still and silent.

Voices attended the footsteps.

"You have your instructions. See that you execute them to the letter. Nothing untoward, mind you. Just get it done and get out of the city. When you get there, make sure the others know."

Grayce heard hints of oily smoothness in that voice, a cool, even tone that spoke of confidence. The sound nibbled at memory.

"We will see to it, lord, never you fear."

"Oh I won't, but you will if you do not do this precisely as I have planned. Now, be off and quickly." Booted feet shuffled as if in departure. "No, wait! What is this? Look! Seems we have had a visitor."

More footsteps and shuffling.

And then a face poked around the corner.

"And they are still here," said the owner of that oily voice.

Tasia squeeled and let go of Grayce's arm. "Run!" she gasped and set off like an arrow back down the narrow way. Grayce followed in her wake, fear making her feet fly.

"After them!" shouted the oily voiced one. "We don't know what they heard!"

Two sets of footsteps sounded pursuit's rhythm behind her as Grayce struggled to catch up with the speedier Tasia. Refuse and old crates choked the way, but the girl navigated like the native she was. Grayce, hampered by unfamiliarity and weakened by hunger quickly fell back. Tasia came to the end of the alley, passed from shadow into light and turned to the right. Grayce tried to follow, but as she came to the spot one of the chasers grabbed the hem of her smock that streamed behind her. The worn out fabric tore, but the sudden arrest disrupted her balance, and she slipped as she turned. She half slid half fell back and sideways into an open space, coming to a stop against a pair of black boots. Those boots side-stepped deftly and moved in between Grayce and her pursuers as she scrambled to her knees. Those two crouched together, breathing hard just outside the shadowed alley. A man dressed all in black to match the boots stood in front of them with a drawn blade held casually at the ready.

"Gentleman," the man said. "I think perhaps you should reconsider. Chasing after women is a bad business even in the shadows. And here in the light there are too many eyes, you see."

"Our master just wanted a word," one of the men wheezed.

"She vandalized the temple," grated the other.

"Ah, yes, so troubling. The pius Reformed Theology Brothers affronted by a girl with some chalk? Really, hardly a reason for a race and grab, don't you think? From the look of both of you, I would hazard thinking is not a frequent part of your devotions. Leave off, boys. Whoever your master is will have to content himself with a water bucket and a brush."

"Master Simson will not be pleased."

"I guessed that already, too, and not my problem, nor this young lady's, either. Back the way you came now fellows. You are done here."

Perhaps it was the way the man carried himself and spoke, perhaps it was the length of his polished sword, but the men merely glared at Grayce before hurrying back the way they came.

The man sheathed his weapon and turned to help Grayce to her feet. As she looked up at him, her heart nearly stopped, for the face from her drawing back in the cave, a face youthful but with experience suggested in the eyes, looked calmly down at her.

"My, my thanks," she managed to stammer. "I'm not sure what I would have done if you—"

"Best not to think of it, then," the man interrupted. The smile on his lips flowed into his eye as he helped her to her feet. "Pity about your smock, though."

Grayce, glanced down, gathered up the ends of the torn cloth, and realized the force of her near capture had disarranged her shirt and one of its buttons. She hastily shifted herself back together, innate caution at war with curiosity. A poem. A face passing in the market. A quiet voice before chaos. Connect.

Impossible.

"My name is Devyn Ambrose," the man said.

Recognition flooded alongside embarrassment as a host of threads tied themselves into a knot in her stomach. She caught sight of Tasia slipping close to stand beside Ambrose, who gave the girl a wry smile.

"I know," Grayce whispered, awed by the moment. "Tasia mentioned you."

"Ah! So you know this miscreant? Is she involved here? Wouldn't surprise me."

Grayce forced herself to meet his gaze. "We just met a few minutes ago, actually, but I have seen her before. She surprised me at my work just before those men...who are they, anyway?"

"They are part of a problem. I would avoid using any of their bare wall space for your work in the future."

"Devyn," Tasia interjected. "This is Grayce Stonesmith. I was going to tell you about her when I saw you next. I have been learning about her for some time now."

Ambrose quirked a curious eyebrow. Tasia continued.

"She's been decorating bare spots all over the city, lovely stuff."

"Really?" Ambrose looked again at Grayce, and, again, she felt her heart pause as she saw the lines of her drawing stare back at her. The naked interest intimidated her.

In a flash she reconsidered all the moments of her life since she left Gallina. She had thought herself hardened by life to overcome Pickson's attempted violation. And yet now, face to face with inspiration, she found open response difficult, as though hesitant at the edge of some self-constructed barrier.

"I meant no harm. Have I broken a law?" she asked, cautiously, almost defensively.

Ambrose chuckled. "Pevana has no laws against art! Hardly, although I think one should choose one's surfaces carefully."

Grayce considered her close call.

"You said those men were part of a problem. I do not understand."

Ambrose waived it off. "No need to concern yourself."

"She said she has known the red robes before," Tasia added.

That brought another frown from Ambrose. "Most of us have, in this city."

"But it wasn't in Pevana! She's from Gallina."

And again Ambrose fixed his compelling eyes on Grayce, but this time the blood drained from his face, and he stared at her as if he, too, were making connections. Then a slow smile drifted across his features.

"Of course," he murmured. "Now it makes sense." He stepped back and sketched a sardonic bow. "Let me guess, shapes and swirls, intersecting lines?"

"And Kembril's Tree!" Tasia exclaimed. "We've got a cover for it and everything!"

"Is that so?"

"What do you mean by *of course*?" Grayce snapped, unnerved by the revelations.

Ambrose must have noted the change in her voice.

"I'm sorry," he responded. "I've seen your work before, in Gallina and again in the hills above the King's Road. He bowed deeper in good humor. "Staig Motta sends his regards."

Grayce fought against the urge to flight as panic gripped her throat and silenced her. Too much, too fast, and too bizarre.

But her stomach saved her by giving out a loud, rumbling grumble that all of them heard.

"Sounds like you could use a meal," Ambrose suggested.

"Let's take her to the Cup!"

"An excellent idea, Tasia!" Ambrose looked reassuringly at Grayce. "Grayce Stonesmith, if you could forego bolting, I'd only find you anyway, perhaps we can swap stories, my treat, over a glass and bowl."

Grayce hesitated, barriers up, but something in Ambrose's tone calmed her. The notion of food overcame caution and despite being tweaked and disheveled, she accepted.

"I've lost the light, anyway," she said. "And I have questions."

"Then we are agreed. Then off, we."

Devyn turned and led Grayce and Tasia back down the narrow way to where it met a regular street. Grayce recognized it, Lampwright's, the avenue that ran along the front of the building where she had her lair. She knew of *The Golden Cup* though her circumstances kept her from going inside. She warmed to the idea as she walked alongside Ambrose. She planned on a bowl, a glass, some information and a quick retreat to her rooftop hole to process the weirdness of the day.

But when the three of them turned to go up the gentle slope to the square fronting the inn, they had to pause to let a carriage pass. Except that it did not pass. It came to a stop just in front of them. Grayce recognized the man sitting imperiously in the back as the same one who discovered her and Tasia hiding in the shadows back by her drawing.

"Well, well, well, and here we have our erstwhile artist, her urchin accomplice and one other." The scorn in the man's voice reminded Grayce of the squishy, caking texture she achieved turning wet clay into a slurry to paint the rocks back during her journey. It covered her, obliterated her sense of calm. She stepped back instinctively and tensed to run anew.

"Surely you have somewhere more important to be, Master Simson, than accosting the king's folk about their business?"

Devyn's cool voice caught Simson's attention, and Grayce felt the shift as a reprieve.

"Oh, yes, it *is* you! I thought I knew your face. You've come a long way since that silly extravagance at the competition finals. So it's you Donari got to replace Arolli. Surprising."

"I see you survived the days as well, Reith Simson."

Simson shrugged. Grayce thought even that move held something feline and slinky about it.

"Dark days, poet, but we are better blessed in our King and our faiths endure, yes?"

"King's eyes and ears, rather, as you already mentioned. Set to watch over things…like making sure the Reformed King's Theology stays as peaceful as it claims to be."

Simson arched his brows in mock surprise. "So high, then? And yet you find time for Maze rats and vandals."

Devyn's sword hand ghosted to the pommel, and Grayce found herself studying the curve of his trembling fingers.

"Are your walls so precious? You placed that structure to minister to the Maze poor, or so we were led to believe."

Simson laughed condescendingly. "It is a slight matter, and I did only want to talk to them." Simson refocused on Grayce. "I intended to have it white-washed again soon anyway. I find a good clean white goes well with red, you see. We profess meekness in our vocation, Ambrose, but we still want folk to be able to find us. Keep at your practice, girl, and I might find a commission for you!" He waved to his driver, who set the matched pair in motion and the carriage trundled off.

"Well, that was not pleasant, eh, Tasia? At least I now have an idea where some of Sevire Anargi's money got to. That carriage looked pretty well-appointed for a *meek vocation.*"

"He's like paint mixed with too much oil," Grayce asserted. "He will stick to nothing, and nothing will stick to him." *And he is a man…a dangerous man…*

"An apt comparison," Devyn agreed. "Though that might be said for many. For him, it fits."

Tasia came to stand alongside Devyn. "None of my friends like going to their places, but it is the best way to keep an eye on them."

Devyn offered both girls an arm. "And you and your friends have done well. Trust me, behind his smug expression, Master Simson is thinking about how we three are connected."

"How are we *connected?*" Grayce tried to keep her voice controlled, but the pressure of his arm against hers disconcerted her; a feeling further intensified when he looked into her eyes.

"I've been following threads for months, Grayce Stonesmith. One of them connects with that man, and then I talked to your Staig Motta and picked up another. You left him worried, girl."

"I had to leave."

Devyn nodded, urging the three of them out into the street. "He told me some of it. We share history, lady. Bad days. And from the look of you, yours here haven't been much better. So come!" he concluded brightly. "I think three bowls of Brimaldi's best will make for a fine tale."

Grayce allowed herself to be swept along, her world a suddenly changing, tilting canvas.

*   *   *

The Golden Cup brought back both bitter and pleasant memories to Grayce. Staig's had been plainer, its customers even more so. As Ambrose re-told her tale as he imagined it, she discovered she missed Staig's ready friendship and concern, but she knew she did not want to go back. Pevana captured her from her first day within the walls. Still, she knew the inside of a tavern, and to her the Cup possessed a combination of shabby and genteel that stopped just short of artifice. Given its location, the effect made sense. The food was as good as promised and the wine smoother than she expected and eventually one bowl became three and one glass turned into two.

At first, Grayce let the other two chat away while she dealt with her hunger, but she was also reluctant to join in. Silence had ruled her life for so long that she had fallen out of practice with words. The first give and take with Tasia was the longest conversation she recalled since her last chat with Staig. It came to her then that there was a risk in living inside onself for extended periods. Careful for so long, Grayce feared sounding harsh and uncouth compared to her new table-mates. But the food and the wine relaxed her, and she grew more at ease listening. She liked the sound of Tasia's sharp-tongued familiarity, but she could tell the girl harbored an infatuated reverence for Ambrose. The more Grayce listened to the man speak the more she understood why. Words slipped out of Devyn Ambrose's mouth like colored water droplets mixing in a fountain. His tone took her back to a memory of a sardonic apology voiced in the act of taking and throwing a votive statue.

She had been near Tasia's age then. Memory crystalized on a face.

Words discovered in a cave nook. Her drawing.

The same voice. The same man. Younger. Dangerous.

But in a different way.

Bit by bit, head and heart aswhirl, she eased her story out to their gentle promptings. Renia help her, she talked, revealing as much as she thought prudent and a little more besides. There is a certain rushing quality to those moments where a person realizes that perhaps it would be acceptable to trust a little. They exist almost as two people; one letting all the pent up information out like a confessional, and the other urging caution, counseling fear of rejection or mischance. In the end the only things she held back were her earliest memories of Devyn and her thoughts about her father. She felt like she had to, really, for Devyn had talked to Staig and knew some of her tale anyway. When she finally fell silent, she saw the empathy and acceptance in their faces. The effect amazed her. For perhaps the first time since her mother's passing, she did not feel judged.

Tasia broke the spell by tossing her spoon into her bowl.

"That was so good, both the stew and your story. I wish I had my pad with me to take it down. I have never caught a rabbit. Taken a stick to a good few rats, but they don't make for as good eating."

"I have done both in my day, young lady," Devyn said, "and a well-seasoned rat will get you through a hard time."

Grayce pushed her own bowl away. "Now you both are making sport of me."

Devyn joshed away her perception. "Not at all. The Maze-born know the truth of things. You are a survivor in your own way as we are in ours."

Tasia got up to leave. "I'm off to Gania's then home. I will spread the word about, Grayce. No pestering from my lot. But have a care to stay away from those priests!"

Tasia left. The proprietor, Saymon Brimaldi joined them with the remains of another bottle. Any lingering caution Grayce might have harbored melted away in the wake of the large, hairy man's affable manner. She surmised the two men shared a deep friendship. By the time Grayce finished her last glass she had promise of a position, a room and a bath.

"I've been short-handed since Sanya whelped her second. She's off in the hills with her man seeing to the king's vines, so you are well-timed and welcome, girl!" Brimaldi said in parting. "Get your things and see Lana in the kitchens about a tub. I could use some help tonight even."

"Yes, absolutely!" Devyn agreed, rising in his turn. "Not all of those smudges are from charcoal. I think you'll like it here. I used your roof top myself once upon a time. *The Cup* is far safer."

He took her hand, and such had been the effect of the food and wine that she did not even flinch when he breathed a kiss over it. He straightened, winking. "Besides, now I know where I can find you. Until next time, then!"

Grayce watched him leave, all but dumbfounded at the changes wrought in the day. She felt caught up in one of those wandering whirling patterns she traced in the dirt during her journey, trapped in a course bounded by attraction and revulsion in equal measure, a palette laden with pigments of fear and hope. She had never felt so exposed, but when she blinked away the confusing reverie, she realized she sat very much alone and ignored by the activity going on around her. She had choices to make. She waved thanks to a busy Brimaldi and left. Outside the afternoon was far along. She hurried down the alley and up the ladder where she bundled her few things together. With a full belly and a slightly fuzzy head, the prospect of a bath sounded particularly appealing.

When she got back to *The Golden Cup*, Brimaldi handed her a folded piece of paper.

"He left this for you," Brimaldi said before turning to deal with a customer.

Mistress Stonesmith, she read, instantly connecting the handwriting to the page from her cave. *Perhaps paper and canvas make better surfaces than other people's walls. I recall Simson urging you to keep practicing. Let us take him at his word. When your duties at The Cup allow, ask Brimaldi how to get to the address below. Talent such as yours needs nurturing.*

When my duties allow, I hope we can unravel some threads together.

Devyn Ambrose

She looked at the address:

Jeril Sandre, Painter/Tutor, #4 Harbor Square St

Sandre. Tasia mentioned that name…

She took extra time in the water.

Chapter 11: A Changing Composition…

"No, no, not quite, Grayce. Here, let me show you."

At Jeril's gruff comment, Grayce stepped back away from the canvas, watching carefully as Jeril took her brush and deftly, with maybe six tiny strokes, brought texture and clarity to her botched rose petal. When he finished, he gave a satisfied grunt.

"There, see? You have to tell the story of the rose with light and motion. See?" He waved a finger over the real flower perched in its vase on the worktable beneath the window. "The rose is all about the motion of her petals, how they weave and circle, how they create little shadow valleys that hide mystery. When I look at the rose, I see a woman in all her magic. Fragile but defended. All linear and curve and folds of meaning. You must think beyond mere shape in this case. Paint the light, texture up, always."

Grayce took back the brush. She did see. In a handful of tiny strokes, Jeril turned her lump of paint, a spot on her canvas that she had labored over, scraped off a number of times and restarted, into something akin to a word in a magic spell. She sighed in frustration. Though she had come a long way in the month since Jeril took her on as a student, she still had a long way to go.

"You make it look so easy."

"Time makes everything easy. Keep at it."

"By the time I 'get' it I'll be old and palsied."

"Wrong," Jeril said. He made her put down the brush and turned her around so that they faced her finished canvasses lined up against the far wall of the studio. "You are stressing on the small difficulties and missing the real design. Look at those! Shape, color and line, alike to your wall scribblings but refined, incorporated into life motifs, it is all there. I have been here for less than a year, girl, but those appear more Pevanese than anything I can boast of. I am just glad I got the king's commission when I did. In time you'll force me into retirement!"

Grayce tried to look at her work with his eyes. She liked them, honestly, without predisposition, as pleasing images in and of themselves. For herself, she still noted hints of those wild days in the hills after Gallina. Pevana in the late spring and early summer was all white walls, red roof tiles and the green-blue sea. It was a profusion of flowers from balcony hangings and bursting through garden boundaries. It was sunlight and maritime haze in the morning. She captured all of that, but sensed beneath the dominance a subtle looseness, a thread of line and color combined to form a wandering path from piece to piece, a figurative animal trail that spoke of the wild.

"Not bad," she offered.

"Not bad?" Jeril scoffed. "Don't be absurd. They are good and you should offer them for sale. It is all well and good to flit about beautifying this place and its forgotten spaces, but you might as well get paid for it. Present yourself, and you just might find yourself invited to paint some not-so-forgotten spaces."

He left her to her thoughts and stumped off downstairs. The sound of the door opening and the gaggle of children come for drawing and sums made up her mind for her. They would be at it until late afternoon. She had to work at *The Golden Cup* that evening. It was still just mid-morning; time enough to risk rejection. She gathered up a handful of the finished paintings, tied them in a bundle, and tossed her pad and pencils into her satchel. Angel padded over while she worked to snif the paintings and rub against her ankles.

"A bit too noisy down there for you too?" She asked, pausing to give the required attention. "I'll give you the run of the studio then. I'm off. Wish me luck."

She took Angel's curt rowl as an answer.

Shouldering her burdens, she clumped down stairs, waded through the chorus of fluted greetings and Jeril's sardonic grin, and shuffled out the door and down the street, heading for the market just inside the Harbor Gate. There, a seamstress allowed her to set up her works on a spare table and even offered a spare stool. All around her, folk shouted out their pitches, trying to draw attention to their wares. It was a noisy place and altogether intimidating at first. Grayce held her tongue. For some reason, verbally advertising things she created out of silence did not seem right. She sat herself down, took up her pad and began sketching. In short order, she lost herself in line and shading, only half-aware of people pausing in their other shopping to examine her offerings.

A gentle touch on her shoulder startled her back to the present. The seamstress stood over her, smiling.

"Sorry to disturb you, Mistress Stonesmith, but here is one with questions."

Grayce followed her gaze. A lady stood before her, holding up her landscape of the headland.

"I have a frame at home that would fit this beautifully," she said. "How much?"

"I haven't the faintest idea," Grayce stammered, stunned by the sudden prospect of a sale. "What do you think it is worth?"

The woman grinned and shook her purse. "That's hardly the way to promote your work, if I may be so bold, but your colors are extraordinary. Several of my friends have already commented on this one. So, of course, I have to have it. What price?"

Grayce gathered her wits, mind racing. Jeril's gentle push had quite changed everything. Suddenly, the prospect of someone else wanting at least a part of what she was charmed her. She glanced at the painting, an early piece and one of her favorites. She looked again at the lady, who shook her purse again and tilted her head in question.

"I'll be honest," Grayce said. "I've never tried selling my work before, so I don't know what to ask for. Should one haggle over art?"

The woman laughed outright. "One can haggle over almost anything girl. That is how the world works! The sooner you learn that, the better off you'll be, excuse me for saying so." She put down the painting and fished out three silver coins. "Here," she continued, placing them in Grayce's palm. "I think this is fair. But make sure to ask for more from the next person who wants to buy. What do you say?"

Grayce fingered the coins. They amounted to a week's wages at *The Cup*. Possibility welled up like mirth. "Agreed," she said. "And be sure to tell your friends. I will be here every day for the next while."

"Not to worry about that, mistress, what is your name?"

"Stonesmith, Grayce Stonesmith."

"Right, as I said, several of my friends have already noticed, but once they see this beauty hanging in my entry hall. Well, clean up your bristles and get to work! Remember, ask for more. That way I get to rub their noses in it when I tell them what I paid for this!"

The woman took her painting and blended away into the crowd. Grayce looked around her with new eyes afterward. She still applied lines to her sketches but quickly grew attuned to the approach of potential customers. She sold another piece by the afternoon and had two people request a portrait drawing.

Her face actually hurt a little from smiling so much. She saw her paintings and drawings as parts of herself slipping away into the city's rhythm to grace hallways and walls. For perhaps the first time since she arrived, she felt less like an outsider looking in, wandering in search of obscure surfaces to leave her tentative lines, and more like the seasmstress working next to her, knitting herself into the fabric of Pevanese life.

As she worked on a drawing of the daughter of the herbalist packing up her simples severals tables down, Reith Simson stopped by her space.

"Ah!" he exclaimed. "So here is where our miscreant vandal has got to! Well, I must say, I like your new style, mistress. Canvas and paper are better suited to your talents than alley walls."

The sound of Simson's pompous voice broke her concentration and sent her subject scurrying away to find her mother's skirts. She looked up at Simson and tried to adopt a calm mein she did not feel.

"I recall apologizing," she said coldly. "And you just cost me a customer. Perhaps we should call it even and leave it at that." She put her pencil away and rose, unwilling to let him loom over her.

"Did I upset the poor thing? So sorry." Simson dug into his purse and spun a coin in the air. He made no effort to catch it, and the coin landed on the unfinished drawing. "Here, recompense. Or shall I buy all your works here? I've a mind to adorn some walls in the temple, and I think some of these would serve nicely."

"I find it hard to believe you would care so for art."

"Mistress, what was it I heard someone call you? *Stonesmith*? Yes? Now I remember! Yes, Grayce Stonesmith. I made a few inquiries, you see, after our little encounter. Employed at Brimaldi's, tutored by Sandre the painter. You've done well."

"Again, why do you care?"

The look in Simson's eye changed then. For a moment, the arrogant glare faded to something almost human.

"Why should I not care for art?" he asked quietly. "I have a responsibility to my faith, true, but isn't that just another form of ornament? I do have a care for art, mistress, and even though I took initial offense at your first efforts on my temple wall, that doesn't mean I didn't appreciate it."

"I went back, after, you had it white-washed over."

That brought a deprecating smile.

"An unfortunate requirement, imposed on me by my associates. They thought it spoiled the purity of the outer facing. Regrettable. So, allow me to make it up to you." He dangled his purse. "Let me purchase your works. All of them."

"No."

"What? Girl, I'm offering—"

"To pay me for my work so you can burn it. It's the same as whitewashing only more permanent."

"I assure you I mean no such thing."

"Still no. I don't trust you."

And that brought a frown, a frank, genuinely disappointed expression that almost made her regret her cold tone. Simson opened his purse, took out two silvers and offered them.

"Let me prove my interest. I want that one over there." He pointed at a midsized effort that showed the river's mouth south of Pevana, one of the first ones she completed after starting up at Sandre's. "Really?" he asked, when she hesitated. "Are you going to make me beg? At least trust my money. Fine, then," he finished with a smile strangely absent of any oily falseness. "Please? I really do think these are quite good. I want that one for my study. I'm serious."

Grayce let him place the coins in her hand, and then he completely surprised her by closing her fingers with his own with a firm yet still gentle grip.

"Thank you, mistress," he said, leaning forward conspiratorially. "I would take back my earlier words if I could. I am not as evil as I must sound. You are well-named, Grayce Stonesmith, both for the delicacy of your fingers and beautiful lines of your work. I will come again. Give the other coin to your lost subject with my apology."

Then he released her, swept up the purchased painting and sauntered off, leaving Grayce stunned and confused. She turned to pack up her things, intent on returning to Jeril's studio to clean up her projects before going to work. Tasia appeared as if from nowhere.

"That was interesting and weird," she said.

"What do you mean?" Grayce asked.

"I saw the whole thing. Gania sent me out for some flowers, and when I saw him, I made sure to wander close. Heard every word."

"And what did you hear?"

"Praise. Worthy, but from him? At least his money is good."

"That part I can deal with, I think. He said nice things about my work. That must count for something."

"Meh. Money is easy cover. He likes you. Even I can see that. What will Ambrose and Sandre say?"

"Ambrose can say what he likes, and Jeril will ask for a commission on my sales."

"Funny. I still say be careful. We were chased, remember?"

"I didn't say I trusted him," Grayce contested. "I'm just not sure what to think. And that happened a month ago."

"Ambrose won't like it."

"What does he have to do with anything? He's been gone, too."

Tasia gave her one of those sly, twelve-year old grins Grayce had come to recognize as humor.

"I remember some looks after that day, too."

"You are being silly, and I am not sure I like what you are implying."

"He likes you, and you like him. Don't deny it."

"I, I—" But Grayce found words unavailable. She considered Devyn's image, intense yet appealing, mirth bubbling underneath a serious mask; darkly handsome yet oddly reticent and vulnerable, like herself. She considered Simson, strange and threatening from distance and by reputation, but also capable of smooth speech and a ready smile. It was as if the man were actually trying.

"I confirm or deny nothing," she said, hoisting her burdens to her shoulder. "I am not sure what I think at the moment. Best to leave it alone. I am sure Mistress Landare expects you, and I have a sketch I want to work on before going to *The Golden Cup*. I'll see you tomorrow."

They parted in the crowd. Grayce hurried back to Jeril's hoping to leave everything alone and just draw. Of course, she did no such thing. While she worked in the studio, she found herself mulling over her reactions to Simson and Ambrose. Her most recent effort, an attempt to recreate from memory the lines she composed on the back of Devyn's poem she found in the cave, did not help matters. He knew more about her than just about anyone else in the world outside of Staig Motta. She missed the freedom of her former anonymity at times. She liked her new friends in Pevana, sure enough. Working for Saymon had proven easy and prosperous. Tasia and the other Maze-children provided ready wit and cheer for her free time. Her pad also contained studies of their earnest faces.

Angel's inquisitive mew brought Grayce back to the present. She bent and scooped her up to plant a kiss between furry ears. The cat's deepening purr put her more at ease.

"How do you think I have done, little one?"

Angel answered her by settling into her embrace. Of all the newness, Angel's quick acceptance had been the easiest to process.

Devyn Ambrose continued to trouble her. She recalled his regular presence during her first days employed at Brimaldi's establishment. He left her alone save for the casual conversation attendant to her service, but at times she felt his eyes upon her as she bustled about and more than once looked up to catch him looking at her with a wry smile on his lips and raised brow. She did not bridle at such a thing, as she would have back in Gallina, as she had done when it was Earvyn Pickson pestering her with his boozy leering, or when Simson showed up at market.

There was nothing of that from Devyn, but the difference actually unnerved her more. She sensed interest there, and, though she constantly reminded herself to take care, realized Tasia was right. She returned it. Reith Simson's interest in her work, and growing interest in her person, just compounded her confusion. Her life had taught her the peril of trusting anyone. Commitment was impossible under such conditions. Devyn intrigued her as much as Simson scared her. The fake priest unsettled her, made her doubt things. Devyn drew her. She sensed a deep compulsion there, but she kept floating indecisively. He, too, had taken her hand.

She put Angel on the railing and flipped open her pad. She traced a finger along the jaw line she had given Devyn in her most recent effort. Almost it was a caress. Almost. She thought back to the moment they shared the night before he left on his most recent mission. She had come out from *The Golden Cup's* kitchen after taking a tray of crockery back for cleaning. He had been on his way out. They came face to face at the end of the bar. He had reached out a hand, half wave, half invitation. She recalled most the look in his eyes and the sound of his voice.

"My thanks, Grayce Stonesmith," he said at the time.

"So, you are off then? Safe journey," she replied, keeping her tone neutral. She thought then that he saw through her, for he gave a wan smile.

"Surely." Then he astounded her by taking her hand and breathing a courtly kiss over her knuckles, keeping hold of her hand when he finished. "And you keep yourself safe as well, and have a care for Tasia."

"What, worried for us, are you?" Again, she had tried to laugh lightly, but the pressure of his hand made it difficult.

In answer, he looked at her, intently, for an awkward moment before letting go.

"Yes," he said quietly as he turned to go. "As a matter of fact, I do, worry about you. I think you know that already. Keep drawing my dreams. I'll look for them when I return."

His last words took away her sense for a moment, and when she finally could draw breath to reply, he had gone out through the door into the night. When she went to retrieve his glass, she found a piece of paper folded on it. The handwriting sent her back to that night in the cave:

Please ward for me my pleasant hours
While the world works its will on me
And keeps me from my frank desire--
To watch and ware
The way the color moves across
Your face when you smile.
I will take with me the image of your
Graceful hand arched around the brush
Delicate yet firm, as new love,
Perhaps...

His touch and poem that night had been the impetus for the drawing. She gave one last whispy brush to the image of Devyn's jawline and let a sigh escape her lips.

Angel must have sensed her unease for she mewed again. She graciously accepted Grayce's caresses before moving on to sniff at the troubling drawing.

"Yes, I know," Grayce whispered in response to Angel's purring. "He vexes me. And I think I want him." She leaned down to receive Angel's tribal head-butt. "I am just not sure I am worthy of him."

The only answer Angel gave was to place a licking kiss on the drawing.

"Ah! Bold one!" Grayce admonished. "Easy for you, perhaps, but not so for me…at least not yet. Besides, he's been gone three weeks."

And what am I to do when he comes back?

She pushed away from the railing, took up her cup and pad, and went back inside to settle herself back at the bench.

"I've been too long on my own, perhaps," she said aloud to the world, taking up her palette. "Or maybe I need to learn patience."

Grayce tried to work but strokes eluded her. Questions ran through her mind like the lines she etched in the hills, swirling and unanswerable. She lost the light with the westering sun and gave up. Giving Angel a final pat, she gathered her things and headed off to work.

* * *

Tasia looked up from her book as Jeril pushed through the open door, arms full of packages. The afternoon sun followed him in aswhirl with street dust. She watched him idly as he hustled about the workroom putting supplies into cupboards. He spared her a smile, bending down to brush Angel's flank as she slunk by him up the stairs.

"Grayce?" he asked.

"She was gone when we got here," she answered. "I think she had work."

Tam and one other, Diran, the youngest son of one of the gate guards, were arguing over answers to their sums at the end of the table.

"Master J, Tam says my numbers are wrong!" Diran announced, waving his paper.

"Well, they are," said Tam. "See where you added wrong?"

"I don't believe you," Diran retorted, proferring Jeril the paper. "He's wrong, isn't he?"

Jeril took up the paper, scanned its contents, and chortled as he gave it back. "I'm afraid Tam is correct, Diran, you left off a number when you subtracted. Nice try, though!" He ruffled the little boy's hair in passing as he moved to wash his hands in the kitchen basin.

"Let's try a new set, and I'll watch you this time," he said. Tasia gave up on her pad and watched as the artist quickly set up both boys with new problems to mull over. They set to with a will. He stood over them thoughtfully, all mirth now subdued.

For Tasia, the effect seemed similar to how the light changed when a cloud passed before the sun. Jeril's expression slackened, and his eyes took on a far away look as though he walked on old paths beset by old dreams. Tasia watched the sweep of his eyes. Story oozed out beyond the wild brows and lids gathered in wrinkled folds in the corners. It was a haunted look. Tasia only knew that Master Sandre had lived in a fishing village called Piling before he came to Pevana, and Piling had burned. Tasia understood that look. All Maze-born knew the painful past, uncertain present, and the daunting expectations of the future.

Jeril must have felt her gaze, for he started and looked over to her, giving her a wink before taking up a pencil. He leaned over the boys and made notations on their problems.

"Much better, Diran! And, Tam, you'll be keeping your father's books in no time."

"I hope so," Tam said. "He wants to add onto the shed and dock. That will mean more berths and fees."

"So? He has done well this last year, then?"

"Yes, Master J. There's more traffic in the harbor this year than ever before that I remember, anyway. Folk need storage and chandlry."

"And will he raise the rates for my little tub?"

Tam laughed. "No, sir! I won't let him! He says I've no time for the queen's school, at my age. I've my letters enough, and you give me my numbers, thank you very much."

"But Tam, you're barely thirteen."

"Old enough to pull an oar in the fishing fleet when my uncle needs the help."

"You come as long as you wish, boy, never forget that. Your da's a good man. I'm sure he wouldn't begrudge your growth. Now, do you have time for another go?"

Tam pushed his paper away and got up from the table. "No more today, Master," he said. "I have to be at the sheds in an hour. I'm off to see about a few things. Bye, Diran!"

Tasia leaned forward in her chair to allow Tam passage. Diran stammered his apologies and followed. Both boys left in a clatter of feet and elbows out the door. Jeril chuckled at the energy released in the boys' departure. He gathered his satchel and hat from its peg by the stairs.

"Well, now that those two have absconded, I'm off to see to a few things myself, Tasia," he said, pausing by her. "You have the run of the place. Lock the door, please."

She wanted to ask him where he had been while watching the boys work on their problems, but something held her back. She always pushed against barriers theses days, but she decided that particular barrier better left alone. She owed him too much to prod.

"I have to leave soon, myself," she responded instead. "Gania needs me. And then I have to stop by *The Golden Cup* on the way home."

"And will you ever *stop by* Mistress Moriah's school?"

Tasia grinned. "Jeril, I do far better here, and I've all but convinced my mother to let it go." She gestured to the literary mess on the table. "I've far more words here, and I'm close to something. I've been reading from the queen's book about Minuet."

"I sense a half-truth, but I won't push. Between you and your friends coming here, I wonder if the woman has any pupils at all. So, you will be a twelve-year old teller of tales. What are you close to, then?"

Tasia picked up her notepad, its topmost page filled with notes. "I think I might have another story to add, maybe."

"You don't sound totally convinced."

"That is because I'm still looking." She picked up a book from the edge of the pile. "Go see to your *things*. I'll lock up."

She recentered her concentration as the door snicked shut. Over the last few weeks, Tasia found herself drawn to the poems and stories collected in the queen's volume. Her early memories of the Maze-poet Kembril Edri accentuated her reading, and she felt he spoke to her in that compelling, wheezy, breathy way. Despite her youth, Tasia could tell Queen Eleni succeeded in capturing some of that quality in her renditions. Tasia also understood that such an insight did not normally come to the average Pevanese twelve-year old.

None of the Pevanese Maze-born were normal. Such descriptors just did not come with the life.

The more time Tasia spent reading from Jeril's expanding personal library, the more she felt changed. For her, even touching the fence tines surrounding Kembril's grave connected her deeply to the pulse and thread of her home. To her mind's eye, it came as a whirling, convoluted word stream: Kembril, Devyn, other unknown poets who added their bits to the volume; all of them part of the whole, and to her that meant continuity, heritage; a legacy she felt compelled to perpetuate.

She felt differently about *her* words. As she grew up, tales of Minuet never failed to draw her complete attention. All those tales ended with some moral point or lesson that, while instructive and fun, always left Tasia disappointed. For her, Minuet was more than someone's theme, a way to explain folklore to children. What if she *was* the adventures? What if she had fears and wonder and all the rest of it? What if she knew dirt?

I know dirt. What if she was me? How would she…or I…tell the stories?

She felt close to something in that moment. Something new. Everyone else told Minuet's stories, but no one let Minuet tell them herself. What did Renia's familiar think about the tasks her mistress set her? Did she ever harbor an ignoble thought? Did she ever question?

She read over the words on her pad, certain somewhere among them lay the start of a new kind of story, and a manner of telling that would be vastly different from the tone and style of the ones in the queen's collection. There are moments in a young person's life when they become aware of things larger than themselves, and that, too, was a truth most Maze-born came to earlier than most.

But this was different. Women had been allowed into the lists for the Poets' Competition since Donari ascended the throne. And each year succeeding had seen less upset among the conservatives in Pevana. Tasia wanted her chance, but she wanted something to mark her as unique. That dirt she wondered if Minuet knew covered everyone in certain parts of Pevana equally. Poverty brought its own kind of sameness to life.

If she were to find her words, she would find her voice. She remembered hearing Devyn tell her about how Kembril showed him the way to find *his* voice back when all the troubles blew up in flames. Devyn called it a last protest, and he found his attitude and his courage in his poem.

But I am twelve, what do I know of courage?

Even as she asked herself the question, she realized she already possessed at least part of the answer. Again, the Maze-born just knew…things.

She tapped her pencil tip against her teeth, waiting, tense yet calm, as though she were a bubble hung suspended in air above multiple possibilities.

"Alright, then," she whispered. "Devyn spoke for the Old Ways. Perhaps I need to speak for Minuet. Maybe in giving her a voice, I will find my own."

The thought sent her surging up out of the chair. Life still called to her, and she had tasks, but now she recognized all would someday come to a pattern. All she need do is become Minuet.

Gania expected her help in the kitchen, but her thoughts compelled her to resist the turning at the Harbor Gate street. Instead, she wove through the folk at the intersection and down a sideway to the green, open space surrounding Kembril's grave, to the place where she first found Minuet in the old poet's raspy-voiced stories. She spent a few minutes pulling weeds from around the fence line, and committed to memory the need for fresh flowers when she came next. The great Tree had been her first playground; the dusty old man her first teacher. She settled back, just as she used to see Devyn do when he came to the place for solace, words, or inspiration. Echoes of both men's voices ran through her head, calming, instructive. She closed her eyes to look again through memory at the wizened but gentle face.

A dog barking in the distance disturbed her reverie. She blinked and noticed Tam staring at Grayce's Tree on the back wall of the warehouse. Curious at what might have made him play hooky from his tasks, too, she scrambled to her feet and went over to join him.

"It's so, so—" he began by way of greeting.

"Large? Grand? Full?" Tasia offered, following his gaze to take in the beloved image.

"Yeah, all of that, but something else, too. I dunno, Tasia, I don't have your words."

Though he was actually half a year older, Tasia noted the respect in his tone. She liked Tam. All the kids she still ran with did. He was genuine and true.

"Ah!" she said. "That's it!"

"What?"

"The word you're looking for. *True*."

Tam giggled. "Yes, that is it. It's so true. It's a grand truth. Grayce is good, isn't she?"

"She must be for Master Sandre to take her on. He sees things, you know, in her, in you, in all of us. He thinks we might be able to do stuff."

"Like sums."

"And stories."

"I like Master Sandre. My da' sometimes frets at me for taking so much time there, but I like it."

"Keep going," Tasia urged him. "I think he needs us as much as we need him."

"He needs us? He has the king's eye."

"Yes, but I think he has his darkness, too."

"You and your stories! But if any of us would know for sure, it would be you, Tasia."

"Someday, maybe. I have a lot to figure out yet."

"And I have to get back to the water. I think I'll try and find a few of Grayce's wall things along the way."

"There is one down along the Harbor wall south," Tasia offered. "And it wouldn't be out of your way, really. I'm for Gania Landare's to help in her kitchen. She has some new lodgers and needs the extra hands."

"Down along the wall, you said?"

"Yes, down off the main way, back in behind the new temple."

Tam dashed off. Tasia followed more slowly, a bit reluctant to leave, but she gave her word to Gania. She got back to the side way that connected to Harbor Street. Congestion in the intersection brought her up short. A procession of King's Theology adherents, a phalanx of red robes and shaven heads led by Reith Simson, who sported a lofty red hat, paced ponderously by. Tasia remembered that hat. She last saw it five years ago perched on the head of the detestable Byrnard Casan. Reith paced along, swinging a smoking bowl of incense on a chain and intoning along with his followers.

Tasia watched, fixated. This was new, different. She thought backward. Ever since the arrival of the Esdan ambassador and the news of the empire's *reguests*, it seemed that every time she turned around she encountered Theology members engaged in some sort of activity.

Reith Simson lay at the center of that visiblility, making a show of refurbishing the temple and sending out followers to do charitable works among the poor. All of it coming after Ambrose left for the north. Last week, one of Simson's fellows tried to put flowers on Kembril Edri's grave, but Tasia made sure to remove them at the first chance. That action, more than any of the others, convinced her everything Simson and his folk did was performance only. Even at twelve, her Maze-born cynicism allowed her to see through such simple subterfuge.

Memories of that ugly, first meeting still instructed her. She made sure to duck down behind a cart until Simson and his lot passed from view. Then she hurried on her way until she spied Gania's house with its decorous fence and bright green door.

"Well, look who gets here on a wish?" Gania boomed when she opened the door. "I wasn't sure you'd remember, girl, but glad I am you did. Lyssa's in the kitchen seeing to dinner. Help me get out a few more chairs. There will be a crowd in here tonight."

She helped Gania organize the table, and then followed her to the kitchen. Lyssa was busy overseeing three different pots of bubbling stuff. A haunch dripped on its spit into the edge of the hearth fire. The place smelled like a feast in preparation. Tasia had never seen such activity in Gania's place before.

"Who do you have staying here?" Tasia asked, setting to with a knife on some potatoes.

"Officers from a trader out of Hallar. The captain wanted a few days off his ship," Gania answered. She took a spoon and slurped from all three pots, adding a pinch of salt to the last. "Lyssa, you have outdone yourself tonight. The king'll be hauling you up to the palace soon, girl! But don't ask for more money 'cos you won't get it."

"I don't want more of your money, G, but if you don't stop booming your voice in my ears I'll be deaf before I get grey!"

"Who's booming?"

"What was that? I couldn't hear you. My ears bleedin' an all."

Gania drew in a breath as if she were about to explode in sound. Tasia tensed for the sonic blow but then noticed the twinkle in her eye. Gania exhaled in a husky chuckle.

"We know each other too well, don't we?" she said, settling on a stool and drawing a bowl of string beans close. She took up a clump in her massive hands and snapped them in half before tossing them in yet another pot. "Now," she continued. "What have we forgot? Bread?"

"Three loaves, fresh this morning."

"Wine?"

"Ellery delivered some when you were out."

"I see the haunch, you're on the pots. Table is ready. Anything else?"

Tasia coughed. Gania swung on her in an instant.

"Don't you cough your timidity at me, little girl. I know you better, too. What is it?"

"Flowers?" Tasia suggested. "For a table setting, maybe?"

"For sailors?" Gania considered the idea, and must have thought it not too outlandish, for she fished out a coin from a pocket and slid it across the worktable. "Good idea. Off to market with you. There should be some fresh cut left. Get what you can and keep any change. Be quick now!"

Tasia fairly ran out the door and down the street. "This," she whispered to herself, "has been a full day."

Chapter 12: Catalyst

Jeril paced pensively once he left for his errands. Tasia's acute comment made him feel a bit exposed. *Still looking.* What was he still looking for? While the children worked at the table, he lost himself in memories of Seri, Dem and the other lost children of Piling. His year in Pevana and rising fortunes served only to recess those ill thoughts. He walked along the street now, looking to replenishing his kitchen needs, feeling vague, indistinct, accompanied by other, older, even more troubling images with voices attached to them.

His mother's voice whispered old herbal wisdom dearly brought to his mind's ear.

"And these are the medicinal plants, Jer-Jer. Wortle for tooth ache, mint bruised and steeped in tea for a sore head and painful joints. Your father uses this all the time."

The remembered words transported him back to that moment in his youth when joy still existed for him. There had been love between his father, the emperor, and Jeril's mother, second wife raised to first after the death of the empress; lost giving birth to Jorian.

The question of succession never entered conversation when they were young. Jeril's mother cared for the king's son as her own, and Jeril, elder by several years, looked after the boy as a blood sibling.

Those had been good years, teaching years, learning how to draw by tracing copies of his mother's plants, endless scrawlings on fine, well-made paper and seemingly unlimited color combinations. He loved it. Jorian had loved it, too, at first. Later his attention waned in favor of expediency. Not the flower for the sensual ark of its petals but, rather, what use could be made of the oils squeezed from them.

Inadvertantly, Jeril's mother taught him how to create but taught Jorian how to destroy.

Memory crystallized anew into a definite, hated tableau: news of the Emperor's fatal stroke, the mad race back to Esda, that last moment discovering mother poisoned and Jorian's mocking insincerity. Like a wave, the sound of that conversation returned and drove him further into himself. Blindly, he stopped and sat on the ledge of a fountain aware that, once *that* memory surfaced, he had no choice but to let it run its course.

"I'm sorry, brother, we did all we could."

The *lie* in Jorian's eyes contradicted the tone of his voice.

"Did you kill father, too?" he asked, stepping close. Jorian's guards crossed spears in front of him. He stared over the barrier.

"That was a rather impertinent question, brother," Jorian answered, his voice grown suddenly colder. "I'd heard duty in the frontier forts took a toll on a man, but you seem to have lost your wits as well."

"I served our father and our people."

"As did I, and given our father's decline, perhaps gave the better service."

Jeril sneered at that. "I get a sense of your 'service' with every passing minute. Mother is dead."

"Not my mother, brother."

"As good as. She cared for you, taught you." His voice caught, almost broke.

Jorian's cruel, condescending laugh seared Jeril's ears. "Yes, I learned my lessons. Useful, all that plant knowledge. I am sure your men all benefited from those green, smelly poltices you concocted for them. My interests ran toward a different pharmacopeia."

"Poison and power."

"I did not kill father. It wasn't necessary. He died in his sleep, possibly dreaming of the two of us acting like heroes for the crown. I let him have his senile fantasy."

"Why mother?"

"Looks like she grew weary of her life and decided to follow father."

"Lie."

Jorian smiled. "Again with the impetuous comments. Foolish, brother."

"Heartsbane is not something a person weary of life would take. There is pain. Heartsbane is a weapon for killers."

Jorian affected a yawn. "This is getting tedious. You are sounding like your mother at one of her lectures."

"How can you stand there so unaffected?" Jeril's sword hand itched. Guards had taken his weapons before allowing him up to the royal residence. He longed to wipe the smirk off his face.

"She got in the way. It seems she actually cared for father in spite of the way he neglected her. She disagreed with my decision."

"Decision?"

"To proclaim myself emperor, of course. I'd worked for too long to let the old man go and name you instead."

"I am eldest."

"From a second wife."

"You are a monster."

Jorian frowned. *"Maybe,"* he mused. *"But I like to think of myself as a realist. That is the biggest difference between us, brother. You think of others far too much for your own good. It will get you nowhere. In the end, it might get you killed."*

"Might? Where is my vial, then?"

Jorian held up a small glass bottle, twin to the one lying next to Jeril's mother on the bed. Jeril stepped back prepared to fight. Jorian's guards uncrossed their spears and held them, points out, gripped short for the killing thrust.

Jorian shook his head, lowered the vial.

"Might," he said. *"I've already dealt with any of the council who would support you. I regret your mother, a little, but there it is. Perhaps I am a monster. But I am a monster who will be proclaimed Emperor in the morning."*

"And I am to be added to the list?"

Jorian's face smoothed, the previous, supercilious expression replaced by something close to open. *"We are brothers, after all."*

"Half."

Jorian's eyebrows came a little closer together.

"When we were little it didn't matter much…"

"But now it does," Jeril interrupted. Jorian's frown deepened.

"Yes, unfortunately for you, it does. But I will let you live just the same."

"But the people…"

"Weren't you listening? The only thing that matters in Esda is the Council. The people will suck up whatever story I decide to tell them. That's how things work here, brother. Really, I think your tour of duty in the north has you quite addled."

"I can't let you do this."

"Why? Because you might rule better? Don't be foolish. You haven't the skill. If you did, your mother would still breathe, but you let honor and duty cloud your sense of things. Frankly, I am doing you a favor this way. I'll shoulder all the responsibility, and you get to go wherever and be as savagely noble as you wish."

"You are mad."

"Well, I'll admit to getting a little angry, but, of course, you mean insane. Sorry, wrong diagnosis. Rather, I consider myself well-equipped to rule this nest of half-witted vipers."

Jorian looked at him, expectant. He was in control and knew it. He raised the vial once again.

"Time to leave, brother. I hope never to see you again."

The creaking sound of a wagon bouncing over the cobblestoned street broke the spell. Those old wounds never completely healed. The potency of this most recent episode troubled him. Something was imminent.

It took an effort to shake off the melancholy and respond to the pleasantries he encountered on his way. He felt like a fraud smiling and nodding away. He finished his few errands and considered what to do next. Tam had mentioned heading back to the boat shed. Jeril decided he needed a distraction. Perhaps he could free Tam from his chores and take him out for some fishing in the bay. He would have the boy bring a book with him, and they could practice reading together. Perhaps that might ease the ill he felt so intently. There was too much of Esda in his thinking and waking life now.

He walked back down Lampwright's Street, waved at Saymon Brimaldi sweeping in front of *The Golden Cup*, and at a client who chanced by in a carriage. He turned down Harbor Street. From there the road crested a small rise. Jeril could see clear out to the bay. A sleek Esdan galley bobbed at anchor in the roads. Another visit. And another reason to free Tam from tasks and go fishing. He wanted a look at that vessel, his previous melancholy serving as a goad to action. He needed to exercise his body and his mind. He always insisted on sharing the rowing duty with Tam on their outings because it helped keep him fit. Memories of Piling and his helplessness on the beach, also served to keep him from excess. That was also why, late at night, with none but Angel to observe, he would haul out his sword and practice until the sweat ran off him and exhaustion stilled his dubious thoughts.

He walked briskly, flowing along with the human stream passed Gania Landare's house and the well square. The pace slowed as he neared the Harbor Gate, a crowd of folk clustered about an alley that ran along the wall, partially blocking the way. When he came to the back of the group, he could hear voices raised in anger and sorrow. Something moved him then, and he shouldered through.

When he got to the source of the upset, he fell to his knees, heart-stopped.

On the ground lay the boy, Tam, legs sprawled akimbo, neck stretched at an angle made possible by the ear-to-ear rent in his poor throat.

For Jeril the scene became a nightmarish collection of sympathetic voices, feet and legs, faces thrust down close to inspect the boy and him.

"Who would do such a thing?" a woman's voice keened through the din.

"So much blood."

"Look at his neck."

"Why?"

"Someone call the watch!"

Jeril struggled to take in air, to calm them, calm himself. He made to rise, but a coarse hand clamped down on his shoulder, stopping him. He turned, took in Gania Landare's stricken face.

"Mistress Gan—" he began.

"Lyssa and me'll see to him," she said gruffly, helping him up. "Step away now, painter, or you'll get his blood all over yourself. Here!" she raised her voice. "One of you, go to the boat storage and tell his da. Let's get the boy cleaned up."

Jeril's voice and senses returned to him. "No!" he grunted. "Leave him for the moment. Let someone get word to the palace, or I will myself. Someone needs to see this."

"But why should the Hill be concerned for a water rat?" someone asked.

Jeril ignored the question. He shuddered, his attention drawn to the reason why he urged them to inaction just yet. Tam's blood had pooled up against the wall, and someone, his murderer, perhaps, had used that precious fluid to scrawl a crude representation of a sprig of heather two feet above the ground.

No. Not possible. It's been five years…but that galley…

Booted feet sounded on the cobblestones as a group of gate guards arrived. Folk moved to clear the space. Jeril ignored them. The bloody sigil drew him, accused him of complacency in the worst degree. The urge to flight surged, but again, Gania's voice, grousing folk back to sense, calmed him.

"Hey! Back away there," she said, even as she steered him back away from the body. "Let the soldier boys get a look. Lyssa, back to the house for that old blanket. Once the helmets are done here, we'll clean the boy up proper."

The crowd dispersed, leaving Jeril and Gania and one or two others to deal with the guards. There was little to say or surmise. The boy lay in the shadows next the wall hidden behind the back of a wagon. The owner of the wagon returned with his team, but the blood smell unnerved the beasts. The man checked, found the body and raised a cry.

Jeril loitered around the edge of the discussion. He had nothing to add and felt any reference to the sign on the wall unnecessary. He did cast his artist's eye on the scene, however, noting a few details that others missed in the initial shock and alarm.

The blood trail ran back down the alley, which faded to shadows from the buildings that encroached upon the wall. He followed a set of bloody footprints a short ways. One of the guards joined him. Wordlessly, they paced back to where the footprints ended, or began as it were, in a splotch of blood.

"This is where the boy got cut," the guard said tonelessly. "But I recall always seeing him about the shoreline. What would have brought him here?"

Jeril avoided comment. The sun moved out from behind a cloud. The midafternoon angle brought light to their corner, and then he knew, with a sickening sense of responsibility, why Tam had found his way to the place where he died.

During their talks while fishing, Jeril had told the child of Grayce and her city-wide irregular art. Tam had been curious and immediately set out to find all of them for himself. He liked to report his findings during their outings. Jeril blinked back a tear as the sunlight settled on one of Grayce's whirling patterns, traced in ink on bare bricks several feet up from the turning. Obviously, the boy had gone exploring after leaving Jeril's, intent on reporting a new find, but instead found his death.

The guard left, leaving Jeril alone with his guilt.

The boy found his picture. That much is clear, but why would it lead to his murder? What is missing?

He recalled Grayce's tale of how she came to meet Tasia and Devyn Ambrose. Tam was not the only one searching out Grayce's art. The priests of the Reformed King's Theology had not been pleased with Grayce's efforts. Jeril recalled other comments overheard in the markets alluding to retribution. Perhaps Tam encountered anger along with his discovery.

"But that doesn't explain murder," he mused aloud. "Unless Tam said something that caused a reaction. Unless…" He paused. Images of Grayce's sketchbook open on the bench; a passing glance, a ruffle of pages, a half-seen representation of the stem of a plant. The moment had not warranted a question, but it welled up now from his other sense as a summons. His mind flashed back to the bloody sign on the wall above Tam's body…and from there back down his own history: spearhead, message, time after time the same thing: driven, mocking, reminders, that insidious craft under Esdan colors. Seri's corpse on the sand, bloody signs on a wall, vengeful priests that proselytized peace despite a militant past, a sprig of heather all somehow connected.

"This isn't just about me," he muttered, turning to go. "Perhaps it never was, but there is a pattern here."

He paused back at Tam's body. Folk had brought water from the well in buckets to wash away the blood. Someone had quickly ministered to Tam, who now lay wrapped in a blanket, limbs composed, only his face showing. Jeril looked hard at the boy's features, searing them in memory. Rage and remorse constricted. He swallowed against the tightness. He had left his home in search of fish, chatter and news, but now he found himself tasked with a deeper, bloodier purpose. He could not find the one who wielded the knife, but he could warn those in power about where the trail might lead.

Piling burned for silence. Seri died for innocence. Tam was a casualty in a conflict that, obviously, had grown to include unusual allies. He left the scene in Gania's capable hands and set his path for the citadel and the palace. Someone said word should get to the king. Who better than himself?

Despite his grief, he quickened his pace.

It was time to tell the truth, finally, even if it was already too late.

Jeril's route would take him back by his house, and Tasia met him at Gania's gate as he made his way up Harbor Street. Seeing her brought a sob pulsing in his throat; they were friends. She must have noted his expression because she reached out to stop him when he made to pass.

"Master Sandre, what is it? You look like you've seen Tolimon or something."

Her question stopped him. "Much worse, I'm afraid, girl, much worse. I've just come from the harbor gate." He searched her eyes, unwilling to spread the pain he felt.

"What happened, tell me!"

"It's Tam, Tasia, murdered. They found him near the wall with his throat cut."

For a moment, the girl stood there, stunned, before tears welled in her eyes to answer his own. Then she fell into his embrace, weeping and keening into his chest. He held her, fought against his own, answering sobs. She pushed away, snuffling and wiping her eyes, her Maze-born control reasserting itself.

"I don't understand," she said, slipping alongside him as he made to continue. "We were supposed to meet later tonight to plan something for Summer Festival. And weren't you off to go fishing?"

"I don't have time to explain, Tasia. Best you get home and keep yourself safe. There's more to this than poor Tam. I'm off to the palace."

"But why?"

"Like I said, there's more to this than poor Tam, much more."

"I'm coming with you," Tasia remonstrated.

Her insistence perplexed Jeril, and he waved his hands, frustrated, in a vain effort to placate her.

"I can't do this now. I think a number of things are involved here, including Grayce's wall art and those priests both of you ran into awhile back…and more besides. Help Gania then get home. You choose."

"I'm coming with you. Bastain works in the palace. He will need to know."

The mature finality in her tone kept him from disagreeing. Together, then, they paced along the stones, upward, towards the citadel.

Chapter 13: False Diplomacy

Jeril's writ from the king garnered him entrance to the citadel, and no one saw fit to question Tasia's presence. Jeril's work took him to many of the great houses on the hill as well as the palace. He became a fixture in the rhythm of the place and so moved somewhat freely. The courtyard before the palace buzzed with activity. A number of carriages sporting merchant house colors lined the inner wall and an escort of Esdan soldiers clustered near the steps to the right. Jeril recognized the formal parade uniforms; it seemed not much had changed in Esda over the last twenty years. These were no common soldiers culled from the galley troops for the purpose, which meant they guarded no common messengers. Between that lot and the smattering of household servants, the place held more armed men than normal.

The sight of them intensified Jeril's fears.

He walked to the palace steps to where some of Donari's personal guard stood in a line before the doors with Cryso, the king's aged valet, next to them. Jeril felt for Tasia's hand and only then realized her absence. He looked around quickly. Out of the corner of his eye, he thought he saw something flit into the royal stable doors. He shook his head in consternation as he mounted the steps to where the guards crossed their spears, barring him entry.

Cryso came to his rescue.

"Master Sandre!" he exclaimed. "But you are a day early, aren't you? I thought we had set up another sitting for the queen for tomorrow."

"I know that, Cryso, but I've just seen something down in the city that might be important. The king is with the Esdans, correct?"

"Ah, so you've seen the galley, then? And those fellows? Yes, he is with the easterners in the main hall. This is not a good time, Jeril. The queen is with him and all the council."

"Cryso, you must let me in. I'll wait, but something has happened in the city that bears looking into."

"You sound worried."

"There's been a murder."

"Worthy of interrupting the king?"

Jeril hesitated. Tam's death and sudden connections he made down by the harbor had decided his own mind and sent him up the hill, but now that he was there, how could he prove his credibility? How was he to convince Donari of what he suspected without exposing his own past? Was it come to that?

The image of Tam's bloodless face compelled him to risk the truth, but only if he could gain entry to the king.

"Cryso, on my honor and talent, the king must hear my story. A child was killed down by the harbor gates, throat slit and placed to be found. There are other aspects to his death that lead me to suspect something wider, more dangerous. The king must know."

"But why? I still do not see…oh very well. Come with me. I will put you in the king's study and contrive something. You really are mysterious today, Jeril, and to be honest I am a little put out myself with all these oily eastern types in the place."

Jeril suppressed a rueful smile.

"I can well imagine, Cryso; especially since rumor has it these meetings prior have not been genteel. That's a warship tied up at the quay, not a trader."

"I have nothing to say about that, of course, but I applaud your observation, painter."

Cryso led him into the palace, depositing him in the king's study as promised.

"Stay here until I come for you," he said. "Everything is on edge, I can tell you that much. I am sure you felt it outside just now."

"Cryso, the whole city feels it. This smells different, bad, somehow."

Cryso dropped his voice, despite the fact they were alone in the room.

"It is," he whispered. "Very, but that must remain just between us. I trust you, Jeril, truly, but you ask much of me here."

"Cryso, I understand, perhaps more than you realize. I need to talk to Donari."

"When the king is free I will tell him you are here. Stay!"

After Cryso left, Jeril tried to sit in one of the over-stuffed chairs, but tension forced him to his feet and pacing. His mind raced, reliving his own past, considering what he saw as a threat to his present and future, the danger to the people who had taken him in and given him a chance at a new life. It was as though no time had passed. He still heard the sound of his brother's voice, silky, convinced, corrupt. His mother's poison contorted face accused him of his own cowardice. He should have known. He should have acted when he had the chance. He ran instead; took the escape Jorian provided him. No mercy there just payment extended over years. All those other faces returned to mouth their silent condemnations: the innocent of Piling, the villagers in the islands. His past followed him like a determined stray dog, forcing him to a choice he spent decades trying to avoid.

He paced in growing impatience and frustration. Finally, he could stand it no longer. He went to the door, opened it carefully, and stuck his head out to check the hallway. Nothing. He knew his way around the palace by now. Donari's study stood just separate from the main hall. Guards stood before the great double doors. He recognized them: two of Donari's more reasonable veterans. Two Esdan guards stood off to one side. The closest, older looking than the other, bore officer's insignia on his uniform that marked him as an Emperial marine.

"Sorry, Master Sandre," the Pevanese guard on the right said as Jeril walked up.

"Rather high level talk going on in there, sir," said the other on the left. Neither of them had lowered spears to bar his way, however, so he kept moving.

"I know," Jeril said affably, "and I have something to add to it. Get these two pieces of eastern shit out of the way."

Before either of the Esdans could react, Jeril braced and swung as hard as he could, catching the older Esdan full in the face. The man's nose shattered from the force of the blow, and he dropped like a stone, blood already gushing from his ruined nose. The other Esdan tried to draw his blade, but Jeril, muscle memory taking over, neatly pirouetted from the momentum of his attack and smashed his right elbow, back-handed, into the throat of the other. The Pevanese guards froze for an instant in the sudden ferocity, and before either could stop him, Jeril shouldered through them to open the doors to the hall. He slammed them shut and locked them.

His entrance brought an immediate response. The king sat across from two others at a small table set before the dias. The queen sat at a small table with her papers and pens recording. The two men sitting opposite to the king drew Jeril's closest attention. The younger one, sporting dark hair pulled tight in the back and braided in typical Esdan fashion, had to be the empire's diplomatic representative because the other one wore a full formal military uniform signifying high rank. Jeril remembered him: Tacidus. Seri's face in death and Piling's flames flared in memory.

"Sandre! What is the meaning of this?" Donari shouted, rising, the Esdans rose with him.

"Jeril?" gasped Eleni. "What—"

"Is this how you treat security, king?" the Esdan ambassador asked. Tacidus interposed himself between Jeril and his countryman, reaching for a blade that was not there. Then he took a pace forward, hands balled into fists.

"Stay behind me Lord," he snarled. "King Donari, you know this man, yes? Then get him to stay clear!"

Jeril stopped three paces away and fixed eyes with Tacidus and waited for recognition to take hold. Jeril answered the slow smile that grew on the easterner's face with one of his own.

"Yes," Jeril breathed in answer to the unasked question. "A bit less hair, but here. Do not feign surprise. You knew. I received your most recent message. It seems you earned a promotion killing innocents and burning a few hovels."

"We always knew, Tandori, well met, again."

Jeril fought back an urge to lash out. Thankfully, Donari strode forward, hand held up imperiously.

"Stop this nonsense, Sandre!" he snarled. "Guards!"

"Sorry, my king, but they are seeing to one of the Esdans. I had to make it in here and did not have time to adequately explain. My apologies for the upset and the Esdan's blood staining the floor outside." He kept his eyes fixed on Tacidus, who seemed to note Donari's reference.

"You mean they don't know?" he asked.

"Know what?" Donari asked. "Sandre, you have much to answer for…wait. He called you *Tandori*. What?"

Jeril cursed under his breath, but then he had intended to reveal everything anyway.

"Sire, forgive me. I have kept secrets from you. My name is actually Jeril Tandori, eldest son of the former emperor of Esda. The ambassador you treat with serves my half-brother, Jorian. And this other has made a career of following me and killing children. I fear the most recent victim lost his life to one following his orders."

"You're mad," sneered Tacidus. "Dare you accuse the emperor's representative? And me, his guard?"

"I do not think there is anyone alive more fit to accuse as I do, pirate." Jeril turned to the king. "Sire, the only madness is even trying to deal with such as these. You know they test you."

"King Donari, it seems you have issues to see to," said the Esdan Lord, rising and gliding by, the oily serenity in his voice at odds with the emotions passing between his assistant and Jeril. "We are done here anyway. Know this, lord, that Esda considers this man a renegade and subject to Esdan justice. Harbor him at your peril."

"He has sworn fealty to me and kept my peace and earned my trust, Lord Piecen."

"Your choice. But be advised, this man's presence in your councils will change the tone and tenor of any further discussions. The Emperor Jorian's patience is at an end. This fellow's allegations are an insult to this embassy. Do not presume on my good nature."

"In Piling, I killed the snakes that attempted to get at my eggs. Used them as bait to catch rats. They tended to hiss at me before I scotched them." Jeril saw his words strike home. The ambassador turned his limpid gaze on him, his eyes beginning to smolder despite the cool effrontery in his voice.

"I remember you," Piecen drawled, "always rushing about, acting noble and speaking your mind. Jorian found you amusing, for a while. You were a fool then. I should think time and travel would have changed you, but you are still intemperate. A pity. Tacidus, let us collect our bloodied compatriot. That was a blow, master Jeril, for which you will have to answer, perhaps to Tacidus here. I am sure your brother will prove indifferent to the matter."

The hall doors opened. Cryso appeared, pocketing his keys, along with another, matronly looking woman. Behind them one of Donari's guards and the other Esdan supported the wounded one.

"Cryso!" Donari exclaimed. "Well-timed. See these gentlemen to the rooms you have prepared for them. Lord, we will take this up in the morning."

"I think not," Piecen sniffed. "We do not trust your security for our party's safety. Tacidus, send word. We sail with the tide."

"Sail? But what of our 'discussions'?"

"As I said, quite clearly, I am sure," the ambassador replied, gliding toward the door. "There will be changes."

They left with Cryso, leaving the woman behind.

"What is it, Manda?" Eleni asked, motioning the woman forward.

"My queen, I'm sorry, but the twins have done it again. I settled them for their nap and stepped out to help with the rooms…"

"Ugh! Again?" Eleni said with disgust. She looked at Donari.

"Go," he said, still looking intently at Jeril. "Jeril *Tandori* and I will stay behind. This day seems filled with news. Come sir, sit. Explain yourself."

Donari led him to a pair of over-stuffed chairs placed before the fireplace. Jeril settled uneasily into his. Donari stared at him, his face a mix of anger and curiosity.

"You weren't the most creative with your choice of name," he said finally, a ghost of a smile teasing across his lips.

Jeril rubbed his temples in frustration. Tam's corpse had driven him to make the decision to reveal the truth. That the Esdans would be in council with the king was just a cruel irony.

"That was what came out after Tam asked when I first arrived here. Tam is, was, the murdered child I came to tell you about. I don't know what I hoped to accomplish, sire."

"Yes, that is a question. Of course, I would want to know about the death of a subject, but was it necessary to barge in here? And how did you get by the guards?"

Jeril hung his head. "I have some old skills, sire, from my former life, that have stayed with me. I deserve arrest."

"I daresay, but I will be the judge of that. I want answers. Those men knew you, especially the military fellow, Tacidus."

"Watch him, sire, and do not trust him. You remember Piling? He was the one responsible."

"You did reference Esda, before, but this is new."

"Again, my king, I regret the ommision. At the time, I was more intent on hiding than the truth. I meant no harm."

"You are telling me this has gone on for a long time?"

"My lord, my half-brother has hounded me across two seas over two decades. They have been watching your coasts for years. That part has less to do with me, I suspect, and more to do with your success, but now that they know I am here, and if we believe Tacidus, they have known for some time, then more than this simpering ambassador will come next."

"I agree. I was leaning toward a similar conclusion when you burst in. They were just beginning to outline demands for tribute and other unpleasant things. I was going to to send them packing in the morning, but it seems they will save me the trouble."

"Send me with them. It might help. I am a danger to you."

"Whether you are the painter Jeril Sandre or the fallen Prince Tandori, you are my subject. Whatever you are to them does not matter now. You have spent half your life running. Time to stop, friend."

"Sire, generous but probably unwise."

"Probably, but that Esdan fellow is irritatingly smug, and Tacidus has the look of a man who will pick a fight. You said this Tam's murder connected somehow to the Esdans?"

Jeril took a moment to collect his thoughts. All he had were his own experience and supposition. Now that it came to it, he doubted his inferences. He looked at the king's face, saw there both concern and consternation. He owed the man truth.

He told the king of how he came to be a royal fugitive. It pained him to recall it; the memory of his mother's face in death brought the cost of his life home to him. He could only imagine what his brother might look like after twenty years. He hoped his dissolute early days might have cost Jorian his vitality, but the energy behind the Esdan moves, and the dedication of the hunt suggested otherwise.

He told of his days in Piling, the joy he took in his work there, and the pain from that last night of death, fire, and terror.

"There has been one constant in all my travels and troubles, sire. Every time, Jorian's agents left a sign, something to remind me of his power. The time before Piling it was a cutting of heather tied to a spear. At Piling it was Tacidus with a message from Jorian himself."

"I see you have no reason to love your former home or your brother, but I still don't see the connections you imply."

"King Donari, Tam was killed and dragged to where he could be found. I followed the blood trail. One of my students, Grayce Stonesmith, spent her early days in Pevana scribbling on any bare surface she could find. She is talented. People have taken to her art. Tam was curious. I think he had gone to see some of them but found his death instead. The picture in question had one thing I am sure Grayce did not put there: a crude representation of heather. Heather is the sigil of my house, sire. I think an Esdan agent put that there. Grayce told me she saw the same thing once back in a town called Gallina. Lord, I think Esda has been watching you, us, me, I do not know—but there is something there that points to trouble. I know it."

"That much is clear. I sent Devyn north with questions three weeks ago. This absurd moment with you just reminds me he is late. Esda has spies in Pevana, so does everybody else. There have always been spies in Pevana. There are two things we have a surplus of here: poets and spies."

"Sire, this is no laughing matter."

"Trust me, I'm not laughing." He rubbed his face, a tired gesture. "But I learned to laugh at difficulty a long time ago. I found it helped me see a way through things."

"Sire, what will you do?"

Donari stared at him for a long, uncomfortable moment. Jeril wondered if he had overstepped a line. His confrontation with Tacidus released those princely instincts and behaviors so long suppressed. His hand and elbow still ached from the unfortunate blows in the hallway. Doubtless, the king thought him presumptuous. Jeril wanted to shrink into himself, appalled at the risk he represented to Pevana. It came as a shock to him to realize how much he cared for the people and place and the royal family, especially the king, so frank and human, decisive yet humane. He was everything a king should be. Despite a twenty-year absence, Jeril knew Jorian possessed none of those qualities.

Jorian had naked ambition supported by the weight of Empire. How could goodness alone stand against such power?

"I am going to do what I must," the king mused. "And the first thing I will do is learn to call you by your right name. My friend, you did not need to hide."

"I did before my life drove me here, sire. What home I have here I owe to you and the queen's kindness. I feel I have given poor payment. You really should use me to bargain. I would be a prize to my brother.

Perhaps he would be satisfied with me and leave you and yours alone. If I had known what Jorian would do, I would have never stayed. I am sorry."

He caught the king's eye and held it. Donari gazed at him as though weighing the difficult absurdity of the whole scene. His brow furrowed momentarily, then softened.

"I believe you, Jeril, I believe you because I have seen you paint my wife's soul. I believe you. Such skill cannot be false."

"I could leave, take my boat and sail with the tide. Maybe--"

"Now you are just being foolish. This situation is not about you. You are merely ancillary to the event."

"Again, sire, use me to bargain. Soften the blow."

"And again, Jeril Tandori, let us have no more of that. This is not a market place squabble. This has been coming for some time. Speaking of time, I think your days in my wife's former home are over, at least in the short term. I will have it watched, but this episode suggests you might be in danger."

"King Donari, that won't be—"

"Call it a royal command if you must. I want you safe. Besides, you still have a canvas to finish for my study! Too bad we won't break bread with these Esdan bullies in the morning. The queen has been keeping notes. I would have you prop a tripod and sketch them to put the bastards off their center."

The king stood, motioned Jeril to join him and together they moved to the hall doors. Cryso waited for them.

"Cryso, Master Sandre, um, Tandori, sorry, will be staying in the palace for a while. He will need an escort to his home to gather what he needs for his comfort. See to it, please. Put him in the rooms we prepared for the Esdans, since they won't be needing them." He reached over and gave Jeril's arm a familiar squeeze. "All is forgiven, sir, now help me deal with the mess. I must look into what mischief the twins caused. I swear they might be more trouble than Esdan spies!"

Jeril, heart and mind all a muddle, watched the king walk away. Cryso touched his elbow to draw his attention.

"I am glad you will be joining us Master Sa—Tandori," the old man said. "I look forward to seeing you work."

"Cryso," Jeril responded resignedly. "I only wish the visit was about work only. There will be storms, my friend."

"And we will survive them, I am sure. There is one thing I have learned in my long life about storms: they trammel up a lot of blow, but usually end up just providing fodder for spectacular sunsets!"

Jeril let the old man's good humor tease him into a smile as they walked down the hall.

Hope is a primary color.

* * *

Tasia had no interest in going into the palace just yet. She wanted to find her brother. Bastain knew Tam as well as she did, and he would want to know what had happened. When Jeril headed off toward the palace steps, Tasia slipped behind the line of carriages to avoid the adults in the area and made for the stable doors off to the right. Bastain had been working as one of the horse grooms since the spring. The family enjoyed the extra money; Tasia took more value in the gossip he would occasionally relate whenever he made it back to the Maze.

Today, however, she had her own news to impart, charged by the tension she felt in Jeril's posture as they paced up the hill through the city. Tasia noticed right away a different set to the painter's shoulders, a soldier's straightness to his spine. The man walked flexing his right hand repeatedly, like muscles moving in memory of other action. Even at twelve, Tasia had seen enough swordplay to recognize the latent skill. There was more to Master Sandre than first appeared. She wondered what his face looked like underneath his beard.

She ducked into the shadows of the stables to confront the smell of hay and horses and the sound of laughter. When her eyes adjusted, she noticed the laughter came from a stall toward the back. Curious, she followed the sound and found it came from two little toe-headed children half hidden in the hay. Two faces popped up at her approach. Tasia recognized Arryn and Ailen, the five-year old twins of King Donari and Queen Eleni.

"Hey!" piped Arryn. "You aren't Basty!"

"No speak, hide-n-seek!" chirped Ailen.

Tasia settled to her knees, infected by the children's humor and absolutely surprised to find them rolling about in stable hay.

"Of course I won't tell," she said. "And *Basty* as you call him, is my brother, and I am looking for him. Do you know where he is?"

Arryn rolled his eyes. "Not here, silly, since he's supposed to be looking for us."

"And we aren't supposed to tell during the game, silly-silly!" added Ailen, standing up and shaking straw from her hair. "If you are Basty's sissy, then your name must be Tasia."

"Yes, that is right. So he told you about me, did he?"

"Yes!" Arryn exclaimed. "He tells us things during riding lessons."

"About the Maze!" added Ailen.

"It sounds like the best place for hide and seek ever," Arryn finished. "We have to stay in the garden most times."

"So why are you here in the stables?"

Both children grinned mischeviously, and Tasia found herself drawn to them, remembering her own younger days and similar looks.

"Sometimes we make nurse tired," explained Arryn.

"And sometimes she naps with us," continued Ailen.

"And sometimes we don't sleep," Arryn went on.

"And that is when we come find Bastain," Ailen elaborated. "There are more places to hide here. We don't go outside the walls by ourselves, and mum and da don't mind. Besides, they are busy with the strange people today, so we had to make our own fun."

"And when no one is out riding, Basty has more time to play with us!"

"So quick, hide!" Ailen squeeked. "He should be here soon."

"Too late," a deeper voice intoned. "He's here and you two are caught!"

Tasia looked up to see her brother, an older, darker copy of herself, grinning down at them from over the stall divider. Despite his humored expression, Tasia immediately detected a tenseness knitting his brow. His smile turned to a frown when he recognized her.

"Tasia! What are you doing here? How'd you get past the gate guards?"

"I came with Sandre. He went in to try and see the king."

"Really? There seems a lot going on today. I've just come from the kitchens. That place is buzzing. And then these two snuck off from the maids again."

"Bastian," Tasia interrupted. "Tam's dead."

"What?"

"Sandre found him earlier, had his throat cut. Sandre thinks it might mean something, so he came straight away. I thought you should know."

Bastian joined them in their stall, slumping down against the slats, face stricken and a tear starting in one eye. The twins must have noted the sudden change in the moment, for they came and sat on either side of him.

"Why?" Bastain whispered. "He never did anything to anyone."

"Sandre seems to have taken it hard."

"And the painter has come? Even more strange."

"Basty, who is Tam," Ailen asked. "Why is he dead?"

"Quiet, Ailee," Arryn scolded. "Can't you tell they were friends?"

"Tam was a boatman's son," Tasia explained. "And, yes, he was our friend."

"Did he play hide and seek with you in the Maze?" Ailen persisted.

Bastain ruffled Ailen's hair, and Tasia took a moment to process the odd scene: two children from Pevana's slums sitting in the palace stables with the royal offspring, talking of death and innocent games.

There is a story here the old poet would have loved to tell.

"Yes," she said aloud. "He played with us from time to time, when we were younger."

"He taught me how to sail," Bastain mused. "I can't believe it."

"Like you teach us how to ride?" Arryn asked.

"Something like that, yes," Bastian answered. "He lived down in the boatsheds with his da." He fixed his eyes on Tasia. "Where?"

"Inside the wall, down from the gate, but Master Sandre thinks it was no accident."

Bastain sighed and suddenly looked far older than his still freckled fifteen years.

"What do you think, Tasia?" he asked in a voice bleak and tired sounding. "I've heard a few things up here, but you are closer to it."

Tasia hesitated. The twins looked at her expectantly, and Tasia saw intelligence there hidden before by play.

"I think Sandre is on to something," she answered. "He seemed angry and afraid. There have been weird things going on in the city. Some strange folk about, and not just the easterners. Poor Tam."

"You are both sad," Ailen asserted. "And we are sad that you are sad. Most times, when we are sad, nurse gets us a treat."

"And mummy tells us a story," Arryn added. "But we aren't good at stories yet."

"But we could ask Cook for a sweet roll!" This from Ailen, who so liked the idea that she jumped up ready to go at once.

Despite contradiction between news and play, Tasia found herself smiling at Ailen's comment.

"Maybe one day I will tell you a story," Tasia said, rising in turn.

"Are you good at stories?" Ailen asked, taking her hand. "Mummy is good at stories."

Arryn rose and took Tasia's other hand.

"Mummy is good," he agreed, "but Devyn is the best! Do you know him? He's from the Maze, too!"

"Every child of the Maze knows Devyn Ambrose," Bastain said, ushering them down toward the door. "And Tasia learned her first stories from him and the old poet Kembril Edri, too! Perhaps one day she will give us a tale, but right now I think we need to get you two back inside. If nurse finds you out here, given what Tasia has told us, she will be cross."

"Nurse is often cross," Ailen said. "And when she gets that way she visits Cook for a bun!"

"Which is why Nurse is so fat and cannot chase us like we want," Arryn added matter of factly.

"Yes," agreed Ailen, beginning to skip. "But at least she shares."

Arryn giggled. "Which is why we like making her cross!"

Tasia paced along, half in wonder, half in awe. She looked a question over her shoulder.

"That is just the way they are," her brother answered. "You can see how interesting things have been up here. Different, in every way. You might want to tuck in your shirt, little prince!" he said, directing his words at Arryn. "The less upset for Nurse the better, sweet buns or no!" He caught Tasia's eye again. "Once we get them back where they belong, we will see if we can find Sandre. We need answers."

They exited the stables, turned right and cut back along the building to another gate that opened to the kitchen garden. Then it was up a row between pole beans and lettuce to a door that led to the ovens.

The kitchen bustled with activity. Apparently, the sight of the royal twins, dirty and disheveled, escorted by the stableboy, was a commonplace occurrence. No one paid them much mind, not even when Ailen and Arryn each grabbed several buns from a basket. The twins shared, and the four of them passed on to the hall that ran alongside the main hall. Tasia walked wide-eyed and intimidated despite the pressure of the little princess's hand in hers and the warmth of the bun. She had heard tales from Bastain about the palace and its clean, quiet halls, well-lit rooms, and the art that graced the walls, but tales paled compared to seeing all of it in person.

"Let's find Nurse," Bastain said, indicating the stairs that led up to the second floor and the royal apartments. Once they reached the rooms where the twins slept, they still had not encountered anyone of significance. Bastain left them at the door.

"Tasia, stay with them. I will go find Cryso. It's a little odd not having anyone in this wing."

"But I'm not supposed to be here!" Tasia retorted. "You're going to get me whipped!"

"You grew up getting into places where you weren't supposed to be. This is no different. Besides, you know the queen. Eleni has better sense. Just keep them from running off. I won't be long."

"I heard Nurse say something about the west wing for the visitors talking with our father," Arryn said. "Maybe that's where they are."

"But where is Nurse, then?"

"Maybe she's helping them! Or still asleep!" chirped Ailen. "Could we have a story while we wait?"

Tasia settled both children on the bed. She sought for a suitable tale while the twins grinned at her expectantly. The whole episode seemed unreal to her, but there she was, and if nothing else, her life had taught her to make the most of the moment presented. She thought about poor Tam and how he had loved the sea.

"Right," she said finally. "A story. Now, I might not be as good as your mother the queen, but this is one of my favorites from when Old Kembril was alive. This is the story of the lost fisherman.

"Once upon a time when the hills were young and Pevana was still just a small place with no walls, towers or gates, the people made their living casting their nets in the waters of the bay hunting fish."

"No walls?" asked Ailen.

"No gates?" added Arryn. "But—"

"Do you want a story or not? Don't interrupt the storyteller. I'm sure your mother has told you about that already."

"We're sorry, Tasia," Arryn soothed. "We promise."

Tasia gave them both her best twelve-year old squint before continuing.

"So, the best of the fisherman was named Ollen. He was always the first one out every day, would always go the farthest out to fish the deeper water, and was always the last to return to shore. He never failed to fill his boat to the gunnels, and when he sent a weighted line to the deeps, he always caught a big one for the market. Folk respected and praised him for his skill and success. At first, he ignored them, but over time he grew proud and would sniff at how his fellow fishermen would fear the sea. He fashioned himself a leader of the fleet and took to criticizing others. He boasted the sea no longer held any secrets for him and laughed at those who still feared it.

And folk accepted his ways because of his success, saying, 'Ollen's words may seem harsh, but look, he has shown us new ways to fish and many of us have increased our catch!'"

'But he is vain and sneering,' said others. 'He paints eyes on his boat and laughs at our scabby craft.'

'His sails catch the same winds as ours,' still others protested. 'His oars dip the same waters. So he is proud, perhaps we all should be so.'

And talk like that ran up and down the beach and especially under the rafters of the town's one tavern until one day an old woman put them all to silence, cackling from her seat near the fire.

'It's a fool that puts aside his better sense for pride,' said she. 'And fools are those that call such men their betters. Ollen will find there are secrets yet waiting for him beneath the waves. Remember: the sea is deepest in the dark.'

Ollen laughed when folk told him of the old woman's prophecy. He continued to fish longer and further out and to have more success than all the others, and his pride grew with his prosperity. And then one day he decided to go as far out as he could, leaving the other boats far behind, going so far out that he even lost sight of the land itself. He went out to where the waves acted different. Instead of the small foam-makers close in, he rode the great swells that rolled like the earth breathing, his boat a small dot of life on the emptiness.

He fished until his boat was almost full, and all that remained were the two lines he set deep, deep into the sea. He hauled in the first one: empty. He hauled on the second one and halfway up he felt a tug, and then a second. He felt the line tense, hold, and then something pulled, pulled so strong that the line cut his hand before he could let it loose. The line ran out like a river in spate. He had to tie the end off to keep from losing all of it and once he did whatever was on the other end of the line began pulling the boat!"

"Pulling the boat?" gasped Ailen. "I've never seen a fish big enough to do that."

"Ah, but that's the thing, you see," Tasia said, and she pitched her voice just so to bring them in the way she remembered Kembril doing when she was little. A small pause, a questioning look, and the thing was done. "It wasn't a fish."

The children stared at her wide-eyed.

"Ollen pulled on the line, while whatever he had hooked dragged his boat along further out to sea. Measure by measure, he brought the line in. His hands ached, his shoulders burned, but eventually he could see what it was he had caught. And no, it was not a fish, nor a whale. What Ollen had on the end of his line was a great turtle as big as the boat it pulled."

"What did Ollen do then?" Arryn asked.

"He took his knife and placed the blade beneath the turtle's jaw and prepared to finish it, but then something amazing happened; the turtle spoke to him."

"Really?" gushed Ailen. "My dolls talk to me all the time. Nurse says I'm just making it up, but I know better."

"Most children do," Tasia agreed. "And sometimes I wonder what would happen if more adults listened to their old toys…" She let the thought slip to silence.

"What did the turtle say?" Arryn asked, touching her forearm. "I want to know!"

Tasia gave him a hug and a smile. She went on.

"The turtle fixed one great, dark eye on Ollen and said, 'Please do not take my life, Ollen, of fisherman greatest and wisest.' Ollen froze, amazed to hear the turtle speak, for its voice sounded like the tolling of a great bell rung from a distant tower. It washed over Ollen like water sluicing by the prow of his boat. He took away the knife.

'How is it that you can speak?' he asked, holding fast the line that held the hook. 'I have caught many creatures of the deep and none of them have ever spoken before.'

'Perhaps in your pride you have lost the power to hear,' said the turtle, 'for the world speaks, fisherman, in many voices.'

'Absurd,' Ollen scoffed, and brandished his blade. 'Here is the only thing that talks.'

'And it has power,' agreed the turtle. 'And serves man well in its limited purpose, but know, Ollen, greatest of fisherman, that with each mindless cut the answers to the world's questions recede further and further.'

'What do you mean?' Ollen asked.

'Remember when you were a child, how the waves would whisper when they spent themselves on the shore? You heard it then.'

'Yes,' Ollen replied. 'I did hear, but that was long ago. I have learned the sea's secrets since then.'

'Oh, have you?' mocked the turtle. 'Such pride you have, man. And yet, even now I can see you doubt yourself, speaking to me rather than taking my life. Perhaps you might still come to understand.'

'Understand what?' Ollen asked. And in truth he no longer wanted to kill the turtle. He sensed something of the magic he had once known as a child pacing the shore, listening to the waves rise and recede. He floated on the edge of something…part of the mystery he had boasted knowledge of.

'That with every taking there must be a giving,' the turtle answered. 'And that taking from pride alone limits the giving. And if all a man does is take without thought, then there will come a time when his nets will surface empty and the world will remove itself from his ken. Take pride in your skills, Ollen, greatest of fisherman, but always remember the sea holds mysteries man will never understand. To think otherwise is to risk the rogue wave that will take you and drown you in the deeps.'

And when the turtle finished speaking it arched its great neck, twisted around and snapped the line just below Ollen's fingers. Ollen fell back in sudden fear, nearly upsetting his boat. When he recovered himself, he looked over the side, but the turtle was gone, descended with its answers back into the depths. Nothing showed on the surface around. Ollen was alone with his thoughts and the westering sun."

"And such thoughts he had," Tasia stressed, warming to her finish. "For as he raised his sail to catch the breeze and follow the sun back to Pevana's beach, he considered what the great turtle told him. He felt certain the goddess Renia spoke to him through the turtle. For the first time since he was a child, wonder filled him and he had to grasp his boat's tiller with both hands to stop his quivering. He rode the great swells homeward abashed and humbled, aware at the same time of his power and his weakness, and he never boasted of his skills ever again. And so it was that Renia found a way to bring conscience to the mind of man. For you see, the turtle was actually Minuet, and the words she spoke to Ollen were Renia's thoughts."

Both children stared, silent and round-eyed.

"You talk like mamma," breathed Ailen. "Only better."

Tasia sat back, stunned and pleased by the praise. Just then the sound of rushing feet pounded down the hall outside the chamber. The door burst open to reveal the queen followed by a red-faced, plump older woman.

"Mummy!" Arryn shouted.

"Nurse!" added Ailen. "We are having stories!"

Tasia scuttled to the edge of the bed. The glamour from her story quickly fading to unease by the sudden intrusion. She felt herself exposed and out of place.

"There you are!" the queen said, advancing to the foot of the bed. "And you've been in the stables again, haven't you? Children, this will not do! And, Tasia, is that you? How did you come here?"

"I, I came with Master Sandre," Tasia stuttered. "And I went to find my brother to tell him about Tam. You remember him? The Chandler's son? Master Sandre found his body down by the harbor wall. Someone had cut his throat." At those last words, her own throat constricted, and she had to blink back tears.

The queen's expression softened. "Ah, I see," she said. "And I can guess some of the rest. There has been cruel mischief of late. Say no more, child. I will get the rest from Sandre later."

Nurse came closer, plucked a stray piece of hay from behind Arryn's ear.

"I am so sorry, my queen," she gushed. "I only left them for a moment to help Cryso, and when I returned they'd slipped away. I'm afraid I can't keep up with them alone anymore."

"Not to worry, Manda. No harm done. They are willful. And yet—" She paused, looked appraisingly at Tasia. "Stories?"

"Yes!" Ailen interjected. "Tasia told us a story about the proud fisherman and a talking turtle!"

"Really?" The queen raised a brow. "Talking turtles?"

"And Renia and Minuet!" added Arryn.

"I see," said the queen, breaking out into a genuine smile. "Manda, I think I might have a solution to your problem. Tasia's brother already works here in the stables. Perhaps we should offer her a position in the palace as well."

"Another Maze-child?"

"Never under estimate the Maze-born, Manda. I have some experience of the place, you know."

"Yes, my queen."

Eleni turned to face Tasia. "So, I think you can see what a pair these two are. Nurse Manda could use some help. I'm sure Gania could spare you, yes? If you wish, you could come and help Nurse with the twins. If your mother agrees, you might stay. I might find other things for you to do. Stories. How would you like access to more?"

Tasia had to fight down the urge to pinch herself. Coming so hard on the heels of her ill news about Tam, the queen's offer felt like a reprieve. Part of her felt guilt for the opportunity while Tam's promise had been taken away from him so sudden and final, and yet the greater part of her turned away from the darkness for the chance at light.

There were books in the palace, stories, the queen's own collection. Her words with Jeril came back to her, haunting in their clarity. This was her chance. She went along with Jeril that afternoon out of fear and remorse for Tam's death only to be handed a pathway to joy. She existed in two emotions at once, speechless. To one born to the dust and rumble of the Maze, the prospect of ease and achieving a heart's desire seemed a contradiction that defied her precocious vocabulary to explain.

She just nodded her head and gave what she hoped was a proper curtsey. The twins understood at least, for they both started cheering and jumping on the bed. For a moment all was chaos and fun before the nurse and their mother could calm them down. Tasia took her opportunity to leave.

"I should probably find Jeril," she said, moving to the door.

"I left him with the king, child, they might not be done," the queen said, hoisting Ailen to her hip like any other ordinary Pevanese mother. "Wait by the entry if you want, but make sure to scuttle home and see what your mother thinks of my offer. In fact, be sure to wait there before you leave. I'll jot down a note for her so she won't think you're making it up."

"No fibs!" popped Ailen.

"Then why are you so good at it, Ails?" laughed her mother. "Manda, why don't you see about that stable dust on Arryn. Ailen can help me write that note." She smiled at Tasia. "You will come and help us, yes?"

"Yes, please come!" Ailen urged.

"Please, please, please?" added Arryn.

Tasia did not need to pinch herself then. It was real.

"Yes, I will gladly come, and thank you, thank you Queen Eleni."

She floated down the hall only half-aware that her feet still made contact with the carpet.

Chapter 14: Two Suitors

When Grayce returned to Sandre's the next afternoon, she found a handful of kids waiting at the door. With Jeril absent, she sent them on their way. As the children trundled off, Jeril arrived sitting in the back of the royal carriage, accompanied by palace guards. He apologized for his absence, then rushed upstairs and ransacked his storage closets and packed up most of his favorite brushes, a sheath of unstretched canvases and a boxful of the ready mixed paints as the guards carried his one large chest down to the waiting cart.

"I've left enough of the dry for you to replace those," he said as he headed off to his bedroom. Grayce followed in growing consternation to lean against the door frame as he bustled about.

"I'm to stay up the hill," he explained. "Until these times ease back, I'm sure you've heard well-gossip, the king thinks I might be in danger—or perhaps 'a' danger to those who truck with me."

His tone disturbed her further. "You, a danger? I don't understand."

He paused in stuffing some shirts into a bag and met her eyes with a somber expression.

"I haven't time to tell you everything, Grayce. Too many lies for a short story. I am afraid you will have to trust me when I say you are probably better off without me. Besides," and he now flashed her one of his most sardonic smiles, "You and Devyn need some time and space. No time like now, and this is a good place."

A cryptic warning followed by an intimacy did nothing to dispel her confusion.

"Me and Devyn? You presume—"

"Oh stop it, girl" Jeril interrupted. "I am a painter, despite all the other tripe in my personal baggage, and I have trained myself to see things. You need some time and space."

He finished shoving the rest of his clothes in the bag, hefted it to his shoulder, and moved to the door, reaching out with his left to lightly brush her hair before turning to the stairs. The casual, paternal touch surprised her, and Grayce suddenly realized how much she had come to regard Jeril with his wild hair, creative intensity, and patient kindness.

"You've been so kind to me."

Jeril's smile faded. "Grayce, we may see dark days soon. I wish I could be more kind and say don't worry, but you have seen enough to know how evil flows. Rely on Devyn. He's a good man, child, and good for you, I think. Good bye for now. Take care."

He stumped down the stairs and out to the waiting carriage. Grayce followed to close the door reluctantly behind him. For a moment she sat at the kitchen table and lay her head on her folded arms trying to process the sudden change in the routines of her world. She missed Jeril already, tried sifting the truth of his comment about Devyn but failed. She sat there immobilized until Angel hopped up and head butted her back to herself.

"Ah, Angel girl! At least he left me you. And this place." She lifted her head at the thought. The light in the room changed as though a cloud had cleared the mid-day sun above. She had grown too used to shadows. The light let her see now with new eyes. She idly stroked Angel into a full-throated, contented rumble and contemplated the possibilities. She heard a real warning in his words, but Jeril's surprise gift felt like a reprieve. A place to call her own. Life called her here. She had work at The Cup. Later, she wanted to sketch the activity around the communal well in the square just up from the Harbor Gate. And Devyn was due to return soon, perhaps even today. Maybe she could capture him in her sketch as he came through the gate. Because of Jeril, anything was possible. She gathered up her things, left milk for Angel, and left. Locking the door this time felt different.

Mine, for now.

* * *

The news of Tam's death made the rounds quickly. Folk talked it up from the harbor to the Land Gate; it served as the main topic of discussion at *The Golden Cup* during that evening's trade and delivered answers for Grayce to her questions about Jeril's behavior.

The boy's death seemed to hit folk hard. Normally, Grayce and Sanya had to spend half their time fending off advances, but not last night. The night passed subdued and ended early. Were it not for the reason, she would have called the experience pleasant.

Well, she would have if Reith Simson had chosen to stay away. He flounced his detestable self into a stool at the bar pretty late in the evening. At the time, Saymon had been busy in the kitchen, forcing Grayce to serve him.

163

He gave her his best smile when she slid over his requested glass of red.

"You match the color of this," he said, raising the glass in toast, "and make a much more attractive complement than old Saymon. Thank you."

"You're welcome, for the wine," Grayce retorted. The man repelled her, and yet he purchased her works in apparent good faith. "And only the wine. You're making it a habit, coming in here. Not what I would expect from a cleric."

Reith's smile deepened; his pleasure in the give and take obvious.

"We are neither a mendicant nor a celibate order, Mistress Stonesmith. And I am from Trenaran stock, myself." He sniggered at his own wit. "And we are not immune to passion."

"Passion is it?" Grayce wiped down the counter, trying to clear away the stain of both wine and words. The moment transported her back to Gallina and the nightly battles between herself and Earvyn Pickson.

"As I said to you before," Reith went on. "I intend to correct my earlier behavior towards you. You have talent. People like your shapes. I have placed the piece I bought earlier in my office and in the vestry. You should hear the comments. Perhaps you should come by and see for yourself?"

"I appreciate the trade, Simson, but that is all. Not a believer, thank you."

"Every man is free to choose; a nice result of our good king's policy, don't you think? And, please, I'm not trying to convert you."

"Really, what are trying to do then?"

"Why, interest you, of course."

Thankfully, a tipped pitcher at one of the back booths took her away from the bar. She felt his eyes on her as she moved about the common room dealing with spills and crockery. She saw him out of the corner of her eye finish his wine and leave, pointedly ignoring his jaunty wave meant for her.

Between that episode and the somber talk at the tables, she went to her bed that night thoroughly depressed.

Sunshine the next day and Angel's ardent attention helped smooth away the unease. She missed Jeril's critical presence. Of all the men connected to her life, he was the only one who did not spark her innate caution. Now he was gone and Tasia, also strangely absent. She made herself a cup of tea and watched Angel take care of a plateful of chicken pieces. A boy bringing a basket of buns from Gania brought the news Tasia had taken service in the palace. No one had word or sight of Devyn.

Grayce liked being alone to create, but this was going too far. Still, Jeril's note gave her the run of the place, so she decided to take advantage of it.

She went back up stairs to the studio and set herself up for a day with pad, pens, brushes, and paint. She stretched a canvas and set up the easel to catch the mid-morning sun. She took up her drawing of Devyn. Thinking about him just then brought a small catch to her thoughts. He created turmoil in her head; the fear of closeness. Men had cost her too much for trust. And yet here she was in a big, sprawling city beset by two. Reith enriched her, but she had drawn Devyn's face just from reading his words. She sensed they spoke the same language; he had hinted at such before he left the last time.

She ran her fingers along the firm jaw she had given him. She braced the drawing against a stack of books, took up her small charcoal pencil, and began laying down lines on the canvas. She sketched quickly, confidently, finding solace in the gestures to tamp down the unease that presented itself yesterday. She let her hand take over, caressing his face from the white, tactile surface, shaping the brow, giving it a hint of that sardonic humor she found so appealing yet confusing. He knew so much, saw something in her that she doubted really existed, made her feel…things.

She paused to mix her colors on Jeril's spare palette. She took up a brush, dipped it in pigment and let it hang over the canvas. It came to her then that once she began, she would paint a different path to her life. All her lines in Gallina, the whirls in the forest, the wandering sketches on Pevana's forgotten, blank spaces, all would pass into the realm of perspective.

Perspective changed everything.

She let the brush descend.

* * *

Devyn took in Pevana's skyline hungrily as his ship weathered the headland to prepare to tack into the calmer waters of the harbor. Ahead of them, outward bound with the last of the tide, a sleek Esdan galley made its

165

offing under oars toward the open sea. Devyn followed its crawling progress. Then the wind his own craft enjoyed reached the other. Oars were swiftly shipped with military precision and the great, red mainsail shaken out. It rode the swell eastward, gaining pace even as Devyn's galley slowed, tiller thrown over to recapture the wind and make their last reach.

Devyn turned his gaze shoreward. The march of stone and wall up to the towers on the hill, the hint of the Maze in its place to the west and south spoke to him as it never had before. Perhaps the news and fear he had to report to the king tinctured his response and set him adrift between emotions even as men took in the sail and applied oars to cross the final distance to the pier and the space flagged for them. He brought change and supposition with him, dangers imminent if he was any decent judge of the signs. He had news of other Esdan ships in the north.

And yet he searched the city scape with other eyes as well. Duty required a visit to the palace, but he contemplated a visit to Grayce Stonesmith after. During his forced idleness aboard ship on the journey south, his thoughts often swung between those two extremes. Her lines claimed him; he admitted it to himself and to her, somewhat, in the lines of verse he left behind. However, duty took him down troubling thought paths that increasingly led him away from words and matters of the heart. It came to him then that his predecessor, Senden Arolli, must have been a lonely man.

He leaped the final yard to the pier as men took hold of lines thrown from the deck to bring the galley in. He gave orders for his limited baggage to follow him and set off on foot in through the Harbor Gate and up the hill. People tried to greet him, but he was too deeply recessed into his thoughts to respond. He did pause at the citadel gates to scrutinize the guards stationed there. There were more of them and on edge; doubtless a response to the ship disappearing over the horizon. He expected to give and receive news that morning.

Action whirled about the palace courtyard. He spied young Bastain exercising one of the mounts in the ring adjacent to the stables. He climbed the palace steps and passed into the shadowed hall intent on heading for his rooms to clean up and await King Donari's pleasure.

He hustled up the side stairs and down the hall to his rooms. Just as he reached his door, Cryso and another man turned the corner and came toward him. Devyn paused in the act of turning the knob when he recognized Cryso's companion: Jeril Sandre.

"Ah, Master Ambrose is returned!" Cryso announced cheerfully. "Have you sent word to the king?"

"Not yet. I wanted to make sure he was alone first. Master Sandre, it is good to see you again."

"And you, Devyn," he responded, and yet even in the brief greeting Devyn detected a note of caution.

"I will go directly to check on him, sir," Cryso said decorously. "I was just having a quiet word with Lord Tandori here."

"Excuse me?" Devyn asked, but Cryso ignored the question and walked off.

"There have been a few *changes* since you've been away," he said, shooting a half-irritated, half-sheepish look at Cryso's back.

"*Lord Tandori?*"

"I can explain."

"Perhaps you should. My rooms?"

"Actually, I'm right next door to you."

Devyn opened the door and ushered the other man inside and listened in growing

sorrow and disgust as Jeril related the real events and connections that had brought him to the palace. So much of the painter's story echoed his own appreciations. When Jeril finished, Devyn gave an exasperated sigh.

"Poor Tam! Renia's Grace, this is a bad time for telling the truth, Jeril."

The painter grimaced. "I know that, and I'm sorry—more than you can know. I hoped to disappear into a new life here. This is home to me now, but I did offer to trade myself to the Esdans if it would help."

"And Donari refused."

That brought a smile. "I admire how well all of you seem to know each other in this city. This truly is a special place. Yes, he refused. Devyn, this is not going to go well."

"I agree, given what I saw in the north, but I will keep my news to myself until I report. I assume that Esdan ship leaving means things went ill?"

"That is correct."

Devyn weighed the unspoken weight of Jeril's words. There was much to unpack here. Changes in identity. Actions taken. Threats north, south and now here in the center.

"And you are placed here for your safety. A sad welcome. Who will look after your house and cat?"

That brought a grin to the painter's face, a more relaxed, good humored expression bereft of old lies or policy; a grin that hinted at mirth. "I left Grayce a note to make free of the place. Good thing, too, for word has it that Tasia now attends the queen by helping out with the twins."

"You are full of news! I wonder how that will work out? As for Grayce, your lack of a beard gave you away, Jeril. Not fair."

"So you deny interest? Then why do I see you with her every time your tasks bring you back to the city?"

"You know better. I am interested, very, but these *tasks* you refer to present persistent obstacles. Plus, the girl is still skittish around me."

"She had a rough time of it, you know, before she made her way here."

"I heard some of it, but I think there's more." Devyn snorted and pointed a finger at the painter. "Just like there seems more to you than at first. What has she told you?"

"Nothing more than what I asked about."

"Explain."

Jeril leaned back, if anything, the sarcasm in his expression deepened.

"I've learned not to think about my own past, why should I force others to reveal theirs? Grayce is a wild talent learning to control her lines. I think that wildness is partly what snared you. If I were a younger man, I might begrudge you the tangle."

Devyn sighed and lay back on the bedding, staring up at the decorated ceiling. A representation of Minuet of the Arrows hunting a basilisk marched across the expanse. Devyn focused on the face of Renia's familiar and saw there a similarity with the look he often caught in Grayce: firm brow, a piercing, determined look, focused, attentive yet passionate, raw but with potential for an earthy softness—something almost tangible for the mortal's ken.

"It is a tangle," he agreed finally. "Women have always intrigued me, but none have caught me like Grayce. I wish I were more like Talyior. He was always the romantic."

"You need to tell her directly. You are a poet, words come easily for you!"

"Most of the time," Devyn said. "But not with her. Jeril, between what both of us have *not* been speaking of, I think something is soon to happen. I have felt that way since seeing Talyior in Desopolis. If things come to an end, what good starting?"

Devyn watched a frown deepen on the painter's brow. The man's eyes greyed and his expression grew thoughtful.

"Or why waste any more time?" he said, almost wistfully. "Devyn Ambrose, I've spent most of my life running from my past in some way or another. I left good memories burned and dead back in Piling. I think that is why I am here now, unmasked, and wanting. You owe the girl and yourself some truth. At least," he finished humbly, "that is how I see it."

Devyn let the moment fall to silence. Jeril's comments pointed Devyn right back to Kembril Edri. The old poet's lesson to that younger, more reckless Devyn all urged truth as an ultimate goal; a noble pursuit worthy of a noble mind. Had he changed so much since then that he could forget? A tear hinted at forming in his eye, but he blinked it away as he swung his feet to the floor and rose.

A knock on his door forestalled futher comment. Cryso stuck his head in, acknowledged Jeril in his chair, and nodded.

"Good," he said. "You are both still here. The king is now free and will see both of you in his study. Lord Tandori, if you please?"

Devyn and Jeril followed Cryso out and down the hall.

"This *Lord Tandori* stuff will take some getting used to," Devyn groused.

"No easier for me," Jeril murmured out of the side of his mouth. "I much preferred my painter's poverty."

"Well, that's all over now," Devyn responded. "If Donari wants you there with us when I report my northern news, then you will have to play the lord whether you like it or not!"

* * *

"So you and Hallan agree that something is brewing north of us?"

Devyn paused before answering the king's question. Donari sat across from Jeril and himself, fingers pressed tips and thumbs into an imprecise triangle. His face bore that tight, suppressed-anger look Devyn had come to recognize since Donari accepted the crown. He recalled a different look years ago; humor balanced by cynicism, an ironic projection that refused to take things too seriously while at the same time working just beneath the surface to do just that.

Devyn remembered that older Donari fondly. Both of them had grown up, and grown too serious. Life and power were equally unfair in that regard. Devyn's life had actually prepared him to take on responsibility. Donari's manner allowed him to accept power's mantel without losing his humanity. Devyn decided both results Goddess gifted.

"Absolutely, sire," he said, taking a deep breath. He had spoken at length of his northern experiences and Hallan's assessment; the king and Jeril listening intently. Occasionally, Donari shot out a question or asked for clarification, but Devyn made sure to be thorough. "He faces growing numbers of refugees on the coast and in the hills above Hallar Port, but the most telling bit came on my way home. A storm kept me port-bound for three days. We sailed by a number of galleys wrecked on the rocks off Emdar. I recognized the devices, sire, Esdan. I think the storm may have stunted an action of some sort. I didn't tarry in the area out of fear there might be others lurking about or coming to investigate the wreckage."

"That might explain some of the blunt talk from our Esdan guests these last few days. They must not know what happened."

"But you can be sure they knew of that force's sailing, sire," Jeril interjected. "My father always knew how all the connected parts moved. That was key to his success. Jorian functions the same."

"You say this despite an absence of twenty years?"

"I say it because of those twenty years," Jeril answered. "Jorian was precise even as a youth. I see the same quality in all these bits and pieces of news we have received. I agree with Devyn; there is too much presence and movement to ignore any longer."

"Hallan is assembling troops, sire," Devyn added. "He thinks we may see trouble along the coast…and perhaps inland. He doesn't trust the river…or the highlands. He fears getting cut off from the bridge at Lomillar, so he has been setting up camps on the southern shore west from the mouth. He wants to be able to move at need."

Donari's eyes flared. He stood and began pacing, flexing his hands intently. The King's aggitation sent a tingle of fear iching along Devyn's spine up to the back of his head where it settled, throbbing, like the first pangs of a wine induced hangover.

"I'm not sure I have the men or ships to spare, that's the pinch of it," Donari muttered, more to himself than the two men watching and listening. "Ill report from the southern coast, flames in the north, ships wrecked where they should not be. This is preposterous! The Esdans sense our weakness. Piecen acted like a cat waiting to pounce. Eleni has always doubted, but I didn't pay attention." He stopped pacing, took a deep breath, expelled it forcibly, and faced them, his expression now direct, controlled. "I wonder how long we have before worse besets us? Prior to Jeril's revelation, the Esdan demands were pretty smug. He expects us to accept client status under Jorian's *protection* and become a vassal state of the empire, gentleman."

"And if you reject?"

"Reject?" Donari asked, amused in the moment. "Already done, Devyn. Don't pretend surprise. You know me better. I did not take this crown to doff it at another's request. I've always enjoyed my freedom too much to accept servitude."

"I suspect Tacidus would like to pull the walls down on us," Jeril murmured from his chair.

The comment drew a sardonic chuckle from the king. "He looked like he wanted a go at you yesterday when you showed up. Perhaps you'll get your chance and soon."

"Then we are agreed?" asked Devyn. "War?"

"No question." Donari stood and turned to look at a map tacked to the wall behind his desk. "I can see it now. We have grown too much to be usefully ignored. Too prosperous by half. Our ships pushing east and south. Before, we were a collection of squabbling city-states with a rough northern, inland polity. Now Pevana sits on her hill above the sea, capital of a realm knit by road and sea-lanes. They test our flanks and distract us with words here in our center. You heard the Esdan, Jeril. 'There will be changes,' he said. We must prepare."

Devyn heard the resolve in Donari's voice and knew what the expression must have cost him. Jeril must have heard something similar, for he shifted forward in his chair.

"I'm sorry, sire," the painter whispered, "for this distress."

Donari sent a quick glance at the painter and then to him. "Nonsense, both of you. New service and old have worth alike here. The question now is what am I to do?"

"Prepare the people. They can find safety in the hills," Devyn offered.

"A panic hurts us worse there, I think," Donari responded. "And yet quiet word given to a trusted few to spread might serve us if it comes to a fight. When. Rather."

"And that is the sick beauty of the Esdan strategy, sire," Jeril asserted. "They force you to defend everything, then strike you where it hurts most."

Donari stared anew at the map with a contemplative frowning concentration. A silence developed. Then he sighed and a ghost of a smile teased over his face.

"It seems I have been worked. How ironic, in the end. I used to congratulate myself on staying a step ahead of my enemies. 'Even kings can be worked' I said. And now here I am the victim of the same." He pushed away from the table. "But the horizon is not full of red sails yet. I will send word to Hallan. His lands will burn for it, as will Emdar. If he pulls back behind the Eloe, he would have space to blunt whatever attack comes. And if it is a diversion as you suggest, Jeril, then he might still be able to come to our aide overland."

"He might be over late, sire," Devyn averred.

"Yes, but we haven't the shipping in place to move masses. He would not abandon his folk anyway without a fight. If Jeril is correct, they will see the first blows. He might come to put out the fires of our defeat, but there it is. Risk. I will send word within the hour. Devyn, make your rounds after you've had a chance to refresh yourself. I will see the galleys out from their sheds. Spies or no, we need to act. This blow will come from the sea, so we will meet it first on the water and defend the walls if we have to."

All three moved toward the door.

"I thought we might have months, but I think we are down to days, gentlemen," Donari said, preceding them into the hallway outside his study. Tandori, look to your guards, please. Devyn, I will expect a meeting tonight after dark."

"Sire, I will do so," Devyn replied. "Plus, I have some personal business to attend to."

"What's that? Personal? What's her name? Be sure and look in on the children if you can. Arryn has been asking after you. See to your business, sir, but see it doesn't intrude on mine!"

"Sire!" Devyn protested, but Jeril's accompanying chuckle made him smile in turn.

"Don't tell me then," Donari joshed, waving them out. "I know I make demands of you, Dev. Take your hour, but return tonight. Eleni will need to record your news after the twins go down. You might be called upon for a story, you know."

"A royal command," Devyn responded.

"No!" Donari asserted. "Just a five-year old's and a father's wish. Good luck. See gentleman, all is not gloom. We cannot let it get the best of us. Until later."

* * *

Grayce made a last touch on a spot near Devyn's cheek, stepped back, and judged the painting finished at least until tomorrow when she would use the early light to check it again. Devyn had not returned for her sketch, but she had compensated herself with the painting.

She moved back, scrutinized the likeness and allowed herself a small, satisfied smile. Devyn's eyes stared back at her. The left, partially covered by a wild lock of hair, seemed to follow her when she shifted from side to side. The brow projected the shadowed humor she intended, and yet the hint of mirth in the lips conveyed a similar message to those dark eyes. As in real life, the work reflected Grayce's tenuous understanding of the subject. To her, Devyn was a contradiction of his parts, but when taken in sum, he loomed like knowledge hidden in words. She wondered if the effect would be the same to the casual viewer. She stood there, hugging herself against the cool sea breeze that pushed into the studio. She left the deck door open the last time she let Angel out. She rubbed goosebumps away and wondered if she would ever let him see it.

She scolded herself for being so sentimental about a man, but deeper down she knew that was a lie. With every brushstroke on the canvas during those last two sessions, she relived their entire association. Jeril was correct. Devyn was good for her. In his more-than-friendship he teased her back toward trust.

He had almost kissed her when he left on his last journey. She knew he wanted more, but she hesitated at the time. In a way, his absence helped avoid decision, and yet those eyes staring back at her made her realize how much she missed him. Her heart whispered *perhaps*, but caution still insisted *not yet*.

Angel startled her by leaping up onto the worktable and hissing at the stairs.

"Now what would you be scolding?" she asked, scooping the cat up and moving toward the stairs. "Let's go down and see what we can find for you." The cat remained tense as Grayce put her foot on the topmost step. When someone pounded on the front door, Angel twisted out of her grip, scratching Grayce's forearm in the process. Grayce froze at the sound, but the knocking continued, followed by a sound as from a handle turning. The door opened. She heard footsteps on the boards approaching the stairs, a shape stopped at their foot. Grayce took in the blond hair, deep, red cloak. She took a step back involuntarily.

Reith Simson raised his arrogant face and smiled benignly at her.

"There you are!" he said brightly. "I've missed you in the market these last few days, and duties kept me from the *Cup*. I thought to myself, how odd. She must be working on something, and then I remembered someone telling me where old Jeril Sandre lived. I took a chance, and here I am, come to see the fruits of your absence."

He did not wait for permission and fairly bounded up the stairs. Grayce retreated to stand beside Devyn's portrait. Somehow, the idea of Simson seeing the work disturbed her. She reached blindly for the cloth she normally used to cover it but missed. Simson reached the studio, took a deep breath of the paint-tinged air, and looked unnaturally pleased wth himself.

"Do you often barge in through closed doors?" Grayce asked, both angry and afraid.

"Only when they have stuff on the otherside of them I want," Simson answered, catching sight of the painting and moving closer to inspect it. "So what's this? Ah, I recognize the intrepid Devyn Ambrose!"

Grayce backed away as he stepped in front of the painting, appaled by the man's effrontery. His confidence and size intimidated her. Simson left her alone for the moment, however, as he gave the painting exaggerated attention.

"I can see why you've been absent from your usual haunts, my dear," Simson said, looking at her and back to the picture. "This is quite good and so different from your other stuff. Not sure I'm convinced the fellow is worth such attention. He seems to like poking about in the shadows too much for my tastes. I wonder what he thinks of it. Oh, that's right, he's gone, isn't he? And this is from memory? Truly impressive then!"

"What do you want?" Grayce tried to feign nonchalance by leaning against the table. She scratched a palm, nervous, wanted something to hold like a brush, and recalled another time and another brush and suppressed a shudder.

Oblivious or indifferent, Simson kept staring at the painting, but his words revealed everything else.

"I like keeping track of things I want to acquire," he murmured, cupping his chin in his hand and squinting. "Like Kings' spies, odd looking painters and talented young women," He turned to face her, looked her up and down speculatively, assessing, "with bewitching hair, like yours, compelling eyes, like yours, and a pleasing shape, again, like yours."

"I have no interest in you. You must know that."

Simson gestured to the painting. "That much is clear or else I, too, might have a likeness in oil loitering about up here. But no matter." He came closer. Grayce put up a hand reflexively against his chest. Part of her wanted to scream but doubted anyone would hear her. Simson had never given her the impression that he might force himself on her, but she had been wrong before.

"Don't touch me," she gasped. He stopped. Her hand was still pushing against his chest.

"But I haven't yet," he whispered, and this time his voice had that throaty rasp of desire. "You're the one touching me, and I don't mean just now," he added when she dropped her hand. "I was not lying about how you affect me, Grayce Stonesmith."

"I'm nobody to you, Simson."

"On the contrary," he replied, and then he did touch her, gently, with just a fingertip underneath her chin. "You might be a great deal to me. You, your friends, your work—all might come to hold real importance, but such things are beyond your interest, I'm sure."

"I have no idea what you are talking about." Grayce tried to move away, but Simson took hold of her arm. In the motion, his hand brushed lightly against her shirt. Grayce felt the pressure against her breast beneath the fabric as an indictment of her helplessness. Simson held her fast but not cruelly, brought his face close to hers.

"You can paint your Maze-boy as fine as you like," he whispered. "I'm better connected by far."

Grayce tried to slap him with her free hand, but he anticipated her, grabbing her wrist in mid-motion and hugging it against his chest. He held her in that caricature of an embrace and stared into her eyes.

"No, please," she breathed, leaning her face as far away as she could.

He bent his face to hers, brushed his lips against her cheek when she turned her face to avoid him. "Yes, *please*, is the word, isn't it, lady? For I could make you a lady and please you," he whispered in her ear. His words made her skin crawl. "There will come a time, maybe soon, when you will look for me. You will need me, want me, to save you." He kissed her forehead. Tears of fear started from her eyes. "And I will save you, Grayce Stonesmith…and have you."

He released her and moved to the stairs. "And then I will burn that painting," he said, once again bestowing on her that insidious, arrogant, cheerful smile. "Good day, mistress, I will call again, soon."

He stumped down the stairs, boots unnaturally loud and jaunty. Angel stuck her head out from under Jeril's favorite, over-stuffed chair and hissed at his disappearing head.

She did not move. The brief episode left her frozen. Her mind ran in a circle of horrorific images. Flames in Gallina, Pickson wheezing in her face, grabbing her, clothes tearing, Pickson's face replaced by Simson's, hands, breath, lips, ill promises and desperation. Tears streamed down her face. Not even Angel's inquisitive mewing and head bumps against her calf could break the spell. She lost time, trapped in lines of her own making, lines tied off by Simson's smug expectations. Vaguely, she grew aware of the pressure of Angel purring in sleep against her hip and a dull ache in her shoulders from holding herself up against the table.

Then faint, as from a distance, the sound of more footsteps on the stairs, quieter, stealthy and precise. She blinked, the portrait swam before her vision. She blinked again and the painting morphed into Devyn's face creased with worry.

"Grayce, what is it, what has happened?" His voice came to her like a summons. She felt his arms around her, holding her up. At once, all the suspended emotion left her like a held breath exhaled. She slumped, weeping into his embrace; all those earlier questions and indecisions forgotten in the relief of his sudden, unlooked for presence. She raised her arms, clasped him in turn, intently, taking in his smell and nearness and all the things from which her fears had kept her.

All the time he mouthed questions and calming words she failed to hear clearly. She raised her face to his, found his lips and kissed him, silencing his questions with the only answer possible.

* * *

Devyn gently eased himself out of the covers, taking care to leave Grayce deep in slumber. She sighed and rolled over. The move revealed her face still smudged with a bit of charcoal. Devyn perched on the edge of the bed and studied her features closely. Innocence in repose welled out from her; the scowl, so frequently a part of her countenance, completely absent. Her breath animated a strand of her hair fallen over her mouth, and in the tiny lock's movement Devyn saw the consummation of all the lines that he had been following since Gallina. Her intensity nearly over-awed him at first, but her insistence broke down his last barriers as well.

Their moment had been much more than physical. He wondered if new lines would now commence for both of them and if they would run together. He rose and moved to look at her representation of him and noticed right away the care and concern, the sum total of a life given wholly over to tasks other than personal, desires greater than those of the heart, a face, no, a soul in need of meaningful distraction.

Or commitment.

He ran a finger down the line she gave his chin. He had forgotten about the scar on his jaw. Even though he was still a young man, his life to that point had been a series of hurts healed over, small joys in words taken as he could find them, wounds of the body and challenges to certainty mixing in the flesh. He reached the same finger to his real face and smiled, reveling in how the muscles contracted under his touch; tangible mirth returned after a long absence. He looked at the drawing again; he might as well have been looking at a mirror. There, in the edges of the eyes, lurked the laughter he now felt welling up inside him.

"Girl," he whispered. "You've done me more justice than I deserve."

"So, I assume that means you like it?"

Devyn turned at the sound of her voice. Grayce had propped herself up on one arm, smoothing back her unruly hair with the other. Her appearance in that moment froze him. She looked a dream. He felt himself respond. She locked eyes with him then let them fall, a smile deepening on her face.

"No need, then," she chuckled. "But I think I meant the picture."

Devyn refused embarrassment. Returning to the bed, he accepted her embrace. He searched her eyes, kissed her then, deeply, slowly, as though tying off the ends of something, final, persistent and decisive.

"You make me nobler than I am," he said. He cupped her body close to his, felt her warmth, carressed her thigh lightly, as if it were flawless marble. In truth, perhaps that was so, for he understood now that every inch their bodies touched expressed truths his life heretofore denied him.

He served Donari and the realm, but Grayce had morphed into a reason to live within it.

"It is just a picture," she said, laying back on the pillows.

"And that mural of the Tree is just a mural, and the designs in the hills were just idle lines. But we both know, especially now, how otherwise it is, how *this* is. Part of me thinks I have taken advantage of you."

"As I recall, I kissed you first, and this is my bed, which I think I led you to. Well, at least it is until Jeril returns to claim it. He said for me to make use of the place for him." She pulled his face close. "Though I doubt he had this in mind."

"About *this*," Devyn murmured into her hair. "This I could like, very much, but why today. I have been gone, but as much as I hoped you missed me I did not, could not, expect this. The look on your face when I arrived, haunted, but by what?"

He felt her tense at the question, but rather than pull away she slipped her arms around him tightly and in a voice equally as tight she told him of her misadventures with Simson. As she spoke, her voice modulated, her grasp turned tender, and by the time she finished she lay against him spent, empty of the pent-up anger and fear that had perplexed her days. Beneath her words, Devyn heard the rest of her story: loss, fear, threat, uncertainty. He lived a similar life as a child. Like knew like. He kissed her forehead.

"We will have no more of Simson, you and I. He is a snake in need of skotching, and I have the blade for it."

"I do not want you fighting my battles for me."

"This is not your battle, Grayce. It is part of something older, bigger."

"Bigger? You have lost me. He wants my pictures and me, or so he said."

Devyn leaned away enough to stare into her eyes, considering the risks of telling her what he knew and decided on a half-measure.

"Wrong, girl. I have just found you. I want you safe. Even if that means you leave. I came home with half answers to many questions. Simson's boldness is a change. I cannot tell you what I mean by something *bigger*, at least not yet, but I will see to it he leaves us alone. There is a connection."

"How? You are so mysterious! And leave? Over Simson? He is a pest we can deal with."

"Yes, but if you had to leave because of threat or danger, then I would find you. Your lines have me, Grayce, always."

She narrowed her eyes. "You give hints. You can't nursemaid me."

"A pleasant thought."

"And a waste of the king's coin, and you know it."

"I think the king would understand."

"Why should he care?"

"Because he is a poet and understands love."

"Oh? So this is love, is it? I take you to bed and suddenly you are all plans and care and—"

Devyn shut her up with another kiss, long, passionate, a verse in touch.

"Yes, my dear," he said, pulling away at last. "It just might be. I feel like I have been following you and your path for a long time. In a way, I suppose I should thank Simson for making you turn around."

"I don't want to talk about him anymore," Grayce sighed, trailing a finger down his chest, and then further. Again, he felt his body respond. She gave a little snigger.

"Are you sure this isn't what you meant by bigger?"

"I was being serious."

"So am I."

"I meant what I said, Grayce. About—This time she stopped him by placing a finger against his lips.

"I know," she said. "And I think so, too."

Chapter 15War Winds

Tasia hunkered down behind a group of rose bushes, taking care to keep her clothes unsnagged in case she had to make a sudden move. She had the twins engaged in a desperate game of hide and seek in the palace garden. After coming to serve in the palace, Tasia and the royal children grew close. She attended their lessons, continued her own at the same time and served as an unofficial nanny to help relieve Eleni's maids for other duties. The queen's request initially left her a bit awestruck. New clothes, the run of the kitchens, a soft bed when she stayed at the palace, and almost daily interaction with the queen, and at times the king, might have overwhelmed a body. However, as a child of the Maze, and one who lived the changes attendant to Donari's reign, she quickly adjusted. She particularly liked having access to the queen's growing library.

She also liked not having to explain burning late-night candles to anyone. In fact, she fell asleep once reading in an over-stuffed chair and let her light melt down to a guttered-out pool of wax. Instead of punishment, she found a basket filled with candles and a sturdy, shapely holder. She suspected the queen had something to do with it. That just added to the mix of emotions she felt for Eleni. At times, close, a young mother in love with her children, her husband and her life. At other times a somewhat distant queen, poet, and practicing historian. For Tasia, she represented words and stories but with a difference; a hint of deeper substance she had yet to access. The effect reminded her of how she felt about some of Grayce Stonesmith's paintings. They held a tincture that always caught her off guard. As the days bled away, she served, played and learned, and counted herself fortunate.

She and Ailen both chose to hide among the plants while Arryn counted. She carefully moved a stalk to take the gate in view, expecting to see his little blond head come bouncing through. Instead of the prince, the king came attended by Devyn Ambrose. By the tone of their voices, Tasia guessed they were nearing the end of an intent discussion. She let the stalk return to its position and tried to make herself smaller, hoping Ailen would stick to the game and remain hidden.

As luck would have it, the two adults stopped right before her clump of rose bushes, and even in undertone, she made out their conversation.

"And I think there is something unsavory, sire. I've had concerns about him for some time now."

"Agreed, but you don't think your new association with Jeril's student has anything to do with it?"

"A little, perhaps, but this isn't jealousy. The man leaves an oil film whenever he bathes."

"And you think he is a threat to her?"

"Absolutely, but not just her. If it were just Grayce, I would find a pretext and contrive and accident or occasion. He is that sort of pest. I think it goes deeper, sire. Since my return, other things have connected. The Esdan's demands, the odd activity to our north and south, Simson's pressure on Grayce, to me it all connects."

"I have prepared as best I can for trouble without, but trouble within? That sect has been quiet these last years. I have heard no clear reports of ill doing except from you."

"I've had their establisments watched, my lord."

"More of your Maze-folk eyes and ears?"

Tasia let a smile steal over her face, for she was one of those Maze-folk. She knew exactly to what Devyn referred. His reference to Grayce as something more than a friend galvanized her attention the most, however. Of all the strangeness in her recent days, that was perhaps the strangest and yet the most fitting. In her view, they belonged together.

"Some of them have grown up watching for me since your crowning, sire," Devyn answered. "When I am in town I hear things. The list of oddities since the winter has grown long. And Jeril spoke of spies."

"And you are concerned enough to have me act inside the city?"

"The timing concerns me most. Simson and his lot have been more visible since our troubles started with Esda."

"And you have fears."

"I fear many things, sire, but I am not certain of any of them, yet. But I think—"

Arryn bursting through the gate cutting off Devyn's comment. The prince skipped down the path, his little voice piping.

"I have finished counting! Ready or not, here I come! Oh! Daddy, Devyn. I did not see you. Are you hiding? Ailen, Tasy! Come out and we will start again. Will you hide this time, father?

Tasia rose from behind her bushes, worked her way carefully around the thorns to stand beside Devyn. Across the path, a giggling Ailen joined them. The king swept up both of his children, his face alight with pleasure; the cares of the moment before submerged beneath a beaming smile.

"So we are playing at hide and seek are we?"

"Yes, but we have never used the garden before," Ailen answered. "I think it is the best spot."

"I'm sure," Donari agreed. "But you know the kitchen garden has lots of nooks and things and," he lowered his voice conspiratorially, "a secret gate."

"But mother and nurse said we were never to go out that way," Arryn asserted, plucking at a lock of his father's hair. "Besides, we have played there before and got dirty between the rows and had to take a bath."

"But you like baths!" Ailen teased, reaching over to poke a finger in her bother's ear.

"Not *all* the time. Hey, stop it."

"Both of you stop, and give me a kiss and settle down. Devyn and I were just talking, but I promise we will have a go later." He turned to Devyn. "We will finish this later as well. As for your concerns, see to them as best you can. Tasia, I will take them for now, if you do not mind. Let us go, you two."

He set both children down and took each one by the hand. For Tasia, the sight of her king acting like a normal parent came as a revelation. In her brief time in the royal family's presence, he had come off to her as a bit distant and intimidating, and yet, there he went, twirling his babies and babbling about stealing some sweet butter buns from the kitchen.

"Huh," she mused, half to herself. "I always thought kings never had any fun."

Devyn must have heard her, for he ruffled her hair. "For ordinary kings, that might be true, Tasia. But in my experience with powerful folk, I would say King Donari is far from ordinary. Surely, a budding poet of Pevana could see that?"

Tasia looked up at Devyn, who had a smile on his face as he watched the king pass through the door into the palace.

"What are you smiling about, Devyn?"

He looked at her then with a knowing look that reached back in time for both of them.

"I was remembering the last time I went out that particular garden gate," he said. "Served me a purpose once. Very useful. You might remember it for yourself, Tasia."

"You mean trouble, don't you? I am sorry. I overheard some of your talk with the king."

"I do. We all might need to practice our hiding one day."

His tone hinted at alarm, but she pushed that aside in favor of what loomed uppermost from her eavesdropping.

"I am glad about you and Grayce."

His expression turned wry. "You caught that too, did you? You have been busy here no doubt, but yes. She and I. It has been, interesting, these last weeks."

"You need her; she needs you."

Her comment brought a frown. "How do you know this? Woman's ways?"

Now it was her turn to smile knowingly.

"Of course," she said. "But anyone could see you both were a little lost, and now you have found each other and all will be well."

"I hope you are right, Tasia. Renia's Grace, I hope you are right."

He left her at the garden gate with a decorous bow and moved off on his own designs. Tasia paused before following him. The cryptic moment teased her. She might be on the edge of a story deeper, more dangerous and yet at the same time more wondrous than she had ever heard or read before. Her curiosity urged her to follow him and find out more about that Reith Simson. She had shared some of Grayce's ill moments with the man. Her younger self intervened with thoughts of perhaps sharing one of those sweet butter buns. She headed for the kitchens.

He called me a poet!

She pilfered several of the pastries from the basket Cook had set on a side-table and made her way out to the Citadel gate tower. This was one of her favorite places because from its summit she could see the entirety of Pevana's valley from the hills west to the sea out beyond the headland. She climbed up into one of the crenallations to munch her treats, sea breeze teasing her hair, mid-morning sun shining down on her world.

Even as she savored the fruits of Cook's labor, she found her pleasure tempered by the notion of threats to her world; a fact with which, in truth, she had lived most of her life. The Maze-born always understood

184

the struggle. She recalled those dangerous days before Donari became king. The fires. The cross talk in the city squares.

Rieth Simson influenced those days, and Devyn, too, but in a good way because he helped end them. She took a bite out of the second bun and tried to bring it all to focus. At seven she fought to keep herself fed, took happiness in small measure as it came to her, mostly in the form of Kembril Edri's stories, and later, Devyn's. Now, at twelve, she had school to skip going to, royal responsibilities and near free range of the palace and the queen's books. She had come a long way from making mudpies out of the dust beneath the Tree.

She recalled a word she came across during one of her study sessions with Eleni: *potential.* Her life now had *potential.* The queen and Devyn saw something in her. She knew she wanted words. Maybe that was it. She teased her mind around the term. She was *potentially* a poet of Pevana. The idea oozed stickiness like a big bite from her bun; all that butter, sugar and bread coating her teeth and tongue, lingering even as she chewed and fought the over-ambitious chunk into something she could swallow. She decided that was the thing with ideas. One had to think them through, chew on them until one could take them in totally. The bigger the idea the longer the chew and the more care one had to take with the swallow. Big ideas had *potential;* they were dangerous. Maybe she was *potentially* dangerous. Devyn was in ways that went beyond the sword. She had something that suggested value, worth, pride, all those big things, but all of it lay still in the future. *Potential,* as she understood it, meant having to deal with hope. It meant surviving the dangers of the present to reach the promise of the future.

She took the last bite of her second bun, licked her fingers clean and scanned the view once more. Devyn always said everything connected in some way. One just had to look closely enough to see how. It came to her then that Pevana, center of a kingdom, ruled by an energetic king, also had potential. She was part of a big idea; one that was both dangerous and in danger. People like Rieth Simson threatened it from within, and, judging by what she overheard in the palace, other things threatened it from without. Like her, Pevana had to survive her present to reach the promise of her future.

Her skin chilled as the sun went behind a cloud. She looked seaward and saw dark shapes dotting the blue on the horizon.

Ships. Lots of them.

A bell sounded from the lighthouse on the headland. Others from the city answered, taking up the warning. Tasia scrambled down from her perch and took a last look at the big, dangerous idea bearing down on Pevana's bay before dashing off back to the palace.

* * *

Devyn checked the guards at the foot of the steps leading to the royal apartments. They assured him the king with twins in tow had gone in search of the queen for some family time. Devyn considered interrupting. The children's play left matters unresolved between them. Everything they discussed pointed towards action. He was uneasy and restless. As he placed a foot on the bottom step, Jeril Tandori walked up, bearing a blade hung at the hip.

"Tell me," Devyn asked. "Did you dye the beard? Every time I see you now, I cannot connect the ages. The blade actually makes you look younger."

Jeril grinned at the jest. "I found it helped me get along. And, as for the blade, if I am to be a burden on the palace for my protection, I figured I could add my own sword to the equation."

"I am sure the king will be relieved. As I recall, there was mention of finishing a canvas? Do you intend to use the tip to mix colors?"

"I might even use it as a pallete knife. I have many talents, you see."

"And as many names." Jeril's face clouded and Devyn quickly waved off the thrust. "Na, na, friend, that was a cut too close, my apologies. Esda fills my head these days, and your revelation only added to it. Donari and I were deep into it just now, but he broke it off before we could finish."

"Ill news?"

"A column along the coast, making for the borders of Hallar. Those wrecks I saw last month were just the start."

"Disturbing."

"You were right. Anything else strike your memories from home that I should know and pass on to the king?"

"If what you say is true, then I have rubbed the rust off this thing none too soon."

"I was just about to interrupt them upstairs. Perhaps you should come with me."

Devyn started to ascend the stairs.

"What was that?" Jeril asked, pausing a step below.

"What was what?" Devyn asked, but Jeril did not answer. He looked back over his shoulder, down the hall to the great doors, propped open to catch the breeze.

Through those doors Devyn heard, faint at first but swelling as others joined, the sounds of Pevana's bells tolling the alarm.

Devyn descended, shoving Jeril forward in the process.

"Bells, all of them. Come on."

He raced out through the palace doors and down the steps, making a beeline for the tower covering the citadel gate, Jeril huffing behind. He pounded up the ramp to the battlements, through the access doors and up the stairs to the top platform. He leaned through a crenellation, catching his breath and staring at the seaward reason for all the bells.

A floating phalanx of war galleys dotted the horizon. Devyn had never seen so many. Behind the armada, far to the south and east, dark clouds showed on the horizon. A great storm boiled there, forming vaporous columns reaching heavenward with a promise of violence; two events of disparate construction foreboding similar destruction. The sight gave him a slight chill despite the warmth of the afternoon. Activity in the boat sheds drew his attention shorward as crews slid Pevana's galleys into the surf. Jeril joined him, coughing. He spat once. Devyn could sense his frustration.

Devyn pointed. "Are those what I think they are?"

"Esdan, certainly, a long ways off yet, but soon we should be able to see the color of their sails. Esdan red. I have always tried to avoid using it."

"Glib? Now?"

Jeril spat again. "Sorry. Does Donari have more, as in many times more, of what I see heading out to the harbor mouth?"

Devyn glanced ruefully to the pitifully small squadron collecting in the harbor.

"No, not here, anyway. Donari has worked hard to replace the losses from Roderran's folly. The southern fiefs have each their number, as do the north. He has knit the realm together with peace, roads and trade, but work has only just begun on signal stations for communication. Geography works against us there."

Jeril grunted. "Piling was my home, but there were folk there who barely knew they had a king. Esda sees your prosperity and unity as a threat. You described those hulks from after that storm. I hazard there is a second move against Desopolis and the other cities."

A chill formed at the base of Devyn's neck. He pointed east. "And yet they still have enough to send that at us?"

"Empire, Devyn. Esda is," he paused, shaking his head, a sad expression dominating his shaven face, "vast," he finished with a sigh. "If my brother hadn't forced me to leave, I would have likely left anyway. Perhaps I needed a small canvas for my life."

Once again, Jeril's tone touched on a familiar pathos for Devyn. The bells continued their peel, the harbor walls now thronged with folk drawn to see if they could spot their fate approaching. Devyn considered the angle and decided they still had no idea beyond the general. In a way, he envied them their temporary ignorance. He had known what approached months ago and still found a way to lose himself in Grayce and her lines; not that he could have done anything to change what floated on the water off the coast.

"You say you are willing to fight for this life you have framed here," he said finally. "But what hope have we against such numbers? An army floats out there. Another marches against Hallar."

"I agree it looks grim," Jeril responded. He traced a finger along the mortar-line of the topmost level of stone. "Esda looks for a quick solution. Pevana is now the heart of the kingdom, a well-built and peopled heart; a place of strength and courage. I have seen it everywhere I look, Devyn, and that is worth defending."

"Of course, we all saw it coming. Now or months later makes no difference from what I see out there."

Jeril spat a third time. "I'm tired of running. I see no other choice. Will the people stay?"

Devyn scanned the harbor walls again. "Many will. And yet I think not all should."

As he spoke three riders, heralds with horns slung swordwise on their backs, rode out through the gate beneath them, each taking a different street and heading into the city.

"Well, there is part of your answer, painter. That should set things stirring." He thought of Grayce. She had come to Pevana, running from pain and found a life, found him. The thought of losing her struck him deep, and yet he would rather see her live than have to face what must come.

Voices in the courtyard shouted his name. He made out Donari's among them. Duty called, and yet he hesitated. "I need to get word to Grayce," he said, grabbing Jeril's arm. "If folk do go, she needs to go with them."

"If I know the girl at all, I do not think you will have much luck there," Jeril sniggered. "And from the sounds below, you will not have time anyway. But I might."

"But you heard the king. He wants you safe."

Jeril half drew his sword. "I am not defenseless, but I'll take his guards with me. I need a few more things from my house. I will put the word to her for you. Like as not, I'll be bringing her back here with me."

Jeril turned to go, but Devyn grabbed his arm again, locking eyes. "Convince her, Jeril, and tell her to leave me a line to follow."

Jeril smiled at the reference. "Oh yes," he murmured. "You two are well-matched. Like I said before, were I younger, I'd be jealous."

Before either of them could leave, the sound of horse hooves on cobblestones took their eyes downward. The king clattered down the slope followed by a squad of palace guards, some still shifting gear into place as they rode.

"Our king moves fast," Jeril commented, "But what does he hope to accomplish? Surely he won't sail?"

"Not without me," Devyn answered. "At least, I hope not. I would be mostly useless in a sea fight, and I know Donari gets seasick. The captains will be gathering at the shore. Perhaps he just goes to give final instructions. I know there have been discussions about such an eventuality, but this is hard on the heels of that false embassy."

Jeril spat again, heading for the stairs. "I would say those ships sailed just after that ambassador's last visit. My father's kind of move, and my brother was always a better pupil. Perhaps if I had paid more attention twenty years ago, I would not have been so outmaneuvered."

Devyn focused on Jeril's tone. "Regrets?" he asked, following.

"My life has been full of regrets, poet," Jeril tossed over his shoulder. "What approaches is just the final act, for me, in a bad drama. Piling should have convinced me. For me, this is personal."

Jeril's words struck a chord in Devyn. Once, he too had thought to find a peace, losing himself in words and Kembril's tales. Events had forced him to choose, to protest. *"With lights going out all around you, you find yourself faced with the need to find expression. None of the old patterns will suffice…that is the way with lies, endlessly convoluted, eminently unsatisfying, and ultimately fruitless."*

As Devyn watched Jeril walk over to collect his protective guards, Kembril's words came back to him now with an ache unexpected. Everything now hung in the balance. All that he had become and worked for faced extinction. The same held true for Tandori. It was time for a final protest, as it were, before the dark.

"Destiny," he mused aloud, "has a bad habit of not asking if one has room in one's schedule before complicating things. Destiny is. You can use it, or be used by it."

Talyior Enmbron's voice rose in his mind's ear as he descended the final steps to the courtyard, *"That sounds like a poem."*

"Perhaps, my friend," he whispered aloud, "Or at least a purpose."

He hurried to the stables, sent Bastian off to get his sword from his room, and saddled a horse. As he walked it out to mount, Bastian and Cryso met him at the palace steps with his sword and helm. He trotted off in the king's wake attended by the ghosts of his youth and memories. It was time to fight.

He found the harbor aswirl in turmoil. Most of the galleys floated on the swell. One ship remained tied to the wharf. He forced his way through the mess. The king stood at the foot of the gangway, barred by his own sailors from going aboard. The ship's master stood behind them.

"Sire, it is no use threatening," he said. "We have talked it out, the men and I, and we will not risk you out on the water."

"You will defy my royal command?" Donari barked. "Have you no sense at all? Clear away. You are wasting time!"

"I'm sorry, sire, but you'll not sway us. Stay."

Devyn pushed through to grab Donari's elbow. Such was the king's focus that he did not even react to the touch. Devyn had to pull him around to make him see him.

"He is right, my lord!" he urged, surging to Donari's front, forcing eye contact. "the painter and I got a good look at what is out there. We cannot stop them on the water, but we might harry them a little. Perhaps then we hold them at the walls, but you out there would be a waste. I will go. The people need to see you here."

Devyn intensified his grip. Donari's eyes fluttered, settled on him, a deep, disapproving frown framing his florid features.

"Even you?" he asked, but Devyn could feel the tension ebbing, as though the king's body heard him before his mind could gather the threads.

"And the Queen Eleni, if she were here. Wisdom now, lord, before bravery. No less courage there. Think. I will go and take the measure of this thing we face. Prepare our defense, lord, against our return."

The frown faded to resigned, smoldering anger. The king turned his gaze to the ship master.

"As you wish, but take no unnecessary risks yourself, either! Test them, slow them, if possible, but leave room for your return." He glared at Devyn. "And that goes treble for you! Bring me information we can use." He shook off Devyn's hand and stepped back. "To the walls, the rest of you! We may see assault on the quayside before long. Let us prepare."

The king turned away and headed shoreward down the pier. Devyn boarded. Men cast off the final lines and shoved the galley clear. Crew took to their oars and rowed out to join the small flotilla. There was no land breeze to help them. As a mass, a small, pitiful mass compared to that sailing toward them, the first Pevanese hope crawled seaward through the bay. Devyn checked the sun, judged it near mid-day and found in that a measure of resolve. The wind should shift in the afternoon, which might grant them speed. With luck, they would strike with the sun setting behind them. They might gain the city a day, perhaps, before the enemy made the bay and forced its way into the inner harbor.

"Kembril, dear, old friend," Devyn whispered to himself as he stared ahead as the galley gained speed and began thrusting with a will through the swell. "Watch over us now."

Spray misted his face. A salty drop touched his lips. Devyn swallowed back fear.

Renia's Tears.

* * *

Darkness cloaked the remnant that felt their way back into port. For the price of information they had taken losses. Their smaller vessels had the advantage in maneuverablilty, and they tried to make the most of it in repeated rushes and thrusts against the Esdan formation. At first they enjoyed some success, throwing the foremost squadrons into disarray. But the larger Esdan vessels had engines fixed to their decking that shot both stone and spears over greater distance, and once these came into range, the Perspan craft took damage as they made their attacks. Some of the missiles burst into flames when they contacted a Perspan deck. Devyn tracked their retreat through the water by the line of burning hulks they left behind. In the end the greater weight of the Esdan artillery forced the Perspans to disengage completely just before sunset.

A cluster of boats set up as fire-ships met them when they returned. While the surviving craft of the flotilla took station at the harbor mouth, the other ships, manned by volunteer skeleton crews, ghosted seaward. Devyn returned to the shore, found Donari, and gave his ill report.

"We had at them, sire, but as you can see, with little real effect I am afraid. Shipmaster Fallon is with the few undamaged craft, taking the fireships out."

Donari wore his full armor. In the torchlight he looked like a representation of the god Borimon himself, all helmed and resolute, but his voice revealed the all too human strain of a lord beset by doubts.

"Little effect, you say?"

"Yes, sire, in the end. They just pushed us aside as though brushing away a fly. We slowed them a little, but that is all."

"Perhaps the fireships may have more effect. If my ships have to burn, I would rather they burn amongst those people rather than tied to my piers."

"Worth a try, my lord."

"As you say, but I wonder. I hate this waiting."

Together they watched the flames from the battlements. Three times they flared during the night, flickering red lights in the darkness, east, north and south. Devyn imagined the carnage those flames must have caused. Donari cursed and paced the walls, gave orders for the city defense and sent word to the citadel.

Dawn showed clusters of still smoking wrecks on the horizon, but closer inshore, floating a league out from the city, lay the bulk of the Esdan force, scarcely diminished in Devyn's opinion. While the sun rose red behind them, the Esdan ships loosed their matching sails and caught the sea breeze. As a mass they thrust into the bay, brushing aside any remaining Perspan ships. Some headed for the river to flank the city, others for the shore to the south, while the majority advanced in a rush toward the piers of the port proper, throwing missiles into the warehouses along the wharf, setting fires to the ship sheds on the northern shore. By mid-morning, smoke hung heavy over the area. Men manned the walls and waited while the smoke and flames grew.

But no assault followed. While the shoreward buildings burned, the Esdans waited just out of range. To Devyn it seemed as if they paused to let the flames clear a path to the walls. Runners brought reports to the king. The Esdans had forced the river mouth to the south of the city, landing troops that marched to the walls then paused just out of arrowshot. Donari stayed where he was. Devyn agreed with his decision. In peace and commerce, the harbor was Pevana's greatest strength, but now it showed as its greatest weakness. The Harbor Gate was the least fortified of the entrances into the city proper. Though walled along its crescent shape, the battlements there were lower than at other places. The Esdans might lay siege to the landward defenses, but their best chance of breaking the city lay in storming the waterfront. To do that they would need space, so shipsheds, boathouses and the warehouse district all burned to clear the way.

The heat rose to beat against them in waves, fanned by the breezes attendant to the tides. Smoke choked the eyes and lungs of the men on the battlements. The heat of the day beat down as a double blow through the smokey veil, and still no assault came. They could see Esdan craft moving about the harbor through the haze. The day passed. Donari ordered refreshment to the garrison, left on a quick tour of the other areas but returned soon to stand next to Devyn in the tower about the gate. The sun set behind them. The flames consumed the last of the buildings as night fell. As the sky turned to cobalt blue and then to black, Devyn noticed glowing spots out on the water, like a collection of blacksmith forges viewed from a distance.

"Look there, sire, see?"

"What new devilry is this?" Donari grunted. "Why do they wait?"

Devyn recalled yesterday's flames.

"Missiles, sire."

On cue, up and down the length of the shore, from those glowing spots flaming orbs launched. Devyn followed their arc through the night as they rose and fell against the area behind the walls. More salvos followed, scattered yet continuous, breaking the night with red-yellow trails of destruction. Soon flames took hold behind the defenders on the walls. Screams and wails rose behind with the flames, but Donari stayed put. Devyn could practically feel his rage as the king gave orders to spare what men he could to go help fight the fires spreading in the areas sheltered by the walls. Devyn's arm ached in memory of other fires. Kembril's face drifted across his mind's eye again. He felt momentarily transported back in time, saw Kembril's shadow beneath the flaming tree as Corvale's sword thrust through his vitals. He half drew his own blade before he remembered where he was. He had taken that old revenge already. He stood to his duty with the king, grieving for what burned behind, throwing thoughts toward Grayce, and vowing to take new vengeance should the chance arise.

The night passed in missiles and flames.

Chapter 16: Hide and Seek

Tasia sped down the steps from the wall, avoided the crush of men and horse crowding the clear space before the palace steps. She looked over to the stables and caught sight of her brother leading out the king's horse.

Tasia caught Bastian's eye when he looked up. He nodded to her, his face a bit pale, eyes rounded with the tension of the moment, intent on his duty. Tasia sensed the warning communicated in that nod and look, something Maze-born and subtle: watch yourself, bad times afoot. They had used that look before to avoid trouble with bullies and angry parents, but this was different. The bell in the citadel tower joined those from the city, reinforcing the difference. Watch yourself. Danger. Bolt.

Tasia had duties of her own. She side-stepped to avoid getting trampled as King Donari stormed out of the palace adjusting a light mail-shirt with one hand and holding his battle helm with its royal circlet in the other. He was all shouted orders and grump, quite a change from the laughing father who, less than an hour ago had swept up his laughing children to go in search of sweets and their mother. Tasia let him stick to his business while she stuck to her own. She knew the twins would need her. They would likely still be with the queen. She ducked inside the great double doors, ignored Cryso's question and darted up the stairs, heading for the royal apartments.

The upper halls were in a turmoil as maids darted about, everyone had worried expressions on their faces, and, strangely enough, no one paused long enough to demand she help them. Tasia checked the twins' nursery: empty. She moved down a door to the queen's sitting room, composed herself, smoothed her dress, a newly found habit, and knocked before entering.

Queen Eleni stood at the window, arms around her children who stood on the sill, the three of them looking out. The window looked southeast, offering a good view of the lower city and the open sea dotted with the ships Tasia had seen from the wall.

"Taizy!" Arryn exclaimed, twisting around at the sound of her entrance. "Ships! Come see!"

Tasia walked over to join them. "I have already seen them, little prince, but this view is fine, too."

"Bells, bells, bong bong!" piped Ailen. "The whole city is ringing. Where is our bell, mama? I want to ring a bell. Bong, bong, bong, sing-a-long."

Eleni's face belied the twin's excitement. She knew what those ships meant, and the look she gave Tasia had Maze-tints of its own, but she kept her tone light to match her children's.

"Tasia," the queen graced. "You come upon a wish. We have just finished our sweets, and cares have called away the king. I may have things to see to, soon. I could use your time with these two. The nursery or garden would do fine, but watch them, please! I may be some time. You and they might prevail on Cook for some dinner later."

"As you wish, my lady. I came as soon as I heard the bells and saw…what was out there." She waved, a vague gesture. "The twins and I will do fine till you need them."

"More hide and seek?" asked Ailen.

"More sweets?" added Arryn.

"No!" Eleni admonished. She moved to the door. "You had quite enough of both. Now, I want you both to mind Tasia. I have things to do. I will look in on you when I can, but keep together! No running about. Not today, children, please." Again, the queen locked eyes with Tasia but pushed a last attempt at the twins. "I'm relying on you."

Eleni motioned Tasia to follow her into the hall. "Tasia, I know this is a lot to ask, but the king insists on finding out what those ships mean. You saw them, and I know you must have heard how things are. This could get bad. I know you have seen enough of the bad to know what to do. Watch them. Keep them occupied for me. I will need to meet with the council, start plans the king has set up. You should expect to stay with them for the rest of the day."

"Yes, my lady. The twins and I will be fine."

The queen left, leaving Tasia alone to face two inquisitive faces.

"Mama looked worried," Arryn said, coming over to take Tasia's hand and lead her back to the window. "I can always tell. She says light things but her right eyebrow goes up."

"And her fingers twitch," Ailen added, climbing up on the window seat. She touched Tasia's temple, still damp with perspiration. "You have been running, Tasia! Why? Is it because of what mama saw outside?"

"Yes, Ailen, I saw the ships and heard the bells and came running back here because I knew you would have questions. Plus, the bells put me in mind of a story neither of you have heard before."

"Can we go to the garden and run?" Arryn asked. "That sounds like fun."

"But mama said to stay in and out of trouble."

"You be quiet, sister. You don't like it just because I'm faster."

"Are not! Snot!"

"Am too, boo!"

"Story?" Tasia interjected, grabbing a hand each and forcing the squablers to sit. "You saw what your mother saw, and you know she has things to deal with, so let us help her by obeying for once!"

"No hide and seek?" Arryn asked with a sweetness that did not quite reach his eyes.

"No having fun?" Ailen sighed.

Tasia suppressed a chuckle. She really did enjoy the two of them; all joy and seriousness and young; protected yet not so different from her memories of herself and her brother.

"And I thought you enjoyed my stories!" she said, faking disappointment.

"We do," Arryn assured her. "But we enjoy hide and seek and running in the garden, too."

"But I have a fun story in mind about how Soralee, the woodland goddess found her voice. The bells reminded me of her." She rose from the window bench. The twins hopped down with her. "And," she continued conspiratorially, "the best place to tell her story is in a tent as if we were camping in the woods. So, a story and a tent, sound good?"

Arryn looked sideways up at her as they moved to the door.

"I like tents, if I can't run and play hide and seek in the garden," he said.

"But the maids will not like us taking our blankets off our beds." Ailen sounded skeptical.

"Oh, but they will be too busy to worry about what we do with your sheets and pillows, I'm sure," she reassured them, crossing the hall to their bedroom. "So let us make a good tent and use everything!"

"And the chair cushions!" the twins added in unison.

"And the cloakstand from the closet," Tasia added.

"A grand tent," Arryn finished, contented.

"And a grand story," Ailen added, giggling.

It ended up being their most impressive tent ever. Every blanket from both beds, plus two others purloined from their parents' draped over the cloak stand made a floor, walls and roof five-year old exotic. They made a mound of pillows and cushions, two extra ones lifted from a bench seat in the hallway, and settled themselves to recover their breath. Tasia waited for them to cease their laughter and punch their pillows into comfortable nests before beginning.

"Settled? Ready then. This is the story of the wood-goddess Soralee, one of Renia's favorites. Soralee is the one who haunts the forest slopes to the south and west of Pevana's valley, caring for the life there but especially the trees. The trees, you see, gave Soralee her voice."

"How?" asked Arryn.

"Does she have a pretty voice, like you and mama?" added Ailen.

Tasia blushed a little at the compliment and the comparison.

"She has the most beautiful of voices," she answered, "for it is made up of the wind passing through leaf and over bough, brushing water in woodland stream, whispering between rocks and mounds. But for long ages she kept her watch over the woodland life in silence for she was mute. Renia thought her into being hurriedly to contest Tolimon's whiles and Borimon's earthy violence. She needed a familiar to act quickly to tame the land but gave no thought to speech. So Soralee tended root and branch, helping them anchor to the earth, to grow tall and spread their canopy over the land, but did so silently, unacknowledged."

"How sad for her," sighed Ailen, "to not be able to sing or call out."

"Ah, but that is the beauty of it, Ailey," Tasia soothed. "Soralee was still happy in her charge. She did not know enough to feel the lack, you see. Renia knows she had enough to do! Imagine having to look after an army of you two? It takes your parents, the maids, Cook and me to keep watch over you!"

"Yes!" Arryn agreed. "And sometimes when I hide especially well, even that is not enough! Did Soralee ever play hide and seek? I bet I could make it hard for her to find me, oh, yes I could!"

Tasia laughed and ruffled the little prince's hair.

"Boasting, really? But you could hide in the deepest crack in the rocks or underneath the hollow of the thickest roots or climb to the tippytoppest of the tallest tree and wrap yourself in leaves and Soralee would always find you. She watches us always when we are in the woods."

"Mama would not like it if you climbed too high, Arry, and you know it," Ailen scolded.

"I climb too good to fall."

"Ha! Mama dislikes us going out to the wall."

"Not by ourselves, but I bet if we took Tasia or Devyn with us, she wouldn't mind."

"Stop it! Or should I stop, instead, and we do sums?" Tasia pitched her voice sharper to get their attention, and it worked instantly.

"Story, please," they both said, wriggling deeper into their pillows.

"Right then. You both be silent so I can tell how Soralee stopped being silent." Tasia punched her pillow into a supportive shape and leaned back, letting her storyteller voice take over.

"For an age Soralee tended to her business, and the forest marched north, west and south, rank upon rank, in every shade of green and brown, size and shape. Roots dug deep into the rocky shoulders of the world, cracking, breaking and knitting the new shapes into the land we know today. But all was not perfect in the world in those days. Tolimon worked his mischief, as he has always done, seeking to mar Renia's design. And in Soralee's case that meant pushing over favorite trees, soiling clean running streams and rolling lumpy boulders to block pathways.

In time, Soralee became aware of Tolimon's presence and took thought, in her silence, for how she might best curb the trickster-god's actions. She watched and waited and soon began to feel Tolimon's presence building, disrupting the woodland goddess' rhythm of root and branch. She would appear before him, a mute presence, forestalling him even as he twisted a trunk to the breaking point or put his spectral shoulder to a stone.

Tolimon found this constant interference unnerving. He was used to having his own way in his little cruelties and upsets. It was all part of the game to him, to visit Man in his dreams with dark thoughts, to goad and push against Minuet's efforts at maintaining order in Renia's realm. It was he who pricked Borimon's rage that set the earth to shaking, the great waves crashing and the lightning striking. He was disorder, the chaos god, and did not like how Soralee's sudden appearances upset his plans.

Tolimon took himself up to the top of the mountain, the very same peak we can see in the west, and searched for a way to take Soralee's silence from her. He sat and listened to the noises of the world, and soon he recognized how even sound was part of Renia's plan. He smiled wickely from his high place, for he realized if he could hear Soralee coming, then he might better avoid her.

Tolimon worked then a great magic, gathering up the threads of the world's winds and knitting them together into a rope, slender and subtle yet possessing great power; all the big and little winds that brush and whisper and roar and rage: the part and parcel of sound itself. Then he took himself deep into the forest to a place where great trees grew among large stones, through which ran a clean, swift stream. He looped his rope of wind in a snare from boughs overhanging the water and set about nudging the great stones loose so that they might choke the streambed. He hummed a ghostly tune as he worked, making no secret of his presence, waiting for Soralee to come.

And come she did. She swept down to the place, and Tolimon's rope slipped over her head and settled around her throat and neck. How she roared! The force of her spirit, given sound by the world's winds, stormed at Tolimon, who withstood its gale laughing, letting the goddess vent and rage as she liked. And when at last the winds subsided, he spoke to her.

'Soralee, I have you now!' he mocked. 'I have given you a voice and will now hear you coming. You will stop me no longer!'

Soralee took her first breath and spoke.

'What have you done, miscreant?' she asked. The sound of her own voice startled her at first. She paused, tested the air, calmed herself and in so doing gently controlled the wind so that it flowed evenly in and around the rocks and boughs. 'This is passing strange,' she continued. 'I am Soralee, silent watcher no more.'

'I have belled you, Soralee. Now you are as the kine controlled by Man, who announce their coming and going with every step. I will always hear you, and so avoid your intrusion. Chaos always finds a way, mistress.'

'You think you have bested me,' Soralee replied in a calm whisper, a soft breath that teased leaf and mold. 'And while it is true I will not be able to stop your childish pranks, I will nonetheless now give sound and sense to the forest. I will be the watcher and the whisperer. You will feel me constantly, easing over bough and stone, brushing against your cheek while you bend to mischief, and you will always hear me though trunk and stone block me from your view. Foolish, foolish, Tolimon, to give voice to little

Soralee. Mar what you will. I will mend. The trees you break and fall will nurse their replacements.

'The streams you choke will flow around, cutting new channels, giving new song to join my own and the life of the forests will take on a new shape, silent no longer. For I will be part of all sounds one hears in the woods, the creak of branch, rustle of leaf, and the chorus of bird song and water babble—all of it will now be part of me. You will never have peace under my living eaves, Tolimon. You may hear me coming, but now I will give warning of your presence! No sound will ease your care. When you walk among my trees, you will be watched by all. Sound will break the silence, and word of your presence will spread, carried by birdsong and breath of wind. The very squirrels will chide and mock you.

'You have given me a great gift, for I can now share speech with Renia herself and give report of you. How will you do then, trickster, when both Minuet and I take you under watch? You will reign only in the dark places; the holes and hollows where light and wind rarely come. You seek to play with the elements, but they are beyond you. Everything is part of Renia's design. You have not stopped me; you have made me. I am Soralee the watcher, the forest spirit, life.'

Tolimon saw his error and yet still smiled through his frustration.

'But mistress, look about us,' he sneered. 'There are shadows and hollows enough for my wants. You will never be able to stop all. We will contest, you and I, for supremacy here. Man will make his way into your woods, bringing his mischief with him. And Man has hollows and dark places enough for my whispers. Look to your trees, mistress.'

'Again, you mistake yourself, Tolimon,' responded she, breathing her words like an echo of a wind, soft yet serious. 'All who walk under my eaves bring their powers with them, but you have given me voice and volition to watch and teach. For those that come to hear the voice of the trees, they will find wisdom enough to reject you.'

Then Soralee drew a great breath and loosed it at Tolimon, and the chaos god could not withstand it for it was full of the truth of him, laying bare all his deceptions, evasions, and lies. He faded from her presence.

"And so it has been for all that go into the woods," Tasia finished. "It is never completely silent. It watches us as we go about our business there. Drafts float and ooze over root and branch. For the unwary, there are accidents and missteps. But for those that wait, children, Soralee's voice will speak to them."

"Have you ever heard Soralee's voice?" Ailen asked, her voice heavy with pending sleep.

"I have," Tasia answered. "When I was your age, before the great fire, I used to climb quite high up the Maze Tree, listening to Kembril Edri tell us stories. Sometimes, after he had finished and all the rest had fallen silent, I would hold my breath and listen to Soralee's voice whisper to me through the leaves."

"I wan' go to the woods," Ailen murmured. "Wanna hear Soralee."

"A good place for hide and see—" But the rest of Arryn's comment fell to a yawn, which left him asleep with his sister on the pile of pillows.

Tasia lay back for a moment, listening to their breathing, but soon grew aware of another sound. She crawled out from the tent to discover Queen Eleni sitting on her knees smiling with tears glistening her cheeks.

"My queen," Tasia whispered. "I'm sorry. The childen are asleep. Should I wake them?"

The queen shook her head no and rose, wiping her face and motioned for Tasia to follow her. They went back across the hall to the queen's sitting room. Papers and ink wells littered her writing table. The queen sat down and gestured for Tasia to join her.

"Is anything wrong, my lady?"

The queen sighed. "Renia's Grace, no, child. I could not help the tears. I only caught about half of it, but by the goddess! I loved it. I do not know what is to come, but while the children sleep, I would like you to write it down if you could. We may face dark days, Tasia, but just now you have given me hope's light."

The queen pushed a tablet and ink well within reach, and Tasia noticed the pen was one the queen often used. She tamped down her emotions. First Devyn and now the queen praised her words, and that made for heady consideration for a Maze-born. Tasia set to after a pause to collect her thoughts. She wrote quickly, strangely confident despite the circumstances. She sensed the queen rise and leave, heard her footsteps on the balcony as an after thought.

Her hand ached when she finished. She was not sure how long she took, but the light outside referenced sunset. She rose, stretched some blood into her backside and went out to join the queen, who stood at the balcony rail looking south and east.

"Thank you," the queen said, and she put an arm around Tasia's shoulders and drew her into a side embrace. Tasia sensed nothing off in the familiarity. Perhaps their shared world of words connected them. Besides, the queen's origins were not much different from her own. Together, they took in the view. Eastward, Tasia could make out the ships she spied earlier. They were closer now. Behind them, just visible on the horizon, smoke rose in isolated tendrils.

The queen anticipated her question.

"Donari sent our fleet out to contest the sea approaches. What is left of them cluster there just inside the bay mouth." She pointed down into the city. "See there. That was what I left you to do. Those with ready transport have been urged to take what they can and head inland. That is attack coming, my dear."

"And you wanted me to copy down a story?"

The queen laughed. "Forgive a mother the desire to have the source of a fine memory. You held them, dear, those squirmy, beautiful children. They need to know you, where you came from, where we all came from. And if we fall or flee, I want them to have that."

Tasia looked to where the queen pointed. Down by the Landgate a line of wagons jostled in the square, and a longish line serpentined along the road running abut the river.

"Why?" Tasia asked.

"Donari felt we would have better defense if as many of the defenseless could be removed to safety, and there is safety in distance."

"I need to get word to my mother." Tasia took herself to task for not thinking about her earlier.

"I took your brother with me. I made sure he knew to offer her shelter here if it came to it—or a place in one of the wains if she wanted."

Tasia knew what her mother would choose. Strangely, she did not feel anything with the news. She and Bastian had lived largely on their own in surviving the Maze. There was love there, surely, but in these last few years less and less closeness. As words took over Tasia's world, her mother's influence waned. Not for her the washtubs and the serving tables. When her mother had given her ready blessing to the offer of palace duty, it had been more of a final goodbye. Bastian knew it, too, and yet he still went with the queen to check on her.

Tasia imagined her mother, her things in a bundle, helped up into a wagon. Tasia could see that. She could not see, however, her mother looking back and up the hill with longing and remorse. Her mother was a survivor. She raised them, such as it were, to survive. She would leave. Tasia and Bastian would stay, and that was the way of it.

"Thank you, my lady," she said. "I'm sure Bastian appreciated at least the chance."

"She will not stay, you mean. Bastian said much the same thing on our way back to the palace. I am sorry, Tasia, but mostly I am glad you are here with us now. Promise me you will look after Arryn and Ailen. Donari will want us to leave, but I will do no such thing. There will be fighting. If I should fall, or events separate us, keep my children safe. I can think of no one better suited and more knowledgeable about those shadows and hollows you mentioned in your story. If it comes to it, indulge my son in some hide and seek!"

They shared the scene until the twins woke a few minutes later. Then it was snacks and actual sums not just a threat followed by fun with pen and ink on the queen's own tablet. Tasia felt the queen unusually indulgent, as though she sought to capture something of the twins' innocence to take with her when duties next called. For their part, Arryn and Ailen seemed to take no outward notice, though Tasia thought she saw Arryn shoot his sister a quick, knowing look before dipping Eleni's favorite pen into the pot.

The four of them shared a meal just after sunset. Donari had yet to return to the palace. When maids came to take the twins for a bath and then to bed, Tasia stayed with the queen. Together they reviewed the draft of her story, and Tasia added details and made small changes on Eleni's advice. For Tasia, the scene bordered on the unreal. She would have thought it too extra-ordinary by half had she not already witnessed the queen's behavior during the day.

A glow not from the city drove them both out to the balcony again. Below them, lights winked here and there in the city. The weird off-light came from the sea. There were flames on the water, clustered in three widely separated spots.

"Fireships," Eleni explained. "We saw them collected in the harbor this afternoon, remember? A great risk and perhaps a waste as well, but Donari must have felt we had no better weapon. We have not had the time, Tasia, to build up that force. We did not think there was a need. Esda seems to have thought otherwise. Once those flames fade, what is left will enter our bay. Renia grant us a wind to blow them away!"

"Will we fight?"

The queen sighed. "Of course, we have no choice. You did not see how the Esdan ambassador behaved, Tasia, lucky you. I had to record his haughty tone and demands. Outrageous and far, far worse than anything we have received before in their official letters. This smells of planning. That is the sadness of it for me. Donari has worked tirelessly to knit this new kingdom together. Peace has a power of its own, and yet that very power is likely what prompted that fleet out there."

"Why can't they leave us alone?"

This time the queen laughed, a wry, rueful sound in the darkness.

"How many times have we asked that question? Why did Roderran try and unit the north and assail the south? When I consider the loss of life and livelihood suffered by our folk, Tasia, I wonder if unity ever really could have served us. We are potential, always, which to Esda means a threat, real, now, that must be dealt with. Silly me, us, for thinking the sea's width protection. So it comes. Donari has built, Tasia, and we will defend it, hoping our walls and spirit are enough. Renia grant us strength."

Once again, Tasia felt the queen's hand touch her brow and then grip her shoulder.

"I do not need to hide the truth from a Maze-born such as you, Tasia. This is not the first darkness you have faced."

Fear and anger swelled in Tasia then at the queen's quiet resolve. She stood a little straighter, remembering how she survived the past.

"I have, my queen," she said, determination filling every syllable. "And I will see to it the twins are kept safe."

This time the queen's laughter sounded more genuine. "I will never doubt you! And I hope it never comes to it, but you ease my heart, Tasia. Just as your story of Soralee put me in mind of my own youth. Maze-wisdom is its own truth, I suppose. I wish her voice heard over the sea. There are men out there who need to stop and listen. The sea wind here blows ill. To me it speaks of ambition and hate."

Tasia had no response. Together they watched the glow fade on the horizon. The night deepened around them. Tasia went to her bed and tried unsuccessfully to sleep. Unrestful thoughts, senses stretched and frayed by change and fear, kept her half-awake.

Instead of chasing dreams, she planned.

Chapter 17: Snared

Jeril descended from the tower and found the two guards assigned to him by the king waiting for him in the courtyard before the palace. Devyn clattered by escorted by two other mounted guards. Jeril considered. He wanted to get down into the city to get a sense of things, to check on Grayce and his house, and even perhaps incite the threat against him to reveal itself prematurely. He had shared with Devyn what his memories of Esdan tactics suggested to him.

But not everything.

That the fleet sailing for the Pevanese bay sailed some time ago was indisputable. Even at distance, Jeril recognized the bulky shapes of transports. This was no raid as on Piling a year ago. This was a killing thrust. That much material took time and logistics even for a realm as capable as Esda. He judged those ships sailed soon after the ambassador Piecen and Tacidus set out on their last, goading diplomatic farce. In fact, he more than half suspected they had sailed together. The timing was too perfect for chance. If he recalled anything useful about his brother the emperor, it was that he never left anything to chance.

Jeril stood there in the courtyard awash in ill feeling and recrimination. He could have done nothing, individually, about how things had played out. His brother had begun preparing for this thrust even as Jeril sailed into Pevana's harbor. He should have screamed his truth as soon as his feet touched the pier. Would it have been too little too late even then as it looked to be now?

Such a question could haunt a man's dreams provided he had enough days left to lose sleep trying.

He felt a strong desire to draw his blade against the assassin Donari and Devyn suspected waited for him in the city. The idea seemed in keeping with how his brother had always operated against him. Those ships outside the bay would be a signal for those elements to make a try at him. Donari's order to stay safe in the citadel limited his choices, and Devyn had asked him to find Grayce. If he was compromised, then so were they all, including his protégé.

Staying put was the same as running away. He wanted action. Let them have their try and trust his remembered skill or die; he would not

207

survive Pevana's fall anyway. Maybe if he could take out the Esdan agents, fate might give him a chance at Tacidus. That thought brought a real, sneering smile he used to hide his disappointment when the two guards assigned to him stepped up smartly.

"Are you sure there isn't a wall where you two could take station?" He kept his tone jocular even as he slipped his swordbelt to wear it over his shoulder. "I'm hardly worth it."

His guards would have none of it. "By the king's orders, sir," the left one snapped.

"Keep you safe, sir," added the right.

"Set to watch me, then? Right, watch me walk out that gate. I've business below."

"Not advisable, Prince Tandori," the left one continued.

"Oh, yes, you will have heard. I'm not overfond of the name, I assure you."

"Yes, sir," said the one on the right. "All the more reason to stay here where we can best protect you."

Jeril gestured to his blade. "Trust me. I know how to use this. The one who confronts me with this drawn will be the one who needs protection. So, I'll give you a choice, young men. You can lose me here, plead the chaos of the moment, go have a beer and a morsel in the mess, and I'll keep it our little secret."

His flood of words must have discommoded them, for he detected doubt in the glances they gave each other.

"Orders, lord," the right one weakly asserted.

"We can't leave you alone," added the other.

"I know all about your orders, but those ships out there have changed things. I tell you I am going out that gate and down to check on my house and a friend of your Devyn Ambrose's. Gave me that particular job himself he did, just now. You might be able to stop me, but think of the scene we will cause. I'll mark both of you like a canvas if I need to."

"Lord, please," the left one began.

"We can't," finished the other.

Jeril pushed by them. "Please yourselves, I'm leaving." He half expected to feel a spear point at his back, but what he got was the sound of the two of them falling into step just behind. Jeril grinned at the compromise.

"Let's go see to some business, then," he said, adjusting his sword belt to a more comfortable position. "I promise to get you back by sundown." He strode purposely out through the gate, leading his guards left at the start of the downward slope heading toward his house.

It was time to check on Grayce and Angel.

* * *

Turmoil stalked the city streets. Jeril and his guards had to weave their way through crowds drawn by the sounds of the bells and rumor. Because of his escort, folk took him for someone official and pestered him with questions he felt he had no right to answer. He limited himself to general references.

"Yes, there are ships on the horizon. King Donari has dispatched a force to investigate. That is all I know. Please, let me pass."

It was variations of the same all the way down to Lampwrights Street and the spaces around his house. Mostly, Jeril wanted to walk, to taunt the agents his brother and Tacidus might have placed in the city. He did not feel any threat in the roiling activity. Folk rushed about their concerns while markets still tried to function. The bells only added to the normal sound and pace of the place.

He fished his key when they came to his door. He unlocked and took inside a look to find Grayce absent. He called, but Angel chose not to come. He took a piece of her extra drawing paper to leave a note but paused before applying the charcoal pencil. What would he say? She had no idea who he actually was. To her he was the bearded painter, a generous teacher who let her stay in the place. He wondered if she would even recognize him clean-shaven and bearing a sword rather than a pallet.

Jeril stood there, sorting out his emotions and for the first time truly understood why Devyn felt as he did about her. Grayce needed someone. He had shown her shape, gave her tools to control her art, but now he worried for her heart. Devyn was correct, of course, she had to be convinced to leave if possible. Would she without Devyn?

Once again, anger and remorse flooded through him. He thought he had built himself a life in Pevana, but the bells tolling exposed the lie. There were costs pending for the lives that touched his. He fished his brother's mocking face from memory and cursed it. Hate suffused him, made potent by his very impotency in getting to Jorian and making the right person pay, finally, for all the evil he caused.

It always comes down to you, brother. I should have killed you even if it meant my own death.

The absurdity of the thought did not keep him from wishing it, fervently. With an effort he composed himself and set charcoal to paper:

Grayce,

I hope this finds you well. The bells toll great changes. Listen to them. Devyn will come if he is able. He sent me to find you and wish you to safety. His words, lady, and wise. There will be fighting. Leave if you can. Devyn needs you safe. I need you safe.

Jeril

Ps. Take Angel with you!

He frowned down at the paper. He mastered colors and shapes a long time ago, but words always left him feeling incomplete, untutored, crass and presumptuous. He considered wadding up the missive and tossing it out the window, but then left it on the table. He knew Grayce would follow her own mind in the end. His poor words would hardly sway her. Devyn might. Grayce would have to choose.

This is no good. I will have to find her.

That thought really gave him pause. He was a target. If he did actually find her and tried to protect her, he would just bring her into his problem. How was that rescue?

He went out on the deck and checked the roofline of his house and the buildings on either side, calling against the sound of the bells tolling, halfway hoping Angel would poke her head up as was her wont. He confessed to a moment's sadness when she did not appear, and yet as with Grayce, perhaps it was a mercy. He had less fear for Angel than anyone else in the drama unfolding.

He gathered up a satchel from the storeroom and started shoving in a few roles of his collected sketches before freezing in mid-motion. No. That was no good either. The assault gathering seaward had forced him to reclaim his past. He doubted he could remain the painter after, if there could be an after. He tossed the half-packed bag onto the table next to the note and left, taking the stairs two at a time.

His escorts waited for him down by the front door. He swept them back out to the street. He had two other stops to make before sunset forced him to return up the hill: *The Golden Cup* to see Saymon Brimaldi and then down Harbor Street to Gania Landare's boarding house. If Grayce were to be found, he hoped they would know where.

He found Brimaldi surveying the scene from in front of his establishment. His glower deepened when he saw Jeril's guards.

"You are either well-risen of late or under arrest," he smirked in greeting.

Jeril allowed himself a small breath of a laugh. "A little of both, actually," he responded.

"That sounds like the beginning of a story. Are your friends allowed to drink on duty?"

"Another time perhaps."

Brimaldi grimaced. "If we are granted that time. All of this," and he gestured to the crowded street and the noise, "seems to suggest otherwise."

Jeril glanced around. Folk clustered in doorways in chattering groups, many looking up to trace the sounds of the bells tolling. Two carts, piled high as though in haste, made their way by, heading for the Landgate square and out of the city. Word must have spread.

"Those who can leave should," Jeril said quietly. "I cannot say more, now, Brimaldi. Forgive me, but this city will face attack soon, I am sure of it. Donari means to fight. The fewer innocent underfoot the better, if you get my meaning."

Brimaldi growled at Jeril's words. "I wondered where you got to, painter. Fell into policy, did you? Mixing with Citadel business? Guards and a sword on your back, and by the pommel, I would say that is no mean weapon. Quality. This really is a story then."

"One with too many twists, Saymon. If we survive what is to come, I promise you a full account. Will you stay?"

Brimaldi scoffed. "Stay? Of course. And so will most of us. I have no interest in the road, living out of a bag. We fought Gaspire Amdoran before. We can see to what is next. So, Esda has done with diplomacy, apparently. I caught a few glimpses of that oily eastern fellow. I'm not surprised."

"Nor I, friend, sadly, but I have no time for more. I am looking for Grayce. Has she been in to work lately?"

"She did a shift at the tables yesterday, mid-day, but I've not seen her since. I know she has been sketching in the fish market down Harbor Street."

The fish reference brought back images of poor Tam's bloody corpse and reminded Jeril, yet again, of how events had spun so quickly into threat. The boy's death would have hit the folk there hard. He imagined Grayce plying her lines, trying to distract the children from fear, their parents from grief and anger.

"I'll look there next," he said, turning to go. "Scrape the rust off of that spear you keep in your back room, Saymon, you will need it."

Jeril and his escorts moved back into the street flow. Next stop, Gania Landare's. The westering sun began to stretch shadows along the street. Jeril's painter self noted the altered light even as the skin of his other self itched with the thought that those same shadows could hide an assassin. He took to scanning the rooftops as he walked.

"If you two want to be really useful," he grated to his guards behind him, "keep your eyes moving."

He took their silence for assent and increased his pace.

The turmoil in the city worsened as he neared the Harbor Gate square. Normally, the place was a busy fishmarket and warefair. Today, however, folk jammed the space, most hardly bothering to shop. Most eyes were on the line of soldiers pacing the parapet on the wall. Folk swarmed the gateway, trying to scry the action out on the water.

Grayce was nowhere to be found, however, but he did find Gania Landare near the well outside her boarding house. Just as with Brimaldi, Jeril's appearance with guards captured interest. Gania yelped a greeting and excused herself from the group of women chattering and drawing water.

"Master Sandre," Landare husked, coming close. "What do you make of all this rot? Bells woke me up out of a sound nap, tolling all afternoon they have. Word has it the king has sailed against the Esdans. An' I'll tell you true, painter, folk are quite upset. Things be gone bad and fast, then, yeh?"

"You are as perceptive as always, Gania. I do not know much more than you, but things have indeed gone bad, as you say. Esda threatens us. Donari has made moves. I'm looking for Grayce."

Landare glanced at Jeril's guards, eyes wide behind a skien of greasy hair that she flicked back with her massive right hand.

"And why these for you, then?" she asked. "You are a question, painter-man. I've not seen Grayce since early today. We took a cup together before she set up her easel at the marketplace. She may have been here all day, I dunno. She's certainly not here now. My Lyssa and I were down at the southern gates since mid-morning checking on some supplies due in overland from Tierne. And I tell you, those are late and that has been rare, but given what is going on here, maybe not so rare anymore, yeh? Can you answer me any of that? Can you?"

Jeril gripped Gania's forearm to calm her as she spoke, the hint of hysteria in her voice, but he had no more time to care. He checked the failing light; the sun was now behind the western mountain.

"I have to let these fellows get me back to the palace, Gania. Do not ask, please. There is no time. 'All of this,' as you say, means war, long planned by all the signs. Protect yourself. And if you come across Grayce, give her my warning. Her Devyn is with the king and terribly concerned."

Gania stared at him, visibly calming as she processed his words, and then she grinned, a gap-toothed, powerful expression that sent a little thrill down Jeril's spine. He marveled momentarily at her sudden transformation from harridan to something close to maternal.

"Ha. Knew that already," she said. "Could see it all over her face when she and I talked yesterday morn. And about time, too, for those two, in my opinion. Scribbler and sketcher, well-matched."

"We are agreed there, woman. I just hope…"

"Don't underestimate us, Master Jeril." Gania shook a meaty finger at him. "I know my queen and our people. The king will see a way through. We Pevanese are tougher than you think. Anyone that tries to spoil things here will have to deal with me!"

Jeril did not doubt her. He had seen her handle her cudgel more than once. If Pevana possessed such as Landare and Brimaldi, then perhaps there was hope.

"I will trust you are right, Gania. Please, look after her for me if you come across her. Dev wants her to leave, but I do not think…and I may not get another chance to see—"

"Because of these two soldier-boys?" Gania interrupted. "You aren't going to tell me anything, that's plain. Keep your secrets. I will lay out for Grayce an' do what I can. I suppose you can use that thing on your back, then? Funny, I never took you for a bladesman. But then I never thought the same of old Talyior, either, and he turned out a rare talent from all the stories I have heard. Luck to you, painter."

"Luck to us all, Gania."

Jeril waited at the gate while Landare lumbered up her walk and entered her house. They would all need luck in abundance to survive what was to come. A cough from one of his guards broke his thought.

"Lord, please, it's time we returned."

Jeril scowled at them but turned to go. They paced back up the street, forced to wind their way through groups of folks lingering, talking out the last light before heading homeward to an uncertain evening.

They came to a side street, a more direct route to the hill, that led off the main way through a lane of storage buildings. As they turned, Jeril heard the distinct thrumb of a bowstring and ducked instinctively. An arrow whizzed over his head to take his left-hand guard in the throat. As the man fell, gurgling and spraying blood another arrow took his right-hand guard square in the chest. He, too, fell lifeless to the stones. Jeril rolled against a wall and reached back to draw his sword, but shapes swarmed him out of the shadows. He swung out wildly, heard a grunt as his fist struck flesh. Voices snarled. He took a blow to the head that brought stars. Another took his legs and he slumped to the ground, arms held, helpless. A face swam before his blurred vision.

Reith Simson leered at him.

"You!" Jeril gasped, spraying blood from broken lips.

"Yes, me," Simson sneered. "Well-met, Prince Tandori. Got you! And now for the other one."

Simson's face receded. The last thing Jeril saw was the man's fist heading toward his face. The blow slammed his jaw and sent him into darkness.

* * *

The day Grayce's world changed forever began with her wandering in the dregs of a dream. She was back in the cave where she found Devyn's poem behind the cleft in the wall. This time, as she drew the face of the then unknown poet, it came to life and rose full-bodied from the paper to embrace her. There were sweet words and a kiss that changed to Angel's raspy tongue licking her cheek and the cat's 'I'm-hungry-purr' rumbling in her ear. Grayce stretched, languid, contented, but full awake brought doubts. Devyn was gone. She flashed back through her life and questioned whether she really deserved the right to be happy. Devyn placed her on the edge of so much change. His scent lingered on her pillow. Memory of his touch made her skin react. This new intimacy brought both surety and new kinds of caution. Before Devyn, she had more intimacy with loss, which made hope difficult.

She rose, put on a robe, and scooped up Angel. She went downstairs to the kitchen, scrounged some bits into a bowl for the cat and listened to her contented rowling for a few minutes, petting and talking soft nonsense, marveling at how much Angel seemed to trust her. She and Angel had shared a connection from the beginning that only deepened once Jeril left for the palace. The effect still partly mystified her. Angel trusted her. Jeril trusted her. Devyn seemed to trust her with his affections. Could she trust herself?

Trust had to happen; these new feelings made it imperative. The life she had formed here in Pevana boded well for the future. She could allow herself to be happy if she persevered. It took an act of will and, most recently, love to show her the way.

The word challenged her. She tested the texture: *love*. Was that how it was between her and Devyn?

The thought drew her back upstairs to take another look at her effort at his portrait. Next to it lay a scrap of her sketch paper with Devyn's bold hand.

> *Lines on a paper, lines among the trees*
> *Lines formed in a smile's crease*
> *That distance takes from view;*
> *Lines along a wandering path,*
> *Lines faint but true:*
> *All lines lead me to you.*
> *And ware the twisted turning*
> *And ware the shadowed face*
> *But never doubt I will find you*
> *No matter time nor place.*

Grayce read the short lines several times, blinking back tears. He possessed the skill to reach inside her and soothe hurts she thought hidden. He unsettled her, pleased her, and made her think of peace even as he hinted at troubles. He was part of her life, of that she was now certain. Where that would take them, she had no idea.

She dressed for the day, packed her things in her satchel, and set out for the fish market over by Gania Landare's close to the Harbor Gate. As she got ready, Angel padded up the stairs, leapt up on the worktable to oversee her preparations, loudly proclaiming her desire for strokes and quiet time. Grayce put her out on the deck with a bowl of water and told her to look afterself. Angel had the run of the neighborhood roofs. Quite often, she would survey her domain from Jeril's deck railing. Grayce went down stairs and out, pausing at the door to heft her two collapsible stools over her shoulder. Then she made sure to lock up and pocket the key.

Unusually thick mid-morning traffic met her outside. She had to weave her way around a line of carts. Bits of over-heard conversation suggested folk leaving in a hurry. Habit made her keep her eyes moving, looking for sign of Simson or his bravos. She did see several of his red-clad priests moving with the stream of people down near *The Golden Cup*, but they were intent on other business. None of them seemed to take notice of her, and no one followed her when she turned up Harbor Street. She saw no sign, nor even sensed his oily, presumptuous presense as she stalked along. Folk she knew waved and greeted her as she turned down Harbor Street. The morning seemed to regain its sense of the ordinary. She relaxed.

Gania accosted her near the well outside her house and insisted they share a cup of tea. They spent a half hour chatting up the news. Even Gania had misgivings about the future. Grayce steered clear of revealing anything about her own hopes and fears with Devyn. Whenever Gania breathed a question, Grayce instead answered with one of her own.

"But enough about me, Gania. Tell me, how are your boarders these days?"

Gania gave her a look then, a flick of greasy hair and a half, gap-toothed smile.

"Oh, my young men, such as they are, all be fine. They pay and Lyssa and I feed 'em. We do well here down by the piers. Good trade these days, lots of coming and going. Though between you an' me, there's too much going and coming of those eastern types. Saw the head-man, the ambassador, leave a while back. Didn't like the look of 'im, I tell you."

"Yes, both Jeril and Devyn mentioned them. Are you worried?"

Gania scowled, a reassuring glare, given the circumstances. "There's not much can scare me, young lady. I've lived through the worst, an' I'll thrive through the best. Rumors don't do anything but raise fear in the meek."

"Devyn suspects evil times may come."

"I dare say, if that Esdan fellow and his crowd are part of it. But there are folk here with roots too deep for fire. Like that Tree picture you put on that wall when you first got here. I remember Tasia telling me about it. Had to go take a look myself. Hit me close to some good old memories it did. Now I'm told folk from all over the city go by to take a look. That's roots, my dear, of a different kind, a good kind."

"I hope you are right, Gania."

"Oh, count on it. Imma' right on most things, had to be, keeping a business in this part of the city free and clear is no easy task. I was wrong about that Talyior Enmbron, your Dev's friend, once—but only the once. Thought he was a skirt chasing fool, but he turned out to be a hero."

Grayce finished her cup and took her leave. She left Gania at the gate and headed for the fish market down near the Harbor Gate. She set up her stools and hung a few sketches from a line holding an awning that shaded the seamstress' table. Her name was Hilea, and over the weeks since that first time selling her art, they had become friendly. The woman's daughter, a little imp of a thing with bright eyes and a fetching smile named Thalia, acted as her assistant.

Grayce set up and over the rest of the morning made four drawings: two sailors, a wine merchant and a Tinsmith. She worked quickly. The hours passed. She noticed the light change when she looked up to take the Tinsmith's coin. She accepted a cup of water from Thalia and took a drink gratefully. Over the rim of the vessel, she saw Reith Simson and four of his fake priest body guards enter the square from a side street that ran along the harbor wall. Grayce almost choked on the water.

Of course, Simson saw her immediately and headed directly towards her.

Grayce nearly panicked. Then Thalia's sweet face swam into view as the girl came over to take the cup. Quickly, Grayce shifted her stools around to gain the light.

"Thalia!" she exclaimed. "You have been such a help. Why don't we do a picture of you as a present for your mother? Have a sit and try to keep still for me, please?"

Thankfully, the girl readily complied, and by the time Grayce sensed Simson's wretched presence she was deeply involved in capturing Thalia's exquisite lines.

"Mistress Stonesmith at her work? How pleasant?" Grayce studiously ignored the man's fatuous tone.

"Hold your head steady for me Thalia, just a minute more, please, thank you." She turned slightly on her stool to give Simson her shoulder, but he ignored the message.

"Such a fine, steady hand." She heard him step closer. "And such a pretty little toppet for a model! Your sales must be going well to allow you to spend time on Pevana's poor."

That was too much. She glared at him over her shoulder.

"I can ignore your insults, Simson, but you have no call to be rude to my subjects. I am working. Leave me alone."

"And I have told you before, I have a commission for you in our main temple hall. Better pay, proper surfaces, or do you intend to scrape dust off of alley walls to practice?"

"You know better, Simson. I told you before, pointedly, that I wanted no part of your offer."

"A sad choice, but what of my other offer?"

Simson's bold insinuation, in a public place no less, made anger flare and her skin crawl.

"You disgust me."

Simson stepped even closer, stopped so that his face swam into her side view.

"I am sorry, mistress, truly, but you take me quite out of myself, you see. You have done so since the day I found you vandalizing my temple's back door. I admit to some early anger, but your lines have grown on me since then. I tried to tell you that when I visited your charming studio home."

Grayce looked full at him at that. His tone almost sounded contrite, and his reference to her lines echoed closely to what Devyn said to her previously. She stared, trying to sift through the nicety and find the man who had all but raped her with his voice in their last meeting.

The face she observed held something of both men, but only on the surface. Simson regarded her with an affable expression, teeth flashed in a winning smile, but his eyes revealed the lie. They were as mocking cold as always. If anything, their smolder seemed dampened, restrained as though from effort. Perhaps he found sounding pleasant a struggle, but Grayce would have none of it.

"I have changed the locks," she said, pitching her voice so that it carried for all around to hear. "And I will have no more of these encounters, sir!"

Instead of reminding him of her public safety, he just laughed.

"Oh! That is good! I would not want you to feel insecure when visitors called."

"Or molesters."

Again, her attempt to shock and embarrass him failed.

"Please, dear," he said, emphasizing the latter word. "Let us avoid upsetting the locals with our spat. I have confused you, and I am sorry. My attraction is quite genuine, I assure you. Perhaps my lack of experience in such worldly things made me clumsy. I am sure you, with more knowledge of such things, could have seen that. All I ask is patience, mistress. A sitting would do wonders to educate us both, don't you think? Come now, let me sit for you."

As the man warmed to his subject, Grayce leaned away as though to physically remove herself from such an odious situation.

"I know all of you I want to. Leave."

"Draw me."

"No."

"Paint my study in the temple."

"Never."

"Eat with me. I have a northern cook who knows his spices."

"Go sod yourself."

That brought another sardonic chuckle.

"I'd rather you helped me."

She shifted the grip on her pencil, recalled Earvyn Pickson, and prepared to stab the man in one of his mocking eyes.

"Leave now, or I will scream, this child will scream, and not even those brutes behind you will save you from the mob."

Simson straightened and blew her a kiss.

"I would truly love to test your theory, girl, but on the faint chance you might be right I'll forebear." He reached down and chucked Thalia's chin. "We don't want to upset this little lamb or all the other sheep. At least not just yet."

"Lord," one of those brutes interjected. "We have preparations to make."

"All in good time," Simson tossed over his shoulder. "We don't have to rush away from this pleasing interchange." He gave Grayce his frankest look yet, direct, piercing, altogether threatening. "And it is always a pleasure sharing words with you, mistress, though I think we would do better with fewer words and in better surroundings. But enough of that. I have other business today. Good bye for now, Grayce Stonesmith."

He bowed and moved away. Grayce watched his back recede until it disappeared in the crowd going down Harbor Street. She took a relieved breath, but something else stuck in her head.

"What did he mean by 'preparations'?" she mused aloud.

"What, mistress?" Thalia asked.

Grayve shook off the ill. "Nothing, Thalia," she responded, re-gripping her pencil in the proper form. "I was just thinking of something the cross man said. It's nothing."

"He was not nice. My mama says stay away from not-nice-people."

The girl's matter of fact tone helped Grayce dump the rest of her upset.

"Your mother is right, Thalia, and I will follow her advice for sure. Now, let me finish this up. See, the sun is westing. Your mama will be closing up shop soon."

She returned to her work, shifting once again to regain the light. She worked swiftly now, adding the fine details to shape the girl's eyes and perfecting the line of her mouth and chin. The act took her, as it almost always did, into another part of herself. If Simson would have returned then, she would not have paused to let him derail her. She became the tip of her pencil, and with each stroke she fixed a bit of the little girl's soul on the paper and part of her own as well.

She made a final smudge and sat back. Thalia hopped off her stool and came around to look and squeeled in delight. Grayce took the drawing, rolled it, and tied it loosely with a piece of twine and sent the girl off to surprise her mother.

Distantly, the bell out on Pevana's headland rang out, followed almost immediately by those in the city. Within minutes, the area transformed into a sea of alarmed folk looking east, asking for news, breaking down tables and stalls.

"What do the bells mean, Hilea?" she asked, helping fold the seamstress's fabrics. Thalia took them and stuffed them into a canvas bag.

"An old warning system," the woman responded. "I've not heard them since I was a girl myself. Strange! But there must be something seaward. That first one was the great headland bell."

"I noticed some odd traffic early, heading toward the Land gate. Strange. What must we do?"

"Wait for news. Some fools will pack up and leave and choke the roads, like as not." Hilea and Thalia shouldered their burdens and made to go. "King Donari will send word out to the people, mark it. We are for home. Perhaps my husband will have news. Good bye mistress!"

Grayce gathered her own things and followed, thinking back to the comment by one of Simson's guards. Preparations. Bells. Her fears suspected a connection, and her fears, sadly, had never led her astray. Home appealed to her, finding Devyn appealed even more, but the bells told her she might not have access to him. Angel would be frightened by the noise. She decided to risk Simson and head home.

The streets became so crowded with folk milling about that it took her nearly an hour to reach her door. Once she let herself in, she set the lock and bolt, dumped her stools in the corner, grabbed a bottle and hung a glass from the top. She swept up Angel's food bowl and went upstairs. If the cat was home, she would be mewling for entry from the deck.

Grayce ascended, let Angel in, poured herself a small measure and sipped to calm her unease.

Then she saw the note propped up on the work table. Relief swelled. Perhaps it was from Devyn and held news. She took it up eagerly, recognized Jeril's spidery hand and cursed the choked city streets when she read the contents, for she had missed him by less than an hour. She read the missive again. Fighting. No Devyn.

"Shit," she muttered, and took a bigger drink.

* * *

The day passed in fitful ignorance for Grayce. Angel, sensing her unease, kept by her side or on her lap. The two of them spent hours on the deck, which afforded them a great view of what caused Pevana's bells to sound. They observed Pevana's galleys massing at the harbor mouth and head out into the bay. Angel's single-minded purr barely served to help her control the fear.

When true dark descended, she tried to sleep, but ill dreams drove rest away. She stared at the ceiling until a strange glow from the east sent her out on the deck again. Flames spotted the sea. Ships burning. While she fretted, desperate action unfolded on the water. Those flames meant death. Again, they reminded her of those tragic days when Roderran's men burned Gallina. All of the flaws in her narrative waited unhappy attention on her as she observed what could perpend to be the end of everything good she had come to treasure.

Eventually, sleep claimed her for a few hours in her deck chair. Angel's solid warmth kept dawn's chill from waking her. She dreamed of a man sipping tea as she passed with her mother and their barrow, who later hurled statuary in Gallina's square with a voice like a summons. She dreamed of a full moon, Earvyn Pickson's insistent, fruitless member, Simson's false breath in her ear and a face which morphed into Devyn, who came and held her, cupped like precious water, whispering things just beyond understanding that calmed her.

She awoke to witness the beginning phases of the Esdan assault on Pevana. Hulks littered the bay outside the harbor. Inside, Esdan ships crowded the area; some anchored just offshore, others tied up alongside the piers. As the light grew, the Esdan craft started launching missiles. She noted where some landed against the harbor wall, where others landed among the buildings and streets in the wall's lee. Smoke began to rise almost immediately. She followed its course and noticed huge clouds reaching heavenward far to the south. Storm. Big one. Black smoke meshed with that white-grey background to create a mottled effect. Any other day she would want to draw or paint it. She pondered rain and thought back to Hilea and her reference to evacuation. Jeril's note had mentioned the same.

She missed Devyn. She needed. The intensity of her thoughts surprised her, but she knew they were true. She could not leave this present. She had run away from her home and the memories of love lost. How could she flee from love newly found? She grew restless with the waiting.

Folk ran by outside, calling on all who could organize their own transport to leave the city and head for the villages up the valley. She ignored them. She peered shoreward through the gathering smoke, tried to imagine Devyn down there alongside the king. Flames spread. They would need help there. Despite Devyn's warning, and Jeril's addition, she decided to go in search of a way to help.

Angel mewed a question at her when she went in to grab some towels and the water bucket. Grayce scooped her up, kissed that fury head and looked deeply into those feline eyes, trying to rationalize what Devyn and Jeril both would say was a foolish choice.

"Angel, sweeting," she whispered. "I have to go. I will come back if I can. Devyn needs me. Jeril, Renia's Grace, is out there, too. I have to do something."

Then she was down and out the door and running for the turning to Harbor Street. She sped around the corner, bumped into a man pushing a barrow piled with fine cloth, and nearly lost her bucket. She kept on, smoke growing dense as she neared the well outside Gania's boarding house. Folk clustered there and dipped cloths and buckets before rushing off to contest flames.

A terrific noise attended the action. The flames consuming that part of the city roared like a stormwind, and yet the sounds of battle coming from the walls contested for mastery. Grayce dipped her bucket and jogged after a small group to toss her water onto the low hanging roof of a shop. It was a pitiful amount, but she felt better for it. Gania passed her, mouth agape and throthing obscenities. Her house was surely threatened. Grayce returned to the trough, dipped her bucket and turned to go back. In the act, she bumped up against someone, upsetting her bucket down her front. A curse pushed against her teeth, but she swallowed it.

Reith Simson stood before her, immaculate, at odds with the soot stained and bedraggled crowd working the water lines. As before, four red robed priest-guards attended him, but this time they bore large cudgels, which they used to clear a space.

"What are you doing?" Grayce gasped. "There is fire!"

Reith grabbed her arm, pinned it behind her, all pretense gone.

"I know," he rasped into her ear. "I set a few of them. The Esdans set the rest. And right now I am saving you from singeing that beautiful hair of yours in a lost cause. I will let you thank me later." He pushed her into the hands of two of his guards and waved them on. "Come, children, our work here is done."

He stalked away. Grayce resisted, but Simson's guards pinned her arms remorselessly, and when she drew breath to shout for help another deftly shoved a cloth into her throat and tied it off with a thong. Half-choking, sobbing in fear and rage, Grayce suffered them to lead her away.

Smoke followed them up the street.

Behind them flames spread.

They turned down an alley. She remembered it: she and Tasia had run down it once before. This time, Simson led them quickly to the back door of the King's Theology temple.

Simson opened the door himself.

"Welcome to my humble establishment," he said. He put his hand under her chin, tilted her head back. "Look, I have kept a few of your lines there above the lintel. I'm such a loyal fan, you know."

She moaned.

"Yes, I know, pretty impressive. You moan deliciously, by the way." He turned to one of his guards. "Take her up to my chambers. Then check on our other guest. I will be along directly. See about some hot water and a cloth for Mistress Stonesmith." He dared to kiss her cheek. "We have but to wait out these events, my dear, plenty of time to get better acquainted."

Her rage as they ushered her into the building threatened to burst her heart. She struggled again, fought for air, then light fell to a candle flame's size and she fainted.

As she slipped into unconsciousness, her hind-brain wondered if darkness was a mercy.

Chapter 18: To Battle Under a Red Sun of Destiny?

Devyn accepted the ladle from the water carrier gratefully. All through the long day, he had stalked the walls with Donari setting the watch as best they could. In the harbor, the Esdan ships dropped anchors and floated on the swell just out of reach of anything the city could launch at them. Though no tactician, he could see the Pevanese lacked the engines their assailants boasted. He drank the water and tried to wash away the bitter realization.

They were in trouble. He knew it. Donari knew it. He suspected the troops knew it, but Donari never let his expression show even a hint of concern. He paced the walls encouraging the men to stand firm, a tireless force in his royal helm and armor. When the bombardment started, he had Devyn take charge of the harbor wall north while he paced the length south. The men huddled behind the battlements as the Esdan vessels sent exploding stones against the walls and flaming bundles over them. This went on all day, fires spreading behind, smoke boiling up, pushed by the land wind to choke them when the tide turned.

Devyn marveled at the Esdans' organization. Their ammunition supply seemed inexhaustible. He stole a long look during a pause in the assault and noticed large, heavy-laden vessels sidle up next to the thicker, wider ships bearing catapults. Wooden cranes levered large mesh bags out from the bowel of the supply ships. Looking deeper into the bay, Devyn noted the Esdans possessed many such ships. He leaned over the parapet. There were scars along the wall, and the harbor gate showed particular wear. Nearly all of the warehouses along the wharf lay in ruins. Flames danced among the fallen timbers. The boathouses were a chaos of broken boats and demolished roofing. It was as if the Esdans wanted a clear field to direct their fire and space to mass their troops once they landed. The sheer volume of the attack intimidated Devyn, but he too, like the king, kept his face impassive and his voice positive.

Flags went up the masts of the enemy ships. Almost immediately, the rain of exploding stones resumed, but this time the Esdans chose to focus on three places where their previous salvos had the most effect: the gate and several hundred paces to either side. Missiles pummeled the stonework there, broke the upper galleries of the left tower, and smashed the harbor facing parapet on the right. While this went on, several other craft kept up the assault on the grounds beyond the wall with flaming bundles. Devyn did a quick check; the flames had begun to spread. Folk would gather to fight them, but they would need order and support, and all that support stood ready at the walls.

Flames. Devyn hated them. Fire had played too much a role in his life: a scarred arm still ached on occasion. Kembril's image killed then consumed still haunted his sleep, and folk had suffered from a fire he had set himself. He felt for those fighting the heat behind and silently cursed the assailants before, who flung cumbustibles and threatened destruction to everything he valued.

Racing thoughts of those he held dear came to him. He worried for Talyior and his new family, the queen and the twins up in the citadel watching their world singe, and Grayce. Her image came to him constantly now. He hoped Jeril had been able to find her. He prayed she took the message and left with the stream of refugees, but a deeper part of him, the part most attuned to her lines and ready to respond to her, still sensed her presense in the chaos growing in the city. She would be afraid, but she would try to help.

Even as he admired that impression of her, it also caused him the most anguish.

Donari came close, returning from his transit of the walls. "Look with me, Devyn, do you see a change in their formation out there?"

Devyn joined him, both of them crouching low against the parapet. To that point, the Esdans had loosed no arrows against the defenders. In fact, no Esdan troops had yet landed on Perspan soil. All the area before the wall lay devoid of life, a no man's land of burned buildings, smoldering piers and wreckage.

Devyn looked and noticed a change. From behind the larger crafts and their engines, smaller ships crawled shoreward under oars. These were crammed with troops. Even from a distance, Devyn could make out their bright red helms. Shields rimmed the gunwales and overhead to provide some protection from arrow flights launched by the Pevanese as the boats came within range. Others swept up to the long pier and used the wooden structure's mass as partial shelter to disgorge the first troops.

"We appear to have reached a new spot in this drama," Donari said, spite and anger dripping from each well-enunciated syllable.

"We have taken little hurt so far, sire," Devyn said, staring at the assembling force. Other activity kept up behind the initial screen of shields, and soon the reason came clear. A portable barrier, a sloping wall covered in what looked to be treated hides, rolled through the first group of Esdan soldiers and continued down the pier towards the wider ground before the walls.

All up and down the shoreline, Esdan ships spilled out their human cargoes. Similar protections showed up, some grouping into mini-walls inching forward, behind which clustered, rank upon rank, red-helmed Esdan soldiery.

"Devyn," Donari announced. "I will take the southern reach here, you the north. Arrows concentrated. Try a few flamers to see if anything will take on those hides. Though I suspect nothing will, we at least need to try. Hearten the men, Dev. Then come find me." The king looked back over the area behind their walls, much of it now burning. "I think your skills might be better used in the city against that."

Devyn agreed. "As you say, sire, but I am ready and willing to have a try at them." He gestured outward. "But I will carve out a small band and see what I can do after I check the walls north. It looks as though there is little pressure there yet."

Donari resettled his helm. "Trust me, Dev. We will have hot work here, but they will have to batter a way in. We will annoy them with our arrows until we run out. Look at them. Well-drilled. We will see ladders in droves soon and a ram at the gate. Check the men. Then off with you."

Devyn made a quick circuit, checking arrow supplies and relaying the king's orders. He kept an eye on the enemy, and, once again marveled at their precision. Despite landing out of boats on a foreign shore, they made their offing as a swarm rather than piecemeal. Portable barriers sprang up to shelter other groups, engineers, likely, who quickly enlarged the protected area. By the time Devyn turned to go back to the gate towers, the fruits of all that precise activity appeared in the form of smaller engines, some throwing stones, others flights of arrows. Added to the continuous fire from the anchored ships in the harbor, this new addition threatened to suppress any response from the Pevanese.

He ran back along the wall, gathered his small squad and went in search of the king. He took a last look at the enemy massing. A slightly different movement caught his eye. A number of vessels moved north to where the hill swelled against the shore in a rocky slope. This was cut by a stream that fell in a series of pools below the wall there before sweeping down into the flats north of the city harbor facilities. He paused, puzzeled, for the ground there provided little room for maneuver; the space between the citadel walls and the water narrow, the defenses high and easily defended by the palace troops. In the same moment, memories of Talyior and his fishing adventures there came to him and, despite the sweat and smoke burning his eyes, he smiled. Those were different days, no less dangerous for them both, back when love and words dominated. Now it was swords and engines, tactics and policy.

Given a double purpose for Donari's orders, he now raced ahead of his squad, down the side steps about the Gate tower, and out into the square and Harbor Street, which boiled with smoke and fire. Even as he descended the steps, warning shouts from the walls rang out. Other voices roaring in a strange tongue responded, and there came a loud bang as of an otherworldly hammer beating against the heart of mortal man. The Esdan assault on the Harbor Gate had begun.

Devyn did not hesitate. People before him needed help with their tasks, and if the gate failed behind him, they would need his protection, feeble though it might be. He pressed on, came to the well fountain, and took stock. Folk here still kept up a semblance of organization, and Devyn soon found out why. Talyior's old landlord, Gania Landare, shucked a soggy towel that smelled of smoke at him.

"Well, about time some new arms showed up!" she sprayed into his face. Several of her greasy locks had smoldered down to her scalp, which gave her usually intimidating face a ghastly power. "We are losing whole sections! Where is our precious king?"

"Defending the walls against those who sent this fire," Devyn responded, tossing back the towel. "He sent me to see what could be done, but you've done well enough despite the loss of some hair."

Gania scowled, put a hand up reflexively and found her crusted stubble.

"You're as cheeky as your old friend, you!" she snapped. "And I've plenty of hair to give to the effort. But don't fool yourself, boy, not all of these flames came from junk flung over the walls. There's been some who have come to me saying things."

"What sort of things?"

"Things like there are some fools among us that also like the color red, if you get my meaning?"

Devyn did understand her. Her grated words confirmed some of his deepest suspicions about Reith Simson and his cadre of fake priests. Now his presence off the wall had a double purpose.

"I will look into that rumor," he said. "And a few other things, besides."

"If you mean Grayce Stonesmith, Jeril Sandre's student, then you're late. Ha, that must be a characteristic you share with old Talyior."

"She was here? How?"

"She came to help, early on as a matter of fact. We shared tea yesterday before she worked the market. That Simson fellow pestered her again. It was just before the bells began, I think. She took off with the rest of them, but when the flames took, she showed up again."

The heat grew unbearable in their area as the flames roared through the buildings clustered along the street. Gania flinched as she slopped her towel in the water.

"I've got to get back to this, scribbler, help if your duties allow. I have my house to save. I have'na seen your Grayce for a while now, but I thought I caught a glimpse of Simson come back here, probably to gloat over our struggles. He is a whoreson a cold one. You would think this heat would melt him a little, but I don' think so."

Devyn let her get back to marshalling her neighbors to defend their homes. He did not have the heart to tell her that her efforts were likely in vain. Behind him, just audible over the roar of the flames, the Esdan attempt at the gate boomed out with a hollow report as a ram continued smashing against the steel reinforced timbers.

Grayce had been here. Simson had been here. Devyn considered the coincidence chilling. He collected his small squad.

"Listen," he told them, mouthing his words clearly over the din. "Help these folk; protect them if the gates do not hold. Try and get as many out of here as you can. I smell treachery. I need to find out. The king will need to know." He grabbed one man by the arm. "Find the king. Tell him I have gone sniffing out our fears."

The man trotted off into the smoke. Devyn sent the others to fan out and help as best they could. He checked to make sure his blade moved freely in its sheath at his hip. His right palm itched; it wanted the sword handle and a clean, clear stroke to give. Beyond reason, but then again, so much of what connected the two of them seemed out of logic, he knew she had always been in danger from that slippery, foppish, fraud Reith Simson.

As he set off to investigate the nearest, and main, King's Theology temple, a great crash range out, its import obvious: the Harbor Gate had failed.

Esda was in the city.

If they haven't been in all this time anyway.

He weighed going back to lose himself in the melee sure to come, but Grayce compelled him. He padded away, left the area of the fires, turned down a side street, the very intersection where he first met Grayce running from Simson's thugs. He paused, recalled a back entry, recalled…other things. The sounds of battle swelled as warriors began trading blows behind him. He raced forward to deliver his own if he could.

"Coming, Grayce," he gasped, speeding through the shadows.

* * *

Grayce regained consciousness to find herself in a room that, from its comfortable appointments, she took to be Simson's. It had that mix of just off effeminancy and masculine forms she associated with the man. She smelled insense, another off-putting taint, but then she sniffed her blouse sleeve and guessed the reason for it. The room was strangely quiet, in stark contrast from the cacophony of fighting the fire. She swallowed, found it painful, remembered the cloth shoved down her throat, sat up and looked for something to swill away the aftertaste. She spied a flagon and cups on a side table next to a window. Shuffling off the bed, she went and poured herself a measure of chilled wine.

She swallowed gratefully despite the odd awareness that someone had cooled the stuff on purpose and placed it on the table while she lay unconscious. There were two cups. She moved to the door: locked. The liquid must have loosened something from her time near the fire for a cough took her then, a painful, wretching expellation of smoke's effects. She poured some more, drank, and then again to quell any more of the tickle.

When she regained control she noticed one of her paintings hung above the bed's headboard. She flung the half-full glass of wine at it. The contents splashed pleasingly over the composition, marring what had been her most accomplished landscape.

She turned away, disgusted, and looked outside. All the eastern parts of Pevana from just south of the harbor proper up to the citadel on the hill spread out before her. Fires still raged near the wall. Folk rushed along the streets in view, fleeing. She thought of Devyn, Jeril, Tasia and the other souls lost in the confusion below. Rather than fear, rage and frustration rose like the smoke clouds boiling skyward. This was wrong. Ill. Her throat constricted anew as she swallowed the bitterness of her state. To be caught so unaware in such a time was beneath her newly won happiness; snatched in mid-career, trying to help, trying to belong. The doorlock rattled. Startled, she tried the window, thinking a leap worth the risk, thinking anything better than what would come through that door.

"Locked, I am afraid," Reith Simson said, entering. Behind him came a priest with a basin of steaming water and some washcloths. Simson himself bore a bundle of what looked like a red skirt and a forest green shirt or blouse. He tossed these on the bed and noticed the vandalized painting.

"Ah, now that was unnecessary, but I suppose you felt you had to. That was my favorite, too. Worth every penny."

"It is worthless now." Grayce's voice came as a grating, unlovely rasp, but her tone left Simson unaffected.

"Well," he drawled. "There are other compensations. Yes?"

He waited by the wine while the priest put the basin on a bench seat against the wall and left. The lock rattled again after he closed the door.

"And that too, as you can see. Sorry," Simson offered in mock apology. "The window is three stories down and the halls here can be confusing. I didn't want you to do anything untoward."

"Untoward?"

"Like running or jumping. Silly choices given the chaos outside."

"You call attack and fire 'chaos'?"

He came close. Grayce backed away slightly. He poured himself a glass. Drank. Made a face as though savoring the taste.

"Ah, so good. Donari might not be long for this world, but at least his vines will survive. I see you have had some. More?" He gestured with the flagon.

"I've had more than enough," Grayce replied. She wished now that she had held on to the cup; it might serve as a weapon however weak. She had looked for anything when she wakened: a brush, knife, stick-pin, anything…paintbrush handle, but Simson had been thorough.

"Well now, 'chaos' and 'enough'; coming from you those terms appear heavy with meaning. He broke eye-contact to look outside. "That is a mess, true, but necessary. In the end there is always fire. My relatives," he continued, turning to her, "in Tarn, made much use of it in the past, and quite successfully, too, I might add. Though in the end, I suppose they used it too often against each other to do any of them much good. But I did not come here to talk about my family history."

"Why have you done this? Why me?"

Her question stopped him for a moment. He looked out the window again, seemed to savor the developing carnage as he had the wine, and let go a short nervous breath. To Grayce, everything about Reith Simson had felt affected, staged, off in some way. And yet that breath, and the way he almost sheepishy avoided looking at her, as though he were suddenly transformed into a bashful schoolboy confronting his first crush, seemed oddly normal.

She still did not find the effect endearing.

"You can't be serious," she interpreted. "I am nothing to you."

He turned and looked at her, his eyes a mix of both desire and demand.

"I assure you, I have never been so serious in all my life." He waved, vaguely at the scene outside the window. "All of that is but to serve my masters. Pevana will fall to Esda, make no mistake, mistress. But I want to save what I can from the Avedun clan's folly."

"Folly? You call peace and unity folly?"

A frown creased his brow, a cloud passing before the sun, but rather than shade, the effect revealed something more like truth.

"What do you know of such things, my dear?" His voice, though pitched calmly, still held a hint of suppressed anger.

Memories flooded Grayce's inward eye of screams in the afternoon, arrows and spears in flight, flames rising, her father's bloodied face in death, ghost voices in the cave and Pickson, Pickson, Pickson, and, like an afterthought, faint voices overhead in a cave above Gallina. The connection shocked her, nearly took her breath such that her next words came as a hoarse whisper.

"I know treachery when I see it."

The frown faded. "Ah, now, I see I have upset you. Please forgive me. I did not want to begin our time together with lessons on dynastic policy, acceptable sacrifices for the greater good, and all that."

"Together? You are mad."

"Well, we will have to wait out the results of what is happening out there, which might take a little time; time for us to mend ourselves to each other, so to speak."

She spat at him. "Traitor! People are dying out there. Homes are burning. Strangers are at the walls, and you want to 'get acquainted'? What is going to spare this building if they or the fire reach it?"

The smile returned and with it a cold, almost serene confidence. Simson drank thoughtfully again before responding.

"Time, yes, time enough, I think. I doubt anything untoward will reach us here. Part of those 'arrangements' I referred to earlier. Plus, this place is almost totally made of stone, rather thick in the outside walls, as a matter of fact." He sniggered. "A nice bit of economy, on my part, actually. Most of this came from former Old Way's temples; nice, sturdy blocks put to a much better use. They also make great surfaces for art, as you recall, I am sure." He must have read her reaction, for his smile deepened. "Yes, I remember that day so well. Took me awhile, you know, to understand why I took such a liking to you. After all, you were all dirt, sweat and anger then, and in company with that nosey Ambrose. I kept those lines on the wall above that back door. They reminded me of others I encountered, once, in a dusty hill town. Nice lines on a stable."

A cold chill formed at the base of Grayce's neck. All of this was almost too much to process: her present and past connected in horrific fashion. She had faced men's lust before, that was easily recognized, but to have it joined with such vaunting treason, from so far down the timeline, defied acceptance.

Simson sniffed. "I have always liked that incense, but the smoke taint from your misadventure out there somewhat spoils the effect. As you can see, I had water brought and some clean clothes. I think you will find them a good fit. I have been observant, you see."

The horror of what Simson intimated fell on Grayce like a wave crashing on a steep shore. She backed away, unfortunately encountering the foot of the bed. Still, she tried to keep courage in her voice.

"You are insane if you think I will consent to this. I will be missed. Devyn—"

"Is dutifully fighting his lord's enemies as he should," Simson finished for her. "Hopefully, some Esdan will spit him for me."

"You would stoop to rape?"

Simson finished his glass of wine, placed it on the table, and sauntered closer.

"Grayce, there will be death and rape all throughout this city by nightfall. You must see how I have spared you that? All we need do now is wait out the mess, sip our wine. You will feel much better after a bit of a wash. That water is warm. Those clothes are clean."

"Absurd."

"I admit the situation isn't perfect, but we can make the best of it."

"You think I will submit, just like that? The last man to try and take me died in the attempt."

Simson shook his head sadly, a mockery of commiseration.

"Then he was a fool. What was name? Ah, yes, I remember now. Unkempt miscreant named Pickson. He deserved it. Besides, he was too greasy for you, my dear. Grayce, I offer you my protection from the storm outside these walls. I am sincere in my regard for you, mistress."

"I would rather take my chances in the streets."

Again, a deep frown and a change in tone. "Wash, change," he said peremptorily. "Or I will wash you myself."

"You will lose the hand you touch me with."

He stepped quickly up and backhanded her accross the face. The sudden violence of the blow stunned her, and she stumbled back across the corner of the bed, lost her balance and fell to the floor, her cheek awash in pain and black spots dancing before her eyes.

She felt his hands upon her then, grabbing her arms, lifting her. He dragged-carried her over to a high backed chair. He must have had some line on his person, for he quickly tied her hands to the chair arms. Grayce drew breath to scream, but another blow took breath and words away. Then his face swam into her vision, unnervingly close.

"Another benefit of thick, fire-resistant walls, my dear, is that they dampen sound quite well. Do not try to scream again."

Grayce tensed for what she expected next: clothes tearing, his hands groping, pinching, his lips questing for hers, his odious skin.

Instead he did something even more disgusting. He became gentle.

He brought over the basin of water, dipped a cup and gathered her smokey-smelling hair and rinsed it, tenderly, carefully, the sluicing wetting Grayce's blouse and shoulders, the excess pooling on the chair and floor.

"I would have preferred to keep the carpet dry, but that cannot be helped now," Simson soothed. "But your clothes are a wet shambles, my dear. Let me help you, since you have indisposed yourself."

The water returned Grayce's senses, and she struggled against the bonds and kicked out, but Simson avoided injury. He took hold of her face, firmly, but without undue pressure on her cheeks. With his free hand, he pinched her nose, shook out a cloth from a pocket and forced it into her mouth when she opened her mouth to breathe. She bit down as he pushed the cloth in, but the material protected him. Still, she drew a curse as he withdrew.

"No!" he said, cold, final. "No more of that. More bruises will just ruin your beauty."

Tears came to her then, a combination of fear, rage and resignation. She moaned against the gag as he deftly undid the buttons of her blouse, and then her undershirt, pulling the fabric aside to expose her breasts. She groaned and kicked out again, helpless.

He bathed her. He started with her face, a mint-scented caress, softly over the eyes and forehead, and down each cheek, and then to her neck. Then more water and careful ministration to each breast, carefully, a whisper of cloth and liquid. His breathing deepened as if with concentration and control. She tried to catch his eyes with hers, to make him see her wrath, but all she got was his voice in her ear, a husky mockery of sensuality.

"I would have preferred to watch," he whispered. "But this is also nice. You are truly beautiful, Grayce Stonesmith. Stunning, especially without that smokey stench you brought with you. But let us see about this skirt."

Before she could react, he stepped before her grabbed one leg and, persevering through her feeble attempts to kick him, secured it to the chair leg. Then he lashed the other. Despite her feeble thrashing, he managed to loosen her belt, half lift her, and slide the skirt off down below her knees, leaving her naked save for her undergarments. He stood before her after double-checking the bonds, admiring the view. He took a small knife from another pocket.

"For my nails," he explained. "But it will suffice for this, too."

He leaned close and carefully cut up either seam and pulled her last protection away.

Now Grayce truly wept and gave up all pretense of struggle. She shut her eyes, willed herself to another place, waited for the inevitable, but Simson went no further. She felt the cloth again on her stomach, down both legs and feet, and again up the insides of her thighs.

"See," he soothed. "So much nicer when there is no struggle. I will forgive the bruised finger. At least I fared better than Pickson. You are a rare talent with a paint brush, madam." He ran a finger now up her still damp thigh.

She felt his offending digit graze her pubic hair, linger there, then agonized as he traced her skin up to cup both breasts, again, gently, a lover's touch, a nightmare.

She opened her eyes, saw the desire there, and glanced down at the evidence of his lust tenting his breeches. She screamed defiance against the gag.

He stepped back again as though admiring his handiwork. A knock sounded on the door.

"You have a key, simpleton, use it!" Simson shouted.

The lock rattled. The door opened. Two of Simson's thuggish attendants entered one after the other.

"My Lord," said the first one. "We've had a runner from the shore. News."

"And our guest downstairs has been disagreeable," said the second.

Simson became all business. "So has our lovely lady here, but she got her bath anyway."

The men looked at Grayce, seemingly unaffected by her nakedness.

"I think another sluicing is in order," Simson continued. "Be thorough. Get her dressed and keep her here until I return." He looked out the window, and then directed his last words to Grayce. "Patience. It will not be long now, my dear. We will have that meal and heart to heart soon."

He swept out of the room, leaving Grayce exposed like a nerve ending.

* * *

Jeril spat into the darkness, still tasted blood, spat again and groaned. He had no idea of the time. His head still throbbed from the blow that sent him into darkness. With that frame of reference, he decided some time had passed but not enough to end pain. His captors tied him, hands bound, to a hook on a wall cool to the touch, meaning he was in a basement or lower floor somewhere. They had either not paid attention to the chain length, or cruelly decided to keep it just short, so that the most comfortable position he could achieve was to sit on his knees, which soon ached from the hard stone floor.

He reviewed what he retained from the ambush. His guards, both killed by skillfully shot arrows, men in red garb but no priests took him to the ground and rained blows at him, and a face. The King's Theology cleric, Reith Simson, a man Grayce feared, a man Devyn distrusted, a man whom Jeril intended to repay for his present iniquity if he could. He shook the chain, pulled again at the hook in hopes of a loose fit, and again frowned into the dark when it proved remarkably firm. Someone came with water, but Jeril upset the bucket when he kicked the man in the groin. That brought more blows. He shouted through the assault in the vain hope that he might be heard. Then darkness.

Bit by bit he pieced his situation clear. Thinking helped keep despair at bay. Obviously, the king and Devyn's fears for his person had been valid. If Simson and his order were not spies in Esda's service, then they answered to one who was. Jeril added a shadow face alongside Simson's in his vow for recompense. He ledgered twenty year's flight, Piling, and Tacidus's arrogance against his account. He told Devyn he would fight for his new life and he meant it, but that was impossible with arms stretched awkwardly, knees numb, and his blade taken.

All he could do was spit what tasted like defeat into the dark, strive for patience, and trammel up his defiance for the time when someone, perhaps Reith or his handler, came by to gloat.

There would be gloating. Jorian always ridiculed those who failed him, and Tacidus took his cue from his lord. Jeril was certain he led the assault on Pevana. The man had been a sneering, cynical expression of spite during their encounter in the palace.

Esda is an empire of sarcastic bastards.

He tried to smile at the ironic thought, but the motion caused his crusted-over lip to split again, and the grin turned into a wince and another copper-tasting spit. He sagged against his bonds tired, thirsty and altogether wretched. He thought his eyes closed, the darkness made certainty impossible since he was so sore he could not even feel his lids.

Footsteps sounded. A key turned in what sounded like a lock. Light flowed in with the opening of a door across the space from him. He flinched against the sudden flare, blinked away the spots that swam and focused on the two men framed in the doorway. The man on the left bore the last face he saw before the darkness: Reith Simson. Next to him stood a short man with olive toned skin and the rounded eyes that screamed 'Esda.'

Jeril struggled to his feet to face them.

"I would like to protest my accommodations."

The Esdan sniggered. Simson grinned good naturedly.

"Painter, or is it, Prince?" he asked. "I do like your sense of humor. Kicking at my fellows will not improve things for you."

Jeril shrugged. "Seemed only fair, given the circumstances." He turned to the Esdan.

"Here to report on me to your masters? I look better, normally."

"I doubt it," the man sneered. "But the commander gave clear instructions to find and hold you for his *special attention.*"

Jeril hefted his chain. "I assure you, I feel plenty special already. Tell Tacidus he and I will have our meeting. There is an account to settle."

The Esdan put hands to his belt and laughed outright. "Bold! I suppose I should count myself blessed! Addressed by the emperor's brother, but I can hardly accept the connection. You look less than the beggars one sees outside the city gates back home."

"You should never have come here, lickspittle," Jeril retorted. "This place will be the death of you."

That brought a laugh from Simson, who restrained the Esdan.

"Can you see through walls, then?" he scoffed. "You saw the beginning. Esda has a force already against the harbor defenses. Fire scours the streets behind, aided by my own feeble efforts. The outcome is inevitable."

The Esdan shook off Simson's grip. "I want him cleaned up and ready to go once the streets are secured. Tacidus has plans for him."

"Tell your master I have no need to grace a triumph back in Esda. He and I can finish our business here. I should have finished it in Piling."

The Esdan smiled deeply. "As it happens, I was on that venture, but I was inland when they took you. I think your memory is inaccurate, but you can tell him whatever you want when the time comes."

"You both have badly underestimated this place and its people."

"Quite the contrary," Simson disagreed. "I think I have the pulse of this pukish place's well-factored. Peace," he scoffed. "Our king thinks power can be let to slip away like hour glass sands with no consequence. He is a happy, weak fool."

"As I recall," Jeril retorted, "he bested your predecessor easily enough."

Simson tossed his red cloak behind his shoulders to reveal his stylish clothes, black breeches and a white shirt, hardly the garb of an attenuated priest.

"You don't understand a third of what you think," he said. "This goes far beyond old failures and figureheads."

"Enlighten me."

"Why do you waste words on this wreck?" the Esdan interrupted. "Call men to toss some water on him and let me have him."

Simson frowned at the other man, and Jeril received the impression that the fake-priest did not much like the fellow's attitude.

"You have other tasks yet, friend," Simson said. "Send a runner to the harbor with word. Then pass the call to my other groups. It's time to move."

"But that is too early yet! We have yet to receive the signal."

"I decide the time to risk my men, stranger. I said I know this city better than both of you. Before I call for the barbers to dandify him for his execution, I think I will chat with him awhile. I do not need your permission."

"Be careful, Perspan," the man grated. "You presume too much."

"Pass the word like a good little minion, and prepare your men. I feel I owe our painter-prince an explanation since he made it possible for me to get other things I wanted. This whole affair has turned into quite a bargain."

The Esdan left, shaking his head and muttering malefactions. Simson's words brought rage and fear to Jeril's forefront.

"You leave her alone," he stressed. "She's an innocent—"

"There are no innocents any more. Not now. Not for a long time. Mistress Stonesmith, yes, I have her. I was always going to. This little invasion allows me to act the savior. I am such a romantic that way. She is upstairs even now, drying off from the bath I just gave her, hopefully dressing, but, frankly, between you and me, she is fabulous with or without the lace. I'll enjoy the conquest."

"You are a heartless, raving piece of excrement."

Simson ignored the insult. "Well, I lost my heart to her, you see. She snatched it clean away, just like I snatched the both of you. Nice blade, by the way. Love the balance."

"Let me have it and I'll show you just how nice."

"Now, you are just being silly," Simson said, shaking his head ruefully. "I am actually instructed to give it back to you! No, really, after you have been properly cleaned up, mended and the city secure. Your hands will be bound, or was it cut off? I cannot remember. Tacidus intends to take it for himself."

"It is a royal blade. Tacidus has ambitions beyond his station. He will likely lose his head first."

"Does he now? Makes no difference to me, in the end. Your brother and I have reached an understanding."

Jeril laughed a little at that. "Look at me, priest, are you sure about that? I'm a test case for the value of Esdan promises."

"A little water helped Grayce. You might require a bit more. You brought it on yourself, you know, fighting back like that. Poor choice."

"You're sick."

Simson nodded. "I am, truly, sick of the Avedun clan, sick of the smarmy Old Ways beliefs, sick of many things. Those flames, and the Esdan masses likely breaking through the Harbor Gate as we chat here, are all part of the cure."

"But why Esda?"

"All bloody and beat about, and yet still curious? I have a moment while the men bring your water." He leaned against the doorjamb. "It won't be warm, mind you, all that stuff went to Grayce's beautiful breasts and delicious thighs."

"Devyn will kill you. He will slice that proud face of yours and peel away your simpering smile."

"Grayce said much the same thing. Not bothered. He will find his death in the mess outside." He patted the door. "Good locks, thick walls regardless."

Jeril shook his head in disbelief. The man appeared completely imperturbable even while he exposed all his actions. Such overweening pride was a flaw. He wished he had a throw knife and a loose hand to exploit it. Simson beamed at him from the doorway, but his eyes had drifted away as though in reverie.

"I still don't understand. Why Esda?"

Simson refocused. "What's that? Oh! Sorry, got a little distracted thinking about our beautiful friend waiting for me upstairs. Why Esda. Well, means to an end, of course. Power. All those things I am told you fled from. There is that. But in the end it was something pretty inoccuous. You recall your brother's sigel?"

"Of course, heather, been cursing the plant for twenty years. When I began seeing it here, I knew something was up."

"Yes: *a sprig of heather/ tells the weather/ when the warm winds blow/ spring will show.* That's part of a child's rhyme from my home: Tarn. The heather sprig is on our coat of arms. When my men began seeing these signs all up and down the coast, I got curious. It is rather funny, really. Donari left us alone after his coronation, thinking us cut deep by getting rid of old Casan and some of his bullyboys. I turned us into a nice, quiet little sect, proselytizing as we went along. That is how I made contact with your brother's spies. Seems he has been watching our lands since just after Donari's coronation. A word here, a letter there, a quick trip over, and a pact made. Better than a magic trick if you ask me."

For Jeril, the clarity brought a sickening twist in the pit of his stomach. Heather twice- cursed this land. Donari thought he ruled in peace, but sedition flowered just the same. Jerile thought he found a home, first in Piling and then here, but the watch found him much sooner.

He never enjoyed a moment of real freedom since he rowed that boat out to sea. Anger and despair contested, threatened to bow his head, but he resisted. At least, now he knew, thanks to the detestable Simson and his self-satisfied chitchat.

"What you call a bargain," he said, "is nothing more than empty treason. Do you think Esda will leave you alone once they squash this place?"

Simson turned serious. "I will return home to Tarn. All my hapless cousins have wasted themselves burning each other's keeps. Small minded idiots the lot of them. The only one I cared for was my older cousin, Roderran's queen. The Avedun's killed her out of hand for that randy old bastard." He shifted as men brought in several tubs and some scraggly looking towels. "One thing I learned from watching Roderran, Casan, and that brigand Gaspire Amdoran is how to be patient. Your brother wants to humble Pevana. So be it. I will take my woman and go reconstruct the north."

Footsteps sounded from down the passage. Simson turned, passed words back and forth with the unseen messenger. Jeril strove to hear as Simson's men flung one pail and then another of frigid water on him. He thought he heard the word *Anargi* and the phrase *in through the back*, but the rest was lost to towels and the ungentle attention of Simson's attendants. While they were at it, Simson turned back for one final comment.

"I'll leave you to these fellows for now. Once they run a comb through that unruly hair of yours, it is off you go to that little Esdan runt for whatever comes next. Thank you for Grayce. It was a boon certain, and if I had the power I would return the favor."

"But that is the point in the end, you fake little shit, you do not have any power. Even your attraction for her is an illusion."

Simson held up his hands and wiggled his slender fingers.

"I'm a tactile person," he said. "And these hands have cupped those perfect breasts. She may have glared at me a bit, but her flesh responded. No illusion there! I will have what power I want and the woman, too. A nice ending, or is it a beginning? Whatever. I like it more than I like what yours will be. Try to take it like a man, and if they take you back to your brother, give him my regards."

Jeril stared at him, dumbfounded, while the man practically danced out of the door and out of sight, laughing loudly at his own wit.

Tasia collected the pieces of colored chalk and put them in their box, carefully folded up the tablecloth to catch the chalk dust and shook it vigorously out the window before putting both box and cloth into the toy bin against the playroom wall. Nurse had taken the children away for a wash and a snack before sums later. Eleni insisted the children's schedule be kept as normal as possible despite the trauma unfolding in the harbor. Tasia did her best, but she could tell from the looks the children shared that they knew something was out of sorts. That did not surprise her given their parentage. The Maze-born survived by knowing more than most suspected. The twins were no different in that respect despite a life of royal privilege. Children could always tell. She cleaned her hands and went in search of the queen.

Tasia found Eleni in the main hall taking reports from a group of armored men. She recognized the insignias of both palace guard and city watch. No one took notice of her entrance save Cryso, who gave her a wink and a nod as she settled on the lowest step of the dais. Almost immediately, she wished she had brought a tablet and pencil along with her.

"You say the king fares well?" the queen asked. Tasia noted the slight taughtness in Eleni's jaw as she spoke. "We can see the destruction in the harbor, the ruin of the warehouses, and now flames have started."

One of the city based troops bowed and stepped forward. Tasia did not recognize him, but then until she came to the palace, most of her experiences with the watch consisted of running away from guardsmen to avoid trouble.

"My queen, the king sends regards and a request for water and food for the wall garrison. He said he dared not leave, but asks that you take care for your and the children's safety and leave with the others."

Tasia looked to see Eleni's response to the expected question. A wry smile stretched the queen's lips.

"Is that how he put it?" she asked.

The man opened his mouth to answer then paused, caught off guard by her question. He coughed to clear his throat.

"Well, um, not exactly," he stuttered.

"Man, out with it. I know my husband."

"He said, 'Tell her to leave, now. Tie her and the kids in a bundle and toss their behinds into a wagon!'" Tasia giggled under her breath, for the man grew visibly paler with each word.

The queen laughed, a sound awash in love and good humor.

"My husband knows me well," she said, "to send such a message. Be easy, sir, there is no offense. Of course, we will not leave, and he knows it. You will have your foodstuffs, and," she looked directly at the palace guardsman, "any that can be spared from the citadel defenses. If I had any real skill with a blade, I would come myself. But there it is," she finished, rising. "I will not abandon Donari and my people for uncertain safety. Tell my husband thank you for the offer, but my behind, and our childen's behinds, will stay."

The soldiers bowed and departed in a stumping, clanking mass down the hall tiles and out the door. The queen sank back onto the throne, slumping a little, a deep frown now marring her beautiful face. She turned and noticed Tasia and gave her a smile that did not quite reach her eyes.

"At least he still lives," she said. "And did I not say he would ask? Foolish man. We have survived fire and war before this, he and I. Are the children with Nurse?"

"Yes, ma'am," Tasia replied, rising. "They are having a snack and promised me they would nap before we do our sums. I almost believe them."

That brought a genuine smile. "That sounds about right," she said, rising in turn and descending the few low steps to the floor. "Did they extort a promise of a story, too?"

"Not this time."

"Now, that is surprising! Come with me to the walls. You heard some of that just now, yes? I hate waiting, but rushing off down there would only add to his problems. So, I wait and watch and send food and spare spears. I feel like a warehouse attendant! Cryso," she gestured the major domo forward. "Have Cook see to the food. Use our royal carriage at need. We're going to take a look for ourselves at this plague of smoke and fire below."

This time they exited the palace and climbed up the gate tower. The action spread out for them like a board game. Together they watched the landings and hyper-organized advance against the walls. The Esdans came against the wall in a wave, with the curl crashing first against the Harbor

Gate. Tasia strained her eyes, trying to make out the shape of King Donari, but smoke and distance hazed everything.

Twice the Esdans and their bright red shields and helms advanced with ladder and engine to contest the walls, rising like snakes to cluster along the battlements, and twice the Pevanese rallied to throw them back. Beside her, the queen stood rigid, tense with fear, expectant yet helpless. Her physical tone infected Tasia likewise and together they observed the scene, life-like statues witnessing the end of their world. Tasia could not help but watch the flames advancing inward from the area behind the wall, heading south and west toward what remained of Pevana's Maze. She glanced up at the queen and followed her gaze to where it focused on the gate. Here motion waxed extreme as the Esdan pressure did not relent.

The king fought there.

Even as the thought formed, she knew it true, as did the queen. Tasia bent her eye there as well and saw the Esdan ranks separate. Through the gap advanced a great cylindric shape slung from what looked like chains in a wheeled frame.

"What is that, my lady?" she asked.

"Ill," the queen relied tersely. "If it breaks the gate there will be fighting in the streets. Captain!" she shouted, and the head of the palace guard stepped smartly up alongside her. "Can we spare the men?"

"Not without compromising the garrison for this place, my queen. The king was adamant. We have sent what we could."

"Will that 'thing' break the Harbor Gate?"

The man hesitated, but at her glare quickly answered.

"If unmolested by our spearmen and archers, lady, in time it will break the gate. Look you how the Esdans swarm to either side of the ram. Not full protection, but they seem well versed in what they do. In every move we have seen, the effect is the same: organized, skilled. We may find ourselves besieged here as well before the day ends."

"And Donari will not pull back."

"No, he cannot, will not. The outer wall provides the best chance to hurt them ere they break through."

"But they will break through."

"Yes, my lady, though it saddens me to have to tell you."

"Have someone find me a serviceable blade. Even if I lack the skill to use it, I at least want something more perilous in my hand than a pen."

Tasia listened to the talk half-distracted, drawn to the rhythm of the combat below. Stick figures gesticulated, the air seemed thick with minute shadows that bespoke arrow flights. Flaming bundles arched over the wall to explode in fire behind the defenders. Death walked the harbor wall of Pevana. She felt a rush of fear and remorse. The flames took her back five years when fire had arched through the night sky to immolate her childhood. She still dreamed of the Tree, flaming, magnificent even in its destruction.

And then, despite all the despair flaring below, she laughed.

Her action startled the adults next to her.

"What is it you see that brings such mirth, child?" the queen asked.

"I was thinking the worst thing the Esdans could do would be to break through, my lady," she responded. "You say they seem well drilled and formidable, but I wonder if they have ever fought in our Maze?" Even as she spoke, the idea blossomed for her like a flower poem and she chortled.

"Oh," she said. "If only Old Kembril were alive to see this!"

She did not see the amazed look on the queen's face; her attention drawn to follow the line of the conflict. She traced it northwards from the embattled gate, noticed the activity diminished to almost nothing as the walls neared the spot where the hill stream descended from its pools and falls to find the flats. That was a narrow space. The wall there climbed the slope in terraced steps shielding the gardens and lawns of the merchant class of Pevana.

Then she saw new smoke, followed by a loud report as though a thundercloud had rent itself asunder in one clap. The tower quivered.

"Lady," Tasia asked, pointing. "What is that?"

The queen and the captain had turned at the sound and her question.

"Treason!" barked the captain.

"Tasia, get back to the children and stay with them," snapped the queen.

"What is it?" Tasia asked, turning to go.

The queen pushed her to the stairs and followed behind.

"The Esdans are over the citadel walls, calamity, Tasia, calamity. Hurry!"

The queen hustled all of them back down the tower, the captain of the guard leaping forward once they hit the cobblestones, shouting orders.

Men rushed to his call to form line astride the wide avenue that led up the slope from the estate region. Red crests and shields populated the ground as they broke through into homes to clear their advance. Tasia lingered beside the queen, transfixed by the swelling spectacle. A column of smoke rose behind the gathering Esdans.

"How did this happen, my lady?" she shouted at the queen. "Where have these come from?"

The queen ignored her at first, slowly back pedaling as men rushed by them to take up their positions, scanning the smoke, assessing the direction.

"Ah!" she gasped finally. "Treason, Tasia. An old treason come back to curse us one last time. That smoke rises above the old Anargi estate: the fount of all our former troubles. Of course, it has lain empty since Sevire's death, forgotten in the wake of bigger events, but someone remembered. That ravine is narrow against the stream there. The Esdans could not hope to assemble a large force unnoticed…" she paused, glanced down at Tasia with sad eyes, "unless others prepared a way for them. I expect that blast took the wall and what few sentries present. Donari feared saboteurs in the city, but not here. We are betrayed."

The queen bent close, grasping Tasia's face in both hands.

"Run, girl," she insisted. "Back to the palace. The children. Your promise. I will follow. Find your brother if you can." The queen's sudden tears dismayed Tasia. The woman's nails pressed into her cheeks as though she tried to physically impress upon her the intensity of her wishes. "Maze-born," the queen finished, "keep my children safe until I come for all of you. Go!"

The queen shoved her roughly in the direction of the palace entrance. She hesitated for a moment, looking past Eleni's stricken face at the enemy force roaring up the street, a swarm of red helms, shields and long, cruel-looking spears. Those few of the guard that had managed to assemble stepped forward to meet them. Tasia sped off as the first sounds of battle rose with metallic clamor. She turned once at the entrance, dodging a squad of men rushing to join the queen. Eleni paced back toward the palace, flanked by two guards, a sword now gripped in her right hand, facing the enemy. The din rose behind, shouts in Perspan and foreign tongue, screams that communicated the same in either language: pain, fear, blood, death.

Tasia touched her still tingling cheek. The queen's will compelled her. She passed through the gate to the courtyard. She looked for her brother as she raced by the stable doors, but the area was aroil with men leaping into saddles and clattering off. If he were there, he had no time for her. She was on her own. She climbed the palace steps. Cryso stood by the doors, armed, a look so at odds with Tasia's usual image of him that she paused, taken aback.

"The queen sent me for the twins," she said, frightened anew by how shrill her own voice sounded.

Cryso gave her a warm look, a remembered calm that helped her. "Of course, she did," the old man said, his tone the quiet of long service and patience. She heard him clearly, despite the rush of activity in the courtyard and the chaos outside. "She has placed great faith in you, child. Well placed, I should say. In with you now, for we will close these doors until the queen should come. Keep them safe, Tasia."

Tasia entered. The great doors shut behind her; the change immediately apparent. She rushed up the carpeted stairs, her pounding pulse the loudest thing in her ears in the relative quiet. Serving maids rushed about, faces intent and scared as news of their peril spread through the halls. Tasia eluded hands that tried to grab her, ignored questions, and pushed on toward the royal apartments. Nurse stood matronly guard by the twins' bedroom door.

"I'm to look in on the children until the queen comes." Her voice must have communicated something of Eleni's intensity because Nurse let her in without a word. The twins had awakened. Arryn's hair was still ruffled from sleep. Ailen sat perched, wide-eyed on her bed.

"Where are mama and papa?" the little girl asked. "We had snack and tried to sleep, like you said, Tazy, but we heard footsteps and shouting. What is it?"

"Where is my father?" Arryn asked, sounding far older than five. Tasia paused before answering, considered the queen's orders, and decided on a partial truth.

"The king is with his soldiers at the harbor gate, keeping watch. The queen is coming soon. She asked me to check on you."

"Is dada watching for Tolimon?" Ailen asked, scrambling out off her bed to join her brother.

"Nah," he answered before Tasia could respond. "He is fighting Borimon. Remember the bells? All that shouting means something."

"It means a story," Tasia blurted, desperate now, despite the memory of those knowing looks the twins had shared earlier, to distract them, to retain the atmosphere of infancy that now stood threatened outside the walls.

"What kind of story?" Ailen asked.

"Minuet?" Arryn added, coming closer.

"More about Soralee? Tolimon?"

More shouts and a woman's scream stunned all of them into silence. A crash, like window glass breaking, sounded close, followed by an even louder bang as of a door breaking under pressure. For Tasia, the import was obvious: the enemy had gained entry into the palace proper.

Tasia ran to the door, but Nurse had locked it from the outside. She pounded on the wood, shouting. The children, infected by her action joined her, adding their piping voices to the call, but no one came. Footsteps pounded in the hallway followed by what sounded like the clash of metal on metal, faint, as though downstairs in the main reception hall.

"Trapped!" Tasia gasped, futilely twisting the handle one last time.

"Why is the door locked?" Ailen asked, sneaking her hand into Tasia's.

"That's never happened before," added Arryn, "not even when mama sent us to bed early for drawing on the walls with her special ink and pens."

Thinking quickly, Tasia took stock of their limited options. They could wait where they were, hoping Cryso or Nurse or the queen herself came to collect them. The sounds about and the unequal contest in the streets outside suggested the only ones likely to come find them would be Esdans intent on either taking or killing them. Children in the palace; strangers would assume them royal, but outside of the palace they could just be kids and anonymous.

She knew all the best hidey-holes in the palace and citadel.

She knew of more outside in the city proper.

She took them each by the hand and led them to the window. The city was a dangerous place under any circumstances, but only to the unaware or untutored; she was neither of those things. Walls and the king's men provided sanctuary, but dead men and compromised walls made for a snare, and traps were things every Maze-born learned to avoid early on. They had made games out of it when she had been the twins' age, darting about among the great Tree's limbs or dashing in and about the warren of poverty, which defined their lives.

The queen told her to keep them safe, but the nursery was no longer safe. She opened the window. Below the sill, a trellis suggested a tenuous route down to the garden below where two days ago they played hide and seek in a different life. Tasia knew she could make it, but the twins were too little to reach all the right hand and footholds. She looked around for an alternative and spied the rumpled bedding.

"This will be a different kind of story," she promised, "an adventure story about us! But first we have to escape from here." She hurried to Ailen's bed, began pulling sheets and blankets off. "You two get the covers off of Arryn's bed and bring them to the window." She gathered up her mass of cloth and returned to the window, tying the separate pieces into a makeshift rope. The twins added their pile and stood by, watching intently as she finished. She tested her knots and tied one end around a bedpost. She looped one end around Arryn's midsection and lifted him up to the windowsill.

"Hold tight, little prince, while I lower you down." Arryn, his fear over the locked door and all the strange noise momentarily forgotten, gave a huge smile.

"This is better than wrestle time with father!" he said as Tasia lowered him down.

The line went slack when Arryn reached the ground.

"Can you untie it?" Tasia shouted. There came a pause.

"No!" Arryn shouted. "It's too tight for me!"

Tasia bit back a curse. Someone pounded on the nursery door. She picked up Ailen. "I have a special ride for you!" she exclaimed cheerfully. She swung the little girl onto her back. "Can you hold on tighter than tight with your arms and legs?" she asked. Ailen answered with a firm squeeze. "Right then. Hold on."

Carefully, she climbed onto the sill and felt for a foothold in the trellis. Gingerly, she moved out and down, trusting the frame and the vines they held to sustain their weight. Ailen clung to her like a baby possum, her arms entwined around Tasia's neck, her breath hot and intense against her ear. Luckily, Ailen was the slighter of the two, and Tasia made easy work of the burden. They joined Arryn on the ground. She untied the prince and led them quickly to the exit opposite their nursery window. Once she had made her decision to leave the palace, their route came to her clearly. The way out the flower garden led to the tended vegetable rows behind the kitchens. At the far end waited the small postern gate Devyn Ambrose pointed out earlier.

She raised the latch and pushed against the door, but it opened just a few inches before sticking fast. The twins joined her but to no avail. Through the partial opening blew cleaner air, a tantalizing presentiment of safety just out of reach. Tasia tamped down another curse at this new check and looked about for anything they could use to lever the door open. The sounds of fighting and screaming filtered into their space. She panicked then, tears of fear and frustration springing to her eyes as she once again threw her shoulder in vain against the door.

A door slammed back in the kitchens. Footsteps sounded of someone running toward them past the ovens. The back door burst open.

"Basty!" cheered Arryn. Tasia's brother slid to a stop before them, breathless, wide-eyed and sporting a gash on his forehead that oozed blood.

"How did you know where we'd be?" Tasia asked.

"Took a guess and got lucky, although I don't think luck has much purchase here today. I was on my way to the back through the garden. The front of this place is a mess, T. Fighting in the courtyard. The queen…"

"Is she?" Tasia left the question unfinished, but Bastian answered anyway.

"Cut off from the palace gates with most of the guard, last time I saw. The enemy flanked them and pushed them down toward the citadel gate. I got this," he gestured to his gash, "by ducking just low enough to avoid a spear point."

He pushed past Tasia and pushed against the door, and with all of their help managed to open the door enough to allow passage.

"There," he said, brushing rust from his hands. "That should do it. Off with you, then."

"Aren't you coming with us?" Tasia asked.

Bastain wiped some blood from his brow. "Tasia, the way I see it, you are here because the queen must have set you a task. Watch over them, yes? Well, Devyn Ambrose is with the king, you have the twins. One of us has to stand by the queen. You know the city as well as I. I am off to get a good knife then round this crazy place to find the queen. Now, no arguments! Find a safer place than this and lay low till…"

"Till the end of the story," Tasia finished for him. He smiled wanly.

"Always with the story, but maybe that is how it should be." He ruffled the prince's hair. "You three out in the city. The enemy won't stand a chance."

He pushed them out the door. Tasia knew better than to dispute with him. In her heart, she knew he was right. He pulled as she pushed, and the door ground shut, leaving them on the outside.

Tasia led them down a steep flight of steps cut into the rock in a zig-zag pattern. Their descent would leave them in the city but shielded temporarily from the conflict down at the harbor gates by the hill's mass. The twins gripped her hands tightly as they negotiated the stairs, neither of them, for perhaps the first time ever, sparing any energy or air for words.

They wound down through narrow streets overhung with houses and bottom floor shops. They met few people about. Most had either gone to fight the flames or fled the city altogether. No one recognized them. Tasia hustled the twins along until they came to the main way that led down from the citadel to the Landgate square. West, they could see folk massed in a jam of carts, wagons and walkers. Tasia crossed over and plunged into the region south of the road, heading for the Maze. She moved by instinct rather than by volition, casting about in her mind all the places where they might go to ground.

Then she knew. She turned onto Lampwright's street, walked quickly by *The Golden Cup* where Saymon Brimaldi stood atop a wagon outside his door shouting instructions to a motly collection of folk armed with rusty old weapons. TThe three of them ducked down an alley between two storage buildings that ended at the edge of the open space that used to be the area immediately around the Tree. Now it sported grass that lapped like a green pond against the fence enclosing Kembril Edri's grave.

She turned to face the back of the building that helped form a border to the place. Grayce's rendition of the tree stood out clear despite the smoke that hazed the city. For Tasia, there could be no more sacred place. She pulled a tarp bunched up against the lower bricks away to reveal a slender ladder, Grayce's old ladder. With difficulty, she managed to heft it upright against the wall.

"Climb, carefully," she instructed the twins.

Up they went, cresting the top and over the low false wall, which, once they squatted down, provided them a clear view all around but kept them hidden from prying eyes. It had been Tasia's favorite hiding place for as long as she could remember.

Devyn Ambrose and Bastain both knew about it. If either survived the tumult now raging, they would come.

She shoved the ladder away until it toppled backwards. If the enemy found them, at least they would have to work at it a little.

She sighed. Wiped sweat from her brow

"Now," she said. "Who wants a story?"

Chapter 20: To Face One's Demons

Devyn padded on down the alley. The flames had yet to reach the area. Most of the conflagration remained focused around the region of the wall and streets into the city from the harbor. He paced down a remembered passage now; it was here that he first encountered Grayce. He hunted semi-blind here, following a hunch, a sense that he and the woman remained connected by lines real and spiritual. He thought back to that other day, half a life ago it seemed, when he had run for his life from Jared Corvale and his thugs. An awareness of how the Tree's roots knit together the elements of life in the Maze had stopped him then, given him a new purpose. After, there had been Senden and words and a choice made to trust a tyrant and serve a king.

His life had been as convoluted and twisted as the Maze itself; the perfect proving ground to solve the puzzle he now faced.

Lines. He had but to follow.

Those lines led him to the back door of the King's Theology temple; the mass of the place muting the sounds of battle beginning to rise back near the harbor. It was almost quiet. He felt time's crunch and the conflict between love and duty. Whispers from his past attended his hoarse breathing as he paused before the door.

"Stop waiting, boy," Kembril's raspy cackle urged.

"You'll never find her, fool," Corvale's arrogant sneer taunted.

"Finish the poem or lose the duel," Talyior's thoughtful tone mused.

"Misguided puppy," Casan's judgemental voice dismissed.

He shook his mind to silence, allowing himself a brief smile at the two pleasant memories. He missed his mentor and friend even more now that he was truly up against unreasonable odds.

He tried the latch, found it locked, saw the remnant of Grayce's work above the doorframe, and heard a different whisper of her desperate need. He was close, could feel it, but how to get in?

He stepped back, swept his gaze back and forth looking for a second story window, anything, but this back temple wall was a whitewashed brick mass from door to roofledge. Anger and frustration surged, and he considered rushing the place from the front. He tamped down the foolish thought. False heroism now might kill them both. He wiped sweat from his eyes and reached out once more to try the door.

The sound of someone pulling back a latch from inside stopped him. Voices rose from inside and the door swung open. Devyn slipped back to crouch behind a refuse bin. Two King's Theology priests exited followed by a squad of rough looking men. All bore swords, even the priests, and the four hindmost carried large sacks. That group made off down the alley to the main way that fronted the temple, leaving a single priest behind. The scene sparked alarms, but Devyn did not have time to wonder about their mission, for the remaining priest turned back inside and the door began to swing closed.

With a grace born more from instinct than practice, Devyn stepped around the bin, drew his knife, grabbed the edge of the door, and using it as a fulcrum, swung around and plunged his blade into the throat of the startled priest attempting to pull it shut. Blood erupted from the wound as Devyn pivoted, pulling out his blade as he moved. The priest slumped gurgling to the ground. Devyn dragged him inside, finished closing the door, and crouched defensively, expecting attack.

He was alone with the bloodsoaked corpse in a dark hallway that ended with a turn to the right. Light showed from around that corner. He slunk down the hall, hugging the wall, sword out and ready, bloody knife in his off-hand. He felt certain Grayce was in here somewhere.

"Fine, then, I'm in," he whispered. "What next?" He had his answer by the time he reached the turning. "'*Finish the poem*', of course!"

The turn led into the temple kitchen. The remains of a hurried meal still lay on a side table. A door stood propped open. Devyn moved to the opening, risked a look, and discovered the door opened on the main hall. Torches lit the area. It was empty except for a small group standing by a staircase set in the middle of the right side. Four spearmen in temple colors framed two others, one taller with arms bound, wet hair and, curiously, a long slender sword hung over his shoulders, one shorter with a red helm, which matched those of the host assailing the city.

Devyn looked closer at the man in the middle and recognized Jeril Tandori. The group looked intent on some mission of mischief, with Tandori apparently a prisoner trussed and ready for transport, and all of it in a temple forced to eschew violence and weapons as part of its revised charter. Devyn wasted no more time. Despite the obvious odds, he stepped out into the hall and began sprinting at the group.

His sudden appearance upset the balance of the scene. The Esdan turned and shouted a warning but too late. As the spearmen turned to lower their weapons, he flung himself among them, hamstringing the one closest to him and slashing the throat of the other. The Esdan tried to back up and draw his blade, but Tandori kicked him viciously in the knee and the man went down in a tumble. The other two fake priests managed to level their spears, but Devyn was inside their guard already. One he took with a thrust to the groin. Tandori threw himself against the other, distracting him enough for Devyn to recover his blade and arc a blow that took half the man's skull.

In less than a breath, four men lay dead or bleeding out. The Esdan moaned and rolled on the floor clutching his knee, in too much pain to call out for help. Devyn helped Tandori to his feet. Jeril, arms still bound, took two steps and kicked the Esdan square in the face. The force of the blow smashed his head against the floor, putting an end to his groaning.

Devyn cleaned his blades, sheathed his sword and used his knife to cut Jeril's bonds.

"I came looking for Grayce and get you instead. I need to check my instincts," he said.

Jeril barked a terse laugh and rubbed blood back into his hands.

"Your instincts are not wrong, friend. Simson does have her. Had me, too, part of a deal he made with my ex-countrymen. Nice timing, by the way."

"Deal?"

Jeril slipped his sword around to hang off the hip. "Treason. All your fears and most of my own have come painfully true. That one," he gestured at the unconscious Esdan, "was about to take me to the harbor and then home after they finished here. Simson has been working for them for longer than you think. There is a tale for you. I would as soon throttle the man as paint him, however."

Devyn moved to the stairs. So far, no one had come to investigate the disturbance in the hall.

"Where did they keep you? Did you see Grayce?"

Jeril joined him. "This place has a rather damp cellar. Simson hinted at an upstairs room. His own, I think." Devyn felt his hand on his arm as he turned to ascend. "Friend," the painter urged, a pained look on his face. "I must warn you. He may have…she might be—"

"Grayce would never let him," Devyn finished for him. "Not willingly. Whether he touched her not, Simson is a dead man as far as I am concerned. He is the last viper in a nest of snakes. I should have taken him before this."

Jeril looked at him closely for a moment, glanced back at the bodies and blood, nodding his head sadly.

"That you are a killer is plain," he said. "But I do not think you are the cold sort. Take your revenge, poet, but do not take pleasure in it. Whatever we find upstairs, I do not think Grayce would want you hating. Though, as for that, perhaps I am out of depth here. It seems we all have our ghosts, old wounds, and pains."

Devyn began ascending. "Trust me, Tandori, I have never grown used to it. Help me find Grayce and get out of here. I fear what we may find outside. It might be a mercy if Grayce were—"

"No," Jeril interrupted. "Best not think that way. Onward."

They went up the flight of stairs, which ended on a landing that led down a hallway with doors to several rooms appearing on the left. The right wall ran blank and obviously formed the upper wall of the lower main hall. The door larger than the others waited at the end of the passage. For Devyn, it spoke of his destination, and yet it seemed altogether too quiet.

"You would think a place like this would be crawling with Simson's thugs," he offered.

"My thought also," Jeril responded. "I was almost insulted they thought four would be enough for me. Simson let slip some of his activities, mentioned fires. Perhaps he loosed his folk to help the chaos?"

"I avoided a group just before I found you. Perhaps we will have a bit of good luck after all."

As they passed the second door on the left it opened, and three of Simson's men spilled out, blades up and looking far more martial than priests should. Devyn and Jeril turned shoulder to shoulder to face the threat. Simson's men effectively blocked their escape route.

"Remind me to keep my mouth shut about luck," Devyn grumbled.

"Keep your mouth shut about luck," Jeril said. "Enough levity. How about you see what is on the other side of that last door? I will entertain our friends."

"Are you sure?"

"Sure enough, but be quick about it!"

Before Jeril finished speaking, Devyn turned and ran at the door. He leaped, kicking at the latch with all his weight and momentum. His blow sent the door crashing open, and he shoulder-rolled into the room, whipping his blade up instinctively. He took in the scene presented in an instant. Simson, shirt half-off, fumbled to draw his sword from its sheath. His cheek dripped blood from some deep scratches. Grayce leaned back half on the bed, clutching her blouse closed. Her face reflected both horror and surprise at his sudden appearance.

Devyn made it to his feet in time to deflect Simson's ineffective thrust. He swept to the attack, drew blood from Simson's arm with a swipe and neatly spun the man's blade from his grasp with a slash at the wrist and a slight twist of his own sword tip.

"Devyn!" Grayce gasped, "How did—"

"Didn't you read my last note?" Devyn responded, keeping his eyes on Simson, who had retreated in pain over towards the window. "I've told you before, love, that you have some powerful lines." He reached for his knife and tossed it on the bed. "Here, you'll need this once we leave."

"You will never make it," Simson said through teeth clenched in anger, frustration and pain. "It is all over for you and your silly king. Look outside, fool, the city is burning. Esda has swarmed the walls and is in the streets."

"And I will go deal with them directly," Devyn said. "But first I will deal with you. Donari will want you saved for questioning."

Behind them, the sounds of blades crossing changed the tone completely.

Simson looked beyond Devyn and smiled in sneering disdain. "You were always presumptuous, poet. Too quick, always, to claim victory. Raised from your dusty Maze to a place too far above your station."

"At least I didn't live a lie for power." Devyn motioned for Grayce to join him and turned sideways to glimpse the action in the hallway. Jeril had lessened the odds to two to one, but his left arm hung slack and dripped blood. Inwardly, Devyn cursed at the time Simson cost them.

Devyn regarded Simson, whose grin had deepened as if he guessed the poet's consternation.

"Yes, quite stopped up here at the end," Simson chortled. "I'm defenseless or am I? You cannot touch me now, boy. The Esdans will require answers for my person." He waved his wounded arm. "This will cost you more than you can pay. Tell you what, I will keep the girl as partial recompense. Already tested the goods, anyway, so I would say that is a barg—"

The rest of his comment ended in a choking gasp because Grayce, snatching up Devyn's knife from the bed, took two quick steps and plunged it almost completely through Simson's open mouth. Blood and teeth spewed everywhere as the priest

stumbled backwards, tottered, and then crashed dead to the floor.

Grayce's violent action stunned Devyn. She bent to retrieve the blade, crossed the room, and planted a kiss on Devyn's lips that defied any questions.

"Ambrose!" Jeril shouted, desperation evident in his voice. "Hurry!"

"Sorry," she said, breaking away. "I just could not take another word from him."

"You just beat me to the thrust is all. Not to worry. We need to get out of here."

He dashed back out of the room, and not a moment too soon. Jeril had fallen to one knee under the rain of blows from Simson's thugs. Devyn took one in the stomach with a thrust from just above Jeril's shoulder level. The other began backing away at the altered odds. Devyn took him in the back when the man turned to run.

Devyn led them past the bodies back to the head of the stairs. No one showed. Simson must have emptied the place except for those few men. Perhaps they had the luck after all. He heard a ripping sound and turned around to see Grayce wrapping her sleeve around Jeril's wounded arm. Her blouse was a ruin, her breasts all but exposed by the torn cloth and loose ties, but, again, the look she shot him defied questions.

"Will you be alright with that arm?" he asked as Grayce made the bandage fast.

Jeril flexed the limb, grimaced, and frowned at the blood that began seeping through the cloth.

"For what awaits us outside, I will do well enough. Might have a little trouble with a brush, however."

Devyn laughed at the absurd comment and raised an imaginary glass in toast. "Here is to hoping we live long enough to give you the chance."

Down the stairs they went, then right and out the hall to the barred main temple doors. Devyn shifted the beam and they exited to a scene worse than any nightmare.

The area before the temple swarmed with people moving in a stream down the street. Many of them looked back over their shoulder, fear obvious on their faces. From the vantage at the top the temple stairs, Devyn saw the reason for those looks. A body of Pevanese troops retreated, shielding the civilians from a larger mass of Esdan infantry.

Devyn pointed. "We need to move, get you both clear of that if we can."

Jeril followed his look, shook his head and urged Grayce and Devyn before him down the steps.

"Too late or near as, friend," he said.

It became immediately apparent to Devyn that he was correct. They gained the street level as the last of the city folk rushed by. As they turned to follow, the Esdan force swarmed forward, crunching brutally against the Pevanese line. Men screamed defiance. Blades rose and fell. The line shivered, splintered, then bled away into groups of running, dying men. The Esdans spilled out into the region near the temple steps, spreading death with ruthless tenacity.

The three of them quickened their pace. The remnants of the Pevanese force reformed their pitifully small line behind them. Devyn and the others reached a turning, slowed as they ran into the back of the mob. The crowd swelled as folk fought to choose their direction. Right or left. Devyn looked behind. The Esdans had reformed their line and advanced, spears forward to push against the mass of folk clustered at the intersection. Panic spread like water over a riverbank. Folk screamed in terror and surged. Behind them battle cries in two languages swelled to complete the din. Devyn reached for Grayce's hand in the press, met her fingers, tried to grasp, but her touch melted away like butter separating on a hot knife. Devyn turned, searched the mass for her face, and caught a glimpse of eyes wide in terror, her hand reaching as the crowd of frightened civilians separated them. He swung around, searching for Jeril, but could not find him in the sea of faces. He tried unsuccessfully to fight the human tide that swept him up the left hand turn. The press pushed and tumbled him up the northern way, leaving him cut off from both Jeril and Grayce. The scope of his world reduced to a collection of strangers.

He gave up fighting against the stream, turned and fell into step with the mass, thinking ahead, trying to recall if a side street exited off the lane that might allow him to double back and rejoin Grayce and Jeril. The mob pressed in as the way narrowed, and Devyn realized it led to the skirts of what remained of the Maze. He darted out of the mass, clung to a doorway against the current of scared humanity, and waited for a space to clear. A group of soldiers, bloodied but still together swam by. He pushed away from his anchor and stopped them.

"Hold!" he shouted. Recognition broke through their collective obscurity. Perhaps his tone or the appearance of his sword held resolutely grabbed them, but they stopped as if on command. They were a bare handful, but they were all he had.

"Face about," he commanded. He had never led men in battle before, but need and anger worked the magic necessary to give him the voice of command because the men focused and fell into line without protest.

"Right then," he continued. "We are going to slow what comes behind, get it? The bastards have dared come into the Maze, and we will make them pay. Small space, men, close quarters and no worries for the flank. We stand here, and we give the people time to clear. We fight for these yards now and trust the king and the others are doing the same. So eyes front! Shields up! Strike and fall back together now. Steady! Here they come."

The men flowed into a semblance of a shield wall as the Esdans closed to trade blows. The first clash sounded like a hammer striking inferior metal, but the line held.

Devyn took his place in a gap, adding his blade to the general weight of the Pevanese counter. And their blows told, beyond all reason. Devyn thrust into a gap and felt a satisfying punch as his sword point met flesh. The man next to him took a spear in the face and fell back in a shower of blood, but Devyn caught the Esdan grasping that weapon with a slashing blow that nearly decapitated the wretch. He stepped back to allow another with a shield to take his place. The pressure in front of them eased slightly. They must have caught the enemy flush in pursuit and stung them. Devyn looked behind them and ordered the group to fall back to where the way narrowed even more. They reformed their line like a plug stopping a tube. The space allowed several of the men to serve now as a second line reserve. Devyn joined them to take a breath. He fought down pangs over losing Grayce and Jeril and let duty take over his thoughts.

The space behind his plug soon cleared of civilians; a small mercy given the tone of what he had observed from the temple steps. Esdan troops invested the city, moving towards the center. He glanced up toward the citadel. The smoke boiling upwards brought the group he saw back at the temple to mind. Treason seemed a plentiful commodity all of a sudden. The enemy had pierced the citadel. The enemy beset the city entire. It would be street to street, house to house throughout.

All he could do was keep twenty men from breaking and running. He remembered fighting in his youth, scrabbling among the dust and hovels to keep his crust and cup from the Maze-bullies. Then it had come down to tenacity in the face of ignorant cruelty. He drew his lines in the dust mostly in his mind, but fought like a wild cat to keep them. Bloody lips and ringing ears did not deter him. He fought for his place, and that was enough.

Now he paced behind his purloined group, mastering his fears and ignorance, calling on every verbal tick he knew to set them to hold; and the line held.

Twice the Esdans surged to the attack, rained blows down on the Pevanese shields and probed for lodgements for their spears, and twice Devyn's Pevanese remnant held them and thrust them back with loss. The ground about them grew slippery with blood. The stench of sweat, shit, and piss comingled in the air, adding to the foul frenzy of the affair.In the short pause after the second encounter, arrows arced over their position, taking several men in the neck as they stepped out of the line to let others take their place. The arrow flight must have been a signal, for the Esdans renewed the pressure immediately and forced them back. Several more of Devyn's group fell. The losses threatened to make their postion untenable.

"Back now, smartly!" he shouted, and he and what remained of his group retreated down the lane. The Esdans pressed behind. They faced about at a turn, took the pressure, flowed back again to another. They ran out of turns or narrow spaces and stumbled out into the cleared space surrounding Kembril Edri's gravesite. All around them, other groups began spilling out from other openings, forming line as best they could opposite the various entrances to the area. Soldiers and shopkeepers now stood shoulder to shoulder trying to keep the Esdan forces from forcing their greater numbers into the clearing.

Devyn swept sweat from his eyes, felt other wet and noticed a gentle rain drizzling over them, the northern skirt of the great storm he noted the day before come to sweep the region with the remnants of its moisture. It might not be enough to quench the fires, but perhaps it might serve to sluice the bitterness he fought to control as he took his place again among his men. A large frame brushed his left shoulder, and he turned in amazement as Gania Landare, brandishing her cudgel in one hand and a large iron skillet in the other, took station next to him.

"Gania, get back," he started to say, but the look she gave him stifled any reasons he might have offered. This fight was for the life of the city, and who was he to deny such a one as Gania the right to strike whatever blows she could?

"No more words, poet," she husked, swinging her skillet up like a shield to deflect a spear thrust. "I'll brain the last of these devils myself, I will!" An Esdan soldier stumbled to a knee before her, and she swung her club down with a sickening crunch on the man's helm. He fell in a bloody senseless pile in front of them. Devyn swallowed the rest of his words and added his own thrusts to hers and the rest of the group fighting with them.They contested their space like heroes, the pressure to their front growing as more and more of the enemy arrived to swell the Esdan ranks.

Devyn lost himself in the death dance of thrust and parry, but he still noticed when Gania went down, clutching a thrown spear that protruded out of her midsection. Devyn spared her a horrified glance, saw the death blood pulsing down the shaft, and her face contorted in rage and agony. Then the press forced him back, and he lost sight of her in the need to defend his front. Back a step. Another. After every thrust and parry, he felt his blade grow heavier. He fought on in an agony of concentration, willing himself to continue. He blocked a blow, felt the shock all the way to his shoulder, but still managed to sweep low and take the man in the leg. He must have hit the artery, for blood erupted over his sword edge like a fountain. He backed another step. Then another. All around, he sensed the same thing as the impacable Esdan assasult pushed the Pevanese back into the cleared space.

Devyn retreated until he came up against a solid structure. He reached out his free hand to feel it and recognized the wrought iron tines of the fence surrounding Kembril's grave. There he fought, sword gripped two-handed, his world reduced to a senseless space the length of his blade and reach, all other awareness fallen to insignifance with the desperate need to keep his space clear. His blade bit over and over again; the concussions numbing his hands and arms. Spear points swam before his sweat-blurred eyes, rain drenched his hair, and his pulse began to match the blows he sent darting out into the fray.

All fell to silence for him save for the memory of a beloved voice leaching through his despair with a final thought:

"One last protest before the dark, boy. You are Renia's Voice, now."

Devyn fought on, an eloquent, silent scream.

* * *

Jeril paused to take shelter in a doorway. The crowd flow that separated him and Grayce from Devyn parted yet again shortly thereafter. He thought he saw her duck down a back alley that ran north towards his home but lost sight of her when the crush pushed him past the turn. He tried to hug the side of a building, as though searching for slack water in a stream to make his way back, but even after the crowd thinned out he realized it was no good. The Esdan forces surged into and through the intersection to engage the squad of Pevanese retreating before them.

Jeril retied Grayce's bandage on his arm and moved out and behind the Pevanese struggling to hold the street. Their leader, a youngish officer with a battered shield and a knotched sword snarled at him to keep moving, but Jeril ignored him. In the swirling action, the top of a red-crested helm kept appearing just behind the foremost Esdan ranks. He had to move forward to lend his blade when the contest intensified. For the next while it was parry and thrust through gaps in the shield wall, a miasma of sweating, cursing men, some screaming defiance, others despair, and after a few crazed moments Jeril could not tell there was a difference.

Then the pressure in front of Jeril eased somewhat as the forces separated for breath and re-order, and in that pause Jeril descried the same Esdan helm, but this time it was attached to a face he recognized.

Tacidus.

In the instant their eyes met, it was as if time stopped. Motion arrested. The sounds of battle fell away. Jeril countenanced destiny with the clarity of a man touched by the gods. Everything flashed to him then: his mother's corpse, his brother, smirking and ironic next to Tacidus in the doorway, Tacidus at the jetty, a spear with Jorian's heather placed among the ashes of an eastern village, Tacidus mocking him at Piling, the promise and threat in the man's eyes in the encounter with Donari. It came to him then that destiny was not something a man could actually choose. Rather, all he could do was face his experiences with honor.

Grace came not with the outcome but with the effort.

All of that flared like a new flame as Jeril observed the rage in Tacidus's expression. The man glared at him, lips and mouth contorted in a shout the surreal silence suppressed. Then he raised his bloodied blade to point the tip right at Jeril.

Jeril's throbbing, dripping left arm broke the spell. He retreated with what remained of the Pevanese force backwards to where the way narrowed somewhat. They redressed their lines and waited for the next onslaught. The Esdans advanced with renewed numbers, and this time Jeril could make out clearly the sound of Tacidus's voice above the tumult.

"Come on, you filthy, arrogant piece of shit," Jeril muttered. "Let's finish this."

The Esdans once again crashed into them, but this time the line wavered despite the smaller front. Men went down, tripped others in their fall, and soon the scene fell to a disorganized melee of individual combats blood-splattered and rain-drenched. Jeril fought then with all his remembered skill ignoring the protest from his back muscles. He took a man in the neck, deftly slicing through the juggler vein, leaned away from the blood splurt to take another in the stomach. He used a foot to free his sword point from the suction before swinging low to take both feet from yet another Esdan. Jeril became a darting, slashing figure, expecting every enemy soldier he faced to be Tacidus.

Every enemy soldier.

The thought only half-surprised him, for they were irrevocably the enemy to him now. He thrust at faces akin to his own but foreign in their aspect and motivation. His sword grew bloody fast as he exculpated the iniquities of half a life spent running. Each blow he landed served as a commentary to his demons.

For Seri and Tam.

For Grayce and Devyn.

"For my king," he said aloud through teeth grit in pressure and pain, and for all that found a modicum of joy because it was truth. "I am Pevanese!" he screamed as he blocked yet another thrust and, spinning, felt his blade bite deep into yet another Esdan neck. That unfortunate fell before him, all but decaptitated, and Jeril came to his senses to realize he and those with whom he fought had come to the end of a side way that exited out onto a cleared space. Tacidus was nowhere in sight. He glanced over his shoulder to get his bearings, took in the wall of the building where Grayce had drawn her vision of the Maze-tree, and swung right to note the desperate line of Pevanese resistance down the length of the field.

The area was a sea of color, smoke and indistinct faces hazed by rain. He blinked away water and recognized the burly form of Saymon Brimaldi hefting a spear alongside him. The incongruity brought a wry smile to his lips. Saymon looked at him but said nothing. Jeril saved his breath as well, for there was nothing left to say that spear point and sword blade could not express.

He flexed his left forearm and found it numbed and thick. All around him and Brimaldi, citizens and soldiers mixed to meet the enemy. There came a lull as the Esdans redressed their ranks to meet this new situation. Jeril took a step forward. If death took him now, he wanted it quick. He brandished his sword, took in the notches and gore along its length, and judged his effort adequate at least for honor. There remained only one thing else, really. Jeril scanned the area, looking for that one thing. As the Esdans advanced, their front rank shifted and from their mass stepped Tacidus himself. He moved forward, sword pointed as before right at Jeril.

Jeril allowed himself one last smile, wiped the blood from his sword hand and slipped into a defensive stance.

"Come then," he spat. "Time to die, you bastard."

Tacidus must have heard him, for he sprinted ahead of the other enemy troops, sweeping his blade up for a mighty blow. Jeril met him at the apex. They bounced off each other as the battle lines met. The crush of bodies and blades brought their faces close together.

"No more room to run, traitor!" Tacidus grunted as he pushed Jeril away to clear space for a thrust. "I would have finished you ages ago, but this is sweeter by far."

"You should have," Jeril agreed. "But you played my brother's games for him. I cannot get him, so I will take you instead." He parried and lunged for Tacidus's knee, hoping to maime and then to finish. Tacidus barely avoided the blow and side-stepped for space.

"I'll take your head for that," he grated. "Fool. You are bloody and old." He levelled a downward slash that rang against Jeril's sword-hilt, followed by sweeping right and leftward blows that forced him backward, stumbling from desparation and exhaustion. Tacidus grinned, a death's head rictus, and he brought a vicious, two-handed overhead smash that nearly disarmed the painter.

Jeril barely blocked the blow, sword swinging wide and useless in the motion. He saw Tacidus's eyes widen in surprise and victory as the man sensed his weakness. The Esdan drew a knife with his off hand and lunged to attack with both blades. Jeril managed to deflect the sword, and spun inside Tacidus's reach to block the knife backhanded, but his left arm failed him. He missed his grab by a handwidth, and instead of the wrist only managed to grasp the forearm. The arm, wounded and weakened, collapsed from the force of Tacidus's blow. The Esdan's dagger bounced along Jeril's ribcage, found a lodgement and pierced deep into his vitals.

Jeril fell to his knees, suddenly out of breath, his side a whitehot searing palette of pain. Tacidus screamed exaltation and raised his sword for the killing blow. Jeril tensed to receive it, but instead, out of the corner of his eye, as if in slow motion, he saw a rusty spear blade slide by. Transfixed, he followed its progress as it punched through Tacidus's breastplate and came to rest deep in his chest. The Esdan staggered for a moment, the shock and surprise changing to visceral agony before his eyes rolled back and he toppled over in death.

Saymon Brimaldi's face, contorted in battle rage swam before Jeril's fading vision. The man turned to him, mouthed words Jeril could not make out, and then his bearded face changed altogether as an arrow shaft replaced his tongue. He crashed to the ground, pulsing blood in his death sprawl.

Bone chilling cold now replaced the heat in Jeril's side. Somehow, he managed to get one leg under himself, tried to use his sword to leverage upright and failed. He sank back to his knees, exhausted beyond all knowledge. He looked around, dumbly, distracted, and recognized Grayce's tree. He might have smiled; he could not be certain for a slackness had overtaken his face. Around him, the scene devolved to a wash of noise and color, abstract representations of action, shape and sorrow. He blinked, forgot how to breathe, and imagined for a second a light as from a studio candle. He saw the spear point coming for him, but merciful darkness took him before he felt its point.

* * *

Grayce felt broken in ways beyond recovery as the wave of folk fleeing Esdan spears swept her up. At first, she tried to work back to Devyn, sick at the thought of losing him. She screamed against the pull, ignored by those intent on flight, but it was no good. Once she lost touch with his hand in the press, she became an oarless craft helplessly adrift in currents antithetical. She felt herself drowning in a choking mix of fear and desparate sorrow. All the power she had reclaimed by dispatching Simson leached away by a near stultifying horror.

The human tide took her ever further back and away. Gradually the press eased and slowed enough for her to regain her breath and bearings. She came upon a remembered turning, slipped out of the crowd that flowed on and padded off on her own. She fled, hartswift, down familiar ways yet unmolested, leaving the noise and terror behind her. All thoughts ran together now: Devyn unreachable in the crush of separation, Jeril locked in combat. Her wrist still ached from the force of the blow she used to kill Simson. She still had the daggar in a white-knuckle grasp. Every part of her throbbed as if fever-driven. She acted now out of instinct only. She broke out into the open near the wall where she had drawn her vision of Pevana's Tree.

The space was strangely quiet compared to the tumult swelling behind her. She ran across the ground, brushed her hand in passing along the wall's surface and drew a measure of strength from the enduring image fixed there. She paused, thought she heard children's voices above, but then a crashing as of spear on shield brought her spinning around to look back. Folk now spilled out from the surrounding areas, soldiers and city folk moving flood-like across the grass. The sight sent her running anew down a narrow way at the far end of the field. She ran until she came to a stumbling, breathless pause outside the door of Jeril's home. She reached for the key in her pocket, realized it lost along with her other clothes back in Simson's rooms, and then duly, insanely calm, she lifted the cobblestone nearest the step to retrieve the spare.

Once inside she threw off the finery Simson forced on her for his pleasure and ran upstairs. She drew out her original pack from the closet and tossed it on the bed, shoving in a blanket and a jacket. From the bottom dresser drawer she drew out her travel clothes and threw them on blindly, wanting speed only. She spied her art satchel on the worktable in the studio and swept pens and inkbottle in along with a pad of paper. She took a frantic look around, saw her picture of Devyn and the poem he left behind, and grabbed them up as well, rolling both into a tight mass that she added to her things. Shouldering her burdens, she turned for the stairs but Angel, perched on the railing, rowling and inquisitive, stopped her dead in her tracks.

"Yes, oh yes, dearheart," Grayce gushed, taking Angel up and kissing the calico forehead. "This is no fit place for either of us."

She went downstairs, settled the cat gently on top of the things in her satchel and wished her to patience, and rushed out of the house. Within moments, she reached the mess of folk exiting the city through the Landgate. Darting in amongst the morass, she forced her way through and joined the human rabble spreading out along the road heading west and north along the river.

She ran and walked alternatively, her thoughts vague, distracted, one moment stopping to go back and find Devyn, even in death, and in the next rushing on mindful of the promise in his last verse. She barely noted the change from fear to hope in the voices of the people around her as the column cleared to allow passage of others coming east. Dumbly, she shuffled off left with the others just out of the way as a long line of horses cantored by. A man with blond hair flowing out from a high helm rode at their head. Alongside him rode another with the Perspan banner snapping behind in their speed. Someone started to cheer. Grayce took more notice, wanted to join, but the column was not a long one, and the horses that passed by were foam-flecked and all but broken. She watched them disappear into the dust of their progress before turning to go on when the others resumed their flight.

When the refugee stream reached the river ford, she turned south rather than continuing with them, her feet changing direction as if from their own accord; a vision in her mind now of a southward road and a path running above it that ended in a cavemouth that faced west.

* * *

When the rain started, Tasia covered the three of them with an old piece of tarp she salvaged from a pile of old building materials. Underneath this tent, she did her best to distract the children with stories. At first, she had great success, for the tarp served to muffle the sounds of battle, and the children enjoyed the whispers in the artificial dark. She talked them down Soralee's pathways in the woods, up into the clouds above to Renia's terrace, and then quickly along the coast with Minuet of the Arrows.

Eventually, however, the battle roar became impossible to ignore, and when Tasia began to run out of words Arryn grew restless and tossed off the tarp and the three of them looked over the edge of the little parapet as life and death began filtering into the field below. The sight filled Tasia with sickening despair. City folk and soldiers crowded the area and formed up to contest the space with Esdan forces come in pursuit. On either side of her, the children looked on the scene without comment at first. Then Ailen sniffed, and Tasia felt the child's shoulders shiver as if she wept.

"Those are bad men," Arryn said, pointing at the Esdans massing to renew the attack. "Where are father and mother? Father should come and deal with them. Where is papa, Tasia?"

"I want mama," added Ailen.

Tasia looked north and west from their vantage, saw the smoke enveloping the region of the citadel, and sought helplessly for soothing words.

"They will come, little ones, we have to be patient and stay hidden here. Look, the old poet stands guard here and Mistress Stonesmith's Tree is below us. Nothing evil will come up here."

As she spoke, battle erupted in the field around Edri's grave, and the Pevanese line began to waver and fold inward. The sight and sounds drove the children to bury their heads into Tasia's shoulders, and she took them and hugged them close against the horror.

She forced herself to watch the carnage, to observe and record the battle for the city if she could because she was a poet of Pevana, perhaps the last poet, and that was what the old man interred beneath the hallowed ground inside the fence would expect of her. It was what Devyn Ambrose would want. As she stared at Edri's grave, she blinked in sorrow and surprise as Devyn himself swam into her field of vision skillfully wielding his sword backed up against the wrought iron tines.

Tasia surveyed the field. Esdan forces swarmed on the right in greater numbers than elsewhere. Movement off to Ambose's left front drew her attention, and despite the distance, she recognized the king and his crowned helm leading men into the fray. Still farther left, from the direction of the Landgate Street, wonder of wonders, a mass of Pevanese calvary spilled out onto the grass, formed line, levelled spears and spurred to the charge. Hope swelled then for Tasia.

"Look, Arryn, Ailen, see! Here comes your papa! See there! The horses! Take courage and look!" She practically shouted, but the battle noise drowned out her words and the children remained as they were.

She swung her gaze back to Ambrose just in time to see three Esdan soldiers slam into him. The weight caused the fence to fail and poet and enemies went down in a tumble. Tasia shut her eyes then against sudden tears, unwilling, not even for honor, to watch the death of the man who had most helped define her world.

And Minuet took up her bow of yew
Set to string arrows straight and true,
And sent her shafts to pierce the gloom
And sent her shafts to pierce the gloom.

She held on to those thoughts like a lifeline, slumped down, back against the parapet and resettled the twins against her. The sounds of battle reverberated against her ears, gale winds against shutters, a crashing human-metallic wave that rose in pitch, held, held, held and then fantastically receded.

Tasia stayed down, clutching the children close as if they alone represented all that remained of life itself.

* * *

Devyn tensed for the collision as the Esdan soldiers rushed him. He swung his blade, but their raised shields turned it easily. They crashed into him, the impact forcing the air from his lungs as they pinned him against the fence. The iron failed, and he fell backward, faint from lack of air with the enemy all a sprawl atop him. He fought for breath, waited for a blade to find his vitals, struck out with his sword pommel at a face that loomed above his, smashing it into a bloody mess as the man rolled away. His remaining assailants rained blows at him with their fists. Devyn could do nothing to avoid them. The world went silent for him as he fought for life and breath, and in that silence he marveled as a spear point passed through the neck of one of the Esdans followed immediately by the foreleg of a horse that struck the other man in the head, sending him somersaulting out of view. Miraculously, the beast's hindquarters missed him altogether as it came to earth.

Breath and sound returned simultaneously to Devyn. He lay back, mouth agape, exhausted and half-stunned as the battle roar rolled away. Vaguely, he noted a change in the timber; a new rhythm attended by the beat of hooves, the beginning swell of cheers and defiance. Hope in the form of a rain-drop found its way to the back of his throat. He coughed, tasted blood and winced as ribs protested. He rolled to his side, got to his knees with difficulty and gasped in amazement at what he saw in front of Kembril's headstone. There, unmarked despite the ruin of fence and ground about, poking maybe a foot above the grass where he remembered burying a single seed five years ago, a slender oak sapling reached heavenward.

The rain failed as a freshening northern wind broke up the clouds and pushed them away. Devyn hurt everywhere. Battle sounds receded farther, heading back toward the harbor area. Folk moved about the field near him, checking for wounded, making sure of the dead. He struggled to his feet and with difficulty shifted the fencing away from the oak sapling. Other hands arrived to help him, younger hands. He looked up from his labor in surprise to find Tasia and the twins.

"What is this?" he asked.

"We had to run from the bad people!" Ailen offered.

"So we ran here!" continued Arryn. "Tasia told us stories until, until—" But his voice trailed off.

Devyn damped down his growing horror at their presence here with so much death around. He had to force lightness back to his tone.

"You ran, you say? Here? How?"

"We made a rope with sheets from mama's bed," Ailen said. "I had to ride pigga-back"

"And then we went out the garden gate," Arryn chimed in.

"We hid on the roof above Grayce's tree," Tasia finished. "Someone heard us, after, and reset the ladder."

Devyn looked up at her and saw there more than perhaps she would want revealed.

"Ah," he said. "That gate has proven useful yet again. "And then stories?"

"Until I ran out of words," Tasia answered. She had tears running down her face now, and looked exhausted and traumatized.

"What do you mean?" Devyn stood and put his arm around her shoulders. The girl slumped against him.

"I'm sorry," she whispered. "I tried to watch at the last, but when you went down I turned away. I couldn't." She choked. "I didn't want the words."

"But you had them for the twins when it counted most," Devyn said. "And you will have them again at need, I am sure!" He looked at the twins. "Well met, prince and princess. Thank you for your help. Old Edri would have appreciated it."

"Is that a tree?" Arryn asked. "It's so little."

"It and you will grow together, little prince. We must tend it."

"Ailen and me will take care of it!" he asserted. "That will be our job."

"We will all look after it," Tasia clarified. "It is the Poets' Tree."

The reference brought a smile to Devyn's face that persisted until the king found him later. He just pointed when Donari looked a question. The king's eyes grew wide when he saw. Then king and poet together set about tending to their master.

"Horses?" Devyn asked.

"Hallan," the king answered, "come on a wish."

"That sounds like a story."

"One that we will hear once we clear the city. His foresight proved prescient. There is work yet, but the Esdans have spent their shafts here. They are flowing back to their boats. Folk report horns from the water, a signal, perhaps. We will let them go."

They walked down the field away from Kembril's grave to where the bodies clustered deepest and found Saymon Brimaldi and Jeril with the Esdan, Tacidus, next to them.

"It seems Jeril had his chance at revenge. Poor Brimaldi," Devyn said. He knelt and gently prised the arrow from the tavern keeper's throat. He looked from one to the other, old friend and new but both dear, and swallowed back a sob.

"If this is victory then it is dearly bought. Too many." Donari said, stooping to close Jeril's eyes. "He deserved better. And Saymon. They will be sorely missed." He placed a hand on Devyn's shoulder, and the familiar gesture brought Devyn's eyes in contact with his lord's.

"Gania Landare fell as well," Devyn said. "Grief enough for all, sire. There are those will need to tell. I do not know if I can find the words."

"We will find the time and words together, Devyn, for Talyior, my Eleni, and your Grayce. But for now we have to see this tragedy finished." Donari helped him rise. "If this wind keeps up we might have a storm. I sent for horses. If you can ride, come with me to see how Hallan is doing. I will send the children back to the palace. We have cleared the hill. Eleni will need to see them."

The king's comment brought thoughts of Grayce rushing back. He wanted to go find her, but duty held him. He closed his eyes tight against the pain in his ribs, felt for her, and sensed, finally, the smallest thread, as whispy as a spiderweb strand parted and undulating in the breeze. Though faint from distance, he took enough certainty from the touch to mount with good will and follow the king down Harbor Street.

They reached the ruined gates and passed beyond to where Hallan marshalled the Pevanese survivors. The Esdans, in an echo of their earlier aggressive precision now held the pier in force to finish their withdrawl. Only a few crafts still bobbed off shore, waiting for the last of the rearguard. Donari held his men back though they growled for revenge. Devyn agreed with the choice, too heartsick over the lives already lost to add more to the tally. The Esdans took ship and sailed away. In the end, the Pevanese would find only a handful of skulkers and wounded left behind.

Devyn observed the scene with a mixture of wonder and despair. The Esdans had devastated much of the city harbor-side and south in their assault. Much of the area immediately behind the wall was a burned out shell. Gania Landare's boarding house would not miss her. What remained of its two stories smoldered in a ruin of blackened, collapsed beams. Despite the rain during the battle, many fires still raged further in. Once again, Pevana's Maze had suffered.

"This has cost us dear, sire."

His comment stirred Donari to look away from the retreating Esdan vessels and take in the devastation behind them.

"Very dear, my friend. This was a near thing, and I suspect we will see other attempts."

And then he did a thing at odds with the situation. He laughed, a long, low, gentle expression of mirth that brought pleasant memories to Devyn.

"Laughter?" he asked.

"Don't you see the delicious irony, Dev? They made a determined try here, but the Maze helped beat them. Renia's Grace! That warren kept the Esdans from concentrating.

We fought them to the one place where Hallan's few could have the most impact."

"We were lucky."

"Sometimes desperation breeds its own luck." He gestured seaward. "But they were not prepared for the narrow lanes. They should have let the fires do their work for them. They rushed it."

"And lost."

"This time. I suspect there will come another."

"What do you intend, my lord?"

The king straightened in the saddle and locked eyes with him. Devyn saw mirth fade to shouldered responsibility, revealing steel beneath the surface, and that, too, brought pleasant memories.

"We will wait for news north and south," the king said. "And then we will see to our people." He glanced searward a last time. "We rebuild what we can, and then we will build a navy."

The image of a tall, white-washed temple with a dead fake priest in an upstairs room came to Devyn. And there were others in the city.

"I know a few buildings we could use for stone," he offered.

Donari caught his meaning clearly. "Yes, and so ordered. We will dispense with that rotten lie once and for all."

The reference brought Grayce to mind once again. Devyn hesitated to ask, but Donari seemed to read his mood, and that was not a new thing, either.

* * *

Epilogue

Devyn stood briefly in the stirrups to relieve the numbness in his backside. He had jogged with his gelding and another mare down the road for a day since fording the river outside Pevana. Now, he felt his his way up through the wooded slopes, following a path dimly remembered from another time, compelled forward and up by another kind of urging. He reached a point where a rocky shoulder of the world punched through soil. The late-morning summer sun shone down on the mouth of a cave, and there sat a woman combing wet auburn hair with a calico cat in her lap and a small satchel at her feet.

Neither one showed the slightest surprise when he halted his little string and dismounted. The woman put the cat aside and came to stand before him, a smile on her lips but a question in her eyes.

"Grayce," he whispered before dispelling her question with a kiss.

She held tightly to him. "I'm sorry," she said. Her voice muffled in his chest. "I couldn't find you. And the flames. I ran."

"You could do nothing less, my dear. I told you I would find you."

She tilted her head back, wonder stealing over her features.

"Yes, yes you did." He noted the slight quiver in her voice as she continued. "But what of the others?"

"There is time enough for that story, later. There was much lost and gained, in the end."

"Devyn, I cannot go back. It is too much. I do not think I could bear it."

"I can see why," he agreed. He gestured to include the horses. "I took the liberty of bringing a few of your belongings. Donari has freed me for a while. To see to things."

"Things?" A smile, tentative and hopeful, teased over her features. "Where will we go?"

He led her over to the mare, helped her mount, and then went back to her camp to scoop up both her satchel and the cat. He gave her Angel and tied her bundle to the pommel of her saddle.

He mounted and looked west toward the mountain.

"Let's go find a new shade of green."

Photo credit: Grace Eide-Gabriel

Mark Nelson is a career educator and for the last twenty-two years has been teaching composition and literature at a small high school located in the rain shadow of the Cascade Mountains in eastern Washington State. He is happily married to his best friend and fellow educator and together they have raised three beautiful daughters and one semi-retired cat. Words, music, food and parenting permeate his life and serve as a constant source for inspiration, challenge and reward. To temper such unremitting joy, Mark plays golf: an addiction that provides a healthy dose of humility.